The Best American
Mystery Stories 1997

The Best American Mystery Stories 1997

Edited and with an Introduction by
Robert B. Parker

Otto Penzler, *Series Editor*

HOUGHTON MIFFLIN COMPANY

BOSTON · NEW YORK   1997

ISSN 1094-8384
ISBN 0-395-83583-6
ISBN 0-395-83584-4

Printed in the United States of America

QUM 10 9 8 7 6 5 4 3 2 1

Contents

Foreword

THE NATURAL FORM for the traditional mystery is not the novel but the short story. It is not uncommon for a detective story to revolve around a single significant clue — which can be discovered, divulged, and its importance explained in a few pages. The rest is embellishment.

Mystery fiction has changed a great deal in recent years, as have virtually all art forms. The classic tale of a murder being committed, the local police called in and responding with utter bafflement, the gifted amateur offering assistance, discovering new clues, breaking down old alibis, and finally identifying the least likely suspect is largely a thing of the past.

Nowadays, much more is expected of the mystery novel, and even of the short story. We have come to expect the same depth of characterization that we do from general fiction, the same sort of intelligent and/or amusing dialogue, the same door opening to let us into a previously unknown or unexplored world. But we also expect a carefully constructed story line that rewards our close attention with a realistic conclusion that answers all the questions posed along the way. No loose ends in these stories; no unexplained activities.

The mystery is the last literary form where serious writers can demonstrate their gifts to provide a thoughtful profile of an individual in the context of society while still being required to plot meticulously. It is the last place a serious reader can have confidence that a literary exercise will also provide a fun, satisfying experience.

Houghton Mifflin, having published the prestigious series *Best American Short Stories,* has this year decided to offer serious readers a new volume, *The Best American Mystery Stories,* which is planned as an annual event.

The methodology for compiling this volume is similar to that used for *The Best American Short Stories.* As the series editor, it is my responsibility to identify and read all the mystery stories published in the calendar year (for this first collection, in the year 1996). From this large number (approximately 500) the goal was to select the best fifty stories and pass them along to the guest editor, who would then choose the best twenty for publication, the others receiving honorable mention.

The source for these stories is, of course, wherever original fiction is published. The most fruitful sources are the mystery specialty magazines, small literary journals, popular consumer publications, and an unusually bountiful crop from anthologies containing all or some original work.

Many editors of non-mystery magazines claimed they didn't publish mystery stories until I provided the definition that has served throughout my varied career in the mystery world. I defined a mystery story as any in which a crime, or the threat of a crime, is central to the theme. Crimes against an individual count, naturally; most frequently murder but also kidnapping, rape, robbery, stalking, or whatever other illegal activity violates another human being. Crimes against the state also fall into my definition, including espionage, terrorism, and whatever other acts directed against a government ultimately do damage to its citizens.

Because of this loose (I prefer to think of it as "generously accepting") definition of a mystery, the stories collected here are enormously diverse. Some are traditional detective stories; others are crime tales, which have become increasingly popular in recent times. Some are as slim and tight as you'd expect from the notion of a short story. Others, like Michael Malone's "Red Clay," James Crumley's "Hot Springs," and S. J. Rozan's "Hoops," are deep enough to be expanded to novels. Two of those have already been optioned for movies. Elmore Leonard liked his female protagonist (and a couple of minor characters) so much that he wrote a novel around them.

As is true of all distinguished literature, some of these stories will linger in the memory for a time, sometimes perhaps even a long time. By the time the last of them fades, it will be time for the 1998 volume of *The Best American Mystery Stories.*

Editors, publishers, and authors who want to be assured that their stories will be considered for the next volume in this series should send material to Otto Penzler, The Mysterious Bookshop, 129 West 56th Street, New York, NY 10019.

O. P.

Introduction

WHOEVER WROTE the first mystery (Job?), Arthur Conan Doyle's invention of Sherlock Holmes created the category. And when American stories about detectives appeared, the category was there to receive them, even though their ancestry is rather different. The unstated, perhaps even unthought assumptions about life that underlie the Holmes stories are that a rational God created a reasonable world. His will is manifest in His creation. Crime is an unreasonable deviation from the norm, and a man of superior reason can restore the norm by solving the crime. It is a triumph of intelligence, smaller in scope but not different in kind from the triumph of intelligence that contrived the original creation. The detective's success is a restoration of the grand design. Since God's will is manifest in His creation, that is to say, nature, then one can understand His will by studying nature. Thus at heart the kind of story that Dr. Doyle was writing celebrates the triumph of science (the rational examination of evidence), which in Dr. Doyle's time seemed well worth celebrating. The kind of story that posits such a universe and such a triumph is often called the English (or ratiocinative) detective story, and the designation is useful enough as long as we know that Americans write that kind of story as well, and that many English writers don't.

The confidence in a rational universe was harder to maintain after war in the trenches, and the sense of a wasteland world modified literature on both sides of the Atlantic. Moreover, the last hundred years have brought to our attention a universe that seems, frankly, not to give a damn. The insights of Freud and Marx suggest that we are much less the products of rational plan and far more the victims of forces we don't understand and often can't control. The experience of several wars has underscored the inefficacy of human planning. If there was design to Verdun, it was of darkness to appall.

The United States was founded by the movement from east to west, from Europe to America, from Boston to St. Louis, from a condition of settled society to one outside of the settlements. We remain to this day the descendants of people who left the settlements and the rule of law to find something else, influenced (even when they didn't approve of it) by the Protestant Reformation, which urged that right conduct was an individual responsibility (every man his own priest), not a hierarchal one. Thus most of us (except the descendants of those who came in slavery, and the descendants of those who were already here and got rolled over by the westward movement) derive from people for whom civilization is perceived as limiting and life outside of it is understood to be freeing. We come from people who in repetitive waves lit out for the territories where heroism was possible. Where anything was possible. It is the American myth. The myth of the West.

Moreover, it was a rather short step from seeing God's design in nature to seeing God in nature. Our founding documents appeal to nature and to "nature's God." The European romanticism of the early nineteenth century, which gave rise to the American transcendental movement of the mid-nineteenth century, reinforced the belief that civilization was the danger and wilderness was the refuge. To be part of civilization was inevitably to be part of the problem.

But, the West being lawless and therefore dangerous, the custodians of the myth, those who actually had to live the imaginings of philosophers and poets, were men with guns (every man his own cop). And the man with a gun became a staple of American fiction. He was alone, outside of society, compelled by his own rules. Neither against the law nor of it, keeping his moral integrity hard and intact. Though he was often the hero of popular fiction written with indiscriminate crudeness, his story still retained some grace of tragedy because he was finally, often reluctantly, but inevitably, a killer of men. "The essential American soul," D. H. Lawrence noted, "is hard, isolate, stoic, and a killer." It is this aspect of the myth of America that informs much of American fiction. The man with a gun filled the pages of dime novels until the frontier closed and the West was gone. Then the dime novels became pulp magazines and the cowboys dismounted, but kept their guns and became detectives. The American detective story has much more to do with James Fenimore Cooper than it does with Edgar Allan Poe.

Like his ancestor, the American detective is usually alone, he is outside the rules of his society; even when he's with the police he is often at odds with his employer. For him the West as a place of purity and freedom is internalized and rarely spoken of. The tragic grace he inherited from his Western ancestors is made more graceful perhaps by the sense of deeply defended innocence that he contains. The price he pays for this innocence is isolation. There are no territories left to light out for. The isolated self is the only refuge from the now pervasive civilization. The kind of detective fiction produced by these circumstances has come to be called American (or hard-boiled), and again the designation will do, with the caveat above.

In fact, of course, the two streams of detective fiction have flowed together often enough so that each has influenced the other, and the changes that they have imposed on each other have been part of the evolution of detective fiction. The English mode has gotten tougher, and the American has become more thoughtful. In the works of Rex Stout, of course, the two streams merged in the persons of Nero Wolfe and Archie Goodwin.

At this point in the twentieth century, except in the most nostalgic of detective fictions, the world of the detective is, in the words of Raymond Chandler, "a world in which gangsters can rule nations and almost rule cities, in which hotels and apartment houses and celebrated restaurants are owned by men who made their money out of brothels, in which a screen star can be the finger man for a mob, and the nice man down the hall is a boss of the numbers racket; a world where a judge with a cellar full of bootleg liquor can send a man to jail for having a pint in his pocket, where the mayor of your town may have condoned murder as an instrument of money making, where no man can walk down a dark street in safety because law and order are things we talk about but refrain from practicing; a world where you may witness a hold-up in broad daylight and see who did it, but you will fade quickly back into the crowd rather than tell anyone because the hold-up men may have friends with long guns, or the police may not like your testimony, and in any case the shyster for the defense will be allowed to abuse and vilify you in open court, before a jury of selected morons, without any but the most perfunctory interference from a political judge."

The detective facing such a world cannot restore the natural order of things through his superior intellect. This is the natural order of things. Crime is not a deviation from the norm. It is the norm. So the smart guy needs to be tougher, and the tough guy needs to be smarter.

The American tough guy was established by Dashiell Hammett, who, like Doyle, may not have been the first, but was obviously the most important. In *The Maltese Falcon*, Spade tells a story to Brigitte O'Shaughnessy about a man named Flitcraft (like so many of Hammett's names, it tells us something about its bearer). Flitcraft was almost killed once by a falling beam at a construction site. This revealed to him that life was random, and he decided to live it randomly. He left his family and his job and drifted. But after a while he found himself in a similar job with a similar family. When beams fell, he adjusted to their falling. When they didn't fall, he adjusted to that. The story seems to Brigitte like an idle way to fill time, but it is not. It is a parable about Spade's understanding of reality and should serve to warn Brigitte of what she can expect from Spade. But Brigitte doesn't get it. No one does. Everyone else reacts to the most recent stimulus. Only Spade understands what life is really like. It is why he wins.

Spade's is a bleak vision of life, and an isolating one. In the stories that follow, Hammett seems to be looking for a way to find connection without denying the world as he, and Spade, understand it. But there were things Hammett seemed unable to say, or had no language to say it with, and the later work suffers, though it may also have suffered from booze and Lillian Hellman. Whatever limited Hammett, it remained for Raymond Chandler to liberate the American detective story from Hammett's desert place.

Chandler infused the American detective story with a life-giving romanticism. In his hands the detective story became a story of a hero (in Northrop Frye's categories, high mimetic) who is superior to other men, though not to nature. Marlowe moves through the sun-blasted streets of Los Angeles, where the butt end of the American dream is sniped out against the end of the continent. He knows everything Spade knows, but he insists on and is tough enough to maintain a high romantic readiness, a deliberate and undeceived sentimentality. The plot doesn't matter much. When we have forgotten the stories, we remember Marlowe. Things do not always come out all right. He cannot restore the grand design. But he remains intact. What comes out all right is Marlowe. It is he who matters. In his romanticism and his courage and the full density of his creation, he provides at least a temporary stay against confusion.

Obviously much has happened in American mystery stories since Chandler. Women have found a comfortable and invigorating place within the form. The story of the hero has diversified in gender, in race, in locale, in sexual preference. But, as you will see in this collection, the stories remain the story of the hero's "adventure in search of a hidden truth." They are stories about a hero "fit for adventure" in a time when stories of far bluer blood are still stuck in that bleak corner of the wasteland where Spade took Hammett.

This is no small thing.

ROBERT B. PARKER

The Best American
Mystery Stories 1997

DOUG ALLYN

Blind Lemon

FROM *Alfred Hitchcock Mystery Magazine*

"HEY, AXTON, WE GONNA DRIVE all night? I need to use the facilities, you know? I promise I won't run."

I glanced at Cootie Keyes. He was a bail jumper, a small-time dope dealer, a user, a snitch. Not one of nature's noblemen. Still, he was worth twenty-five hundred bucks to the Saheen Bail Bond Agency back in Detroit, plus the mileage I'd run up on my old Buick driving down to Knoxville to pick him up. And he hadn't been much trouble. So far.

"We'll take a break at the next place I see," I said. "But only if they've got chicken."

"Very funny," he said gloomily, staring out into the rainy Indiana night. He'd been hiding in a chicken coop when I rousted him. Which was appropriate. Cootie looked a bit like a chicken: scrawny neck, a beak nose, no chin to speak of. He even had a few scraps of feathers in his hair.

The neon sign said THE 3-B BARRELHOUSE, BURGERS, BEER 'N' BLUES. I wheeled into the half-filled parking lot.

"C'mon, Ax," Cootie whined. "I was thinkin' maybe someplace nice. It's my last night of freedom, man."

"I'm not on an expense account, Cootie," I said. "Of course, if you'd rather wait in the trunk . . ."

"Okay, okay, I'm cool," he said. "How about takin' the cuffs off? It's embarrassing."

"No chance," I said. "Besides, from the looks of this place, half the people in here may be wearing cuffs."

I was wrong. The old log building was surprisingly pleasant inside, massive dark pine tables and chairs, checkered tablecloths, and a magnificent old Wurlitzer jukebox from the fifties pumping out roadhouse blues from the same era. Home sweet home.

We sat in the shadows at a corner table. Cootie kept his hands out of sight while we ordered cheeseburgers and beer from a surprisingly young and sweet waitress.

Most of the customers were college types, gathered at the far end of the building near a small bandstand. Some of them had Fighting Irish jackets, and it occurred to me that this place was probably only twenty miles or so from Notre Dame.

The burgers were great, flame-broiled, dripping with their own juices and homemade mustard. Cootie and I tore into them like wolves, and I made a mental note to remember the 3-B's. Not that I'm likely to forget it now.

A small combo took the stage, took a moment to tune their instruments, then ripped into their opening number without so much as a "howdy, folks." They were blues dynamite, jamming on a hard-driving Elmore James shuffle, "Dust My Broom." The lead guitarist was a woman and a killer player, passionate and precise. And they weren't even warmed up yet. I was truly sorry I was only passing through . . . and then she started to sing.

I froze, my beer mug posed in midair. I knew that voice. I'd know it anywhere. Cheryl Vanetti. I glanced sharply at Cootie, but he was busy making carnage of his burger, oblivious to the music. He was young enough that he might not have heard her anyway. Or remember, if he had. But I wasn't likely to forget her. She'd helped kill a friend of mine.

It was back in the eighties. Detroit was still Murder City then. I was a lot younger and hadn't gotten my private eye ticket yet. So I bounced in clubs or collected cash from folks who weren't altogether sure they owed it. And in those days, I still had friends. Danny Liebman was one. A chubby Jewish kid from Grosse Pointe who'd parlayed a master's in economics and a passion for music into a hole-in-the-wall dive a few blocks from the University of Detroit. He called the Place Yo Mama's, a thoughtful touch, since the rumor was that he'd conned his mother into putting up most of the money for it.

Mama Liebman's investment was paying off, though. Danny hired a young chick singer with a halfway decent band behind her, Cherry and the Pit. They were drawing a yuppie college trade six nights a week. It wasn't my scene, the crowd was too young even then and the music was white bread, but I'd filled in as a bouncer there a few times as a favor to Danny, and I'd collected a few bad debts for him from guys who'd forgotten how to add up a bar tab. We couldn't have been more different, Danny and I. He was a Detroiter, born into old Dodge motor money, and I'd drifted up to Motown from a Mississippi dirt farm looking for work a few years before.

We both loved music, though, and we whiled away many an early morning after Yo Mama's closed listening to scratchy old 78's of Big Mama Thornton, Tampa Red, and Blind Lemon Jefferson. Danny was heavy into old-time bluesers and did his best to turn me on to them, too. It might have worked eventually, but my business got in the way and our lives separated for a while, the way they do when you're young. Or any time, for that matter. Stuff happens.

I hadn't seen him for a few months when he called me out of the blue and said he needed to see me at the club the next day. Emergency.

Business at Yo Mama's was slow that afternoon. Two U. of Detroit sophs were trying to score with a barmaid old enough to mother 'em. Three coeds with cropped hair, no makeup, and Goodwill duds were sharing a back booth and a pitcher of beer, arguing earnestly about things academic. They looked familiar. Either I'd seen them around or there's a trio like them in every college bar every afternoon.

A deafening delta blues jam was thumping over the house sound system. I didn't recognize the singer. Robert Johnson? Leadbelly? Definitely one of Danny Liebman's precious dead bluesmen. The guy's wailing was unintelligible, but it was a safe bet his life wasn't going very well. No wonder the joint was nearly deserted. I limped across the postage stamp dance floor to the office, rapped once, and went in.

Danny Liebman was lost in the music, slumped in his swivel chair with an old Martin Flattop guitar cradled in his ample lap. He was playing along with the tape. Or trying to. Butchering the same lick over and over again. His timing was so lame I couldn't tell if he was improving or not. Danny loved to play. And had zero aptitude for it.

"Yo, Danny," I said. No response. I gimped over to the sound system and turned it down. Danny blinked up at me through his steel-framed granny glasses. He was dressed in his usual street-grunge duds, faded flannel shirt, ripped jeans, shaggy hair. And still looked exactly like a well-fed Jewish kid from Grosse Pointe. Genes will out.

"Are you limping?" Danny asked.

"I got kicked by some yo-yo's girlfriend over at the Bucket of Blood," I said, easing painfully down on the corner of the desk. "Thirty seconds earlier he'd been beatin' hell out of her, but as soon as I step in, she boots me on the ankle. Hurts like a bitch. That's my sad story, what's yours? What's the big emergency? You got a collection problem for me, I hope?"

"Au contraire," Danny said, "somebody's trying to give me money for a change. A guy stopped by to see me last night while I was closing up. Said he was seriously interested in buying the club."

"No kidding," I said, surprised. "I didn't know you were looking to get out. How long have you been open? Six months?"

"Sell hell, this is a dream job. Running a blues bar near the campus, great music, many brews, and friendly coeds who think I'm too cool for school. I'm as happy as the proverbial pig."

"Which you're going to resemble soon if you don't back off on the Bud Lite, bud," I said. "But if you don't have a collection job for me, what am I doing here?"

"I want to tell you about the offer."

"Why? I'm jealous enough of you as it is."

"Maybe you shouldn't be. The guy offered to take over my mortgage, double the points I paid up front, plus ten grand."

"Ten? That's chicken feed considering the sweat equity you put into remodeling this place. Who made the offer? Some stud from the Afro student union who figures you're an ofay cashing in on black culture?"

"He'd be dead right about that," Danny said mildly. "But this guy's no brother, he's Chinese, Ax. From across the border at Windsor. And he knew the numbers, my mortgage and points. To the nickel. He definitely did some homework."

"So who asked him to? If you don't want to sell, tell him to stick it."

"Actually, I did. Sort of. I said I wasn't interested. At which point he said the price was nonnegotiable. And it would drop a thousand a day until I took it."

"A thousand a day?" I said. "Interesting. Did he threaten you?"

"Don't be a schmuck, Ax. I may have had a sheltered upbringing, but I know a threat when I hear one."

"Yeah, you're probably right. Subtle, though. Not much to complain to the law about. So what do you want me to do?"

"Woof him off," Danny said simply. "The guy weighs one forty tops, and you can pass for a facsimile of lusty American manhood in bad light. I figured you'd scowl a little, maybe threaten him with grievous bodily harm; end of problem. Of course, that was before you came gimping in here like somebody's granny."

"So I'll woof him sittin' down," I said. "Unless you don't think I'm up to it, in which case woof him yourself, Liebman. You weigh more than a hundred and forty. A lot more."

"Get real," a girl said from the doorway. "Danny couldn't intimidate a bat mitzvah class. You're Axton, right?"

I swiveled to face her. She was gaunt, gangly, and looked about sixteen. Her blonde hair was short as a boy's, barely more than peach fuzz. She was pretty enough if you're into the starving gamin type. Personally, I prefer grownups.

"Ax, this is Cheryl Vanetti, of Cherry and the Pit? My house band."

"Right, I've heard the group," I said.

"And?" she prompted.

"And it has . . . real potential. With a little work."

The room chilled about ten degrees. "Gee, thanks so much, Mister Axton, sir. Are you a music critic? Or just a hired goon?"

"I do what I do," I said. "And I'd rather do it somewhere other than this office, Danny. It's too private in here. When's this guy due?"

"Five minutes ago, and I've got a feeling he'll be prompt."

"Then let's take a table," Cherry said.

"Hold it," I said. "No offense, but I don't remember inviting you."

"I don't need an invitation, at least not from you, jack. I just signed a long-term development contract with Danny, so what affects him affects me. Besides, Danny says I need to learn more about life to be a better singer. What could be more lively than this? Oughtta be a hoot, right, Danny?"

"It might not hurt to have a witness present anyway, Ax," Danny said sheepishly, leading us out to a table near the dance floor. "The guy's just coming to talk, and with you here, there won't be any trouble."

"It's your party," I said, shrugging.

"Good, I like parties," Cherry said, taking a seat at the table. "But you'd better turn that noise down, Danny. We want to woof the guy off, not bore him to death."

"Bore him?" Danny echoed with mock indignation. "You little philistine. That's Blind Lemon Jefferson. 'Bed Spring Blues.' It's a classic."

"Which is a synonym for outdated, passé, and boooring." Cherry groaned. "If you played some new stuff once in a while, maybe your daytime business would pick up."

"It's kinda tough to find new Blind Lemon songs, miss," I put in. "He froze to death in a Chicago alley back in 1930."

"No wonder he sounds lame. Jeez, Danny, a guy who's been dead sixty years isn't relevant to . . . Is that your friend?"

Danny didn't bother to answer. A couple was standing just inside the front door, waiting for their eyes to adjust to the murk after the coppery brightness of the Motown afternoon. Orientals. Taller than I expected. The man was six feet or so, slender as a clarinet, in a designer leather jacket, all gleaming zippers and studs. Slacks and tassel loafers. She was nearly as tall, but more conservatively dressed; dark suit, a pastel orange Oldham scarf that vaguely matched her shoulder bag. I couldn't guess their ages; tough to do with Asians. Young, though. Thirtyish at the outside.

They spotted Danny and came directly back, moving between the tables with wary grace, like feral cats. And I felt my shoulders tensing, my gut knotting up. It was an intuitive response, not a rational one. The guy didn't look threatening. More like a yuppie stockbroker. Or a lawyer. Hell, maybe that's what was bugging me.

"Mr. Chen," Danny said, "this is my partner, Mr. Axton."

Chen glanced at me but didn't offer to shake hands. Just as well. Up close he had a slightly rancid air, as though his cologne had passed its expiration date. There was a smudge on his jaw where he'd shaved around an acne patch.

"This lady will translate for me if I need," he said. He slouched into a chair across from Danny. "Wouldn't want no misunderstandings."

The woman lit beside him, hovering near his shoulder like a pilot fish. Orientals are supposedly inscrutable, but this one wasn't hard to read. She was jumpy as a bat in a barn fire. Her brow and upper lip were dewy, and she avoided looking at us, even at Cherry, which was odd. Women usually check each other out for at least a split second. I was picking up seriously bad vibes from these two. Something was definitely wrong. I gave Chen my ugliest thousand-yard stare and he barely noticed. He seemed more interested in looking over the room, as if he already owned it. And us.

But the thing was, he wasn't exactly a physical type, and I could see by the cut of his jacket that he wasn't packing iron. So what was I missing?

"I told Liebman our offer yesterday," Chen said, addressing me directly, sizing me up. His accent was odd, more British than Chinese. "He said he had a . . . silent partner? Must be pretty silent. The cosigner on the mortgage and incorporation papers is Mavis Liebman, his mother. So you got no legal . . . standing in this thing. Is that not so?"

"My standing is really none of your business," I said. "And it doesn't matter anyway. Mr. Liebman isn't interested in selling. And for a ten grand walkaway? That was a joke, right?"

"No, not a joke," Chen said with a faint smile. "I promise you it is a . . . serious offer. Deadly serious. You understand? We'll take over the bank debts and give you a good profit. Nine thousand."

"Nine? You said ten," Danny protested.

"Yesterday's price," Chen noted. "Tomorrow it will be eight. Maybe less. It's a good offer. You should take it." Chen's eyes met mine and held. There was a flat challenge in them. "But the price isn't the only number. There's one more number you should know."

"What number?" I asked. "What are you talking about?"

Chen made a production of it. He took out an engraved silver lighter and a matching case that held cigarette papers. Took out a single sheet, jotted a figure on it, and held it up: 23K. He flicked the lighter and touched the flame to the corner of the paper. It flared instantly and vanished into the air. Flash paper. Very theatrical. Very effective. It impressed the hell out of me, and not because I thought it was magic.

Twenty-three K was a Chinese triad, one of the gangs that had been carving up Windsor and Toronto like so many won tons.

Gambling, drugs, extortion. Murder. Serious gangsters. International. And now they were moving into Detroit. Or at least one smug weasel was. And then it hit me. That was what was wrong with his attitude. He was way too cool. About me, about this whole situation. He didn't care whether Danny took his offer or not. Because his gang was just beginning its move on Motown, and at this point a few dead bodies to serve as examples would be as valuable to them as Danny's club.

And the woman with him? Translator my foot. She hadn't said a word and didn't even seem to be listening. She wasn't there to talk, she was a mule. Chen wouldn't risk packing his own gun, that was her job. It was probably in her purse, which was below the table now, beside Chen's knee. And that's why she was so edgy. She knew what was going down here. There wouldn't be any more offers. If Danny said no, Chen meant to settle things today.

He was coolly scanning the room again, probably counting the witnesses. Danny was saying something about thinking things over, but Chen wasn't listening anymore. His eyes had gone empty. In his mind Danny was probably already dead. He shifted his position slightly, with his left hand beneath the table. My God! He was getting ready to take us out, right here and now. And I was unarmed and didn't have a prayer of getting to him before he could fire, unless . . .

His accent. I wondered how long he'd been off the boat. And how sharp he really was.

"You must be new to this country, Mr. Chen," I said.

He hesitated. "I'm here long enough."

"For Toronto or Windsor, maybe. This is Detroit. Things are different here. We're only a small business, but we have a friend. Every business on this street has a friend. A big friend."

I had his attention now. This was something he could understand. "So what?" he said. "I got friends. Probably more than you."

"Then you can see our problem," I said. "The truth is, Danny couldn't sell to you if he wanted to. Nor could I. It wouldn't mean anything. And our friend wouldn't like it. We could get hurt. So could you. So you're wasting your time talking to us. If you're serious about doing business, you need to speak to our friend."

Chen's eyes zeroed in on mine. "Really? And what's his name, this friend?"

"I can't mention his name to strangers, you understand. But a man with your . . . resources should have no trouble getting it."

"Maybe he isn't nobody, this friend. Maybe he don't exist."

"He exists," Cherry put in, the first time she'd spoken. "He's a Cuban. He has one eye."

Chen glanced at her. Through her, really. As a woman, she counted as less than nothing to him. "What's the matter? He's so bad, this friend, you're afraid of his name? Say it. If it's real."

"Delagarza," Cherry said. "Eladio Delagarza."

Chen glanced back to me. "Is what she says true?"

"That's right," I said, swallowing. "Delagarza."

Chen eyed me for what seemed like a very long time, then shrugged, mildly annoyed. He'd probably been looking forward to waxing us. "Name like that, he'll be easy to find," Chen said, rising abruptly. The woman rose with him. Her hands were trembling. With fear or relief? I couldn't be sure.

"You better understand somethin'," Chen said quietly. "Whether I find your friend or not, my offer won't change. I'll be back in a few days. Price then will be five thousand. You better take it. These are hard times. Will get harder. For you." He turned and sauntered out of the room without a backward glance. The woman trailed him like a shadow, zipping her purse closed.

Danny shifted in his chair and stared at me. His face was slick with perspiration. "Have both of you gone absolutely psycho?" he said at last. "What the hell was that about?"

"Your pal here was trying to run a bluff," Cherry snapped. "Only he couldn't think of a name, so I tossed one in."

"Some name," I said.

"Who is this — Delagarza, anyway?" Danny asked.

"A crime boss," Cherry said. "A big one. Or so I read in the papers."

"That's crazy," Danny said. "I don't know him."

"No, but Chen doesn't either," I said. "And while he's asking around, we'll have time to figure what to do next."

"There won't be any next," Cherry said flatly. "Delagarza's in some kind of federal trouble. So if Chen asks, Delagarza will just blow him off. Chen'll do some checking, find out Delagarza's nobody to mess with, and back off. End of problem."

"It won't be that simple," I said.

"Maybe you just hope it won't so you can collect another fee," Cherry said. "I thought you were supposed to scare this guy off, Axton, not run some kind of a scam on him."

"Lady, you don't have any idea what was going on. Danny, this guy didn't come here to do a deal, he isn't bright enough. I make him as a stone shooter who'd rather whack you out than buy your place. You'd better go to the police about this. Or seriously think about giving him what he wants."

"Give him what he wants?" Cherry said, aghast. "Are you nuts? Some guy sits at a table with you, runs his mouth, and you wanna pack it in? Jesus, Danny, where did you —"

"Okay, okay, cool it you two," Danny interrupted. "All's well that ends well, right?"

"That's just it, Danny," I said. "This isn't over. He'll be back."

"In which case I'll give a yell and you can muscle him off again," Danny said. "Or maybe Cherry's right and he's history. Either way, the problem's settled for now, and I could use a beer. Why don't you both join me?"

"No, thanks," Cherry said, rising. "I've got a rehearsal, and I'd better not be late if I want to live up to the promise Axton thinks I've got, though I doubt he knows any more about music than he does about muscle. I'll see you tonight, Danny. And just for the record, whatever you're paying your goon friend here, it's way too much." She turned and stalked off.

"How much am I paying you, Ax?" Danny asked as I got painfully to my feet. "Things happened so quickly we didn't discuss the details."

"No charge," I said grimly. "If Chen's gone for good, then it was as much Cherry's doing as mine. I was just trying to come out of this alive."

"That's a bit of an exaggeration, isn't it?" Danny said.

"I don't think it is. Look, you know me, Danny. You know I don't spook easily, and I'm telling you this guy is serious trouble. What are you gonna do?"

"I . . . don't know," Danny said hesitantly. "I need to think."

"I doubt he'll give you much time."

"I expect I've got at least a few days, and if Cherry's right, maybe a lot more than that. I can't just hand over my place to some thug, Ax."

"Then you'd better talk to the police. And soon. And no matter what, if Chen contacts you again, don't meet him alone, okay? You get hold of me."

"Okay," Danny said simply. "Whatever you say. But I wish you'd try to get along with Cheryl. She's young, but she's got a good head on her shoulders, and she's got a world of talent."

"I'll just bet she has," I said.

"No, man, it's not like that at all," Danny said, smiling. "Even if she was my type, I wouldn't be hers, and neither would you. She's gay, man. Got a steady girlfriend mean enough to whip Godzilla. But I'm dead serious about her talent. Maybe it isn't shining through yet, but it will. She's gonna be a keeper someday. You mark my words. So cut her some slack, okay? I like my friends to get along."

"Well, I'll admit she could be right on one small point," I said. "Your daytime trade might improve if you lightened up on the music. Maybe bag Blind Lemon and play something newer."

"I'd rather listen to the real thing, thanks."

"It's your place," I grumbled. "At least for now."

My ankle turned out to be severely sprained. I stopped at a doc-in-the-box infirmary on Jefferson, and a medic taped me into a plastic walking cast, which meant I was temporarily unemployable as a bouncer, bill collector, or anything else I knew how to do. Terrific.

I decided to call it a day, pick up some barbecued ribs on my way home, and fort up for the evening.

Papa Henry's Hickory Hut serves the best barbecued ribs in the city of Detroit. Bar none. The rotisserie in the storefront window revolves slowly, cradling racks of ribs and chicken flame-kissed by the fire below. The aroma alone could turn Gandhi into a carnivore.

I was in a back booth finishing off an order of spiced slaw when I caught a name on the TV newscast from the set above the counter. I turned slowly to face the screen. The volume on the set was low. I couldn't catch it all.

"Alleged mob figure Eladio Delagarza . . . luxurious Eastpointe home . . . explosion." The flames blazing on the screen were nearly as bright as the barbecue pit, greedily licking the skeleton of what had once been a mansion. "Victims' names are being withheld pending notification of next of kin . . ."

Coincidence. That's all it was. Just a freaking coincidence. Dela-garza was in trouble with the law, maybe one of his rivals . . . Be-sides, I was lame and my rack of short ribs wouldn't be ready for another ten minutes. Best barbecue in the city of Detroit.

Damn.

I dropped a twenty on the table and gimped out to my rusty Buick.

I parked on McNichols, around the corner from the club. Dusk in Detroit. The street was deserted. A wino crouched in the entry-way of the vacant barbershop next door. A chill wind nipped at my jacket as I limped cautiously into Yo Mama's Blues.

The place was empty. No surprise. Blind Lemon Jefferson's moaning on the sound system would have driven off any customers who weren't deaf or too drunk to stagger out. Damn Danny anyway. A bar's supposed to be a business, not a freaking history of music seminar.

I stumped quickly across the dance floor to the office. And stopped in the doorway. Danny was slumped in his chair. A slather of crimson was leaking down his cheek. He'd been shot. Once. In the eye. Through the right lens of his glasses.

Triad. I'd read somewhere it was their trademark. A way to tell their killings from the two dozen others in a Motown month.

Stepping into that room was maybe the hardest thing I've ever done. I managed, somehow. I touched Danny's throat, just to be certain. His skin was already cooling.

Sweet Jesus. Nine-one-one. Call 911. I reached for the phone but hesitated, not wanting to smear any fingerprints. The thundering blues tape was so loud I couldn't think . . .

There was a clatter from the other room, and I froze. Then I took a deep breath and edged silently to the open door. I peered around the corner of the jamb. The bar still looked empty, but someone was out there, I knew it at the core of my soul. As I'd known about Danny somehow, the moment I saw those flames on the TV screen. I glanced back into the office, desperately scanning the room for some kind of a weapon. Damn it, with my ankle in a cast I couldn't even run for it . . .

"Danny?" Cheryl Vanetti called from the shadows near the bar.

"No, it's me, Axton," I said, stepping out where she could see me. "Danny's . . . had it."

"What do you mean, had it?" she said, stalking angrily toward me. "You're lying."

"No," I said, grabbing her arm, trying to keep her away from the office. She stared into my face for a moment, then shrugged off my grip and moved to the office doorway. And looked inside.

"Oh." She said it so softly I barely heard. I gave her a moment, then touched her arm. She drew away.

"We have to get out of here," I said.

"But . . . what about the police?"

"We'll call 'em," I said, "from somewhere on the road."

"What are you talking about? Chen —"

"Didn't do this," I said.

"What?"

"He didn't do this," I repeated. "Not personally, anyway. He knows we can tie him to it, so he'll have an alibi that will hold up long enough for his people to take us out. This isn't just a murder, it's first blood in a gang war. They hit Delagarza's house an hour ago, and if they're up for that, they can swat us like flies whenever they want. We've got to get out of here, now."

"But what about my band? I can't just leave."

"You have to, and right now. My car's outside. Let's go."

"But —"

"Dammit, girl, we've both made enough mistakes for one day. If you don't think so, ask Danny. Now move it, or I'll by God leave you here."

She looked up at me, blinking as though I'd slapped her. Then her eyes cleared, the anguish in them erased by anger. "You bastard," she said. "This is your fault."

"You're half right," I admitted. "Which is the only reason I'm willing to take you along. Are you coming or not?"

"Just a minute." She disappeared into Danny's office and came out carrying his old Martin guitar. I just stared. "It's a good guitar and he loved it," she said defiantly. "It shouldn't go to strangers. Besides, he never could play it worth a damn anyway."

I started to say something, but her eyes stopped me. They were brimming, and the hurt in them was deep. She was only a word away from falling apart. So I turned away and went out to my car. She followed, carefully stowed the guitar in the back seat, and climbed in.

We drove all night, south mostly. And neither of us said a solitary word to the other. Not one.

I dropped her at a truck stop in Tennessee. She said she could make a few calls, find a friend to stay with. Under the circumstances it would be best if I didn't know where she was going. Danny was right, she had a good head on her shoulders.

I drove all the next day, wound up at a cousin's farm in Mississippi, and called a friend on the Detroit P.D. to fill him in on what happened. He told me Chen was dead already, whacked by Delagarza's people, but the shooting was still going on. It might be wise if I stayed gone for a while.

So I did. I picked up a few odd jobs repossessing cars for a detective agency in Biloxi, worked a few skip traces, and kept body and soul together. It took most of a year for things to shake out between the triads and the Cubans. I kept in touch with my contacts in Detroit. Eventually they told me things were cool, that nobody in particular was looking for me. So I moved back and picked up the pieces of my life.

That was ten years ago, maybe a little more. And Danny's memory had faded some, like an old photograph. It happens. I'd never seen Cheryl Vanetti again. Until tonight.

She looked different, of course, and it was more than just the years. Her hair was waist-length now, and dark, though whether she was coloring it then or now, I couldn't tell. Her face had a few character lines, but they weren't unbecoming.

I glanced at a poster on the wall. The band was called Truth in Packaging. She wasn't billed separately, so I couldn't tell whether she was using her own name. I could have asked a waitress, I suppose, but that might have alerted Cootie, so I didn't risk it. If she was still hiding, it was none of my business.

Her band was really good. A lot better than promising now. I couldn't tell if she'd spotted me or not. She was wearing sunglasses, so it was impossible to follow her eyes. Or read anything in them.

They ended their set to enthusiastic applause. And I noticed that Cootie was getting restless, which was a bad sign. He was dumb enough to make a run for it, and I didn't feel like chasing him around a redneck roadhouse in freaking Indiana.

I asked the waitress for our tab, but while she was totting it up, the background noise in the room tapered off.

Cherry had returned to the stage alone, carrying a battered old Martin guitar that I recognized instantly. She tuned it, then glanced around the room, waiting for the audience to quiet, and began to fingerpick a tune, Blind Lemon Jefferson's "Bed Spring Blues."

It's an old song, a classic, but there was nothing derivative in her version of it. She sang it with power and anguish and heart. With soul. She'd always had the voice, the talent, but now what her singing had was passion, and the pain was real.

I didn't know whether the song was meant for me or just part of her show, but I think it was for me. When she played a short solo before the final verse, she built it around a mistake, a broken lick, note for note, the same lame way Danny used to butcher it all those years ago. The timing was off, the tune was wrong, but in her hands it was brilliant, as imperfect as real life.

She sang the last verse, and maybe she and I were the only ones in the room who knew what the loss in that song was really about, but it didn't matter. She was singing the truth and the audience sensed it.

When she finished, there was a stunned moment of silence before the roar of applause began, and it was far more telling than all the hooting and hollering in the world. Even Cootie joined in.

I left without speaking to her. I had Cootie in tow, but it was more than that.

The truth is, I don't know what we can say to each other now. Some hurts never heal. They just scar over. It's best to let them be.

I hadn't liked her much, and her recklessness had helped get a friend of mine killed. But most of the blame was mine. Cherry had no way of knowing how dangerous Chen was. But I should have.

Still, we were both younger then, and when you're green, the world's a superstore, with everything you want. The catch is, the prices aren't marked. So you make choices, but you don't know what they're going to cost you until later. Or how much your friends and loved ones will pay. Sometimes, if you're lucky, you can make it up to them in some way. Not this time, though.

A few hours later, cruising through Toledo, halfway to the morning with Cootie snoring in the back seat, damned if I didn't hear another Blind Lemon blues tune on a college station out of Lansing. And for a moment it brought Danny back so clearly I could almost sense his presence in the car.

And I had to smile, remembering how crazy we were in those days, about music and life and all of it. And it occurred to me that if Danny had been with me earlier, if he'd come back from Shadowland to hear Cherry sing that one Blind Lemon song . . . if I'd asked him if the price we paid was too high, I know what his answer would have been.

JAMES CRUMLEY

Hot Springs

FROM *Murder for Love*

AT NIGHT, EVEN IN THE chill mountain air, Mona Sue insisted on cranking the air conditioner all the way up. Her usual temperature always ran a couple of degrees higher than normal, and she claimed that the baby she carried made her constant fever even worse. She kept the cabin cold enough to hang meat. During the long, sleepless nights Benbow spooned to her naked, burning skin, trying to stay warm.

In the mornings, too, Mona Sue forced him into the cold. The modern cabin sat on a bench in the cool shadow of Mount Nihart, and they broke their fast with a room-service breakfast on the deck, a robe wrapped loosely about her naked body while Benbow bundled into both sweats and a robe. She ate furiously, stoking a furnace, and recounted her dreams as if they were gospel, effortlessly consuming most of the spread of exotic cheeses and expensively unseasonable fruits, a loaf of sourdough toast and four kinds of meat, all the while aimlessly babbling through the events of her internal night, the dreams of a teenage girl, languidly symbolic and vaguely frightening. She dreamt of her mother, young and lovely, devouring her litter of barefoot boys in the dark Ozark hollows. And her father, home from a Tennessee prison, his crooked member dangling against her smooth cheek.

Benbow suspected she left the best parts out and did his best to listen to the soft southern cadences without watching her face. He knew what happened when he watched her talk, watched the soft moving curve of her dark lips, the wise slant of her gray eyes. So he picked at his breakfast and tried to focus his stare downslope at the

steam drifting off the large hot-water pool behind the old shagbark
lodge.

But then she switched to her daydreams about their dubious
future, which were as deadly specific as a .45 slug in the brainpan:
after the baby, they could flee to Canada; nobody would follow
them up there. He listened and watched with the false patience of a
teenage boy involved in his first confrontation with pure lust and
hopeless desire.

Mona Sue ate with the precise and delicate greed of a heart
surgeon, the pad of her spatulate thumb white on the handle of her
spoon as she carved a perfect curled ball from the soft orange meat
of her melon. Each bite of meat had to be balanced with an equal
weight of toast before being crushed between her tiny white teeth.
Then she examined each strawberry poised before her darkly red
lips as if it might be a jewel of great omen and she some ancient
oracle, then sank her shining teeth into the fleshy fruit as if it were
the mortal truth. Benbow's heart rolled in his chest as he tried to
fill his lungs with the cold air to fight off the heat of her body.

Fall had come to the mountains, now. The cottonwoods and
alders welcomed the change with garish mourning dress, and in
the mornings a rime of ice covered the windshield of the gray
Taurus he had stolen at the Denver airport. New snow fell each
night, moving slowly down the ridges from the high distant peaks of
the Hard Rock Range and slipped closer each morning down the
steep ridge behind them. Below the bench the old lodge seemed to
settle more deeply into the narrow canyon, as if hunkering down
for eons of snow, and the steam from the hot springs mixed with
wood smoke and lay flat and sinuous among the yellow creek wil-
lows.

Benbow suspected, too, that the scenery was wasted on Mona
Sue. Her dark eyes seemed turned inward to a dreamscape of her
life, her husband, R. L. Dark, the pig farmer, his bull-necked son,
Little R. L., and the lumpy Ozark offal of her large worthless family.

"Coach," she'd say — she thought it funny to call him Coach —
interrupting the shattered and drifting narrative of her dreams.
Then she would sweep back the thick black Indian hair from her
face, tilt her narrow head on the slender column of her neck, and
laugh. "Coach, that ol' R. L., he's a-comin'. You stole somethin'
belonged to him, and you can bet he's on his way. Lit'l R. L., too,

prob'ly, 'cause he tol' me once he'd like to string your guts on a bob-wire fence," she recited like a sprightly but not very bright child.

"Sweetheart, R. L. Dark can just barely cipher the numbers on a dollar bill or the spots on a card," Benbow answered, as he had each morning for the six months they'd been on the run. "He can't read a map that he hasn't drawn himself, and by noon he's too drunk to fit his ass in a tractor seat and find his hog pens. . . ."

"You know, Puddin', an ol' boy's got enough a them dollar bills, or stacks a them Franklins like we do," she added, laughing, "he can hire-out that readin' part, and the map part too. So he's a-comin'. You can put that in your momma's piggy bank."

This was a new wrinkle in their morning ritual, and Benbow caught himself glancing down at the parking lot behind the lodge and at the single narrow road up Hidden Springs Canyon, but he shook it off quickly. When he made the fateful decision to take Mona Sue and the money, he vowed to go for it, never glancing over his shoulder, living in the moment.

And this was it. Once more. Leaving his breakfast untouched, again, he slipped his hand through the bulky folds of Mona Sue's terry cloth robe to cradle the warm ripening fullness of her breasts and the long, thick nipples, already rock hard before his touch, and he kissed her mouth, sweet with strawberry and melon. Once again, he marveled at the deep passionate growl from the base of her throat as he pressed his lips into the hollow, then Benbow lifted her small frame — she nestled the baby high under the smooth vault of her rib cage and even at seven months the baby barely showed — and carried her to the bedroom.

Benbow knew, from recent experience, that the horse wrangler who doubled as room-service waiter would be waiting to clear the picnic table when they came out of the house to finish the coffee. The wrangler might have patience with horses but not with guests who spent their mornings in bed. But he would wait for long minutes, silent as a Sioux scout, as Mona Sue searched her robe for his tip, occasionally exposing the rising contour of a breast or the clean scissoring of her long legs. Benbow had given him several hard looks, which the wrangler ignored as if the blunt stares were spoken in a foreign tongue. But nothing helped. Except to take the woman inside and avoid the wrangler altogether.

This morning Benbow laid Mona Sue on the featherbed like a gift, opened her robe, kissed the soft curve of her swollen belly, then blew softly on her feathery pubic hair. Mona Sue sobbed quickly, coughed as if she had a catfish bone caught in her throat, her long body arching. Benbow sobbed, too, his hunger for her more intense than the hunger growling in his empty stomach.

While Mona Sue had swelled through her pregnancy, Benbow had shed twenty-seven pounds from his blocky frame. Sometimes, just after they made love, it seemed as if her burning body had stolen the baby from his own muscled flesh, something stolen during the tangle of love, something growing hard and tight in her smooth, slim body.

As usual, they made love, then finished the coffee, ordered a fresh pot, tipped the wrangler, then made love again before her morning nap.

While Mona Sue slept, usually Benbow would drink the rest of the coffee as he read the day-old Meriwether newspaper, then slip into his sweats and running shoes, and jog down the switchbacks to the lodge to laze in the hot waters of the pools. He loved it there, floating in the water that seemed heavier than normal, thicker but cleaner, clearer. He almost felt whole there, cleansed and healthy and warm, taking the waters like some rich foreign prince, fleeing his failed life.

Occasionally, Benbow wished Mona Sue would interrupt her naps to join him, but she always said it might hurt the baby and she was already plenty hot with her natural fevers. As the weeks passed, Benbow learned to treasure his time alone in the hot pool and stopped asking her.

So their days wound away routinely, spooling like silk ribbons through their fingers, as placid as the deeply still waters of the pool.

But this noon, exhausted from the run and the worry, the lack of sleep and food, Benbow slipped effortlessly into the heated gravity of Mona Sue's sleeping body and slept, only to wake suddenly, sweating in spite of the chill, when the air conditioner was switched off.

R. L. Dark stood at the foot of their bed. Grinning. The old man stretched his crinkled neck, sniffing the air like an ancient snapping turtle, testing the air for food or fun, since he had no natural enemies except for teenage boys with .22's. R. L. had dressed for the occasion. He wore a new Carhart tin coat and clean bib overalls with the old Webley .455 revolver hanging on a string from his neck and bagging the bib pocket.

Two good ol' boys flanked him, one bald and the other wildly hirsute, both huge and dressed in Kmart flannel plaid. The bald one held up a small ball-peen hammer like a trophy. They weren't grinning. A skinny man in a baggy white suit shifted from foot to foot behind them, smiling weakly like a gun-shy pointer pup.

"Well, piss on the fire, boys, and call the dogs," R. L. Dark said, hustling the extra .455 rounds in his pocket as if they were his withered privates, "this hunt's done." The old man's cackle sounded like the sunrise cry of a cannibalistic rooster. "Son, they say you coulda been some kinda football coach, and I know you're one hell of a poker player, but I'd a never thought you'd come to this sorry end — a simpleminded thief and a chickenfuckin' wife stealer." Then R. L. brayed like one of the old plow mules he kept in the muddy bottoms of the White. "But you can run right smart, son. Gotta say that. Sly as an old boar coon. We might still be a-lookin' if'n Baby Doll there ain't a called her momma. Collect. To brag 'bout the baby."

Jesus, Benbow thought. Her mother. A toothless woman, now shaped like a potato dumpling, topped with greasy hair, seasoned with moles.

Mona Sue woke, rubbing her eyes like a child, murmuring, "How you been, Daddy Honey?"

And Benbow knew he faced a death even harder than his unlucky life, knew even before the monster on the right popped him behind the ear with the ball-peen hammer and jerked his stunned body out of bed as if he were a child and handed him to his partner, who wrapped him in a full nelson. The bald one flipped the hammer and rapped his nuts smartly with it, then flipped it again and began breaking the small bones of Benbow's right foot with the round knob of the hammerhead.

Before Benbow fainted, harsh laughter raked his throat. Maybe this was the break he had been waiting for all his life.

Actually, it had all been Little R. L.'s fault. Sort of. Benbow had spotted the hulking bowlegged kid with the tiny ears and the thick neck three years earlier when the downward spiral of his football coaching career had led him to Alabamphilia, a small town on the edge of the Ozarks, a town without hope or dignity or even any convincing religious fervor, a town that smelled of chicken guts, hog manure, and rampant incest, which seemed to be the three main industries.

Benbow first saw Little R. L. in a pickup touch football game played on the hardscrabble playground and knew from the first moment that the boy had the quick grace of a deer, combined with the strength of a wild boar. This kid was one of the best natural running backs he'd ever seen. Benbow also found out just as quickly that Little R. L. was one of the redheaded Dark boys, and the Dark boys didn't play football.

Daddy R. L. thought football was a silly game, a notion with which Benbow agreed, and too much like work not to draw wages, with which once again Benbow agreed, and if'n his boys were going to work for free, they were damn well going to work for him and his hog operation, not some dirt-poor pissant washed-up football bum. Benbow had to agree with that, too, right to R. L.'s face, had to eat the old man's shit to get to the kid. Because this kid could be Benbow's ticket out of this Ozark hell, and he intended to have him. This was the one break Benbow needed to save his life. Once again.

It had always been that way for Benbow, needing that one break that never seemed to come. During his senior year at the small high school in western Nebraska, after three and a half years of mostly journeyman work as a blocking back in a pass-crazy offense, Benbow's mother had worked double shifts at the truck-stop café — his dad had been dead so long nobody really remembered him — so they could afford to put together a videotape of his best efforts as a running back and pass receiver to send down to the university coaches in Lincoln. Once they had agreed to send a scout up for one game, Benbow had badgered his high school coach into a promise to let him carry the ball at least twenty times that night.

But the weather screwed him. On what should have been a lovely early October Friday night, a storm raced in from Canada, days early, and its icy wind blew Benbow's break right out of the water. Before the game it rained two hard inches, then the field froze.

During the first half it rained again, then hailed, and at the end of the second quarter it became a blinding snow squall.

Benbow had gained sixty yards, sure, but none of it pretty. And at halftime the Nebraska scout came by to apologize but if he was to get home in this weather, he had to start now. The lumpy old man invited Benbow to try a walk-on. Right, Benbow thought. Without a scholarship, he didn't have the money to register for fall semester. *Damn,* Benbow thought as he kicked the water cooler, and *damn it to hell,* he thought as his big toe shattered and his senior season ended.

So he played football for some pissant Christian college in the Dakotas where he didn't bother to take a degree. With his fused toe, he had lost a step in the open-field and his cuts lost their precision, so he haunted the weight room, forced thick muscle over his running back's body, and made himself into a solid if small fullback, but good enough to wrangle an invitation to one of the postseason senior bowl games. Then the first-string fullback, who was sure to be drafted by the pros, strained his knee in practice and refused to play. *Oh, God,* Benbow thought, *another break.*

But God foxed this one. The backfield coach was a born-again fundamentalist named Culpepper, and once he caught Benbow neither bowing his head nor even bothering to close his eyes during a lengthy team prayer, the coach became determined to convert the boy. Benbow played along, choking on his anger at the self-righteous bastard until his stomach cramped, swallowing the anger until he was throwing up three times a day, twice during practice and once before lights-out. By game day he'd lost twelve pounds and feared he wouldn't have the strength to play.

But he did. He had a first half to praise the football gods, if not the Christian one: two rushing touchdowns, one three yards dragging a linebacker and a corner, the other thirty-nine yards of fluid grace and power; and one receiving, twenty-two yards. But the quarterback had missed the handoff at the end of the first half, jammed the ball against Benbow's hip, and a blitzing linebacker picked it out of the air, then scored.

In the locker room at halftime, Culpepper was all over him like stink on shit. *Pride goeth before a fall!* he shouted. *We're never as tall as we are on our knees before Jesus!* And all the other soft-brain clichés. Benbow's stomach knotted like a rawhide rope, then rebelled. Ben-

bow caught that bit of vomit and swallowed it. But the second wave
was too much. He turned and puked into a nearby sink. Culpepper
went mad. Accused him of being out of shape, of drinking, smoking, and fornicating. When Benbow denied the charges, Culpepper
added another, screamed *Prevaricator!* his foamy spittle flying into
Benbow's face. And that was that.

Culpepper lost an eye from the single punch and nearly died
during the operation to rebuild his cheekbone. Everybody said
Benbow was lucky not to do time, like his father, who had killed a
corrupt weighmaster down in Texas with his tire thumper, and was
then killed himself by a bad Houston drug dealer down in the Ellis
Unit at Huntsville when Benbow was six. Benbow was lucky, he
guessed, but marked "Uncoachable" by the pro scouts and denied
tryouts all over the league. Benbow played three years in Canada,
then destroyed his knee in a bar fight with a Chinese guy in Vancou-
ver. Then he was out of the game. Forever.

Benbow drifted west, fighting fires in the summers and dealing
poker in the winter, taking the occasional college classes until he
finally finished a P.E. teaching degree at Northern Montana and
garnered an assistant coach's job at a small town in the Sweetgrass
Hills, where he discovered he had an unsuspected gift for coaching,
as he did for poker: a quick mind and no fear. A gift, once discovered, that became an addiction to the hard work, long hours, loving
the game, and paying the price to win.

Head coach in three years, then two state championships, and a
move to a larger school in Washington State. Where his mother
came to live with him. Or die with him, as it were. The doctors said
it was her heart, but Benbow knew that she died of truck-stop food,
cheap whiskey, and long-haul drivers whose souls were as full of
stale air as their tires.

But he coached a state championship team the next year and was
considering offers from a football power down in northern California when he was struck down by a scandalous lawsuit. His second-
string quarterback had become convinced that Benbow was sleeping with his mother, which of course he was. When the kid attacked
Benbow at practice with his helmet, Benbow had to hit the kid to
keep him off. He knew this part of his life was over when he saw the
kid's eye dangling out of its socket on the grayish pink string of the
optic nerve.

Downhill, as they say, from there. Drinking and fighting as often as coaching, low-rent poker games and married women, usually married to school-board members or dumb-shit administrators. Downhill all the way to Alabamphilia.

Benbow came back to this new world propped in a heap on the couch in the cottage's living room with a dull ache behind his ear and a thousand sharp pains in his foot, which was propped in a white cast on the coffee table, the fresh cast the size of a water-melon. Benbow didn't have to ask what purpose it served. The skinny man sat beside him, a syringe in hand. Across the room, R. L.'s bulk stood black against a fiery sunset, Mona Sue sitting curled in a chair in his shadow, slowly filing her nails. Through the window, Benbow could see the Kmart twins walking slow guard tours back and forth across the deck.

"He's comin' out of it, Mr. Dark," the old man said, his voice as sharp as his pale nose.

"Well, give him another dose, Doc," R. L. said without turning. "We don't want that boy a-hurtin' none. Not yet."

Benbow didn't understand what R. L. meant as the doctor stirred beside him, releasing a thin, dry stench like a limestone cavern or an open grave. Benbow had heard that death supposedly hurt no more than having a tooth pulled and he wondered who had brought back that bit of information as the doctor hit him in the shoulder with a blunt needle, then he slipped uneasily into an enforced sleep like a small death.

When he woke again, Benbow found little changed but the light. Mona Sue still curled in her chair, sleeping now, below her hus-band's hulk against the full dark sky. The doctor slept, too, leaning the fragile bones of his skull against Benbow's sore arm. And Ben-bow's leg was also asleep, locked in position by the giant cast resting on the coffee table. He sat very still for as long as he could, waiting for his mind to clear, willing his dead leg to awaken, and wondering why he wasn't dead too.

"Don't be gettin' no ideas, son," R. L. said without turning.

Of all the things Benbow had hated during the long Sundays shoveling pig shit or dealing cards for R. L. Dark — that was the trade he and the old man had made for Little R. L.'s football services — he hated the bastard calling him "son."

"I'm not your son, you fucking old bastard."

R. L. ignored him, didn't even bother to turn. "How hot's that there water?" he asked calmly as the doctor stirred.

Benbow answered without thinking. "Somewhere between ninety-eight and one-oh-two. Why?"

"How 'bout half a dose, Doc?" R. L. said, turning now. "And see 'bout makin' that boy's cast waterproof. I'm thinkin' that hot water might take the edge off my rheumatism and I for sure want the coach there to keep me company. . . ."

Once again Benbow found the warm, lazy path back to the darkness at the center of his life, half listening to the old man and Mona Sue squabble over the air conditioner.

After word of his bargain with R. L. Dark for the gridiron services of his baby son spread throughout every tuck and hollow of the county, Benbow could no longer stop after practice for even a single quiet beer at any one of the rank honky-tonks that surrounded the dry town without hearing snickers as he left. It seemed that whatever he might have gained in sympathy, he surely lost in respect. And the old man treated him worse than a farting joke.

On the Saturdays that first fall, when Benbow began his days exchanging his manual labor for Little R. L.'s rushing talents, the old man dogged him all around the hog farm on a small John Deere tractor, endlessly pointing out Benbow's total ignorance of the details of trading bacon for bread and his general inability to perform hard work, complaining at great length, then cackling wildly and jacking the throttle on the tractor as if this was the funniest thing he'd ever seen. Even knowing that Little R. L. was lying on the couch in front of the television and soothing his sore muscles with a pint jar of 'shine couldn't make Benbow even begin to resent his bargain, and he never even bothered to look at the old man, knowing that this was his only escape.

Sundays, though, the old man left him alone. Sunday was Poker Day. Land-rich farmers, sly country lawyers with sharp eyes and soft hands, and small-town bankers with the souls of slave traders came from as far away as West Memphis, St. Louis, and Fort Smith to gather in R. L.'s double-wide for a table stakes hold 'em game, a game famous in at least four states, and occasionally in northern Mexico.

On the sabbath he was on his own, except for the surly, lurking presence of Little R. L., who seemed to blame his coach for every ache and pain, and the jittery passage of a slim, petulant teenage girl who slopped past him across the muddy farmyard in a shapeless feed-sack dress and oversized rubber boots, trailing odd, throaty laughter, the same laughter she had when one of the sows decided to dine on her litter. Benbow should have listened.

But these seemed minor difficulties when balanced against the fact that Little R. L. gained nearly a hundred yards a game his freshman year.

The next fall, the shit-shoveling and the old man's attitude seemed easier to bear. Then when Benbow casually let slip that he had once dealt and played poker professionally, R. L.'s watery blue eyes suddenly glistened with greed, and the Sunday portion of Benbow's bargain became both easier and more complicated. Not that the old man needed him to cheat. R. L. Dark always won. The only times the old man signaled him to deal seconds was to give hands to his competitors to keep them in the game so the old man could skin them even deeper.

The brutal and dangerous monotony of Benbow's life continued, controlled and hopeful until the fall of Little R. L.'s junior year, when everything came apart. Then back together with a terrible rush. A break, a dislocation, and a connection.

On the Saturday afternoon after Little R. L. broke the state rushing record the night before, the teenage girl stopped chuckling long enough to ask a question. "How long you have to go to college, Coach, to figure out how to scoot pig shit off concrete with a fire hose?"

When she laughed, Benbow finally asked, "Who the fuck are you, honey?"

"Mrs. R. L. Dark, Senior," she replied, the perfect arch of her nose in the air, "that's who." And Benbow looked at her for the first time, watched the thrust of her hard, marvelous body naked beneath the thin fabric of her cheap dress.

Then Benbow tried to make conversation with Mona Sue, made the mistake of asking Mona Sue why she wore rubber boots. "Hookworms," she said, pointing at his sockless feet in old Nikes. *Jesus,* he thought. Then *Jesus wept* that night as he watched the white worms slither through his dark, bloody stool. Now he knew what the old man had been laughing about.

On Sunday a rich Mexican rancher tried to cover one of R. L.'s raises with a Rolex, then the old man insisted on buying the fifteen-thousand-dollar watch with five K cash, and when he opened the small safe set in the floor of the trailer's kitchen, Benbow glimpsed the huge pile of banded stacks of one-hundred-dollar bills that filled the safe.

The next Friday night Little R. L. broke his own rushing record with more than a quarter left in the game, which was good because in the fourth quarter the turf gave way under his right foot, which then slid under a pursuing tackle. Benbow heard the *pop* all the way from the sidelines as the kid's knee dislocated.

Explaining to R. L. that a bargain was a bargain, no matter what happened with the kid's knee, the next day Benbow went about his chores just long enough to lure Mona Sue into a feed shed and out of her dress. But not her rubber boots. Benbow didn't care. He just fucked her. The revenge he planned on R. L. Dark a frozen hell in his heart. But the soft hunger of her mouth and the touch of her astonishing body — diamond-hard nipples, fast-twitch cat muscle slithering under human skin, her cunt like a silken bag of rich, luminous seed pearls suspended in heavenly fucking fire — destroyed his hope of vengeance. Now he simply wanted her. No matter the cost.

Two months later, just as her pregnancy began to show, Benbow cracked the safe with a tablespoon of nitro, took all the money, and they ran.

Although he was sure Mona Sue still dreamed, she'd lost her audience. Except for the wrangler, who still watched her as if she were some heathen idol. But every time she tried to talk to the dark cowboy, the old man pinched her thigh with horny fingers so hard it left blood blisters.

Their mornings were much different now. They all went to the hot water. The doctor slept on a poolside bench behind Mona Sue, who sat on the side of the pool, her feet dangling in the water, her blotched thighs exposed, and her eyes as vacant as her half-smile. R. L. Dark, Curley, and Bald Bill, wearing cutoffs and cheap T-shirts, stood neck-deep in the steamy water, loosely surrounding Benbow, anchored by his plastic-shrouded cast, which loomed like a giant boulder under the heavy water.

A vague sense of threat, like an occasional sharp sniff of sulphur, came off the odd group and kept the other guests at a safe distance, and the number of guests declined every day as the old man rented each cabin and room at the lodge as it came empty. The rich German twins who owned the place didn't seem to care who paid for their cocaine.

During the first few days, nobody had much bothered to speak to Benbow, not even to ask where he had hidden the money. The pain in his foot had retreated to a dull ache, but the itch under the cast had become unbearable. One morning, the doctor had taken pity on him and searched the kitchen drawers for something for Benbow to use to scratch beneath the cast, finally coming up with a cheap shish kebab skewer. Curly and Bald Bill had examined the thin metal stick as if it might be an Arkansas toothpick or a bowie knife, then laughed and let Benbow have it. He kept it holstered in his cast, waiting, scratching the itch. And a deep furrow in the rear of the cast.

Then one morning as they stood silent and safe in the pool, a storm cell drifted slowly down the mountain to fill the canyon with swirling squalls of thick, wet snow, the old man raised his beak into the flakes and finally spoke: "I always meant to come back to this country," he said.

"What?"

Except for the wrangler slowly gathering damp towels and a dark figure in a hooded sweatshirt and sunglasses standing inside the bar, the pool and the deck had emptied when the snow began. Benbow had been watching the snow gather in the dark waves of Mona Sue's hair as she tried to catch a spinning flake on her pink tongue. Even as he faced death, she still stirred the banked embers glowing in Benbow's crotch.

"During WW Two," the old man said softly, "I got in some trouble over at Fort Chaffee — stuck a noncom with a broomstick — so the army sent me up here to train with the Tenth Mountain. Stupid assholes thought it was some kinda punishment. Always meant to come back someday. . . ."

But Benbow watched the cold wind ripple the stolid surface of the hot water as the snowflakes melted into it. The rising steam became a thick fog.

"I always liked it," Benbow said, glancing up at the mountain as it appeared and disappeared behind the roiling clouds of snow. "Great hunting weather," he added. "There's a little herd of elk bedded just behind that first ridge." As his keepers' eyes followed his upslope, he drifted slowly through the fog toward Mona Sue's feet aimlessly stirring the water. "If you like it so much, you old bastard, maybe you should buy it."

"Watch your tongue, boy," Curly said as he cuffed Benbow on the head. Benbow stumbled closer to Mona Sue.

"I just might do that, son," the old man said, cackling, "just to piss you off. Not that you'll be around to be pissed off."

"So what the fuck are we hanging around here for?" Benbow asked, turning on the old man, which brought him even closer to Mona Sue.

The old man paused as if thinking. "Well, son, we're waitin' for that baby. If'n that baby has red hair and you tell us where you hid the money, we'll just take you home, kill you easy, then feed you to the hogs."

"And if it doesn't have red hair, since I'm not about to tell you where to find the money?"

"We'll just find a hungry sow, son, and feed you to her," the old man said, "startin' with your good toes."

Everybody laughed then: R. L. Dark threw back his head and howled; the hulks exchanged high fives and higher giggles; and Benbow collapsed underwater. Even Mona Sue chuckled deep in her throat. Until Benbow jerked her off the side of the pool. Then she choked. The poor girl had never learned to swim.

Before either the old man or his bodyguards could move, though, the dark figure in the hooded sweatshirt burst through the bar door in a quick, limping dash and dove into the pool, then lifted the struggling girl onto the deck and knelt beside her while enormous amounts of steaming water poured from her nose and mouth before she began breathing. Then the figure swept the hood from the flaming red hair and held Mona Sue close to his chest.

"Holy shit, boy," the old man asked unnecessarily as Bald Bill helped him out of the pool. "What the fuck you doin' here?"

"Goddammit, baby, lemme go," Mona Sue screamed. "It's a-comin'!"

Which roused the doctor from his sleepy rest. And the wrangler from his work. Both of them covered the wide wooden bench with dry towels, upon which Little R. L. gently placed Mona Sue's racked body. Curly scrambled out of the pool, warning Benbow to stay put, and joined the crowd of men around her sudden and violent contractions. Bald Bill helped the old man into his overalls and the pistol's thong as Little R. L. helped the doctor hold Mona Sue's body, arched with sudden pain, on the bench.

"Oh, Lordy me!" she screamed. "It's tearin' me up!"

"Do somethin', you pissant," the old man said to the wiry doctor, then slapped him soundly.

Benbow slapped to the side of the pool, holding on to the edge with one hand as he dug frantically at the cast with the other. Bits of plaster of paris and swirls of blood rose through the hot water. Then it was off, and the skewer in his hand. He planned to roll out of the pool, drive the sliver of metal through the old man's kidney, then grab the Webley. After that, he'd call the shots.

But life should have taught him not to plan.

As Bald Bill helped his boss into the coat, he noticed Benbow at the edge of the pool and stepped over to him. Bald Bill saw the bloody cast floating at Benbow's chest. "What the fuck?" he said, kneeling down to reach for him.

Benbow drove the thin shaft of metal with the strength of a lifetime of disappointment and rage into the bottom of Bald Bill's jaw, up through the root of his tongue, then up through his soft palate, horny brainpan, mushy gray matter, and the thick bones of his skull. Three inches of the skewer poked like a steel finger bone out of the center of his bald head.

Bald Bill didn't make a sound. Just blinked once dreamily, smiled, then stood up. After a moment, swaying, he began to walk in small airless circles at the edge of the deck until Curly noticed his odd behavior.

"Bubba?" he said as he stepped over to his brother.

Benbow leapt out of the water; one hand grabbed an ankle and the other dove up the leg of Curly's trunks to grab his nut sack and jerk the giant toward the pool. Curly's grunt and the soft clunk of his head against the concrete pool edge was lost as Mona Sue delivered the child with a deep sigh, and the old man shouted boldly, "Goddamn, it's a girl! A black-headed girl!"

Benbow had slithered out of the pool and limped halfway to the

old man's back as he watched the doctor lay the baby on Mona
Sue's heaving chest. "Shit fire and save the matches," the old man
said, panting deeply as if the labor had been his.

Little R. L. turned and jerked his father toward him by the front
of his coat, hissing, "Shut the fuck up, old man." Then he shoved
him violently away, smashing the old man's frail body into Benbow's
shoulder. Something cracked inside the old man's body, and he
sank to his knees, snapping at the cold air with his bloody beak like
a gut-shot turtle. Benbow grabbed the pistol's thong off his neck
before the old man tumbled dead into the water.

Benbow cocked the huge pistol with a soft metallic click, then his
sharp bark of laughter cut through the snowy air like a gunshot.
Everything slowed to a stop. The doctor finished cutting the cord.
The wrangler's hands held a folded towel under Mona Sue's head.
Little R. L. held his gristled body halfway into a mad charge. Bald
Bill stopped his aimless circling long enough to fall into the pool.
Even Mona Sue's cooing sighs died. Only the cold wind moved,
whipping the steamy fog across the pool as the snowfall thickened.

Then Mona Sue screamed, "No!" and broke the frozen moment.

The bad knee gave Benbow time to get off a round. The heavy
slug took Little R. L. in the top of his shoulder, tumbled through his
chest, and exited just above his kidney in a shower of blood, bone
splinters, and lung tissue, and dropped him like a side of beef on
the deck. But the round had already gone on its merry way through
the sternum of the doctor as if he weren't there. Which, in moments, he wasn't.

Benbow threw the pistol joyfully behind him, heard it splash in
the pool, and hurried to Mona Sue's side. As he kissed her blood-
spattered face, she moaned softly. He leaned closer, but only mis-
took her moans for passion until he understood what she was saying. Over and over. The way she once called his name. And Little
R. L.'s. Maybe even the old man's. "Cowboy, Cowboy, Cowboy," she
whispered.

Benbow wasn't even mildly surprised when he felt the arm at his
throat or the blade tickle his short ribs. "I took you for a backstab-
ber," he said, "the first time I laid eyes on your sorry ass."

"Just tell me where the money is, *old man*," the wrangler whispered, "and you can die easy."

"You can have the money," Benbow sobbed, trying for one final break, "just leave me the woman." But the flash of scorn in Mona Sue's eyes was the only answer he needed. "Fuck it," Benbow said, almost laughing, "let's do it the hard way."

Then he fell backward onto the hunting knife, driving the blade to the hilt above his short ribs before the wrangler could release the handle. He stepped back in horror as Benbow stumbled toward the hot waters of the pool.

At first, the blade felt cold in Benbow's flesh, but the flowing blood quickly warmed it. Then he eased himself into the hot water and lay back against its compassionate weight like the old man the wrangler had called him. The wrangler stood over Benbow, his eyes like coals glowing through the fog and thick snow. Mona Sue stepped up beside the wrangler, Benbow's baby whimpering at her chest, snow melting on her shoulders.

"Fuck it," Benbow whispered, drifting now, "it's in the air conditioner."

"Thanks, old man," Mona Sue said, smiling.

"Take care," Benbow whispered, thinking, *This is the easy part,* then leaned farther back into the water, sailing on the pool's wind-riffled, snow-shot surface, eyes closed, happy in the hot, heavy water, moving his hands slightly to stay afloat, his fingers tangled in dark, bloody streams, the wind pushing him toward the cool water at the far end of the pool, blinking against the soft cold snow, until his tired body slipped, unwatched, beneath the hot water to rest.

JEFFERY DEAVER

The Weekender

FROM *Alfred Hitchcock Mystery Magazine*

I LOOKED IN THE REAR-VIEW mirror and didn't see any lights, but I knew they were after us and it was only a matter of time till I'd see the cops.

Toth started to talk, but I told him to shut up and got the Buick up to eighty. The road was empty, nothing but pine trees for miles around.

"Oh brother," Toth muttered. I felt his eyes on me, but I didn't even want to look at him, I was so mad.

They were never easy, drugstores.

Because, just watch sometime, when cops make their rounds they cruise drugstores more often than anyplace else. Because of the prescription drugs.

You'd think they'd stake out convenience stores. But those're a joke, and with the closed circuit TV you're going to get your picture took, you just are. So nobody who knows the business, I mean really *knows* it, hits them. And banks, forget banks. Even ATMs. I mean, how much can you clear? Three, four hundred tops? And around here the Fast Cash button gives you twenty bucks. Which tells you something. So why even bother?

No. We wanted cash and that meant a drugstore, even though they can be tricky. Ardmore Drugs. Which is a big store in a little town. Liggett Falls. Sixty miles from Albany and a hundred or so from where Toth and me lived, farther west into the mountains. Liggett Falls is a poor place. You'd think it wouldn't make sense to hit a store there. But that's exactly why — because like everywhere else people there need medicine and hairspray and makeup only they don't have credit cards. Except maybe a Sears or Penney's. So they pay cash.

"Oh brother," Toth whispered again. "Look."

And he made me even madder, him saying that. I wanted to shout, Look at what, you son of a bitch? But then I could see what he was talking about, and I didn't say anything. Up ahead. It was like just before dawn, light on the horizon. Only this was red, and the light wasn't steady. It was like it was pulsing, and I knew that they'd got the roadblock up already. This was the only road to the interstate from Liggett Falls. So I should've guessed.

"I got an idea," Toth said. Which I didn't want to hear but I also wasn't going to go through another shootout. Sure not at a road-block where they was ready for us.

"What?" I snapped.

"There's a town over there. See those lights? I know a road'll take us there."

Toth's a big guy, and he looks calm. Only he isn't really. He gets shook easy, and he now kept turning around, skittish, looking in the back seat. I wanted to slap him and tell him to chill.

"Where's it?" I asked. "This town?"

"About four, five miles. The turnoff, it ain't marked. But I know it."

This was that lousy upstate area where everything's green. But dirty green, you know. And all the buildings're gray. These gross little shacks, pickups on blocks. Little towns without even a 7-Eleven. And full of hills they call mountains but aren't.

Toth cranked down the window and let this cold air in and looked up at the sky. "They can find us with those, you know, satellite things."

"What're you talking about?"

"You know, they can see you from miles up. I saw it in a movie."

"You think the state cops do that? Are you nuts?"

This guy, I don't know why I work with him. And after what happened at the drugstore, I won't again.

He pointed out where to turn, and I did. He said the town was at the base of The Lookout. Well, I remembered passing that on the way to Liggett Falls that afternoon. It was this huge rock a couple of hundred feet high. Which if you looked at it right looked like a man's head, like a profile, squinting. It'd been some kind of big deal to the Indians around here. Blah, blah, blah. He told me, but I didn't pay no attention. It was spooky, that weird face, and I looked once and kept on driving. I didn't like it. I'm not really superstitious, but sometimes I am.

"Winchester," he said now, meaning what the name of the town was. Five, six thousand people. We could find an empty house, stash the car in a garage, and just wait out the search. Wait till tomorrow afternoon — Sunday — when all the weekenders were driving back to Boston and New York and we'd be lost in the crowd.

I could see The Lookout up ahead, not really a shape, mostly this blackness where the stars weren't. And then the guy on the floor in the back started to moan all of a sudden and just about give me a heart attack.

"You. Shut up back there." I slapped the seat, and the guy in the back went quiet.

What a night.

We'd got to the drugstore fifteen minutes before it closed. Like you ought to do. 'Cause mosta the customers're gone and a lot've the clerks've left and people're tired, and when you push a Glock or Smitty into their faces, they'll do just about anything you ask.

Except tonight.

We had our masks down and walked in slow. Toth getting the manager out of his little office, a fat guy started crying and that made me mad, a grown man doing that. He kept a gun on the customers and the clerks, and I was telling the cashier, this kid, to open the tills and, Jesus, he had an attitude. Like he'd seen all of those Steven Seagal movies or something. A little kiss on the cheek with the Smitty and he changed his mind and started moving. Cussing me out, but he was moving. I was counting the bucks as we were going along from one till to the next, and sure enough, we were up to about three thousand when I heard this noise and turned around and what it was, Toth was knocking a rack of chips over. I mean, Jesus. He's getting Doritos!

I look away from the kid for just a second, and what's he do? He pitches this bottle. Only not at me. Out the window. Bang, it breaks. There's no alarm I can hear, but half of them are silent anyway and I'm really pissed. I could've killed him. Right there. Only I didn't. Toth did.

He shoots the kid, blam, blam, blam. And everybody else is scattering and he turns around and shoots another one of the clerks and a customer, just bang, not thinking or nothing. Just for no reason. Hit this girl clerk in the leg, but this guy, this customer, well, he was dead. You could see. And I'm going, What're you doing, what're you doing? And he's going, Shut up, shut up, shut up. . . . And we're like we're swearing at each other when we figured out we hadta get outa there.

So we left. Only what happens is, there's a cop outside. That's why the kid threw the bottle. And he's outa his car. So we grab another customer, this guy by the door, and we use him like a shield and get outside. And there's the cop, he's holding his gun up, looking at the customer we've got, and the cop, he's saying, It's okay, it's okay, just take it easy.

And I couldn't believe it, Toth shot him, too. I don't know whether he killed him, but there was blood so he wasn't wearing a vest it didn't look like, and I could've killed Toth there on the spot. Because why'd he do that? He didn't have to.

We threw the guy, the customer, into the back seat and tied him up with tape. I kicked out the taillights and burned rubber outa there. We made it out of Liggett Falls.

That was all just a half-hour ago, but it seems like weeks.

And now we were driving down this highway through a million pine trees. Heading right for The Lookout.

Winchester was dark.

I don't get why weekenders come to places like this. I mean, my old man took me hunting a long time ago. A couple of times, and I liked it. But coming to places like this just to look at leaves and buy furniture they call antiques but's really just busted-up crap . . . I don't know.

We found a house a block off Main Street with a bunch of newspapers in front, and I pulled into the drive and put the Buick behind it just in time. Two state police cars went shooting by. They'd been behind us not more than a half mile, without the lightbars going. Only they hadn't seen us 'causa the broke taillights, and they went by in a flash and were gone, going into town.

Toth got into the house, and he wasn't very clean about it, breaking a window in the back. It was a vacation place, pretty empty and the refrigerator shut off and the phone, too, which was a good sign — there wasn't anybody coming back soon. Also, it smelled pretty musty and had stacks of old books and magazines from the summer.

We took the guy inside, and Toth started to take the hood off this guy's head and I said, "What the hell're you doing?"

"He hasn't said anything. Maybe he can't breathe."

This was a man talking who'd just laid a cap on three people back there, and he was worried about this guy *breathing?* Man. I just laughed. Disgusted, I mean. "Like maybe we don't want him to see us?" I said. "You think of that?" See, we weren't wearing our ski masks anymore.

It's scary when you have to remind people of stuff like that. I was thinking Toth knew better. But you never know.

I went to the window and saw another squad car go past. They were going slower now. They do that. After like the first shock, after the rush, they get smart and start cruising slow, really looking for what's funny — what's *different*, you know? That's why I didn't take the papers up from the front yard. Which would've been different from how the yard looked that morning. Cops really do that Columbo stuff. I could write a book about cops.

"Why'd you do it?"

It was the guy we took.

"Why?" he whispered again.

The customer. He had a low voice, and it sounded pretty calm, I mean considering. I'll tell you, the first time I was in a shootout I was totally freaked for a day afterwards. And I had a gun.

I looked him over. He was wearing a plaid shirt and jeans. But he wasn't a local. I could tell because of the shoes. They were rich-boy shoes, the kind you see all the yuppies wear in TV shows about Connecticut. I couldn't see his face because of the mask, but I pretty much remembered it. He wasn't young. Maybe in his forties. Kind of wrinkled skin. And he was skinny, too. Skinnier'n me, and I'm one of those people can eat what I want and I don't get fat. I don't know why. It just works that way.

"Quiet," I said. There was another car going by.

He laughed. Soft. Like he was saying, What? So they can hear me all the way outside?

Kind of laughing *at* me, you know? I didn't like that at all. And sure, I guess you *couldn't* hear anything out there, but I didn't like him giving me any crap so I said, "Just shut up. I don't want to hear your voice."

He did for a minute and just sat back in the chair where Toth put him. But then he said again, "Why'd you shoot them? You didn't have to."

"Quiet!"

"Just tell me why."

I took out my knife and snapped that sucker open, then threw it down so it stuck in a tabletop. Sort of a *thunk* sound. "You hear that? That was a eight-inch Buck knife. Carbon tempered. With a locking blade. It'd cut clean through a metal bolt. So you be quiet. Or I'll use it on you."

And he gave this laugh again. Maybe. Or it was just a snort of air. But I was thinking it was a laugh. I wanted to ask him what he meant by that, but I didn't.

"You got any money on you?" Toth asked and took the wallet out of the guy's back pocket. "Lookit," Toth said and pulled out what must've been five or six hundred. Man.

Another squad car went past, moving slow. It had a spotlight and the cop turned it on the driveway, but he just kept going. I heard a siren across town. And another one, too. It was a weird feeling, knowing those people were out there looking for us.

I took the wallet from Toth and went through it.

Randall C. Weller, Jr. He lived in Boston. A weekender. Just like I thought. He had a bunch of business cards that said he was vice president of this big computer company. One that was in the news, trying to take over IBM or something. All of a sudden I had this thought. We could hold him for ransom. I mean, why not? Make a half million. Maybe more.

"My wife and kids'll be sick worrying," Weller said. It spooked me, hearing that. First, 'cause you don't expect somebody with a hood over his head to say anything. But mostly 'cause there I was, looking right at a picture in his wallet. And what was it of? His wife and kids.

"I ain't letting you go. Now, just shut up. I may need you."

"Like a hostage, you mean? That's only in the movies. They'll shoot you when you walk out, and they'll shoot me, too, if they have to. That's the way they do it. Just give yourself up. At least you'll save your life."

"Shut up!" I shouted.

"Let me go and I'll tell them you treated me fine. That the shooting was a mistake. It wasn't your fault."

I leaned forward and pushed the knife against his throat, not the blade 'cause that's real sharp but the blunt edge, and I told him to be quiet.

Another car went past, no light this time but it was going slower, and all of a sudden I got to thinking what if they do a door-to-door search?

"Why did he do it? Why'd he kill them?"

And funny, the way he said *he* made me feel a little better 'cause it was like he didn't blame me for it. I mean, it was Toth's fault. Not mine.

Weller kept going. "I don't get it. That man by the counter? The tall one. He was just standing there. He didn't do anything. He just shot him down."

But neither of us said nothing. Probably Toth because he didn't know why he'd shot them. And me because I didn't owe this guy any answers. I had him in my hand. Completely, and I had to let him know that. I didn't have to talk to him.

But the guy, Weller, he didn't say anything else. And I got this weird sense. Like this pressure building up. You know, because nobody was answering his damn stupid question. I felt this urge to say something. Anything. And that was the last thing I wanted to do. So I said, "I'm gonna move the car into the garage." And I went outside to do it.

I was a little spooked after the shootout. And I went through the garage pretty good. Just to make sure. But there wasn't nothing inside except tools and an old Snapper lawnmower. So I drove the Buick inside and closed the door. And went back into the house.

And then I couldn't believe what happened. I mean, Jesus . . .

When I walked into the living room, the first thing I heard was Toth saying, "No, way, man. I'm not snitching on Jack Prescot."

I just stood there. And you should've seen the look on his face. He knew he'd blown it big.

Now this Weller guy knew my name.

I didn't say anything. I didn't have to. Toth started talking real fast and nervous. "He said he'd pay me some big bucks to let him go." Trying to turn it around, make it Weller's fault. "I mean, I wasn't going to. I wasn't even thinking 'bout it, man. I told him forget it."

"I figured that," I said. "So? What's that got to do with tellin' him my name?"

"I don't know, man. He confused me. I wasn't thinking."

I'll say he wasn't. He hadn't been thinking all night.

I sighed to let him know I wasn't happy, but I just clapped him on the shoulder. "Okay," I said. "S'been a long night. These things happen."

"I'm sorry, man. Really."

"Yeah. Maybe you better go spend the night in the garage or something. Or upstairs. I don't want to see you around for a while."

"Sure."

And the funny thing was, it was that Weller gave this little snicker or something. Like he knew what was coming. How'd he know that? I wondered.

Toth went to pick up a couple of magazines and the knapsack with his gun in it and extra rounds.

Normally, killing somebody with a knife is a hard thing to do. I say normally even though I've only done it one other time. But I remember it, and it was messy and hard work. But tonight, I don't know, I was all filled up with this . . . feeling from the drugstore. Mad. I mean, really. Crazy, too, a little. And as soon as Toth turned his back, I went to work, and it wasn't three minutes later it was over. I drug his body behind the couch and then — why not — I pulled Weller's hood off. He already knew my name. He might as well see my face.

He was a dead man. We both knew it.

"You were thinking of holding me for ransom, right?"

I stood at the window and looked out. Another cop car went past, and there were more flashing lights bouncing off the low clouds and off the face of The Lookout, right over our heads. Weller had a thin face and short hair, cut real neat. He looked like every ass-kissing businessman I'd ever met. His eyes were dark and calm, and it made me even madder he wasn't shook up looking at that big bloodstain on the rug and floor.

"No," I told him.

He looked at the pile of stuff I'd taken from his wallet and kept going like I hadn't said anything. "It won't work. A kidnapping. I don't have a lot of money, and if you saw my business car and're thinking I'm an executive at the company, they have about five hundred vice presidents. They won't pay diddly for me. And you see those kids in the picture? It was taken twelve years ago. They're both in college now."

"Where," I asked, sneering. "Harvard?"

"One's at Harvard," he said, like he was snapping at me. "And one's at Northwestern. So the house's mortgaged to the hilt. Besides, kidnapping somebody by yourself? No, you couldn't bring that off."

He saw the way I looked at him, and he said, "I don't mean you personally. I mean somebody by himself. You'd need partners."

And I figured he was right. The ransom thing was looking, I don't know, tricky.

That silence again. Nobody saying nothing and it was like the room was filling up with cold water. I walked to the window and the floors creaked under my feet, and that only made things worse. I remember one time my dad said that a house had a voice of its own, and some houses were laughing houses and some were forlorn. Well, this was a forlorn house. Yeah, it was modern and clean and the *National Geographic*s were all in order, but it was still forlorn.

Just when I felt like shouting because of the tension, Weller said, "I don't want you to kill me."

"Who said I was going to kill you?"

He gave me this funny little smile. "I've been a salesman for twenty-five years. I've sold pets and Cadillacs and typesetters, and lately I've been selling mainframe computers. I know when I'm being handed a line. You're going to kill me. It was the first thing you thought of when you heard him —" nodding toward Toth "— say your name."

I just laughed at him. "Well, that's a damn handy thing to be, sorta a walking lie detector," I said, and I was being sarcastic.

But he just said, "Damn handy," like he was agreeing with me.

"I don't want to kill you."

"Oh, I know you don't *want* to. You didn't want your friend to kill anybody back there at the drugstore either. I could see that. But people *got* killed, and that ups the stakes. Right?"

And those eyes of his, they just dug into me, and I couldn't say anything.

"But," he said, "I'm going to talk you out of it."

He sounded real certain and that made me feel better. 'Cause I'd rather kill a cocky son of a bitch than a pathetic one. And so I laughed. "Talk me out of it?"

"I'm going to try."

"Yeah? How you gonna do that?"

Weller cleared his throat a little. "First, let's get everything on the table. I've seen your face, and I know your name. Jack Prescot. Right? You're, what?, about five-nine, a hundred fifty pounds, black hair. So you've got to assume I can identify you. I'm not going to play any games and say I didn't see you clearly or hear who you were. Or anything like that. We all squared away on that, Jack?"

I nodded, rolling my eyes like this was all a load of crap. But I gotta admit I was kinda curious what he had to say.

"My promise," he said, "is that I won't turn you in. Not under any circumstances. The police'll never learn your name from me. Or your description. I'll never testify against you."

Sounding honest as a priest. Real slick delivery. Well, he was a salesman, and I wasn't going to buy it. But he didn't know I was onto him. Let him give me his pitch, let him think I was going along. When it came down to it, after we'd got away and were somewhere in the woods upstate, I'd want him relaxed. Thinking he was going to get away. No screaming, no hassles. Just two fast cuts and that'd be it.

"You understand what I'm saying?"

I tried to look serious and said, "Sure. You're thinking you can talk me out of killing you. Which I'm not inclined to do anyway. Kill you, I mean."

And there was that weird little smile again.

I said, "You think you can talk me out of it. You've got reasons?"

"Oh, I've got reasons, you bet. One in particular. One that you can't argue with."

"Yeah? What's that?"

"I'll get to it in a minute. Let me tell you some of the practical reasons you should let me go. First, you think you've got to kill me because I know who you are, right? Well, how long you think your identity's going to be a secret? Your buddy shot a cop back there. I don't know police stuff except what I see in the movies. But they're going to be looking at tire tracks and witnesses who saw plates and makes of cars and gas stations you might've stopped at on the way here."

He was just blowing smoke. The Buick was stolen. I mean, I'm not stupid.

But he went on, looking at me real coy, "Even if your car was stolen, they're going to check down every lead. Every shoeprint around where you or your friend found it, talk to everybody in the area around the time it vanished."

I kept smiling like it was nuts what he was saying. But this was true, shooting the cop part. You do that and you're in big trouble. Trouble that sticks with you. They don't stop looking till they find you.

"And when they identify your buddy," he nodded toward the couch where Toth's body was lying. "They're going to make some connection to you."

"I don't know him that good. We just hung around together the past few months."

Weller jumped on this. "Where? A bar? A restaurant? Anybody ever see you in public?"

I got mad, and I shouted, "So? What're you saying? They gonna bust me anyway, then I'll just take you out with me. How's that for an argument?"

Calm as could be he said, "I'm simply telling you that one of the reasons you want to kill me doesn't make sense. And think about this — the shooting at the drugstore? It wasn't premeditated. It was, what do they call it? Heat of passion. But you kill me, that'll be first degree. You'll get the death penalty when they find you."

When they find you. Right. I laughed to myself. Oh, what he said made sense, but the fact is, killing isn't a making-sense kind of thing. Hell, it *never* makes sense, but sometimes you just have to do it. But I was kind of having fun now. I wanted to argue back. "Yeah, well, I killed Toth. That wasn't heat of passion. I'm going to get the needle anyway for that."

"But nobody gives a damn about him," he came right back. "They don't care if he killed *himself* or got hit by a car accidentally. You can take that piece of garbage out of the equation altogether. They care if you kill *me*. I'm the 'Innocent Bystander' in the headlines. I'm the 'Father of Two.' You kill me, you're as good as dead."

I started to say something, but he kept going.

"Now, here's another reason I'm not going to say anything about you. Because you know my name, and you know where I live. You know I have a family, and you know how important they are to me. If I turn you in, you could come after us. I'd never jeopardize my family that way. Now let me ask you something. What's the worst thing that could happen to you?"

"Keep listening to you spout on and on."

Weller laughed hard at that. I could see he was surprised I had a sense of humor. After a minute he said, "Seriously. The worst thing."

"I don't know. I never thought about it."

"Lose a leg? Go deaf? Lose all your money? Go blind . . . Hey, that looked like it hit a nerve. Going blind?"

"Yeah, I guess. That'd be the worst thing I could think of."

That *was* a pretty damn scary thing, and I'd thought on it before. 'Cause that was what happened to my old man. And it wasn't not seeing anymore that got to me. No, it was that I'd have to depend on somebody else for, Christ, for everything, I guess.

"Okay, think about this," he said. "The way you feel about going blind's the way my family'd feel if they lost me. It'd be that bad for them. You don't want to cause them that kind of pain, do you?"

I didn't want to, no. But I knew I *had* to. I didn't want to think about it anymore. I asked him, "So what's this last reason you're telling me about?"

"The last reason," he said, kind of whispering. But he didn't go on. He looked around the room, you know, like his mind was wandering.

"Yeah?" I asked. I was pretty curious. "Tell me."

But he just asked, "You think these people, they have a bar?"

And I'd just been thinking I could use a drink, too. I went into the kitchen, and of course they didn't have any beer in the fridge on account of the house being all closed up and the power off. But they did have scotch, and that'd be my first choice anyway.

I got a couple of glasses and took the bottle back to the living room. Thinking this was a good idea. When it came time to do it, it'd be easier for him and for me both if we were kinda tanked. I shoved my Smitty into his neck and cut the tape his hands were tied with, then taped them in front of him. I sat back and kept my knife near, ready to go, in case he tried something. But it didn't look like he was going to be a hero or anything. He read over the scotch bottle, kind of disappointed it was cheap. And I agreed with him there. One thing I learned a long time ago, you going to rob, rob rich.

I sat back where I could keep an eye on him.

"The last reason. Okay, I'll tell you. I'm going to *prove* to you that you should let me go."

"You are?"

"All those other reasons — the practical ones, the humanitarian ones . . . I'll concede you don't care much about those — you don't look very convinced. All right? Then let's look at the one reason you should let me go."

I figured this was going to be more crap. But what he said was something I never would've expected, and it made me laugh.

"For your own sake."

"For me? What're you talking about?"

"See, Jack, I don't think you're lost."

"Whatta you mean, lost?"

"I don't think your soul's beyond redemption."

I laughed at this, laughed out loud, because I just had to. I expected a hell of a lot better from a hotshot vice president sales-man like him. "Soul? You think I got a soul?"

"Well, everybody has a soul," he said, and what was crazy was, he said it like he was surprised that I didn't think so. It was like I'd said, Wait a minute you mean the earth ain't flat? or something.

"Well, if I got a soul it's taken the fast lane to hell." Which was this line I heard in this movie and I tried to laugh, but it sounded flat. Like Weller was saying something deep and I was just kidding around. It made me feel cheap. I stopped smiling and looked down at Toth, lying there in the corner, those dead eyes of his just staring, staring, and I wanted to stab him again I was so mad.

"We're talking about your soul."

I snickered and sipped the liquor. "Oh yeah, I'll bet you you're the sort that reads those angel books they got all over the place now."

"I go to church, but no, I'm not talking about all that silly stuff. I

don't mean magic. I mean your conscience. What Jack Prescot's all
about."

I could tell him about social workers and youth counselors and
all those guys who don't know nothing about the way life works.
They think they do. But it's the words they use. You can tell they
don't know a thing. Some counselors or somebody'll talk to me and
they say, Oh, you're maladjusted, you're denying your anger, things
like that. When I hear that, I know they don't know nothing about
souls or spirits.

"Not the afterlife," Weller was going on. "Not mortality. I'm talking about life here on earth that's important. Oh sure, you look
skeptical. But listen to me. I really believe if you have a connection
with somebody, if you trust them, if you have faith in them, then
there's hope for you."

"Hope? What does that mean? Hope for what?"

"That you'll become a real human being. Lead a real life."

Real . . . I didn't know what he meant, but he said it like what he
was saying was so clear that I'd have to be an idiot to miss it. So I
didn't say nothing.

He kept going. "Oh, there're reasons to steal, and there're reasons to kill. But on the whole, don't you really think it's better not
to? Just think about it: Why do we put people in jail if it's all right
for them to murder? Not just us but all societies."

"So, what? I'm gonna give up my evil ways?" I laughed at him.

And he just lifted his eyebrow and said, "Maybe. Tell me, Jack,
how'd you feel when your buddy — what's his name?"

"Joe Roy Toth."

"Toth, when he shot that guy by the counter? How'd you feel?"

"I don't know."

"He just turned around and shot him. For no reason. You knew
that wasn't right, didn't you?" And I started to say something. But
he said, "No, don't answer me. You'd be inclined to lie. And that's
all right. It's an instinct in your line of work. But I don't want you
believing any lies you tell me. Okay? I want you to look into your
heart and tell me if you didn't think something was real wrong
about what Toth did. Think about that, Jack. You knew something
wasn't right."

All right, I did. But who wouldn't? Toth screwed everything up.
Everything went sour. And it was all his fault.

"It dug at you, right, Jack? You wished he hadn't done it."

I didn't say nothing but just drank some more scotch and looked out the window and watched the flashing lights around the town. Sometimes they seemed close, and sometimes they seemed far away.

"If I let you go, you'll tell 'em."

Like everybody else. They all betrayed me. My father — even after he went blind, the son of a bitch turned me in. My first P.O., the judges. Sandra. . . . My boss, the one I knifed.

"No, I won't," Weller said. "We're talking about an agreement. I don't break deals. I promised I won't tell a soul about you, Jack. Not even my wife." He leaned forward, cupping the booze between his hands. "You let me go, it'll mean all the difference in the world to you. It'll mean that you're not hopeless. I guarantee your life'll be different. That one act — letting me go — it'll change you forever. Oh, maybe not this year. Or for five years. But you'll come around. You'll give up all this, everything that happened back there in Liggett Falls. All the crime, the killing. You'll come around. I know you will."

"You just expect me to believe you won't tell anybody?"

"Ah," Weller said and lifted his taped-up hands to drink more scotch. "Now we get down to the big issue."

Again that silence, and finally I said, "And what's that?"

"Faith."

There was this burst of siren outside, and I told him to shut up and pushed the gun against his head. His hands were shaking, but he didn't do anything stupid and a few minutes later, after I sat back, he started talking again. "Faith. That's what I'm talking about. A man who has faith is somebody who can be saved."

"Well, I don't have any goddamn faith," I told him.

But he kept right on talking. "If you believe in another human being, you have faith."

"Why the hell do you care whether I'm saved or not?"

"Because life's hard, and people're cruel. I told you I'm a church-goer. A lot of the Bible's crazy. But some of it I believe. And one of the things I believe is that sometimes we're put in these situations to make a difference. I think that's what happened tonight. That's why you and I both happened to be at the drugstore at the same time. You've felt that, haven't you? Like an omen? Like something happens and is telling you you ought do this or shouldn't do that."

Which was weird 'cause the whole time we were driving up to Liggett Falls I kept thinking, something funny's going on. I don't know what it is, but this job's gonna be different.

"What if," he said, "everything tonight happened for a purpose? My wife had a cold, so I went to buy NyQuil. I went to that drugstore instead of 7-Eleven to save a buck or two. You happened to hit that store at just that time. You happened to have your buddy —" he nodded toward Toth's body "— with you. The cop car just happened by at that particular moment. And the clerk behind the counter just happened to see him. That's a lot of coincidences. Don't you think?"

And then — this sent a damn chill right down my spine — he said, "Here we are in the shadow of that big rock, that face."

Which is one hundred percent what I was thinking. Exactly the same — about The Lookout, I mean. I don't know why I was. But I happened to be looking out the window and thinking about it at that exact same instant. I tossed back the scotch and had another and, oh man, I was pretty freaked out.

"Like he's looking at us, waiting for you to make a decision. Oh, don't think it was just you, though. Maybe the purpose was to affect everybody's life there. That customer at the counter Toth shot. Maybe it was just his time to go — fast, you know, before he got cancer or had a stroke. Maybe that girl, the clerk, had to get shot in the leg so she'd get her life together, maybe get off drugs or give up drinking."

"And you? What about you?"

"Well, I'll tell you about me. Maybe you're the good deed in my life. I've spent years thinking only about making money. Take a look at my wallet. There. In the back."

I pulled it open. There were a half-dozen of these little cards, like certificates. RANDALL WELLER — SALESMAN OF THE YEAR. EXCEEDED TARGET TWO YEARS STRAIGHT. BEST SALESMAN OF 1992.

Weller kept going. "There are plenty of others back in my office. And trophies, too. And in order for me to win those, I've had to neglect people. My family and friends. People who could maybe use my help. And that's not right. Maybe you kidnapping me, it's one of those signs to make me turn my life around."

The funny thing was this made sense. Oh, it was hard to imagine not doing heists. And I couldn't see myself, if it came down to a fight, not going for my Buck or my Smitty to take the other guy out. That turning the other cheek stuff, that's only for cowards. But maybe I *could* see a day when my life'd be just straight time. Living with some woman, maybe a wife, living in a house. Doing what my father and mother, whatever she was like, never did.

"If I was to let you go," I said, "you'd have to tell 'em something."

He shrugged. "I'll say you locked me in the trunk and then tossed me out somewhere near here. I wandered around, looking for a house or something, and got lost. It could take me a day to find somebody. That's believable."

"Or you could flag down a car in an hour."

"I could. But I won't."

"You keep saying that. But how do I *know*?"

"That's the faith part. You don't know. No guarantees."

"Well, I guess I don't have any faith."

"Then *I'm* dead. And *your* life's never gonna change. End of story." He sat back, and it was crazy but he looked calm, smiling a little.

That silence again but it was like it was really this roar all around us, and it kept going till the whole room was filled up with the sound of a siren.

"You just want . . . what do you want?"

He drank more scotch. "Here's a proposal. Let me walk outside."

"Oh, right. Just let you stroll out for some fresh air or something?"

"Let me walk outside and I promise you I'll walk right back again."

"Like a test?"

He thought about this for a second. "Yeah. A test."

"Where's this faith you're talking about? You walk outside, you try to run and I'd shoot you in the back."

"No, what you do is you put the gun someplace in the house. The kitchen or someplace. Somewhere you couldn't get it if I ran. You stand at the window, where we can see each other. And I'll tell you up front. I can run like the wind. I was lettered track and field in college, and I still jog every day of the year."

"You know if you run and bring the cops back everything's gonna get bloody. I'll kill the first five troopers come through that door. Nothing'll stop me, and that blood'll be on your hands."

"Of course I know that," he said. "But if this's going to work, you can't think that way. You've got to assume the worst is going to happen. That if I run I'll tell the cops everything. Where you are and that there're no hostages here and that you've only got one or two guns. And they're going to come in and blow you to hell. And you're not going to take a single one down with you. You're going to die and die painfully 'cause of a few lousy hundred bucks. . . . But, but, but . . ." He held up his hand and stopped me from saying anything. "You gotta understand, faith means risk."

"That's stupid."

"I think it's just the opposite. It'd be the smartest thing you ever did in your life."

"What'll it prove?" I asked. But I was just stalling. And he knew it. He said patiently, "That I'm a man of my word. That you can trust me."

"And what do I get out of it?"

And then this son of a bitch smiled that weird little smile of his. "I think you'll be surprised."

I tossed back another scotch and had to think about this.

Weller said, "I can see it there already. Some of that faith. It's there. Not a lot. But some."

And yeah, maybe there was a little. 'Cause I was thinking about how mad I got at Toth and the way he ruined everything. I didn't want anybody to get killed tonight. I *was* sick of it. Sick of the way my life had gone. Sometimes it was good, being alone and all. Not answering to anybody. But sometimes it was real bad. And this guy, Weller, it was like he was showing me something different.

"So," I said. "You just want me to put the gun down?"

He looked around. "Put it in the kitchen. You stand in the doorway or window. All I'm gonna do is walk down to the street and walk back."

I looked out the window. It was maybe fifty feet down the driveway. There were these bushes on either side of it. He could just take off, and I'd never find him.

All through the sky I could see lights flickering.

"Naw, I ain't gonna. You're nuts."

And I expected begging or something. Or getting pissed off, more likely — which is what happens to me when people don't do what I tell them. Or don't do it fast enough. But, naw, he just nodded. "Okay, Jack. You thought about it. That's a good thing. You're not ready yet. I respect that." He sipped a little more scotch, looking at the glass. And that was the end of it.

Then all of a sudden these searchlights started up. They was some ways away, but I still got spooked and backed away from the window. Pulled my gun out. Only then I saw that it wasn't nothing to do with the robbery. It was just a couple of big spotlights shining on The Lookout. They must've gone on every night, this time.

I looked up at it. From here it didn't look like a face at all. It was just a rock. Gray and brown and these funny pine trees growing sideways out of cracks.

Watching it for a minute or two. Looking out over the town, and something that guy was saying went into my head. Not the words, really. Just the *thought*. And I was thinking about everybody in that town. Leading normal lives. There was a church steeple and the roofs of small houses. A lot of little yellow lights in town. You could just make out the hills in the distance. And I wished for a minute I was in one of them houses. Sitting there. Watching TV with a wife next to me. Like Sandy or somebody.

I turned back from the window and I said, "You'd just walk down to the road and back? That's it?"

"That's all. I won't run off, you don't go get your gun. We trust each other. What could be simpler?"

Listening to the wind. Not strong but a steady hiss that was comforting in a funny way even though any other time I'da thought it sounded cold and raw. It was like I heard a voice. I don't know from where. Something in me said I ought to do this.

I didn't say nothing else 'cause I was right on the edge and I was afraid he'd say something that'd make me change my mind. I just took the Smith & Wesson and looked at it for a minute, then put it on the kitchen table. I came back with the Buck and cut his feet free. Then I figured if I was going to do it I ought go all the way. So I cut his hands free, too. Weller seemed surprised I did that. But he smiled like he knew I was playing the game. I pulled him to his feet and held the blade to his neck and took him to the door.

"You're doing a good thing," he said.

I was thinking, Oh man, I can't believe this. It's crazy.

I opened the door and smelled cold fall air and woodsmoke and pine, and I heard the wind in the rocks and trees above our heads.

"Go on," I told him.

Weller didn't look back to check up on me. . . . Faith, I guess. He kept walking real slow down toward the road.

I felt funny, I'll tell you, and a couple of times when he went past some real shadowy places in the driveway and could disappear I was like, oh man, this is all messed up. I'm crazy.

I almost panicked a few times and bolted for the Smitty but I didn't. When Weller got down near the sidewalk, I was actually holding my breath. I expected him to go, I really did. I was looking for that moment — when people tense up, when they're gonna swing or draw down on you or bolt. It's like their bodies're shouting what they're going to be doing before they do it. Only Weller wasn't doing none of that. He walked down to the sidewalk real casual. And he turned and looked up at the face of The Lookout, like he was just another weekender. Then he turned around. He nodded at me. Which is when the car came by. It was a state trooper. Those're the dark cars, and he didn't have the lightbar going. So he was almost on us before I knew it. I guess I was looking at Weller so hard I didn't see nothing else.

There it was, two doors away, and Weller saw it the same time I did.

And I thought, That's it. Oh, hell.

But when I was turning to get the gun, I saw this like flash of motion down by the road. And I stopped cold.

Could you believe it? Weller'd dropped onto the ground and rolled underneath a tree. I closed the door real fast and watched from the window. The trooper stopped and turned his light on the driveway. The beam — it was real bright — it moved up and down and hit all the bushes and the front of the house, then back to the road. But it was like Weller was digging down into the pine needles to keep from being seen. I mean, he was *hiding* from those sons of bitches. Doing whatever he could to stay out of the way of the light.

Then the car moved on, and I saw the lights checking out the house next door and then it was gone. I kept my eyes on Weller the whole time, and he didn't do nothing stupid. I seen him climb out from under the trees and dust himself off. Then he came walking back to the house. Easy, like he was walking to a bar to meet some buddies.

He came inside and shook his head. Gave this little sigh, like relief. And laughed. Then he held his hands out. I didn't even ask him to.

I taped 'em up again with adhesive tape, and he sat down in the chair, picked up his scotch, and sipped it.

And damn, I'll tell you something. The God's truth. I felt good. Naw, naw, it wasn't like I'd seen the light or anything like that. But I was thinking that of all the people in my life — my dad or Sandy or Toth or anybody else — I never did really trust them. I'd never let myself go all the way. And here, tonight, I did. With a stranger and somebody who had the power to do me some harm. It was a pretty scary feeling, but it was also a good feeling.

It was a little thing, real little. But maybe that's where stuff like this starts. I realized then that I'd been wrong. I could let him go. Oh, I'd keep him tied up here. Gagged. It'd be a day or so before he'd get out. But he'd agree to that. I knew he would. And I'd write his name and address down, let him know I knew where him and his family lived. But that was only part of why I was thinking I'd let him go. I wasn't sure what the rest of it was. But it was something about what'd just happened, something between me and him.

"How you feel?" he asked.

I wasn't going to give too much away. No, sir. But I couldn't help saying, "I thought I was gone then. But you did right by me."

"And you did right, too, Jack." And then he said, "Pour us another round."

I filled the glasses to the top. We tapped 'em.

"Here's to you, Jack. And to faith."

"To faith."

I tossed back the whiskey, and when I lowered my head, sniffing air through my nose to clear my head, well, that was when he got me. Right in the face.

He was good, that son of a bitch. Tossed the glass low so that even when I ducked, automatically, the booze caught me in the eyes, and man, that stung like nobody's business. I couldn't believe it. I was howling in pain and going for the knife. But it was too late. He had it all planned out, exactly what I was going to do. How I was gonna move. He brought his knee up into my chin and knocked a couple of teeth out, and I went over onto my back before I could get the knife out my pocket. Then he dropped down on my belly with his knee — I remembered I'd never bothered to tape his feet up again

— and he knocked the wind out, and there I was lying, like I was paralyzed, trying to breathe and all. Only I couldn't. And the pain was incredible, but what was worse was the feeling that he didn't trust me.

I was whispering, "No, no, no. I was going to, man. You don't understand. I was going to let you go."

I couldn't see nothing and couldn't really hear nothing either, my ears were roaring so much. I was gasping, "You don't understand you don't understand."

Man, the pain was so bad. So bad . . .

Weller must've got the tape off his hands, chewed through it, I guess, 'cause he was rolling me over. I felt him tape my hands together, then grab me and drag me over to a chair, tape my feet to the legs. He got some water and threw it in my face to wash the whiskey out of my eyes.

He sat down in a chair in front of me. And he just stared at me for a long time while I caught my breath. He picked up his glass, poured more scotch. I shied away, thinking he was going to throw it in my face again, but he just sat there, sipping it and staring at me.

"You . . . I was going to let you go. I *was*."

"I know," he said. Still calm.

"You know?"

"I could see it in your face. I've been a salesman for twenty-five years, remember? I know when I've closed a deal."

I'm a pretty strong guy, 'specially when I'm mad, and I tried real hard to break through that tape but there was no doing it. "Goddamn you!" I shouted. "You said you weren't going to turn me in. You, all your goddamn talk about faith . . ."

"Shhhh," Weller whispered. And he sat back, crossing his legs. Easy as could be. Looking me up and down. "That fellow your friend shot back at the drugstore. The customer at the counter?"

I nodded slowly.

"He was my friend. It's his place my wife and I are staying at this weekend. With all our kids."

I just stared at him. His friend? What was he saying?

"I didn't know —"

"Be quiet," he said, real soft. "I've known him for years. Gerry was one of my best friends."

"I didn't want nobody to die. I —"

"But somebody did die. And it was your fault."

"Toth . . ."

He whispered, "It was your fault."

"All right, you tricked me. Call the cops. Get it over with, you goddamn liar."

"You really don't understand, do you?" He shook his head. Why was he so calm? His hands weren't shaking. He wasn't looking around, nervous and all. Nothing like that. He said, "If I'd wanted to turn you in, I would just've flagged down that squad car a few minutes ago. But I said I wouldn't do that. And I won't. I gave you my word I wouldn't tell the cops a thing about you. And I won't."

"Then what do you want?" I shouted. "Tell me." Trying to bust through that tape. And as he unfolded my Buck knife with a click, I was thinking of something I told him.

Oh man, no . . . Oh, no.

"Yeah, being blind, I guess. That'd be the worst thing I could think of."

"What're you going to do?"

"What'm I going to do, Jack?" Weller said. He cut the last bit of tape off his wrists with the Buck, then looked up at me. "Well, I'll tell you. I spent a good bit of time tonight proving to you that you shouldn't kill me. And now . . ."

"What, man? What?"

"Now I'm going to spend a good bit of time proving to you that you should've."

Then, real slow, Weller finished his scotch and stood up. And he walked toward me, that weird little smile on his face.

BRENDAN DUBOIS

The Dark Snow

FROM *Playboy*

WHEN I GET TO THE STEPS of my lakeside home, the door is
open. I slowly walk in, my hand reaching for the phantom weapon
at my side, everything about me extended and tingling as I enter
the strange place that used to be mine. I step through the small
kitchen, my boots crunching the broken glassware and dishes on
the tile floor. Inside the living room with its cathedral ceiling the
furniture has been upended, as if an earthquake had struck.

I pause for a second, looking out the large windows and past the
enclosed porch, down to the frozen waters of Lake Marie. Off in
the distance are the snow-covered peaks of the White Mountains. I
wait, trembling, my hand still curving for that elusive weapon. They
are gone, but their handiwork remains. The living room is a jumble
of furniture, torn books and magazines, shattered pictures and
frames. On one clear white plaster wall, next to the fireplace, two
words have been written in what looks to be ketchup: GO HOME.

This is my home. I turn over a chair and drag it to the windows. I
sit and look out at the crisp winter landscape, my legs stretched out,
holding both hands still in my lap, which is quite a feat.

For my hands at that moment want to be wrapped around someone's throat.

After a long time wandering, I came to Nansen, New Hampshire, in
the late summer and purchased a house along the shoreline of
Lake Marie. I didn't waste much time, and I didn't bargain. I made
an offer that was about a thousand dollars below the asking price,
and in less than a month it belonged to me.

At first I didn't know what to do with it. I had never had a residence that was actually mine. Everything before this had been apartments, hotel rooms, or temporary officer's quarters. The first few nights I couldn't sleep inside. I would go outside to the long dock that extends into the deep blue waters of the lake, bundle myself up in a sleeping bag over a thin foam mattress, and stare up at the stars, listening to the loons getting ready for their long winter trip. The loons don't necessarily fly south; the ones here go out to the cold Atlantic and float with the waves and currents, not once touching land the entire winter.

As I snuggled in my bag I thought it was a good analogy for what I'd been doing. I had drifted too long. It was time to come back to dry land.

After getting the power and other utilities up and running and moving in the few boxes of stuff that belonged to me, I checked the bulky folder that had accompanied my retirement and pulled out an envelope with a doctor's name on it. Inside were official papers that directed me to talk to him, and I shrugged and decided it was better than sitting in an empty house getting drunk. I phoned and got an appointment for the next day.

His name was Ron Longley and he worked in Manchester, the state's largest city and about an hour's drive south of Lake Marie. His office was in a refurbished brick building along the banks of the Merrimack River. I imagined I could still smell the sweat and toil of the French Canadians who had worked here for so many years in the shoe, textile, and leather mills until their distant cousins in Georgia and Alabama took their jobs away.

I wasn't too sure what to make of Ron during our first session. He showed me some documents that made him a Department of Defense contractor and gave his current classification level, and then, after signing the usual insurance nonsense, we got down to it. He was about ten years younger than I, with a mustache and not much hair on top. He wore jeans, a light blue shirt, and a tie that looked as if about six tubes of paint had been squirted onto it, and he said, "Well, here we are."

"That we are," I said. "And would you believe I've already forgotten if you're a psychologist or a psychiatrist?"

That made for a good laugh. With a casual wave of his hand, he said, "Makes no difference. What would you like to talk about?"

"What should I talk about?"

A shrug, one of many I would eventually see. "Whatever's on your mind."

"Really?" I said, not bothering to hide the challenge in my voice. "Try this one on then, doc. I'm wondering what I'm doing here. And another thing I'm wondering about is paperwork. Are you going to be making a report down south on how I do? You working under some deadline, some pressure?"

His hands were on his belly and he smiled. "Nope."

"Not at all?"

"Not at all," he said. "If you want to come in here and talk baseball for fifty minutes, that's fine with me."

I looked at him and those eyes. Maybe it's my change of view since retirement, but there was something trustworthy about him. I said, "You know what's really on my mind?"

"No, but I'd like to know."

"My new house," I said. "It's great. It's on a big lake and there aren't any close neighbors, and I can sit on the dock at night and see stars I haven't seen in a long time. But I've been having problems sleeping."

"Why's that?" he asked, and I was glad he wasn't one of those stereotypical head docs, the ones who take a lot of notes.

"Weapons."

"Weapons?"

I nodded. "Yeah, I miss my weapons." A deep breath. "Look, you've seen my files, you know the places Uncle Sam has sent me and the jobs I've done. All those years, I had pistols or rifles or heavy weapons, always at my side, under my bed or in a closet. But when I moved into that house, well, I don't have them anymore."

"How does that make you feel?" Even though the question was friendly, I knew it was a real doc question and not a from-the-next-barstool type of question.

I rubbed my hands. "I really feel like I'm changing my ways. But damn it. . . ."

"Yes?"

I smiled. "I sure could use a good night's sleep."

As I drove back home, I thought, Hell, it's only a little white lie.

The fact is, I did have my weapons.

They were locked up in the basement, in strongboxes with heavy combination locks. I couldn't get to them quickly, but I certainly hadn't tossed them away.

I hadn't been lying when I told Ron I couldn't sleep. That part was entirely true.

I thought, as I drove up the dirt road to my house, scaring a possum that scuttled along the side of the gravel, that the real problem with living in my hew home was so slight that I was embarrassed to bring it up to Ron.

It was the noise.

I was living in a rural paradise, with clean air, clean water, and views of the woods and lake and mountains that almost broke my heart each time I climbed out of bed, stiff with old dreams and old scars. The long days were filled with work and activities I'd never had time for. Cutting old brush and trimming dead branches. Planting annuals. Clearing my tiny beach of leaves and other debris. Filling bird feeders. And during the long evenings on the front porch or on the dock, I tackled thick history books.

But one night after dinner — I surprised myself at how much I enjoyed cooking — I was out on the dock, sitting in a fifties-era web lawn chair, a glass of red wine in my hand and a history of the Apollo space program in my lap. Along the shoreline of Lake Marie, I could see the lights of the cottages and other homes. Every night there were fewer and fewer lights, as more of the summer people boarded up their places and headed back to suburbia.

I was enjoying my wine and the book and the slight breeze, but there was also a distraction: three high-powered speedboats, racing around on the lake and tossing up great spray and noise. They were dragging people along in inner tubes, and it was hard to concentrate on my book. After a while the engines slowed and I was hoping the boats would head back to their docks, but they drifted together and ropes were exchanged, and soon they became a large raft. A couple of grills were set up and there were more hoots and yells, and then a sound system kicked in, with rock music and a heavy bass that echoed among the hills.

It was then too dark to read and I'd lost interest in the wine. I was sitting there, arms folded tight against my chest, trying hard to breathe. The noise got louder and I gave up and retreated into the house, where the heavy *thump-thump* of the bass followed me in. If I'd had a boat I could have gone out and asked them politely to turn it down, but that would have meant talking with people and putting myself in the way, and I didn't want to do that.

Instead, I went upstairs to my bedroom and shut the door and windows. Still, that *thump-thump* shook the beams of the house. I lay down with a pillow wrapped about my head and tried not to think of what was in the basement.

Later that night I got up for a drink of water, and there was still noise and music. I walked out onto the porch and could see movement on the lake and hear laughter. On a tree near the dock was a spotlight that the previous owners had installed and which I had rarely used. I flipped on the switch. Some shouts and shrieks. Two powerboats, tied together, had drifted close to my shore. The light caught a young muscular man with a fierce black mustache standing on the stern of his powerboat and urinating into the lake. His half a dozen companions, male and female, yelled and cursed in my direction. The boats started up and two men and a young woman stumbled to the side of one and dropped their bathing suits, exposing their buttocks. A couple others gave me a one-fingered salute, and there was a shower of bottles and cans tossed over the side as they sped away.

I spent the next hour on the porch, staring into the darkness.

The next day I made two phone calls, to the town hall and the police department of Nansen. I made gentle and polite inquiries and got the same answers from each office. There was no local or state law about boats coming to within a certain distance of shore. There was no law forbidding boats from mooring together. Nansen being such a small town, there was also no noise ordinance.

Home sweet home.

On my next visit Ron was wearing a bow tie, and we discussed necktie fashions before we got into the business at hand. He said, "Still having sleeping problems?"

I smiled. "No, not at all."

"Really?"

"It's fall," I said. "The tourists have gone home, most of the cottages along the lake have been boarded up and nobody takes out boats anymore. It's so quiet at night I can hear the house creak and settle."

"That's good, that's really good," Ron said, and I changed the subject. A half-hour later, I was heading back to Nansen, thinking about my latest white lie. Well, it wasn't really a lie. More of an oversight.

I hadn't told Ron about the hang-up phone calls. Or how trash had twice been dumped in my driveway. Or how a week ago, when I was shopping, I had come back to find a bullet hole through one of my windows. Maybe it had been a hunting accident. Hunting season hadn't started, but I knew that for some of the workingmen in this town, it didn't matter when the state allowed them to do their shooting.

I had cleaned up the driveway, shrugged off the phone calls, and cut away brush and saplings around the house, to eliminate any hiding spots for . . . hunters.

Still, I could sit out on the dock, a blanket around my legs and a mug of tea in my hand, watching the sun set in the distance, the reddish pink highlighting the strong yellows, oranges, and reds of the fall foliage. The water was a slate gray, and though I missed the loons, the smell of the leaves and the tang of woodsmoke from my chimney seemed to settle in just fine.

As it grew colder, I began to go into town for breakfast every few days. The center of Nansen could be featured in a documentary on New Hampshire small towns. Around the green common with its Civil War statue are a bank, a real estate office, a hardware store, two gas stations, a general store, and a small strip of service places with everything from a plumber to video rentals and Gretchen's Kitchen. At Gretchen's I read the paper while letting the mornings drift by. I listened to the old-timers at the counter pontificate on the ills of the state, nation, and world, and watched harried workers fly in to grab a quick meal. Eventually, a waitress named Sandy took some interest in me.

She was about twenty years younger than I, with raven hair, a wide smile, and a pleasing body that filled out her regulation pink uniform. After a couple weeks of flirting and generous tips on my part, I asked her out, and when she said yes, I went to my pickup truck and burst out laughing. A real date. I couldn't remember the last time I had had a real date.

The first date was dinner a couple of towns over, in Montcalm, the second was dinner and a movie outside Manchester, and the third was dinner at my house, which was supposed to end with a rented movie in the living room but instead ended up in the bedroom. Along the way I learned that Sandy had always lived in Nansen, was divorced with two young boys, and was saving her money so she could go back to school and become a legal aide. "If you think I'm going to keep slinging hash and waiting for Billy to send his support check, then you're a damn fool," she said on our first date.

After a bedroom interlude that surprised me with its intensity, we sat on the enclosed porch. I opened a window for Sandy, who needed a smoke. The house was warm and I had on a pair of shorts; she had wrapped a towel around her torso. I sprawled in an easy chair while she sat on the couch, feet in my lap. Both of us had glasses of wine and I felt comfortable and tingling. Sandy glanced at me as she worked on her cigarette. I'd left the lights off and lit a couple of candles, and in the hazy yellow light, I could see the small tattoo of a unicorn on her right shoulder.

Sandy looked at me and asked, "What were you doing when you was in the government?"

"Traveled a lot and ate bad food."

"No, really," she said. "I want a straight answer."

Well, I thought, as straight as I can be. I said, "I was a consultant, to foreign armies. Sometimes they needed help with certain weapons or training techniques. That was my job."

"Were you good?"

Too good, I thought. "I did all right."

"You've got a few scars there."

"That I do."

She shrugged, took a lazy puff off her cigarette. "I've seen worse."

I wasn't sure where this was headed. Then she said, "When are you going to be leaving?"

Confused, I asked her, "You mean, tonight?"

"No," she said. "I mean, when are you leaving Nansen and going back home?"

I looked around the porch and said, "This is my home."

She gave me a slight smile, like a teacher correcting a fumbling but eager student. "No, it's not. This place was built by the Gerrish family. It's the Gerrish place. You're from away, and this ain't your home."

I tried to smile, though my mood was slipping. "Well, I beg to disagree."

She said nothing for a moment, just studied the trail of smoke from her cigarette. Then she said, "Some people in town don't like you. They think you're uppity, a guy that don't belong here."

I began to find it quite cool on the porch. "What kind of people?"

"The Garr brothers. Jerry Tompkins. Kit Broderick. A few others. Guys in town. They don't particularly like you."

"I don't particularly care," I shot back.

A small shrug as she stubbed out her cigarette. "You will."

The night crumbled some more after that, and the next morning, while sitting in the corner at Gretchen's, I was ignored by Sandy. One of the older waitresses served me, and my coffee arrived in a cup stained with lipstick, the bacon was charred black, and the eggs were cold. I got the message. I started making breakfast at home, sitting alone on the porch, watching the leaves fall and days grow shorter.

I wondered if Sandy was on her own or if she had been scouting out enemy territory on someone's behalf.

At my December visit, I surprised myself by telling Ron about something that had been bothering me.

"It's the snow," I said, leaning forward, hands clasped between my legs. "It's going to start snowing soon. And I've always hated the snow, especially since . . ."

"Since when?"

"Since something I did once," I said. "In Serbia."

"Go on," he said, fingers making a tent in front of his face.

"I'm not sure I can."

Ron tilted his head quizzically. "You know I have the clearances."

I cleared my throat, my eyes burning a bit. "I know. It's just that it's . . . Ever see blood on snow, at night?"

I had his attention. "No," he said, "no, I haven't."

"It steams at first, since it's so warm," I said. "And then it gets real dark, almost black. Dark snow, if you can believe it. It's something that stays with you, always."

He looked steadily at me for a moment, then said, "Do you want to talk about it some more?"

"No."

I spent all of one gray afternoon in my office cubbyhole, trying to get a new computer up and running. When at last I went downstairs for a quick drink, I looked outside and there they were, big snowflakes lazily drifting to the ground. Forgetting about the drink, I went out to the porch and looked at the pure whiteness of everything, of the snow covering the bare limbs, the shrubbery, and the frozen lake. I stood there and hugged myself, admiring the softly accumulating blanket of white and feeling lucky.

Two days after the snowstorm I was out on the frozen waters of Lake Marie, breathing hard and sweating and enjoying every second of it. The day before I had driven into Manchester to a sporting goods store and had come out with a pair of cross-country skis. The air was crisp and still, and the sky was a blue so deep I half-expected to see brushstrokes. From the lake, I looked back at my home and liked what I saw. The white paint and plain construction made me smile for no particular reason. I heard not a single sound, except for the faint drone of a distant airplane. Before me someone had placed signs and orange ropes in the snow, covering an oval area at the center of the lake. Each sign said the same thing: DANGER! THIN ICE! I remembered the old-timers at Gretchen's Kitchen telling a story about a hidden spring coming up through the lake bottom, or some damn thing, that made ice at the center of the lake thin, even in the coldest weather. I got cold and it was time to go home.

About halfway back to the house is where it happened.

At first it was a quiet sound, and I thought that it was another airplane. Then the noise got louder and louder, and separated, becoming distinct. Snowmobiles, several of them. I turned and they came speeding out of the woods, tossing up great rooster tails of snow and ice. They were headed straight for me. I turned away and kept up a steady pace, trying to ignore the growing loudness of the approaching engines. An itchy feeling crawled up my spine to the base of my head, and the noise exploded in pitch as they raced by me.

Even over the loudness of the engines I could make out the yells as the snowmobiles roared by, hurling snow in my direction. There were two people to each machine and they didn't look human. Each was dressed in a bulky jump suit, heavy boots, and a padded helmet. They raced by and, sure enough, circled around and came back at me. This time I flinched. This time, too, a couple of empty beer cans were thrown my way.

By the third pass, I was getting closer to my house. I thought it was almost over when one of the snowmobiles broke free from the pack and raced across about fifty feet in front of me. The driver turned so that the machine was blocking me and sat there, racing the throttle. Then he pulled off his helmet, showing an angry face and thick mustache, and I recognized him as the man on the powerboat a few months earlier. He handed his helmet to his passenger, stepped off the snowmobile, and unzipped his jump suit. It took only a moment as he marked the snow in a long, steaming stream, and there was laughter from the others as he got back on the machine and sped away. I skied over the soiled snow and took my time climbing up the snow-covered shore. I entered my home, carrying my skis and poles like weapons over my shoulder.

That night, and every night afterward, they came back, breaking the winter stillness with the throbbing sounds of engines, laughter, drunken shouts, and music from portable stereos. Each morning I cleared away their debris and scuffed fresh snow over the stains. In the quiet of my house, I found myself constantly on edge, listening, waiting for the noise to suddenly return and break up the day. Phone calls to the police department and town hall confirmed what I already knew: Except for maybe littering, no ordinances or laws were being broken.

On one particularly loud night, I broke a promise to myself and went to the tiny, damp cellar to unlock the green metal case holding a pistol-shaped device. I went back upstairs to the enclosed porch, and with the lights off, I switched on the night-vision scope and looked at the scene below me. Six snowmobiles were parked in a circle on the snow-covered ice, and in the center, a fire had been made. Figures stumbled around in the snow, talking and laughing. Stereos had been set up on the seats of two of the snowmobiles, and the loud music with its bass *thump-thump-thump* echoed across the flat ice. Lake Marie is one of the largest bodies of water in this part of the country, but the camp was set up right below my windows.

I watched for a while as they partied. Two of the black-suited figures started wrestling in the snow. More shouts and laughter, and then the fight broke up and someone turned the stereos even louder. *Thump-thump-thump.*

I switched off the nightscope, returned it to its case in the cellar, and went to bed. Even with foam rubber plugs in my ears, the bass noise reverberated inside my skull. I put the pillow across my face and tried to ignore the sure knowledge that this would continue all winter, the noise and the littering and the aggravation, and when the spring came, they would turn in their snowmobiles for boats, and they'd be back, all summer long.

Thump-thump-thump.

At the next session with Ron, we talked about the weather until he pierced me with his gaze and said, "Tell me what's wrong."

I went through half a dozen rehearsals of what to tell him, and then skated to the edge of the truth and said, "I'm having a hard time adjusting, that's all."

"Adjusting to what?"

"To my home," I said, my hands clasped before me. "I never thought I would say this, but I'm really beginning to get settled, for the first time in my life. You ever been in the military, Ron?"

"No, but I know —"

I held up my hand. "Yes, I know what you're going to say. You've worked as a consultant, but you've never been one of us, Ron. Never. You can't know what it's like, constantly being ordered to uproot yourself and go halfway across the world to a new place with a different language, customs, and weather, all within a week. You never settle in, never really get into a place you call home."

He swiveled a bit in his black leather chair. "But that's different now?"

"It sure is," I said.

There was a pause as we looked at each other, and Ron said, "But something is going on."

"Something is."

"Tell me."

And then I knew I wouldn't. A fire wall had already been set up between Ron and the details of what was going on back at my home. If I let him know what was really happening, I knew that he would make a report, and within the week I'd be ordered to go somewhere else. If I'd been younger and not so dependent on a monthly check, I would have put up a fight.

But now, no more fighting. I looked past Ron and said, "An adjustment problem, I guess."

"Adjusting to civilian life?"

"More than that," I said. "Adjusting to Nansen. It's a great little town, but . . . I feel like an outsider."

"That's to be expected."

"Sure, but I still don't like it. I know it will take some time, but . . . well, I get the odd looks, the quiet little comments, the cold shoulders."

Ron seemed to choose his words carefully. "Is that proving to be a serious problem?"

Not even a moment of hesitation as I lied: "No, not at all."

"And what do you plan on doing?"

An innocent shrug. "Not much. Just try to fit in, try to be a good neighbor."

"That's all?"

I nodded firmly. "That's all."

It took a bit of research, but eventually I managed to put a name to the face of the mustached man who had pissed on my territory. Jerry Tompkins. Floor supervisor for a computer firm outside Manchester, married with three kids, an avid boater, snowmobiler, hunter, and all-around guy. His family had been in Nansen for generations, and his dad was one of the three selectmen who ran the town. Using a couple of old skills, I tracked him down one dark afternoon and pulled my truck next to his in the snowy parking lot of a tavern on the outskirts of Nansen. The tavern was called Peter's Pub and its windows were barred and blacked out.

I stepped out of my truck and called to him as he walked to the entrance of the pub. He turned and glared at me. "What?"

"You're Jerry Tompkins, aren't you."

"Sure am," he said, hands in the pockets of his dark-green parka. "And you're the fella that's living up in the old Gerrish place."

"Yes, and I'd like to talk with you for a second."

His face was rough, like he had spent a lot of time outdoors in the wind and rain and an equal amount indoors, with cigarette smoke and loud country music. He rocked back on his heels with a little smile and said, "Go ahead. You got your second."

"Thanks," I said. "Tell you what, Jerry, I'm looking for something."

"And what's that?"

"I'm looking for a treaty."

He nodded, squinting his eyes. "What kind of treaty?"

"A peace treaty. Let's cut out the snowmobile parties on the lake by my place and the trash dumped in the driveway and the hang-up calls. Let's start fresh and just stay out of each other's way. What do you say? Then, this summer, you can all come over to my place for a cookout. I'll even supply the beer."

He rubbed at the bristles along his chin. "Seems like a one-sided deal. Not too sure what I get out of it."

"What's the point in what you're doing now?"

A furtive smile. "It suits me."

I felt like I was beginning to lose it. "You agree with the treaty, we all win."

"Still don't see what I get out of it," he said.

"That's the purpose of a peace treaty," I said. "You get peace."

"Feel pretty peaceful right now."

"That might change," I said, instantly regretting the words.

His eyes darkened. "Are you threatening me?"

A retreat, recalling my promise to myself when I'd come here. "No, not a threat, Jerry. What do you say?"

He turned and walked away, moving his head to keep me in view. "Your second got used up a long time ago, pal. And you better be out of this lot in another minute, or I'm going inside and coming out with a bunch of my friends. You won't like that."

No, I wouldn't, and it wouldn't be for the reason Jerry believed. If they did come out I'd be forced into old habits and old actions, and I'd promised myself I wouldn't do that. I couldn't.

"You got it," I said, backing away. "But remember, Jerry. Always."

"What's that?"

"The peace treaty," I said, going to the door of my pickup truck. "I offered."

*   *   *

Another visit to Ron, on a snowy day. The conversation meandered along, and I don't know what got into me, but I looked out the old mill windows and said, "What do people expect, anyway?"

"What do you mean?" he asked.

"You take a tough teenager from a small Ohio town, and you train him and train him and train him. You turn him into a very efficient hunter, a meat eater. Then, after twenty or thirty years, you say thank you very much and send him back to the world of quiet vegetarians, and you expect him to start eating cabbages and carrots with no fuss or muss. A hell of a thing, thinking you can expect him to put away his tools and skills."

"Maybe that's why we're here," he suggested.

"Oh, please," I said. "Do you think this makes a difference?"

"Does it make a difference to you?"

I kept looking out the window. "Too soon to tell, I'd say. Truth is, I wonder if this is meant to work, or is just meant to make some people feel less guilty. The people who did the hiring, training, and discharging."

"What do you think?"

I turned to him. "I think for the amount of money you charge Uncle Sam, you ask too many damn questions."

Another night at two A.M. I was back outside, beside the porch, again with the nightscope in my hands. They were back, and if anything, the music and the engines blared even louder. A fire burned merrily among the snowmobiles, and as the revelers pranced and hollered, I wondered if some base part of their brains was remembering thousand-year-old rituals. As I looked at their dancing and drinking figures, I kept thinking of the long case at the other end of the cellar. Nice heavy-duty assault rifle with another night-vision scope, this one with crosshairs. Scan and track. Put a crosshair across each one's chest. Feel the weight of a fully loaded clip in your hand. Know that with a silencer on the end of the rifle, you could quietly take out that crew in a fistful of seconds. Get your mind back into the realm of possibilities, of cartridges and windage and grains and velocities. How long could it take between the time you said go and the time you could say mission accomplished? Not long at all.

"No," I whispered, switching off the scope.

I stayed on the porch for another hour, and as my eyes adjusted, I saw more movements. I picked up the scope. A couple of snow machines moved in, each with shapes on the seats behind the drivers. They pulled up to the snowy bank and the people moved quickly, intent on their work. Trash bags were tossed on my land, about eight or nine, and to add a bit more fun, each bag had been slit several times with a knife so it could burst open and spew its contents when it hit the ground. A few more hoots and hollers and the snowmobiles growled away, leaving trash and the flickering fire behind. I watched the lights as the snowmobiles roared across the lake and finally disappeared, though their sound did not.

The nightscope went back onto my lap. The rifle, I thought, could have stopped the fun right there with a couple of rounds through the engines. Highly illegal, but it would get their attention, right?

Right.

In my next session with Ron, I got to the point. "What kind of reports are you sending south?"

I think I might have surprised him. "Reports?"

"How I'm adjusting, that sort of thing."

He paused for a moment, and I knew there must be a lot of figuring going on behind those smiling eyes. "Just the usual things, that's all. That you're doing fine."

"Am I?"

"Seems so to me."

"Good." I waited for a moment, letting the words twist about on my tongue. "Then you can send them this message. I haven't been a hundred percent with you during these sessions, Ron. Guess it's not in my nature to be so open. But you can count on this. I won't lose it. I won't go into a gun shop and then take down a bunch of civilians. I'm not going to start hanging around 1600 Pennsylvania Avenue. I'm going to be all right."

He smiled. "I have never had any doubt."

"Sure you've had doubts," I said, smiling back. "But it's awfully polite of you to say otherwise."

On a bright Saturday, I tracked down the police chief of Nansen at one of the two service stations in town, Glen's Gas & Repair. His cruiser, ordinarily a dark blue, was now a ghostly shade of white from the salt used to keep the roads clear. I parked at the side of the garage, and walking by the service bays, I could sense that I was being watched. I saw three cars with their hoods up, and I also saw a familiar uniform: black snowmobile jump suits.

The chief was overweight and wearing a heavy blue jacket with a black Navy watch cap. His face was open and friendly, and he nodded in all the right places as I told him my story.

"Not much I can do, I'm afraid," he said, leaning against the door of his cruiser, one of two in the entire town. "I'd have to catch 'em in the act of trashing your place, and that means surveillance, and that means overtime hours, which I don't have."

"Surveillance would be a waste of time anyway," I replied. "These guys, they aren't thugs, right? For lack of a better phrase, they're good old boys, and they know everything that's going on in Nansen, and they'd know if you were setting up surveillance. And then they wouldn't show."

"You might think you're insulting me, but you're not," he said gently. "That's just the way things are done here. It's a good town and most of us get along, and I'm not kept that busy, not at all."

"I appreciate that, but you should also appreciate my problem," I said. "I live here and pay taxes, and people are harassing me. I'm looking for some assistance, that's all, and a suggestion of what I can do."

"You could move," the chief said, raising his coffee cup.

"Hell of a suggestion."

"Best one I can come up with. Look, friend, you're new here, you've got no family, no ties. You're asking me to take on some prominent families just because you don't get along with them. So why don't you move on? Find someplace smaller, hell, even someplace bigger, where you don't stand out so much. But face it, it's not going to get any easier."

"Real nice folks," I said, letting an edge of bitterness into my voice.

That didn't seem to bother the chief. "That they are. They work hard and play hard, and they pay taxes, too, and they look out for one another. I know they look like hell-raisers to you, but they're more than that. They're part of the community. Why, just next week, a bunch of them are going on a midnight snow run across the lake and into the mountains, raising money for the children's camp up at Lake Montcalm. People who don't care wouldn't do that."

"I just wish they didn't care so much about me."

He shrugged and said, "Look, I'll see what I can do. . . ." but the tone of his voice made it clear he wasn't going to do a damn thing.

The chief clambered into his cruiser and drove off, and as I walked past the bays of the service station, I heard snickers. I went around to my pickup truck and saw the source of the merriment.

My truck was resting heavily on four flat tires.

At night I woke up from cold and bloody dreams and let my thoughts drift into fantasies. By now I knew who all of them were, where all of them lived. I could go to their houses, every one of them, and bring them back and bind them in the basement of my home. I could tell them who I was and what I've done and what I can do, and I would ask them to leave me alone. That's it. Just give me peace and solitude and everything will be all right.

And they would hear me out and nod and agree, but I would know that I had to convince them. So I would go to Jerry Tompkins, the mustached one who enjoyed marking my territory, and to make my point, break a couple of his fingers, the popping noise echoing in the dark confines of the tiny basement.

Nice fantasies.

I asked Ron, "What's the point?"

He was comfortable in his chair, hands clasped over his little potbelly. "I'm sorry?"

"The point of our sessions?"

His eyes were unflinching. "To help you adjust."

"Adjust to what?"

"To civilian life."

I shifted on the couch. "Let me get this. I work my entire life for this country, doing service for its civilians. I expose myself to death and injury every week, earning about a third of what I could be making in the private sector. And when I'm through, I have to adjust, I have to make allowances for civilians. But civilians, they don't have to do a damn thing. Is that right?"

"I'm afraid so."

"Hell of a deal."

He continued a steady gaze. "Only one you've got."

So here I am, in the smelly rubble that used to be my home. I make a few half-hearted attempts to turn the furniture back over and do some cleanup work, but I'm not in the mood. Old feelings and emotions are coursing through me, taking control. I take a few deep breaths and then I'm in the cellar, switching on the single lightbulb that hangs down from the rafters by a frayed black cord. As I maneuver among the packing cases, undoing combination locks, my shoulder strikes the lightbulb, causing it to swing back and forth, casting crazy shadows on the stone walls.

The night air is cool and crisp, and I shuffle through the snow around the house as I load the pickup truck, making three trips in all. I drive under the speed limit and halt completely at all stop signs as I go through the center of town. I drive around, wasting minutes and hours, listening to the radio. This late at night and being so far north, a lot of the stations that I can pick up are from Quebec, and there's a joyous lilt to the French-Canadian music and words that makes something inside me ache with longing.

When it's almost a new day, I drive down a street called Mast Road. Most towns around here have a Mast Road, where colonial surveyors marked tall pines that would eventually become masts for the Royal Navy. Tonight there are no surveyors, just the night air and darkness and a skinny rabbit racing across the cracked asphalt. When I'm near the target, I switch off the lights and engine and let the truck glide the last few hundred feet or so. I pull up across from a darkened house. A pickup truck and a Subaru station wagon are in the driveway. Gray smoke is wafting up from the chimney.

I roll down the window, the cold air washing over me like a wave of water. I pause, remembering what has gone on these past weeks, and then I get to work.

The nightscope comes up and clicks into action, and the name on the mailbox is clear enough in the sharp green light. TOMPKINS, in silver and black stick-on letters. I scan the two-story Cape Cod, checking out the surroundings. There's an attached garage to the right and a sunroom to the left. There is a front door and two other doors in a breezeway that runs from the garage to the house. There are no rear doors.

I let the nightscope rest on my lap as I reach toward my weapons. The first is a grenade launcher, with a handful of white phosphorus rounds clustered on the seat next to it like a gathering of metal eggs. Next to the grenade launcher is a 9mm Uzi, with an extended wooden stock for easier use. Another night-vision scope with cross-hairs is attached to the Uzi.

Another series of deep breaths. Easy enough plan. Pop a white phosphorus round into the breezeway and another into the sun-room. In a minute or two both ends of the house are on fire. Our snowmobiler friend and his family wake up and, groggy from sleep and the fire and the noise, stumble out the front door onto the snow-covered lawn.

With the Uzi in my hand and the crosshairs on a certain face, a face with a mustache, I take care of business and drive to the next house.

I pick up the grenade launcher and rest the barrel on the open window. It's cold. I rub my legs together and look outside at the stars. The wind comes up and snow blows across the road. I hear the low *hoo-hoo-hoo* of an owl.

I bring the grenade launcher up, resting the stock against my cheek. I aim. I wait.

It's very cold.

The weapon begins trembling in my hands and I let it drop to the front seat.

I sit on my hands, trying to warm them while the cold breeze blows. Idiot. Do this and how long before you're in jail, and then on trial before a jury of friends or relatives of those fine citizens you gun down tonight?

I start up the truck and let the heater sigh itself on, and then I roll up the window and slowly drive away, lights still off.

"Fool," I say to myself, "remember who you are." And with the truck's lights now on, I drive home. To what's left of it.

Days later, there's a fresh smell to the air in my house, for I've done a lot of cleaning and painting, trying not only to bring everything back to where it was but also to spruce up the place. The only real problem has been in the main room, where the words GO HOME were marked in bright red on the white plaster wall. It took me three coats to cover that up, and of course I ended up doing the entire room.

The house is dark and it's late. I'm waiting on the porch with a glass of wine in my hand, watching a light snow fall on Lake Marie.

Every light in the house is off and the only illumination comes from the fireplace, which needs more wood.

But I'm content to dawdle. I'm finally at peace after these difficult weeks in Nansen. Finally, I'm beginning to remember who I really am.

I sip my wine, waiting, and then comes the sound of the snowmobiles. I see their wavering dots of light racing across the lake, doing their bit for charity. How wonderful. I raise my glass in salute, the noise of the snowmobiles getting louder as they head across the lake in a straight line.

I put the wineglass down, walk into the living room, and toss the last few pieces of wood onto the fire. The sudden heat warms my face in a pleasant glow. The wood isn't firewood, though. It's been shaped and painted by man, and as the flames leap up and devour the lumber, I see the letters begin to fade: DANGER! THIN ICE!

I stroll back to the porch, pick up the wineglass, and wait.

Below me, on the peaceful ice of Lake Marie, my new home for my new life, the headlights go by.

And then, one by one, they blink out, and the silence is wonderful!

ELIZABETH GEORGE

The Surprise of His Life

FROM *Women on the Case*

WHEN DOUGLAS ARMSTRONG had his first consultation with Thistle McCloud, he had no intention of murdering his wife. His mind, in fact, didn't turn to murder until two weeks after consultation number four.

Douglas watched closely as Thistle prepared herself for a revelation from another dimension. She held his wedding band in the palm of her left hand. She closed her fingers around it. She hovered her right hand over the fist that she'd made. She hummed five notes that sounded suspiciously like the beginning of "I Love You Truly." Gradually, her eyes rolled back, up, and out of view beneath her yellow-shaded lids, leaving him with the disconcerting sight of a thirtysomething female in a straw boater, striped vest, white shirt, and polka-dotted tie, looking as if she were one quarter of a barbershop quartet in desperate hope of finding her partners.

When he'd first seen Thistle, Douglas had appraised her attire — which in subsequent visits had not altered in any appreciable fashion — as the insidious getup of a charlatan who wished to focus her clients' attention on her personal appearance rather than on whatever machinations she would be going through to delve into their pasts, their presents, their futures, and — most importantly — their wallets. But he'd come to realize that Thistle's odd getup had nothing to do with distracting anyone. The first time she held his old Rolex watch and began speaking in a low, intense voice about the prodigal son, about his endless departures and equally endless returns, about his aging parents who welcomed him always with open arms and open hearts, and about his brother who watched all this with a false fixed smile and a silent shout of *What about me? Do I mean nothing?* he had a feeling that Thistle was exactly what she purported to be: a psychic.

He'd first come to her storefront operation because he'd had forty minutes to kill prior to his yearly prostate exam. He dreaded the exam and the teeth-grating embarrassment of having to answer his doctor's jovial, rib-poking "Everything up and about as it should be?" with the truth, which was that Newton's law of gravity had begun asserting itself lately to his dearest appendage. And since he was six weeks short of his fifty-fifth birthday, and since every disaster in his life had occurred in a year that was a multiple of five, if there was a chance of knowing what the gods had in store for him and his prostate, he wanted to be able to do something to head off the chaos.

These things had all been on his mind as he spun along Pacific Coast Highway in the dim gold light of a late December afternoon. On a drearily commercialized section of the road — given largely to pizza parlors and boogie board shops — he had seen the small blue building that he'd passed a thousand times before and read PSYCHIC CONSULTATIONS on its hand-painted sign. He'd glanced at his gas gauge for an excuse to stop, and while he pumped super unleaded into the tank of his Mercedes across the street from that small blue building, he made his decision. What the hell, he'd thought. There were worse ways to kill forty minutes.

So he'd had his first session with Thistle McCloud, who was anything but what he'd expected of a psychic since she used no crystal ball, no tarot cards, nothing at all but a piece of his jewelry. In his first three visits, it had always been the Rolex watch from which she'd received her psychic emanations. But today she'd placed the watch to one side, declared it diluted of power, and set her fog-colored eyes on his wedding ring. She'd touched her finger to it, and said, "I'll use that, I think. If you want something further from your history and closer to your heart."

He'd given her the ring precisely because of those last two phrases: *further from your history and closer to your heart.* They told him how very well she knew that the prodigal son business rose from his past while his deepest concerns were attached to his future.

With the ring now in her closed fist and with her eyes rolled upward, Thistle stopped the four-note humming, breathed deeply

six times, and opened her eyes. She observed him with a melancho-
lia that made his stomach feel hollow.

"What?" Douglas asked.

"You need to prepare for a shock," she said. "It's something
unexpected. It comes out of nowhere and because of it, the essence
of your life will be changed forever. And soon. I feel it coming very
soon."

Jesus, he thought. It was just what he needed to hear three weeks
after having an indifferent index finger shoved up his ass to see
what was the cause of his limp-dick syndrome. The doctor had said
it wasn't cancer, but he hadn't ruled out half a dozen other possibilities. Douglas wondered which one of them Thistle had just now
tuned her psychic antennae onto.

Thistle opened her hand and they both looked at his wedding
ring where it lay on her palm, faintly sheened by her sweat. "It's an
external shock," she clarified. "The source of upheaval in your life
isn't from within. The shock comes from outside and rattles you to
your core."

"Are you sure about that?" Douglas asked her.

"As sure as I can be, considering the armor you wear." Thistle
returned the ring to him, her cool fingers grazing his wrist. She
said, "Your name isn't David, is it? It was never David. It never will be
David. But the *D*, I feel, is correct. Am I right?"

He reached into his back pocket and brought out his wallet.
Careful to shield his driver's license from her, he clipped a fifty-dol-
lar bill between his thumb and index finger. He folded it once and
handed it over.

"Donald," she said. "No. That isn't it, either. Darrell, perhaps.
Dennis. I sense two syllables."

"Names aren't important in your line of work, are they?" Douglas
said.

"No. But the truth is always important. Someday, Not-David,
you're going to have to learn to trust people with the truth. Trust is
the key. Trust is essential."

"Trust," he told her, "is what gets people screwed."

Outside, he walked across the Coast Highway to the cramped
side street that paralleled the ocean. Here he always parked his car
when he visited Thistle. With its vanity license plate DRIL4IT virtually announcing who owned the Mercedes, Douglas had decided

early on that it wouldn't encourage new investors if anyone put the word out that the president of South Coast Oil had begun seeing a psychic regularly. Risky investments were one thing. Placing money with a man who could be accused of using parapsychology rather than geology to find oil deposits was another. He wasn't doing that, of course. Business never came up in his sessions with Thistle. But try telling that to the board of directors. Try telling that to anyone.

He unarmed the car and slid inside. He headed south, in the direction of his office. As far as anyone at South Coast Oil knew, he'd spent his lunch hour with his wife, having a romantic winter's picnic on the bluffs in Corona del Mar. The cellular phone will be turned off for an hour, he'd informed his secretary. Don't try to phone and don't bother us, please. This is time for Donna and me. She deserves it. I need it. Are we clear on the subject?

Any mention of Donna always did the trick when it came to keeping South Coast Oil off his back for a few hours. She was warmly liked by everyone in the company. She was warmly liked by everyone period. Sometimes, he reflected suddenly, she was too warmly liked. Especially by men.

You need to prepare for a shock.

Did he? Douglas considered the question in relation to his wife.

When he pointed out men's affinity for her, Donna always acted surprised. She told him that men merely recognized in her a woman who'd grown up in a household of brothers. But what he saw in men's eyes when they looked at his wife had nothing to do with fraternal affection. It had to do with getting her naked, getting down and dirty, and getting laid.

It's an external shock.

Was it? What sort? Douglas thought of the worst.

Getting laid was behind every man-woman interaction on earth. He knew this well. So while his recent failures to get it up and get it on with Donna frustrated him, he had to admit that he was feeling concerned that her patience with him was trickling away. Once it was gone, she'd start looking around. That was only natural. And once she started looking, she was going to find or be found.

The shock comes from outside and rattles you to your core.

Shit, Douglas thought. If chaos was about to steamroller into his life as he approached his fifty-fifth birthday — that rotten bad luck integer — Douglas knew that Donna would probably be at the wheel. She was thirty-five, four years in place as wife number three, and while she acted content, he'd been around women long enough to know that still waters did more than simply run deep. They hid rocks that could sink a boat in seconds if a sailor didn't keep his wits about him. And love made people lose their wits. Love made people go a little bit nuts.

Of course, *he* wasn't nuts. He had his wits about him. But being in love with a woman twenty years his junior, a woman whose scent caught the nose of every male within sixty yards of her, a woman whose physical appetites he himself was failing to satisfy on a nightly basis . . . and had been failing to satisfy for weeks . . . a woman like that . . .

"Get a grip," Douglas told himself brusquely. "This psychic stuff is baloney, right? Right." But still he thought of the coming shock, the upset to his life, and its source: external. Not his prostate, not his dick, not an organ in his body. But another human being. "Shit," he said.

He guided the car up the incline that led to Jamboree Road, six lanes of concrete that rolled between stunted liquidambar trees through some of the most expensive real estate in Orange County. It took him to the bronzed glass tower that housed his pride: South Coast Oil.

Once inside the building, he navigated his way through an unexpected encounter with two of SCO's engineers, through a brief conversation with a geologist who simultaneously waved an ordnance survey map and a report from the EPA, and through a hallway conference with the head of the accounting department. His secretary handed him a fistful of messages when he finally managed to reach his office. She said, "Nice picnic? The weather's unbelievable, isn't it?" followed by "Everything all right, Mr. Armstrong?" when he didn't reply.

He said, "Yes. What? Fine," and looked through the messages. He found that the names meant nothing to him, absolutely nothing.

He walked to the window behind his desk and looked at the view through its enormous pane of tinted glass. Below him, Orange County's airport sent jet after jet hurtling into the sky at an angle so acute that it defied both reason and aerodynamics, although it did protect the delicate auditory sensibilities of the millionaires who lived in the flight path below. Douglas watched these planes without really seeing them. He knew he had to answer his telephone messages, but all he could think about was Thistle's words: *an external shock.*

What could be more external than Donna?

She wore Obsession. She put it behind her ears and beneath her breasts. Whenever she passed through a room, she left the scent of herself behind.

Her dark hair gleamed when the sunlight hit it. She wore it short and simply cut, parted on the left and smoothly falling just to her ears.

Her legs were long. When she walked, her stride was full and sure. And when she walked with him — at his side, with her hand through his arm and her head held back — he knew that she caught the attention of everyone. He knew that together they were the envy of all their friends and of strangers as well.

He could see this reflected in the faces of people they passed when he and Donna were together. At the ballet, at the theater, at concerts, in restaurants, glances gravitated to Douglas Armstrong and his wife. In women's expressions he could read the wish to be young like Donna, to be smooth-skinned again, to be vibrant once more, to be fecund and ready. In men's expressions he could read desire.

It had always been a pleasure to see how others reacted to the sight of his wife. But now he saw how dangerous her allure really was and how it threatened to destroy his peace.

A shock, Thistle had said to him. *Prepare for a shock. Prepare for a shock that will change your world.*

That evening, Douglas heard the water running as soon as he entered the house: fifty-two-hundred square feet of limestone floors, vaulted ceilings, and picture windows on a hillside that offered an ocean view to the west and the lights of Orange County to the east. The house had cost him a fortune, but that had been all right with him. Money meant nothing. He'd bought the place for Donna. But if he'd had doubts about his wife before — born of his own performance anxiety, growing to adulthood through his consultation with Thistle — when Douglas heard that water running, he began to see the truth. Because Donna was in the shower.

He watched her silhouette behind the blocks of translucent glass that defined the shower's wall. She was washing her hair. She hadn't noticed him yet, and he watched her for a moment, his gaze traveling over her uplifted breasts, her hips, her long legs. She usually bathed — languorous bubble baths in the raised oval tub that looked out on the lights of the city of Irvine. Taking a shower suggested a more earnest and energetic effort to cleanse herself. And washing her hair suggested . . . Well, it was perfectly clear what that suggested. Scents got caught up in the hair: cigarette smoke, sautéing garlic, fish from a fishing boat, or semen and sex. Those last two were the betraying scents. Obviously, she would have to wash her hair.

Her discarded clothes lay on the floor. With a hasty glance at the shower, Douglas fingered through them and found her lacy underwear. He knew women. He knew his wife. If she'd actually been with a man that afternoon, her body's leaking juices would have made the panties' crotch stiff when they dried, and he would be able to smell the afterscent of intercourse on them. They would give him proof. He lifted them to his face.

"Doug! What on earth are you doing?"

Douglas dropped the panties, cheeks hot and neck sweating. Donna was peering at him from the shower's opening, her hair lathered with soap that streaked down her left cheek. She brushed it away.

"What are *you* doing?" he asked her. Three marriages and two divorces had taught him that a fast offensive maneuver threw the opponent off balance. It worked.

She popped back into the water — clever of her, so he couldn't see her face — and said, "It's pretty obvious. I'm taking a shower. God, what a day."

He moved to watch her through the shower's opening. There was no door, just a partition in the glass-block wall. He could study her body and look for the telltale signs of the kind of rough lovemaking he knew that she liked. And she wouldn't know he was even looking, since her head was beneath the shower as she rinsed off her hair.

"Steve phoned in sick today," she said, "so I had to do everything at the kennels myself."

She raised chocolate Labradors. He had met her that way, seeking a dog for his youngest son. Through a reference from a veterinarian, he had discovered her kennels in Midway City — less than one square mile of feedstores, other kennels, and dilapidated post-war stucco and shake roofs posing as suburban housing. It was an odd place for a girl from the pricey side of Corona del Mar to end up professionally, but that was what he liked about Donna. She wasn't true to type, she wasn't a beach bunny, she wasn't a typical southern California girl. Or at least that's what he had thought.

"The worst was cleaning the dog runs," she said. "I didn't mind the grooming — I never mind that — but I hate doing the runs. I completely reeked of dog poop when I got home." She shut off the shower and reached for her towels, wrapping her head in one and her body in the other. She stepped out of the stall with a smile and said, "Isn't it weird how some smells cling to your body and your hair while others don't?"

She kissed him hello and scooped up her clothes. She tossed them down the laundry chute. No doubt she was thinking, Out of sight, out of mind. She was clever that way.

"That's the third time Steve's phoned in sick in two weeks." She headed for the bedroom, drying off as she went. She dropped the towel with her usual absence of self-consciousness and began dressing, pulling on wispy underwear, black leggings, a silver tunic. "If he keeps this up, I'm going to let him go. I need someone consistent, someone reliable. If he's not going to be able to hold up his end . . ." She frowned at Douglas, her face perplexed. "What's wrong, Doug? You're looking at me so funny. Is something wrong?"

"Wrong? No." But he thought, That looks like a love bite on her neck. And he crossed to her for a better look. He cupped her face for a kiss and tilted her head. The shadow of the towel that was wrapped around her hair dissipated, leaving her skin unmarred. Well, what of it? he thought. She wouldn't be so stupid as to let some heavy breather suck bruises into her flesh, no matter how turned on he had her. She wasn't that dumb. Not his Donna.

But she also wasn't as smart as her husband.

At five forty-five the next day, he went to the personnel department. It was a better choice than the Yellow Pages because at least he knew that whoever had been doing the background checks on incoming employees at South Coast Oil was simultaneously competent and discreet. No one had ever complained about some two-bit gumshoe nosing into his background.

The department was deserted, as Douglas had hoped. The computer screens at every desk were set to the shifting images that preserved them: a field of swimming fish, bouncing balls, and popping bubbles. The director's office at the far side of the department was unlit and locked, but a master key in the hand of the company president solved that problem. Douglas went inside and flipped on the lights.

He found the name he was looking for among the dog-eared cards of the director's Rolodex, a curious anachronism in an otherwise computer-age office. *Cowley and Son, Inquiries,* he read in faded typescript. This was accompanied by a telephone number and by an address on Balboa Peninsula.

Douglas studied both for the space of two minutes. Was it better to know or to live in ignorant bliss? he wondered at this eleventh hour. But he wasn't living in bliss, was he? And he hadn't been living in bliss from the moment he'd failed to perform as a man was meant to. So it was better to know. He had to know. Knowledge was power. Power was control. He needed both.

He picked up the phone.

Douglas always went out for lunch — unless a conference was scheduled with his geologists or the engineers — so no one raised a hair of an eyebrow when he left South Coast Oil before noon the following day. He used Jamboree once again to get to the Coast Highway, but this time instead of heading north toward Newport where Thistle made her prognostications, he drove directly across the highway and down the incline where a modestly arched bridge spanned an oily section of Newport Harbor that divided the mainland from an amoeba-shaped portion of land that was Balboa Island.

In summer the island was infested with tourists. They bottled up the streets with their cars and rode their bicycles in races on the sidewalk around the island's perimeter. No local in his right mind ventured onto Balboa Island during the summer without good reason or unless he lived there. But in winter, the place was virtually deserted. It took less than five minutes to snake through the narrow streets to the island's north end where the ferry waited to take cars and pedestrians on the eye-blink voyage across to the peninsula.

There a stripe-topped carousel and a Ferris wheel spun like two opposing gears of an enormous clock, defining an area called the

Fun Zone, which had long been the summertime bane of the local
police. Today, however, no bands of juveniles roved with cans of
spray paint at the ready. The only inhabitants of the Fun Zone were
a paraplegic in a wheelchair and his bike-riding companion.

Douglas passed them as he drove off the ferry. They were intent
upon their conversation. The Ferris wheel and carousel did not
exist for them. Nor did Douglas and his blue Mercedes, which was
just as well. He didn't particularly want to be seen.

He parked just off the beach, in a lot where fifteen minutes cost a
quarter. He pumped in four. He armed the car and headed west
toward Main Street, a tree-shaded lane some sixty yards long that
began at a faux New England restaurant overlooking Newport Harbor and ended at Balboa Pier, which stretched out into the Pacific
Ocean, gray-green today and unsettled by roiling waves from a
winter Alaskan storm.

Number 107-B Main was what he was looking for, and he found
it easily. Just east of an alley, 107 was a two-story structure whose
bottom floor was taken up by a time-warped hair salon called JJ's —
heavily devoted to macramé, potted plants, and posters of Janis
Joplin — and whose upper floor was divided into offices that were
reached by means of a structurally questionable stairway at the
north end of the building. Number 107-B was the first door upstairs — JJ's Natural Haircutting appeared to be 107-A — but when
Douglas turned the discolored brass knob below the equally discolored brass nameplate announcing the business as COWLEY AND
SON, INQUIRIES, he found the door locked.

He frowned and looked at his Rolex. His appointment was for
twelve-fifteen. It was currently twelve-ten. So where was Cowley?
Where was his son?

He returned to the stairway, ready to head to his car and his
cellular phone, ready to track down Cowley and give him hell for
setting up an appointment and failing to be there to keep it. But he
was three steps down when he saw a khaki-clad man coming his way,
sucking up an Orange Julius with the enthusiasm of a twelve-year-
old. His thinning gray hair and sun-lined face marked him at least
five decades older than twelve, however. And his limping gait — in
combination with his clothes — suggested old war wounds.

"You Cowley?" Douglas called from the stairs.

The man waved his Orange Julius in reply. "You Armstrong?" he
asked.

"Right," Douglas said. "Listen, I don't have a lot of time."

"None of us do, son," Cowley said, and he hoisted himself up the stairway. He nodded in a friendly fashion, pulled hard on the Orange Julius straw, and passed Douglas in a gust of aftershave that he hadn't smelled for a good twenty years. Canoe. Jesus. Did they still sell that?

Cowley swung the door open and cocked his head to indicate that Douglas was to enter. The office comprised two rooms: one was a sparsely furnished waiting area through which they passed; the other was obviously Cowley's demesne. Its centerpiece was an olive-green steel desk. Filing cabinets and bookshelves of the same issue matched it.

The investigator went to an old oaken office chair behind the desk, but he didn't sit. Instead, he opened one of the side drawers, and just when Douglas was expecting him to pull out a fifth of bourbon, he dug out a bottle of yellow capsules instead. He shook two of them into his palm and knocked them back with a long swig of Orange Julius. He sank into his chair and gripped its arms.

"Arthritis," he said. "I'm killing the bastard with evening primrose oil. Give me a minute, okay? You want a couple?"

"No." Douglas glanced at his watch to make certain Cowley knew that his time was precious. Then he strolled to the steel bookshelves.

He was expecting to see munitions manuals, penal codes, and surveillance texts, something to assure the prospective clients that they'd come to the right place with their troubles. But what he found was poetry, volume after volume neatly arranged in alphabetical order by author, from Matthew Arnold to William Butler Yeats. He wasn't sure what to think.

The occasional space left at the end of a bookshelf was taken up by photographs. They were clumsily framed, snapshots mostly. They depicted grinning small children, a gray-haired grandma type, several young adults. Among them, encased in Plexiglas, was a military Purple Heart. Douglas picked this up. He'd never seen one, but he was pleased to know that his guess about the source of Cowley's limp had been correct.

"You saw action," he said.

"My butt saw action," Cowley replied. Douglas looked his way, so the PI continued. "I took it in the butt. Shit happens, right?" He moved his hands from their grip on the arms of his chair. He folded them over his stomach. Like Douglas's own, it could have been flatter. Indeed, the two men shared a similar build: stocky, quickly given to weight if they didn't exercise, too tall to be called short and too short to be called tall. "What can I do for you, Mr. Armstrong?"

"My wife," Douglas said.

"Your wife?"

"She may be . . ." Now that it was time to articulate the problem and what it arose from, Douglas wasn't sure that he could. So he said, "Who's the son?"

"What?"

"It says Cowley and Son, but there's only one desk. Who's the son?"

Cowley reached for his Orange Julius and took a pull on its straw. "He died," he said. "Drunk driver got him on Ortega Highway."

"Sorry."

"Like I said. Shit happens. What shit's happened to you?"

Douglas returned the Purple Heart to its place. He caught sight of the graying grandma in one of the pictures and said, "This your wife?"

"Forty years my wife. Name's Maureen."

"I'm on my third. How'd you manage forty years with one woman?"

"She has a sense of humor." Cowley slid open the middle drawer of his desk and took out a legal pad and the stub of a pencil. He wrote ARMSTRONG at the top in block letters and underlined it. He said, "About your wife . . ."

"I think she's having an affair. I want to know if I'm right. I want to know who it is."

Cowley carefully set his pencil down. He observed Douglas for a moment. Outside, a gull gave a raucous cry from one of the rooftops. "What makes you think she's seeing someone?"

"Am I supposed to give you proof before you'll take the case? I thought that's why I was hiring you. To give *me* proof."

"You wouldn't be here if you didn't have suspicions. What are they?"

Douglas raked through his memory. He wasn't about to tell Cowley about trying to smell up Donna's underwear, so he took a moment to examine her behavior over the last few weeks. And when he did so, the additional evidence was there. Jesus. How the hell had he missed it? She'd changed her hair; she'd bought new underwear — that black lacy Victoria's Secret stuff; she'd been on the phone twice when he'd come home and as soon as he walked into the room, she'd hung up hastily; there were at least two long absences with insufficient excuse for them; there were six or seven engagements that she said were with friends.

Cowley nodded thoughtfully when Douglas listed his suspicions. Then he said, "Have you given her a reason to cheat on you?"

"A reason? What is this? I'm the guilty party?"

"Women don't usually stray without there being a man behind them, giving them a reason." Cowley examined him from beneath unclipped eyebrows. One of his eyes, Douglas saw, was beginning to form a cataract. Jeez, the guy was ancient, a real antique.

"No reason," Douglas said. "I don't cheat on her. I don't even want to."

"She's young, though. And a man your age . . ." Cowley shrugged. "Shit happens to us old guys. Young things don't always have the patience to understand."

Douglas wanted to point out that Cowley was at least ten years his senior, if not more. He also wanted to take himself from membership in the club of *us old guys.* But the PI was watching him compassionately, so instead of arguing, Douglas told the truth.

Cowley reached for his Orange Julius and drained the cup. He tossed it into the trash. "Women have needs," he said, and he moved his hand from his crotch to his chest, adding, "A wise man doesn't confuse what goes on here" — the crotch — "with what goes on here" — the chest.

"So maybe I'm not wise. Are you going to help me out or not?"

"You sure you want help?"

"I want to know the truth. I can live with that. What I can't live with is not knowing. I just need to know what I'm dealing with here."

Cowley looked as if he were taking a reading of Douglas's level of veracity. He finally appeared to make a decision, but one he didn't like because he shook his head, picked up his pencil, and said, "Give me some background, then. If she's got someone on the side, who are our possibilities?"

Douglas had thought about this. There was Mike, the poolman

who visited once a week. There was Steve, who worked with Donna at her kennels in Midway City. There was Jeff, her personal trainer. There were also the postman, the FedEx man, the UPS driver, and Donna's too youthful gynecologist.

"I take it you're accepting the case?" Douglas said to Cowley. He pulled out his wallet from which he extracted a wad of bills. "You'll want a retainer."

"I don't need cash, Mr. Armstrong."

"All the same . . ." All the same, Douglas had no intention of leaving a paper trail via a check. "How much time do you need?" he asked.

"Give it a few days. If she's seeing someone, he'll surface eventually. They always do." Cowley sounded despondent.

"Your wife cheat on you?" Douglas asked shrewdly.

"If she did, I probably deserved it."

That was Cowley's attitude, but it was one that Douglas didn't share. He didn't deserve to be cheated on. Nobody did. And when he found out who was doing the job on his wife . . . Well, they would see a kind of justice that Attila the Hun was incapable of extracting.

His resolve was strengthened in the bedroom that evening when his hello kiss to his wife was interrupted by the telephone. Donna pulled away from him quickly and went to answer it. She gave Douglas a smile — as if recognizing what her haste revealed to him — and shook back her hair as sexily as possible, running slim fingers through it as she picked up the receiver.

Douglas listened to her side of the conversation while he changed his clothes. He heard her voice brighten as she said, "Yes, yes. Hel*lo* . . . No . . . Doug just got home and we were talking about the day. . . ."

So now her caller knew he was in the room. Douglas could imagine what the bastard was saying, whoever he was: *"So you can't talk?"*

To which Donna, on cue, answered, "Nope. Not at all."

"Shall I call later?"

"Gosh, that would be nice."

"Today was what was nice. I love to fuck you."

"Really? Outrageous. I'll have to check it out."

"I want to check you out, baby. Are you wet for me?"

"I sure am. Listen, we'll connect later on, okay? I need to get dinner started."

"Just so long as you remember today. It was the best. You're the best."

"Right. Bye." She hung up and came to him. She put her arms round his waist. She said, "Got rid of her. Nancy Talbert. God. Nothing's more important in her life than a shoe sale at Neiman-Marcus. Spare me. Please." She snuggled up to him. He couldn't see her face, just the back of her head where it reflected in the mirror.

"Nancy Talbert," he said. "I don't think I know her."

"Sure you do, honey." She pressed her hips against him. He felt the hopeful but useless heat in his groin. "She's in Soroptimists with me. You met her last month after the ballet. Hmm. You feel nice. Gosh, I like it when you hold me. Should I start dinner or d'you want to mess around?"

Another clever move on her part: he wouldn't think she was cheating if she still wanted it from him. No matter that he couldn't give it to her. She was hanging in there with him and this moment proved it. Or so she thought.

"Love to," he said, and smacked her on the butt. "But let's eat first. And after, right there on the dining room table . . ." He managed what he hoped was a lewd enough wink. "Just you wait, kiddo."

She laughed and released him and went off to the kitchen. He walked to the bed where he sat, disconsolately. The charade was torture. He had to know the truth.

He didn't hear from Cowley and Son, Inquiries, for two agonizing weeks, during which he suffered through three more coy telephone conversations between Donna and her lover, four more phony excuses to cover unscheduled absences from home, and two more midday showers sloughed off to Steve's absence from the kennels again. By the time he finally made contact with Cowley, Douglas's nerves were shot.

Cowley had news to report. He said he'd hand it over as soon as they could meet. "How's lunch?" Cowley asked. "We could do Tail of the Whale over here."

No lunch, Douglas told him. He wouldn't be able to eat anyway. He would meet Cowley at his office at twelve forty-five.

"Make it the pier, then," Cowley said. "I'll catch a burger at Ruby's and we can talk after. You know Ruby's? The end of the pier?"

He knew Ruby's. A fifties coffee shop, it sat at the end of Balboa

Pier, and he found Cowley there as promised at twelve forty-five, polishing off a cheeseburger and fries with a manila envelope sitting next to his strawberry milkshake.

Cowley wore the same khakis he'd had on the day they'd met. He'd added a Panama hat to his ensemble. He touched his index finger to the hat's brim as Douglas approached him. His cheeks were bulging with the burger and fries.

Douglas slid into the booth opposite Cowley and reached for the envelope. Cowley's hand slapped down onto it. "Not yet," he said.

"I've got to know."

Cowley slid the envelope off the table and onto the vinyl seat next to himself. He twirled the straw in his milkshake and observed Douglas through opaque eyes that seemed to reflect the sunlight outside. "Pictures," he said. "That's all I've got for you. Pictures aren't the truth. You got that?"

"Okay. Pictures."

"I don't know what I'm shooting. I just tail the woman and I shoot what I see. What I see may not mean shit. You understand?"

"Just show me the pictures."

"Outside."

Cowley tossed a five and three ones onto the table, called "Catch you later, Susie," to the waitress, and led the way. He walked to the railing, where he looked out over the water. A whale-watching boat was bobbing about a quarter-mile offshore. It was too early in the year to catch sight of a pod migrating to Alaska, but the tourists on board probably wouldn't know that. Their binoculars winked in the light.

Douglas joined the PI. Cowley said, "You got to know that she doesn't act like a woman guilty of anything. She just seems to be doing her thing. She met a few men — I won't mislead you — but I couldn't catch her doing anything cheesy."

"Give me the pictures."

Cowley gave him a sharp look instead. Douglas knew his voice was betraying him. "I say we tail her for another two weeks," Cowley said. "What I've got here isn't much to go on." He opened the envelope. He stood so that Douglas only saw the back of the pictures. He chose to hand them over in sets.

The first set was taken in Midway City not far from the kennels, at the feed and grain store where Donna bought food for the dogs. In these, she was loading fifty-pound sacks into the back of her Toyota pickup. She was being assisted by a Calvin Klein type in tight jeans and a T-shirt. They were laughing together, and in one of the pictures Donna had perched her sunglasses on top of her head the better to look directly at her companion.

She appeared to be flirting, but she was a young, pretty woman and flirting was normal. This set seemed okay. She could have looked less happy to be chatting with the stud, but she was a businesswoman and she was conducting business. Douglas could deal with that.

The second set was of Donna in the Newport gym where she worked with a personal trainer twice a week. Her trainer was one of those sculpted bodies with a head of hair on which every strand looked as if it had been seen to professionally on a daily basis. In the pictures, Donna was dressed to work out — nothing Douglas had not seen before — but for the first time he noted how carefully she assembled her workout clothes. From the leggings to the leotard to the headband she wore, everything enhanced her. The trainer appeared to recognize this because he squatted before her as she did her vertical butterflies. Her legs were spread and there was no doubt what he was concentrating on. This looked more serious.

He was about to ask Cowley to start tailing the trainer when the PI said, "No body contact between them other than what you'd expect," and handed him the third set of pictures, saying, "These are the only ones that look a little shaky to me, but they may mean nothing. You know this guy?"

Douglas stared with *know this guy, know this guy* ringing in his skull. Unlike the other pictures in which Donna and her companion-of-the-moment were in one location, these showed Donna at a view table in an oceanfront restaurant, Donna on the Balboa ferry, Donna walking along a dock in Newport. In each of the pictures she was with a man, the same man. In each of the pictures there was body contact. It was nothing extreme because they were out in public. But it was the kind of body contact that betrayed: an arm around her shoulders, a kiss on her cheek, a full-body hug that said, Feel me up, baby, 'cause I ain't limp like him.

Douglas felt that his world was spinning, but he managed a wry grin. He said, "Oh hell. Now I feel like a class-A jerk."

"Why's that?" Cowley asked.

"This guy?" Douglas indicated the athletic-looking man in the picture with Donna. "This is her brother."

"You're kidding."

"Nope. He's a walk-on coach at Newport Harbor High. His name is Michael. He's a free-spirit type." Douglas gripped the railing with one hand and shook his head with what he hoped looked like chagrin. "Is this all you've got?"

"That's it. I can tail her for a while longer and see —"

"Nah. Forget it. Jesus, I sure feel dumb." Douglas ripped the photographs into confetti. He tossed this into the water, where it formed a mantle that was quickly shredded by the waves that arced against the pier's pilings. "What do I owe you, Mr. Cowley?" he asked. "What's this dumb ass got to pay for not trusting the finest woman on earth?"

He took Cowley to Dillman's on the corner of Main and Balboa Boulevard, and they sat at the snakelike bar with the locals, where they knocked back a couple of brews apiece. Douglas worked on his affability act, playing the abashed husband who suddenly realizes what a dickhead he's been. He took all Donna's actions over the past weeks and reinterpreted them for Cowley. The unexplained absences became the foundation of a treat she was planning for him: the purchase of a new car, perhaps; a trip to Europe; the refurbishing of his boat. The secretive telephone calls became messages from his children who were in the know. The new underwear metamorphosed into a display of her wish to make herself desirable for him, to work him out of his temporary impotence by giving him a renewed interest in her body. He felt like a total idiot, he told Cowley. Could they burn the damn negatives together?

They made a ceremony of it, torching the negatives of the pictures in the alley behind JJ's Natural Haircutting. Afterward, Douglas drove in a haze to Newport Harbor High School. He sat numbly across the street from it. He waited two hours. Finally, he saw his youngest brother arrive for the afternoon's coaching session, a basketball tucked under his arm and an athletic bag in his hand.

Michael, he thought. Returned from Greece this time, but always the prodigal son. Before Greece, it was a year with Greenpeace on the *Rainbow Warrior*. Before that, it was an expedition up the Amazon. And before that, it was marching against apartheid in South

Africa. He had a resumé that would be the envy of any prepubescent kid out for a good time. He was Mr. Adventure, Mr. Irresponsibility, and Mr. Charm. He was Mr. Good Intentions without any follow-through. When a promise was due to be kept, he was out of sight, out of mind, and out of the country. But everyone loved the son of a bitch. He was forty years old, the baby of the Armstrong brothers, and he always got precisely what he wanted.

He wanted Donna now, the miserable bastard. No matter that she was his brother's wife. That made having her just so much more fun.

Douglas felt ill. His guts rolled around like marbles in a bucket. Sweat broke out in patches on his body. He couldn't go back to work like this. He reached for the phone and called his office.

He was sick, he told his secretary. Must have been something he ate for lunch. He was heading home. She could catch him there if anything came up.

In the house, he wandered from room to room. Donna wasn't at home — wouldn't be at home for hours — so he had plenty of time to consider what to do. His mind reproduced for him the pictures that Cowley had taken of Michael and Donna. His intellect deduced where they had been and what they'd been doing prior to those pictures being taken.

He went to his study. There, in a glass curio cabinet, his collection of ivory erotica mocked him. Miniature Asians posed in a variety of sexual postures, having themselves a roaring good time. He could see Michael and Donna's features superimposed on the creamy faces of the figurines. They took pleasure at his expense. They justified their pleasure by using his failure. No limp dick here, Michael's voice taunted. What's the matter, big brother? Can't hang on to your wife?

Douglas felt shattered. He told himself he could have handled her doing anything else, he could have handled her seeing anyone else. But not Michael, who had trailed him through life, making his mark in every area where Douglas had previously failed. In high school it had been in athletics and student government. In college it had been in the world of fraternities. As an adult it had been in embracing adventure rather than in tackling the grind of business. And now it was in proving to Donna what real manhood was all about.

Douglas could see them together as easily as he could see his pieces of erotica intertwined. Their bodies joined, their heads thrown back, their hands clasped, their hips grinding against each other. God, he thought. The pictures in his mind would drive him mad. He felt like killing.

The telephone company gave him the proof he required. He asked for a printout of the calls that had been made from his home. And when he received it, there was Michael's number. Not once or twice, but repeatedly. All of the calls had been made when he — Douglas — wasn't at home.

It was clever of Donna to use the nights when she knew Douglas would be doing his volunteer stint at the Newport suicide hotline. She knew he never missed his Wednesday evening shift, so important was it to him to have the hotline among his community commitments. She knew he was building a political profile to get himself elected to the city council, and the hotline was part of the picture of himself he wished to portray: Douglas Armstrong, husband, father, oilman, and compassionate listener to the emotionally distressed. He needed something to put into the balance against his environmental lapses. The hotline allowed him to say that while he may have spilled oil on a few lousy pelicans — not to mention some miserable otters — he would never let a human life hang there in jeopardy.

Donna had known he'd never skip even part of his evening shift, so she'd waited till then to make her calls to Michael. There they were on the printout, every one of them made between six and nine on a Wednesday night.

Okay, she liked Wednesday night so well. Wednesday night would be the night that he killed her.

He could hardly bear to be around her once he had the proof of her betrayal. She knew something was wrong between them because he didn't want to touch her any longer. Their thrice-weekly attempted couplings — as disastrous as they'd been — fast became a thing of the past. Still, she carried on as if nothing and no one had come between them, sashaying through the bedroom in her Victoria's Secret selection-of-the-night, trying to entice him into making a fool of himself so she could share the laughter with his brother Michael.

No way, baby, Douglas thought. You'll be sorry you made a fool out of me.

When she finally cuddled next to him in bed and murmured, "Doug, is something wrong? You want to talk? You okay?" it was all he could do not to shove her from him. He wasn't okay. He would never be okay again. But at least he'd be able to salvage a measure of his self-respect by giving the little bitch her due.

It was easy enough to plan once he decided on the very next Wednesday.

A trip to Radio Shack was all that was necessary. He chose the busiest one he could find, deep in the barrio in Santa Ana, and he deliberately took his time browsing until the youngest clerk with the most acne and the least amount of brainpower was available to wait on him. Then he made his purchase with cash: a call diverter, just the thing for those on-the-go SoCal folks who didn't want to miss an incoming phone call. No answering machine for those types. This would divert a phone call from one number to another by means of a simple computer chip. Once Douglas programmed the diverter with the number he wanted incoming calls diverted to, he would have an alibi for the night of his wife's murder. It was all so easy.

Donna had been a real numbskull to try to cheat on him. She had been a bigger numbskull to do her cheating on Wednesday nights because the fact of her doing it on Wednesday nights was what gave him the idea of how to snuff her. The volunteers on the hotline worked it in shifts. Generally there were two people present, each manning one of the telephone lines. But Newport Beach types actually didn't feel suicidal very frequently, and if they did, they were more likely to go to Neiman-Marcus and buy their way out of their depression. Midweek especially was a slow time for the pill poppers and wrist slashers, so the hotline was manned on Wednesdays by only one person per shift.

Douglas used the days prior to Wednesday to get his timing down to a military precision. He chose eight-thirty as Donna's death hour, which would give him time to sneak out of the hotline office, drive home, put out her lights, and get back to the hotline before the next shift arrived at nine. He was carving it out fairly thin and allowing only a five-minute margin of error, but he needed to do that in order to have a believable alibi once her body was found.

There could be neither noise nor blood, obviously. Noise would arouse the neighbors. Blood would damn him if he got so much as a drop on his clothes, DNA typing being what it was these days. So he chose his weapon carefully, aware of the irony of his choice. He would use the satin belt of one of her Victoria's Secret slay-him-where-he-stands dressing gowns. She had half a dozen, so he would remove one of them in advance of the murder, separate it from its belt, dispose of it in a Dumpster behind the nearest Vons in advance of the killing — he liked that touch, getting rid of evidence *before* the crime, what killer ever thought of that? — and then use the belt to strangle his cheating wife on Wednesday night.

The call diverter would establish his alibi. He would take it to the suicide hotline, plug the phone into it, program the diverter with his cellular phone number, and thus appear to be in one location while his wife was being murdered in another. He made sure Donna was going to be at home by doing what he always did on Wednesdays: by phoning her from work before he left for the hotline.

"I feel like dogshit," he told her at five-forty.

"Oh, Doug, no!" she replied. "Are you ill or just feeling depressed about —"

"I'm feeling punk," he interrupted her. The last thing he wanted was to listen to her phony sympathy. "It may have been lunch."

"What did you have?"

Nothing. He hadn't eaten in two days. But he came up with shrimp because he'd gotten food poisoning from shrimp a few years back and he thought she might remember that, if she remembered anything at all about him at this point. He went on, "I'm going to try to get home early from the hotline. I may not be able to if I can't pull in a substitute to take my shift. I'm heading over there now. If I can get a sub, I'll be home pretty early."

He could hear her attempt to hide dismay when she replied. "But Doug . . . I mean, what time do you think you'll make it?"

"I don't know. By eight at the latest, I hope. What difference does it make?"

"Oh. None at all, really. But I thought you might like dinner . . ."

What she really thought was how she was going to have to cancel her hot romp with his baby brother. Douglas smiled at the realization of how nicely he'd just unhooked her little caboose.

"Hell, I'm not hungry, Donna. I just want to go to bed if I can. You be there to rub my back? You going anywhere?"

"Of course not. Where would I be going? Doug, you sound strange. Is something wrong?"

Nothing was wrong, he told her. What he didn't tell her was how right everything was, felt, and was going to be. He had her where he wanted her now: she'd be home, and she'd be alone. She might phone Michael and tell him that his brother was coming home early so their tryst was off, but even if she did that, Michael's statement after her death would conflict with Douglas's uninterrupted presence at the suicide hotline that night.

Douglas just had to make sure that he was back at the hotline with time to disassemble the call diverter. He'd get rid of it on the way home — nothing could be easier than flipping it into the trash behind the huge movie theater complex that was on his route from the hotline to Harbour Heights where he lived — and then he'd arrive at his usual time of nine-twenty to "discover" the murder of his beloved.

It was all so easy. And so much cleaner than divorcing the little whore.

He felt remarkably at peace, considering everything. He'd seen Thistle again and she'd held his Rolex, his wedding band, and his cuff links to take her reading. She'd greeted him by telling him that his aura was strong and that she could feel the power pulsing from him. And when she closed her eyes over his possessions, she'd said, "I feel a major change coming into your life, not-David. A change of location, perhaps, a change of climate. Are you taking a trip?"

He might be, he told her. He hadn't had one in months. Did she have any suggested destinations?

"I see lights," she responded, going her own way. "I see cameras. I see many faces. You're surrounded by those you love."

They'd be at Donna's funeral, of course. And the press would cover it. He was somebody after all. They wouldn't ignore the murder of Douglas Armstrong's wife. As for Thistle, she'd find out who he really was if she read the paper or watched the local news. But that made no difference since he'd never mentioned Donna and since he'd have an alibi for the time of her death.

He arrived at the suicide hotline at five fifty-six. He was relieving a UCI psych student named Debbie who was eager enough to be gone. She said, "Only two calls, Mr. Armstrong. If your shift is like mine, I hope you brought something to read."

He waved his copy of *Money* magazine and took her place at the desk. He waited ten minutes after she'd left before he went back out to his car to get the call diverter.

The hotline was located in the dock area of Newport, a maze of narrow one-way streets that traversed the top of Balboa Peninsula. By day, the streets' antique stores, marine chandleries, and secondhand clothing boutiques attracted both locals and tourists. By night, the place was a ghost town, uninhabited except for the new-wave beatniks who visited a dive called the Alta Cafe three streets away, where anorexic girls dressed in black read poetry and strummed guitars. So no one was on the street to see Douglas fetch the call diverter from his Mercedes. And no one was on the street to see him leave the suicide hotline's small cubbyhole behind the real estate office at eight-fifteen. And should any desperate individual call the hotline during his drive home, that call would be diverted onto his cellular phone and he could deal with it. God, the plan was perfect.

As he drove up the curving road that led to his house, Douglas thanked his stars that he'd chosen to live in an environment in which privacy was everything to the homeowners. Every estate sat, like Douglas's, behind walls and gates, shielded by trees. On one day in ten, he might actually see another resident. Most of the time — like tonight — there was no one around.

Even if someone had seen his Mercedes sliding up the hill, however, it was January dark and his was just another luxury car in a community of Rolls-Royces, Bentleys, BMWs, Lexuses, Range Rovers, and other Mercedes. Besides, he'd already decided that if he saw someone or something suspicious, he would just turn around, go back to the hotline, and wait for another Wednesday.

But he didn't see anything out of the ordinary. He didn't see anyone. Perhaps a few more cars were parked on the street, but even these were empty. He had the night to himself.

At the top of his drive, he shut off the engine and coasted to the house. It was dark inside, which told him that Donna was in the back, in their bedroom.

He needed her outside. The house was equipped with a security system that would do a bank vault proud, so he needed the killing to take place outside where a peeping Tom gone bazooka or a burglar or a serial killer might have lured her. He thought of Ted Bundy and how he'd snagged his victims by appealing to their maternal need to come to his aid. He'd go the Bundy route, he decided. Donna was nothing if not eager to help.

He got out of the car silently and paced over to the door. He rang the bell with the back of his hand, the better to leave no trace on the button. In less than ten seconds, Donna's voice came over the intercom. "Yes?"

"Hi, babe," he said. "My hands are full. Can you let me in?"

"Be a sec," she told him.

He took the satin belt from his pocket as he waited. He pictured her route from the back of the house. He twisted the satin around his hands and snapped it tight. Once she opened the door, he'd have to move like lightning. He'd have only one chance to fling the cord around her neck. The advantage he already possessed was surprise.

He heard her footsteps on the limestone. He gripped the satin and prepared. He thought of Michael. He thought of her together with Michael. He thought of his Asian erotica. He thought of betrayal, failure, and trust. She deserved this. They both deserved it. He was only sorry he couldn't kill Michael right now too.

When the door swung open, he heard her say, "Doug! I thought you said —"

And then he was on top of her. He leapt. He yanked the belt around her neck. He dragged her swiftly out of the house. He tightened it and tightened it and tightened it and tightened it. She was too startled to fight back. In the five seconds it took her to get her hands to the belt in a reflex attempt to pull it away from her throat, he had it digging into her skin so deeply that her scrabbling fingers could find no slip of material to grab on to.

He felt her go limp. He said, "Jesus. Yes. Yes."

And then it happened.

The lights went on in the house. A mariachi band started playing. People shouted, "Surprise! Surprise! Sur —"

Douglas looked up, panting, from the body of his wife, into popping flashes and a video camcorder. The joyous shouting from within his house was cut off by a female shriek. He dropped Donna to the ground and stared without comprehension into the entry and beyond that the living room. There, at least two dozen people were gathered beneath a banner that said SURPRISE, DOUGIE! HAPPY FIVE-FIVE!

He saw the horrified faces of his brothers and their wives and children, of his own children, of his parents, of one of his former wives. Among them, his colleagues and his secretary. The chief of police. The mayor.

He thought, What is this, Donna? Some kind of joke?

And then he saw Michael coming from the direction of the kitchen, Michael with a birthday cake in his hands, Michael saying, "Did we surprise him, Donna? Poor Doug. I hope his heart —" And then saying nothing at all when he saw his brother and his brother's wife.

Shit, Douglas thought. What have I done?

That, indeed, was the question he'd be answering for the rest of his life.

JEREMIAH HEALY

Eyes That Never Meet

FROM *Unusual Suspects*

One

MARLA VAN DORN OWNED a condo in one of those bay-windowed brownstones on Commonwealth Avenue. The living room had a third-floor view of the Dutch-elmed mall as it runs eastward through Back Bay to Boston's Public Garden. The view westward tends toward the bars and pizza joints of Kenmore Square and derelicts on public benches, so most people with bay windows look eastward for their views. As I was.

Behind me, Van Dorn said, "When the leaves are off the trees, you can see straight across Commonwealth to the buildings on the other side. Even into the rooms, at night with the lights on."

I nodded. Ordinarily, I meet clients in my office downtown, the one with JOHN FRANCIS CUDDY, CONFIDENTIAL INVESTIGATIONS stenciled in black on a pebbled-glass door. But I live in Van Dorn's neighborhood, so stopping on the way home from work at her place, at her request, wasn't exactly a sacrifice.

She said, "It might be helpful if we sat and talked for a while first, then I can show you some things."

I turned and looked at her. Early thirties, *Cosmo* cover girl gone straight into a high-rise investment house. Her head was canted to the right. The hair was strawberry blond and drawn back in a bun that accented the cords in her long neck. The eyes were green and slightly almond-shaped, giving her an exotic, almost oriental look. The lipstick she wore picked up a minor color in the print blouse that I guessed was appropriate business attire in the dog days of

July. Her skirt was pleated and looked to be the mate to a jacket that I didn't see tossed or folded on the burlappy, sectional furniture in the living room. The skirt ended two inches above the knee while she was standing and six inches farther north as she took a seat across a glass and brass coffee table from me. Van Dorn made a ballet of it.

The head canted to the left. "Shall I call you 'John' or 'Mr. Cuddy'?"

"Your dime, your choice."

The tip of her tongue came out between the lips, then back in, like it was testing the wind for something. "John, then. Tell me, John, do you find me attractive?"

"Ms. Van —"

"Please, just answer the question."

I gave it a beat. "I think you're attractive."

"Meaning, you find me attractive?"

"Meaning based on your face and your body, you'd get admiring glances and more from most of the men in this town."

"But not from you."

"Not for long."

"Why?"

"You're too aware of yourself. The way you move your head and the rest of you. I'd get tired of that and probably tired of trying to keep up with it."

Her lips thinned out. "You're a blunt son of a bitch, aren't you?"

"If you don't like my answers, maybe you shouldn't ask me questions."

A more appraising look this time. "No. No, on the contrary. I think you're just what I need."

"For what?"

"I'm being . . . I guess the vogue-ish expression is 'stalked.'"

"There's a law against that now. If you go to —"

"I can't go to the police on this."

"Why not?"

"Because a policeman may be the one stalking me."

Uh-oh. "Ms. Van Dorn —"

"Perhaps it would be easier if I simply summarized what's happened."

She didn't phrase it as a question.

I sat back, taking out a pad and pen, show her I was serious before probably turning her down. "Go ahead."

She settled her shoulders and resettled her hands in her lap. "I was burglarized two months ago, the middle of May. I came home from work to find my back window here, the one on the alley, broken. I've since had security bars installed, so that can't happen again. Whoever it was didn't take much, but I reported it to the police, and they sent a pair of detectives out to take my statement. One of them . . . He called me on a pretext, about checking a fact in my statement, and he . . . asked me to go out with him."

Van Dorn stopped.

I said, "Did you?"

"Did I what?"

"Go out with him?"

"No. He was . . . unsuitable."

"Did you hear from him again?"

"Yes. I'm afraid I wasn't quite clear enough the first time I turned him down. Some of them just don't get it. The second time, I assure you he did."

"What'd you tell him?"

"I told him I don't date black men."

I looked at her, then said, "His name?"

"Evers, Roland Evers. But he told me I could call him 'Rollie.'"

"Then what happened?"

"Nothing for a week. I travel a good deal in my job, perhaps ten days a month. When I'd get back from a trip, there would be . . . items waiting for me, downstairs."

When I came into her building, there had been a double set of locked doors with a small foyer between them and a larger lobby beyond the inner door. "What do you mean by 'downstairs'?"

"In the space between the doors, as though somebody had gotten buzzed in and just dropped off a package."

"Buzzed in by one of your neighbors, you mean?"

"Yes. The buzzer can get you past the outer door to the street but not the second one."

"What kind of package?"

"Simple plain-brown-wrappers, no box or anything with a name on it."

"What was in the packages?"

"Items of women's . . . The first one was a bra, the second one panties, the third . . ." Van Dorn's right hand went from her lap to her hair, and she looked away from me. "The bra was a peek-a-boo, the panties crotchless, the third item was a . . . battery-operated device."

I used my imagination. "Escalation."

"That's what I'm afraid. . . . That's the way it appears to me as well."

"You said the burglar didn't take much."

Van Dorn came back to me. "Excuse me?"

"Before, when you told me about the break-in, you said not much was taken."

"Oh. Oh, yes. That's right."

"Exactly what did you lose?"

"A CD player, a Walkman. Camera. They left the TV and VCR, thank God. More trouble hooking them up than replacing them."

"No items of . . . women's clothing, though."

"Oh, I see what . . ." A blush. "No, none of my . . . things. At first I assumed the burglary wasn't related to all this, beyond bringing this Evers man into my life. But now, well, I'm not so sure anymore."

"Meaning he might have pulled the burglary hoping he'd get assigned to the case and then have an excuse for meeting with you?"

Van Dorn didn't like the skepticism. "Far-fetched, I grant you, but let me tell you something, John. You've no doubt heard burglary compared to violation. Violation of privacy, of one's sense of security."

"Yes."

"Well, let me tell you. Living in this part of the city, being such a target for the scum that live off drugs and need the money to buy them and get that money by stealing, I've come to expect burglary. It's something you build in, account for in the aggravations of life, like somebody vandalizing your Beemer for the Blaupunkt."

Beemer. "I see what you mean."

"I hope you do. Because this man, whoever it is, who's leaving these . . . items, is grating on me a lot more than a burglary would. Than my own burglary *did*. It's ruining my peace of mind, my sense of control over my own life."

"You just said, 'whoever it is.'"

"I did."

"Does that mean it might not be Evers?"

"There's someone else who's been . . . disappointed in his advances toward me."

"And who is that?"

"Lawrence Fadiman."

"Can you spell it?"

"F-A-D-I-M-A-N. 'Lawrence' with a 'W,' not a 'U.'" Van Dorn opened a folder on the coffee table and took out a photo. A nail the color of her lipstick tapped on a face among three others, one of them hers. "That's Larry."

Thirtyish, tortoiseshell glasses, that hairstyle that sweeps back from the forehead in clots like the guys in Ralph Lauren clothes ads. The other two people in the shot were older men, everybody in business suits. "How did you come to meet him?"

"We work together at Tower Investments."

"For how long?"

"I started there three years ago, Larry about six months later."

"What happened?"

"We were on a business trip together. To Cleveland of all places, though a lot of people don't know what that city is famous for in an investment sense."

"It has the highest number of Fortune 500 headquarters outside New York?"

Van Dorn gave me the appraising look again. "Very good, John."

"Not exactly a secret. What happened in Cleveland?"

"A few too many drinks and 'accidental' brushings against me. I told him I wasn't interested."

"Did that stop him?"

"From the unwanted physical contact, yes. But he's made some other . . . suggestions from time to time."

"And that makes him a candidate."

"For the items, yes."

"You talk with Fadiman or his superior about sexual harassment?"

"No."

"Why not?"

Van Dorn got steely. "First, Larry and I are peers. I'm not his subordinate, not in the hierarchy and not in talent, either. However, if I can't be seen to handle his . . . suggestions without running to a father figure in the firm, there would be some question about my capability to handle other things — client matters."

"Your judgment. Evers and Fadiman. That it?"

"No."

"Who else?"

"A bum."

"A bum?"

"A homeless man. A beggar. What do you call them?"

I just looked at her again. "'Homeless' will do."

Van Dorn said, "He's always around the neighborhood. He stinks and he leers and he whistles at me when I walk by, even across the street when I'm coming from the Copley station."

The subway stop around the corner. "Anything else?"

"He says things like 'Hey, lovely lady, you sure look nice today,' or 'Hey, honey, your legs look great in those heels.'"

She'd lowered her voice and scrunched up her face imitating him. In many ways, Van Dorn was one of those women who got less attractive the more you talked with them.

I said, "Any obscenities?"

"No."

"Unwanted physical contact?"

Van Dorn looked at me, trying to gauge whether I was making fun of the expression she'd used. She decided I wasn't. "Not yet."

"You have a name for this guy?"

"You can't be serious?"

"How about a description?"

"Easier to show you."

She stood, again making a production of it, and swayed past me to the bay window. "Over here."

I got up, moved next to her.

Van Dorn pointed to a bench on the mall with two men on it. "Him."

One wore a baseball cap, the other was bareheaded. "Which one?"

"The one closer to us."

"With the cap on?"

"Yes."

"Does he always wear that cap?"

"No."

"You're sure that he's the one?"

"What do you mean?"

"Well, it's kind of hard to see his face under the cap."

Van Dorn looked at me as though I were remarkably dense. "I couldn't describe his face if I tried. I mean, you don't really *look* at them, do you? It's like . . . it's like the eyes that never meet."

"I don't get you."

"It was an exhibit, a wonderful one from Greece at the Met in New York the last time I was there. There were a dozen or so funeral stones from the classical period, 'stelae' I think is the plural for it. In any case, they'll show a husband and wife in bas relief, her sitting, giving some symbolic wave, him standing in front of her, sort of sadly? The idea is that she's died and is waving goodbye, but since she's dead, the eyes — the husband's and the wife's — never meet."

I thought of a hillside in South Boston, a gravestone that had my wife's maiden and married names carved into it. "And?"

"And it's like that with the homeless, don't you find? You're aware of them, you know roughly what they look like — and certainly this one's voice — but you never look into their faces. Your eyes never meet theirs."

It bothered me that Van Dorn was right. "So, you think the guy in the cap might be leaving these items for you?"

"He's around all the time, seeing me get into cabs with a garment bag. God knows these bums don't do anything, they have all the time in the world to sit on their benches, planning things."

"The items . . . the pieces of underwear in the packages, were they new?"

"Well, I didn't examine them carefully, of course. I threw them away."

"But were they new or old?"

"They seemed new."

"And the device."

The blush again. "The same."

"Where would a homeless man get the money to buy those things new?"

"Where? Begging for it, stealing for it. For all I know, he's the one who broke into this place. Fence the CD and such for whatever money he needed."

I looked down at the guy in the cap. He didn't look like he was going anywhere for a while. "Anybody else?"

"Who could be leaving the packages, you mean?"

"Yes."

"No."

"How about a neighbor?"

"No."

"Jilted boyfriend?"

"John, I haven't had a *boy*friend in a long time."

She looked at me, catlike. "I do have some very good *men*friends from time to time, but one has to be so much more careful these days."

I nodded and changed the subject. "What exactly is it that you want me to do, Ms. Van Dorn?"

She swayed back to the couch, rolling her shoulders a little, as though they were stiff. "What I want you to do is pay all these men a visit, rattle their cages a little. Let them know that I've hired you and therefore that I treat this as a very serious issue."

I waited for her to sit again. "It's not very likely one of them's going to break down and confess to me."

"I don't care about that. Frankly, I don't even care who it is who's been doing these things. I just want it to stop because I made it stop through hiring you."

Through her getting back in control. "I can talk to them. I can't guarantee results."

A smile, even more like a cat now. "I realize that. But somehow I think you achieve results, of all different kinds, once you put your mind to it."

I folded up my pad.

Van Dorn let me see the tip of the tongue again. "You may regret not finding me attractive, John."

"Our mutual loss."

The tongue disappeared, rather quickly.

Two

I left Marla Van Dorn's building through the front doors, holding open the outer one for a nicely dressed man carrying two Star Market bags and fumbling to find his keys. He thanked me profusely, and I watched to be sure he had a key to open the inner door, which he did. Most natural thing in the world, holding a door open for someone, especially so they could just drop off a package safely for someone in the building.

Before crossing to the mall, I walked around the corner to the mouth of the alley behind Van Dorn's block, the side street probably being the one she'd use walking from the subway station. The alley itself was narrow and typical, cars squeezed into every square inch of pavement behind the buildings in a city where parking was your worst nightmare. I moved down the alley, a hot breeze on my face, counting back doors until I got to the one I thought would be Van Dorn's. There were bars across a back window on the third floor, but a fire escape that accessed it. Before the bars, nobody would have needed anything special to get up and in there, just hop on a parked car and catch the first rung of the escape like a stationary trapeze.

I walked the length of the alley and came out on the next side street, turning right and taking that back to Commonwealth. I crossed over to the mall and started walking down the macadam path that stretched like a center seam on the eighty-foot-wide strip of grass and trees. And benches.

The way I was approaching them, the guy in the baseball cap was farther from me than the other man, who looked brittly old and seemed asleep. The guy in the cap was sitting with his legs straight out, ankles crossed, arms lazing over the back of the bench. He wore blue jeans so dirty they were nearly black, with old running shoes that could have been any color and a chamois shirt with tears through the elbow. He was unshaven but not yet bearded, and the eyes under the bill of the cap picked me up before I gave any indication I was interested in talking to him.

The guy in the cap said, "Now who might you be?"

"John Cuddy." I showed him my ID folder.

"Private eye. Didn't think you looked quite 'cop.'"

"You've had some experience with them."

"Some. Mostly Uncle Sugar's, though."

The eyes. I'd seen eyes like that when I strayed out of Saigon or they came into it. "What's your name?"

"Take your pick, John Cuddy, seeing as how I don't have no fancy identification to prove it to you."

I said, "What outfit, then?"

The shoulders lifted a little. "Eighty-second. You?"

"Uncle Sugar's cops."

The cap tilted back. "MP?"

"For a while."

"In-country?"

"Part of the while."

He gestured with the hand closest to me. "Plenty of bench. Set a spell."

"I won't be here that long."

The hand went back to where it had been. "Why you here at all?"

"A woman's asked me to speak to you about something that's bothering her."

"And that would be?"

"You."

A smile, two teeth missing on the right side of the upper jaw, the others yellowed and crooked. "Miss Best of Breed?"

"Probably."

"Saw you going into her front door over there."

"You keep pretty good tabs on the building?"

"Passes the time."

"You seen anybody leaving things in the foyer?"

"The foyer? You mean inside the door there?"

"That's what I mean."

"Sure. United Parcel, Federal Express."

"Anybody not in a uniform and more than once?"

"This about what's bothering her?"

"Partly."

"What does 'partly' mean?"

"It means she isn't nuts about you grizzling her every time she walks by."

The cap tilted down. "I don't grizzle her."

"She doesn't like it."

"All's I do, I tell her how good she looks, how she makes my day better."

"She doesn't appreciate it."

The guy tensed. "Fine. She won't hear it no more, then."

"That a promise?"

The guy took off the cap. He had a deep indentation scar on his forehead, one you didn't notice in the shadow of the bill. "Got this here from one of Charlie's rifle butts. The slope that done it thought he'd killed me, but he learned he was mistaken, to his everlasting regret. When I was in, I found I liked hand-to-hand, picked up on it enough so's the colonel had me be an instructor."

"What's your point?"

"My point, John Cuddy, is this. You come over here to deliver a message, and you done it. Fine, good day's work. But you come back to roust me some more, and you might find you're mistaken and regret it, just like that slope I told you about."

"No more comments, no more whistles, no more packages."

"I don't know nothing about no packages. What the hell's in them, anyways?"

"Things that bother her."

"What, you mean like . . . scaring her?"

"You could say that."

The head dropped, the arms coming off the back of the bench, hands between his knees, kneading the flesh around his thumbs. "That ain't right, John Cuddy. Nossir. That ain't right at all."

Three

The Area D station that covers my neighborhood is on Warren Street, outside Back Bay proper. The building it's in would remind you of every fifties black-and-white movie about police departments. Inside the main entrance, I was directed to the Detective Unit. Of eight plainclothes officers in the room, there was one Asian male, one black female, and one black male.

The black male looked to be about my size and a good stunt double for the actor Danny Glover. He was sitting behind a desk while a shorter, older white detective perched his rump on the edge of it. The black guy wore a tie and a short-sleeved dress shirt, the white guy a golf shirt and khaki pants. They were passing documents from a file back and forth, laughing about something.

I walked up to the desk, and the black detective said, "Help you?"

"Roland Evers?"

"Yeah?"

"I wonder if I could talk to you."

"Go ahead."

"In private?"

The white guy swiveled his head to me. Brown hair, clipped short, even features, the kind of priestlike face you'd tell your troubles to just before he sent you away for five-to-ten. "Who's asking?"

I showed them my ID holder.

The white guy said, "Jesus, Rollie, a private eye. I'm all a-quiver."

Evers said, "Can't hardly stand it myself, Gus. Alright, Cuddy, what do you want?"

"Without your partner here might be better."

Gus looked at Evers, but Evers just watched me. "Partner stays."

Gus said, "You need to use a name, mine's Minnigan."

I decided to play it on the surface for a while. "You two respond to a B & E couple months back, condo belonging to Marla Van Dorn?"

Evers blinked. "We did."

"The lady's been getting some unwelcome mail. She'd like it to stop."

Minnigan said, "We never made a collar on that, did we, Rollie?"

Evers said, very evenly, "Never did."

Minnigan looked at me. "Seems we can't help you, Cuddy. We don't even know who did it."

"You spend much time trying?"

"What, to find the guy?"

"Yes."

Minnigan shook his head. "She lost, what, a couple of tape things, am I right?"

I said, "Walkman, CD player, camera."

"Yeah, like that. She never even wrote down the serial numbers. That always amazes me, you know? These rich people, can afford to live like kings and never keep track of that stuff."

"Meaning no way to trace the goods."

Evers said, "And no way to tie them to any of our likelies."

"That's alright. I'm not sure one of your likelies is the problem, anyway."

Minnigan said, "I don't get you."

"Van Dorn's not sure it's the burglar who's become her admirer."

Evers said, "Who does she think it is?"

"She's not sure." I looked from Evers to Minnigan, then back to Evers and stayed with him. "That's why I'm talking to you."

Minnigan said, "We already told you, we can't help you any."

Evers said, "That's not what Cuddy means, Gus. Is it?"

I stayed with Evers. "All she cares about is that it stops, not who's doing it or why. Just that it stops."

Minnigan glared at me.

Evers said, "You don't push cops, Cuddy."

"Is that what I'm doing?"

"You push a man, you find out he can hurt you, lots of different ways."

"I'm licensed, Evers."

"Licenses get revoked."

"Not without some kind of cause, and when you stop to think about it, everybody's licensed, one way or the other."

Minnigan came down off the glare. "Hey, hey. What are we talking about here?"

Evers glanced at him, then back to me. "Okay, let me give you the drill. I ask the woman out one time, she says 'no' like she maybe means 'maybe.' Fine. I ask her a second time, she gives me a real direct lecture on why she thinks the races shouldn't mix. I got the hint, you hear what I'm saying?"

I looked at both of them, Minnigan trying to look reasonable, Evers just watching me with his eyes as even as his voice.

I nodded. "Thanks for your time."

Outside the building, I took a deep breath. Halfway down the block, I heard Gus Minnigan's voice say, "Hey, Cuddy, wait up a minute."

I stopped and turned.

Minnigan reached me and lowered his voice. "Let me tell you something, okay?"

"Okay."

"Rollie's going through a divorce. I know I been there, maybe you have, too."

"Widowed."

"Wid — jeez, I'm sorry. Really. But look, he's just out on his own a month, maybe two, when we answer the call on that Van Dorn woman. And you've seen her, who wouldn't try his luck, am I right? But that don't mean Rollie'd do anything more than that."

"So?"

"So, cut him a little slack, okay?"

"As much as he needs."

Minnigan nodded, like I meant what he meant, and turned back toward the Area D door.

Four

When I got off the elevator on the forty-first floor, I let my ears pop, then turned toward the sign that said TOWER INVESTMENTS, INC. The receptionist was sitting at the center of a mahogany horseshoe and whispered into a minimike that curved from her ear toward her mouth like a dentist's mirror. She gave me the impression she'd hung up however you have to in that kind of rig, then smiled and asked if she could help me.

"Lawrence Fadiman, please."

As she looked down in front of her, a man came through the internal doorway behind her. He wore no jacket, but suspenders held up pin-striped suit pants and a bow tie held up at least two chins. He looked an awful lot like one of the two older men in the photo Marla Van Dorn had shown me.

The receptionist pushed a button I could see and stared at a screen that I couldn't. "I'm afraid Mr. Fadiman's out of the office for at least another hour. Can someone else help you?"

"No, thanks. I'll catch him another time."

As I left, I heard the older man say, "Fadiman's not back yet?" and the receptionist say, "No, Mr. Tice."

The lobby of the building had a nice café with marble tabletops over wrought-iron bases that Arnold Schwarzenegger would have had a time rearranging. I chose a table that gave me a good view of the elevator bank servicing floors 25 through 50. I'd enjoyed most of a mint-flavored iced tea before the man in the tortoiseshell glasses and clotted hair came through the revolving door from outside. He wore a khaki suit against the heat, the armpits stained from sweat as he checked his watch and shook his head.

I said, "Larry!"

He stopped and looked around. Seeing no one he knew, Fadiman started for the elevator again.

"Larry! Over here."

This time he turned completely around. "Do I know you?"

"Only by telephone. John Cuddy."

"Cuddy . . . Cuddy . . ."

"Mr. Tice upstairs said I might catch you if I waited here."

The magic word in the sentence was "Tice," which made Fadiman move toward me like he was on a tractor beam.

He said, "Well, of course I'd be happy to help. What's this about?"

As we shook hands and he sank into the chair opposite me, I said, "It's about those nasty little packages Marla's been getting."

Fadiman looked blank. "Marla Van Dorn?"

"How many Marlas you know, Larry?"

"Well, just —"

"The packages have to stop."

"What packages?"

"*The* packages."

"I don't know what —"

"Larry. No more of them, understand?"

He looked blanker. If it was an act, he was very, very good. "I'm sorry, but I don't have a clue as to what —"

"Just remember, Larry. I want them to stop, Marla wants them to stop, and most important of all, Mr. Tice would want them to stop if I were to tell him about them."

Blank was replaced by indignant. "Is this some sort of . . . veiled threat?"

I stood to leave. "No, I wouldn't call it 'veiled,' Larry."

Five

When I got back to the office, I called her at Tower Investments.

"Marla Van Dorn."

"John Cuddy, Ms. Van —"

"What the hell did you say to Larry?"

"Not much. If he isn't the one who's been sending the packages, he wouldn't have guessed what was in them."

"Yes, well, that's great, but you should have seen him fifteen minutes ago."

"What did he do?"

"He grabbed me by the arm, pulled me into a cubbyhole, and hissed at me."

"Hissed at you?"

"Yes. At least, that's what it sounded like. He told me he didn't appreciate my 'goon' accosting him across a crowded lobby."

I liked "accosted." "The lobby wasn't that crowded."

A pause. "What I mean is, I think you've rattled his cage enough."

"He say anything else?"

"Just that if I stood in the way of any opportunities he had here, he'd know what to do about it."

I didn't like that. "Maybe I rattled a little too hard."

"Don't worry about it. I can't say I feel sorry for him. Did you see the others?"

I told her about Evers and the guy in the cap.

"Well, then, I guess we just . . . wait and see if the packages stop?"

"I guess."

"Unless you have something else in mind, John?"

"No."

"Well then." Brusquely. "I have things to do if I'm going to be out of here by six."

She hung up. I pushed some papers around my desk for a while, trying to work on other cases, but I kept coming back to Marla Van Dorn. I turned over what I'd learned. Lawrence Fadiman may have confronted her at work, but he wasn't likely to do anything violent there. Her condo was a better bet, and with the back window barred, that left the front entrance as maybe the best bet of all.

The paperwork on my desk could wait. I locked the office and headed home to change.

The guy in the baseball cap was already on the bench with the best view of Marla Van Dorn's likely route from the subway station down the side street toward Commonwealth. Even with me wearing sunglasses and a Kansas City Royals cap of my own above and a Hawaiian shirt, Bermuda shorts, and black kneesocks below, I thought he might recognize me. So I sat with my Boston guidebook and unfolded map on the next bench up the mall, keeping my eye on the side street as best I could, which really meant just from the alley mouth to Commonwealth. I checked my watch. Five-forty.

While I waited, taxis stopped, dropping off some fares and picking up others. United Parcel and Federal Express trucks plied the double-parked lane, moving down a few doors at a time. Owners

walked dogs and summer-school students played Frisbee and nobody thought to ask the obvious tourist if he needed any help.

Out of the corner of my eye, I noticed the guy in the cap
straighten. Looking over to the side street, I saw Marla Van Dorn
walking, left hand holding a bag of some kind, hurrying a little as
she approached the mouth of the alley, accentuating her figure
under the cream-colored dress she wore.

Then one of the UPS trucks entered the intersection, its opaque,
beetle-brown mass blocking my eyes for a frame. Before it passed,
the guy in the ball cap was up and running hard, crossing Commonwealth toward the side street. As I got up, the UPS truck went
by, and I could see the mouth of the alley again. But not my client.

I started running, too.

The guy in the cap disappeared into the alley, and I heard two
cracks and a man's yell and a woman's scream. I drew a Smith &
Wesson Chief's Special from under the Hawaiian shirt and flat-
tened myself against the brick wall at the mouth of the alley, using
my free hand as a stop sign to the people starting to stream down
the side street. The two cracks had sounded to me like pistol shots,
and both the man and the woman in the alley were still making
noise, him more than her.

That's when I looked around the wall.

Marla Van Dorn was on her hands and knees, the front of the
dress torn enough to see she was wearing a white bra and white
panties. On his back on the ground in front of her was the guy in
the cap, but he was bareheaded now, the cap still boloing near him
from the hot breeze in the alley. The yelling was coming from
Detective Gus Minnigan, whose right arm was pointing at an angle
from his shoulder that God never intended, a four-inch revolver
about twenty feet away from him.

I came into the alley fast, Minnigan clenching his teeth and
yelling to me now. "The goddamn bum broke my arm, he broke my
goddamn arm!"

Hoarsely, Van Dorn said, "This bastard . . . was waiting for me . . .
grabbed me and pulled me into the alley."

Minnigan said, "She don't know what she's saying!"

Van Dorn looked up at me. "He put his gun in my . . . between my
legs and said, 'What, you don't care about who's sending you the
undies and the toy, I don't mean that much to you?'"

I remembered Minnigan in the Area D station, glaring at me when I told him and Evers that.

Minnigan said, "She's lying, I tell you!"

I said, "Shut up or I'll break your other arm."

Rocking back onto her ankles, Van Dorn pointed at the guy lying in front of her. "Then he came out of . . . nowhere. He ran right at us, against the gun. . . . The shots . . . He broke this bastard's arm and kicked the gun away, then fell. He came right through the bullets."

I looked down at the guy in the cap. His eyes were open, but unfocused, and I knew he was gone. Two blossoms of red, one where a lung would be, the other at his heart, grew toward each other as they soaked the chamois shirt.

"Why?" said Van Dorn staring at the man's face from communion height above his body. "Why did you do that?"

I thought, eyes that never meet, but kept it to myself.

MELODIE JOHNSON HOWE

Another Tented Evening

FROM *Ellery Queen's Mystery Magazine*

MAURICE HAMLIN PEERED OUT from the party tent that covered a grassy section of his vast backyard. His shrewd eyes came to an uneasy rest on the Ferris wheel. It spun around in a blur of colorful lights. Well-dressed men and bejeweled women seemed to sit as high as the moon in their swaying chairs. They laughed and waved to one another with that slight embarrassment adults feel when they think they should be enjoying themselves more than they really are.

Disgusted, Hamlin turned his assessing gaze back to the interior of the tent and surveyed the frolicking clowns, the mimes frozen in mocking imitations of his guests, the balloon sellers, the cotton-candy vendors, and the white-jacketed waiters serving Moët & Chandon champagne.

Hamlin had a familiar look in his eyes; the look of a producer whose movie has gone over budget and out of control. It was an expression I had seen many times in my years of being an actress. But this was not one of Hamlin's movies; this was his wife's fortieth birthday party.

"It's costing me a fortune. Where the hell is she, Diana?" he demanded.

"It's an important birthday. It's not easy for some women." I spoke from experience.

"The party's been going on for almost an hour. Robin's the one who wanted all this."

He tilted his round head toward me. His hair was obviously dyed a reddish-brown color. Hamlin didn't stay up nights worrying about the loss of subtlety in his search for youth, money, and a box office hit.

"Oh, God, I can't believe I'm married to a forty-year-old woman." He eyed a lithe redhead swaying past him. A blue balloon was tied by a long string to the thin silvery strap of her low-cut dress. Printed on the balloon was HAPPY BIRTHDAY ROBIN.

"Will you go hurry her up, Diana?"

He didn't wait for an answer. Producers never do.

"I hope Robin doesn't sing tonight," he mumbled, walking quickly away to catch up with the young woman. I couldn't remember her name but she had done two movies and was poised to "make it big" or to disappear. It was another tented evening in Hollywood.

I made my way across the sparkling black AstroTurf, grabbed two glasses and a champagne bottle from a waiter's tray, and stepped out of the tent.

"Diana!"

It was Joyce Oliphant. She had just been named head of Horizon Studios. I knew her, many years ago, when she and I were the last of the starlets.

"Congratulations, Joyce."

"I didn't know you'd be here." She meant: *I thought you were out of the business and no longer important enough to be invited to the Hamlins'.*

Forcing her thin lips into a smile, she purposely did not introduce me to the men standing on each side of her. This was not just a lack of good manners. This was intended to intimidate, to make me feel ill at ease. Their eyes hunted the party for more important people.

"What are you doing with yourself?" She tossed her highlighted brown hair back from her lined, tense face. Her hair was too long for her age. It's difficult for some women to let go of the decade of their youth — ours was the sixties — no matter how successful they are in the present.

"I've got a small role in Hamlin's next picture," I said.

"I heard you had gone back to work. I do miss Colin."

And once again I felt that sharp, isolating pain of loss. Colin was my husband. He had died of a heart attack just fourteen months ago.

"I miss his wit," Joyce continued. "Where has all the wit gone?"

Her greedy eyes searched the yard as if she could pluck wit from one of the guests' heads. "Colin had it. There are times, Diana, when a script isn't working, I want to pick up the phone and say get me Colin Hudson, the greatest writer Hollywood ever had."

"I wish you could," I said.

One of the men whispered in her ear. New prey had been found and she and I had talked too long. A conversation at a Hollywood party should not last over thirty seconds.

"We'll talk. God, I hope Robin doesn't sing tonight." Her Chanel shoulder bag, dangling on a gold and leather strap, hit me in the stomach as she spun away.

I was a middle-aged woman, still good-looking enough for a middle-aged woman who was starting over in a business meant for very young women. I had no choice but to work. Colin and I had spent everything he had earned. No regrets. Besides, I had three things in my favor: I could act, I had contacts, and I knew how to play the game.

The Ferris wheel turned and the music blared as I made my way up the veranda steps to the enormous neo-Mediterranean house that curved like a lover's arm around a mosaic-lined pool.

"Hello, Diana." Oscar Bryant, my ex-business manager, stood smoking a cigar. Next to him, lurking in the shadow of a banana palm, was Roland Hays, the director.

"How are you, Oscar?"

"Still hoping you'll go out with me."

Dating your ex-business manager would be like dating your ex-gynecologist. He knows too much about your internal affairs.

"You know Roland Hays, don't you?" He turned to Hays. "This is Diana Poole."

The director was a slight man with receding black hair. He had a talent for getting the studios to make his movies even though they never turned a profit. For this reason he was referred to as an artist. His evasive dark eyes almost looked at me.

"Colin Hudson's widow," Oscar explained my existence.

"Great writer," the director muttered. "God, I hope Robin doesn't sing tonight."

"Why?" I asked.

"Have you ever heard her sing?" Oscar asked.

"No."

"Wait. Wait." He stared at the glasses and champagne bottle in my hands. "What's all that?"

"Robin's having trouble making an entrance."

He opened the French door for me. "Maybe you should just leave her up there." He chuckled.

"Better for all of us." The director stepped farther back into the swordlike shadows of the palm.

The house was eerily quiet in contrast to the noise outside. Contemporary art haunted the walls. My high heels clicked out their lonely female sounds as I made my way across a limestone floor to the stairs.

I'd met Robin Hamlin six months ago in acting class. I had gone back to brush up on the craft I had left when I married Colin. I have to admit — and these things are important to admit — I would not be walking up these stairs, and I would not have made friends with Robin in acting class, if she were not Maurice Hamlin's wife. I say these things are important to admit because at least I'm not lying to myself. Not yet, anyway. As I said, I know how to play the games.

There was a side to Robin that was spontaneous and delightful. There was another side that was petulant, insensitive, and demanding. But she had thought of me for the role in her husband's new movie and got me to read for him and the director. In Hollywood that makes her a person of character. There was also something poignant about Robin. At the age of forty she still dreamed, like a young girl dreams, of being a movie star, a performer, or just famous. Her husband had given her some small roles in his movies. And that's all they were — small roles doled out by a powerful husband to his wife.

I made my way down the long hallway to her bedroom suite.

"Robin? It's Diana," I announced to the closed door. "I come bearing champagne. Robin?" I waited. "Robin? Maurice is worried about you."

I tapped the door with my toe. I pushed it with my foot. It opened. I stepped into a mirrored foyer. My blond hair, black evening suit, one strand of pearls, red lips, reflected in a jagged kaleidoscopic maze.

"Robin? It's Diana."

A mirrored door opened. Robin stood there holding a sterling silver candelabra. Two of the four candles were missing. The ones that remained were tilted at a funny angle. Her black hair caressed her bare shoulders. The famous diamond and emerald necklace that Maurice had given Robin for her last birthday dazzled around her long, slim neck. The necklace and the candelabra were her only attire.

"Nice outfit," I said.

"Thank God, Diana. Come in here quick."

I followed her into the bedroom. She locked the door. Setting the bottle and the glasses on her mauve, taffeta-skirted vanity, I saw William DeLane reflected in the beveled mirror. Fully clothed, he leaned against the white velvet headboard. His misty gray eyes, full of surprise, stared into mine. I whirled around. The right side of his head was caved in. Blood spattered the white coverlet and his green jacket. Little drops of blood dotted the headboard near his thick brown hair. I didn't have to check his pulse to know he was dead. On the floor next to the bed was a white cocktail dress. Blood streaked the shimmery fabric. "I ruined my dress." Robin stamped her foot. Her implanted breasts never moved.

"Jesus Christ, Robin, what happened?"

Her voice went off into a whine. "I'm not going to cry. I'm not going to cry." She took a deep breath and didn't cry.

I pried the candelabra from her hand and set it on a table between two lavender-striped chairs.

"It doesn't go there. It goes on the mantel." She gestured toward an ornate marble fireplace.

"Robin, that's William DeLane." DeLane was a young and very successful screenwriter.

"Don't you think I know that? At least give me credit for knowing who I killed. Nobody gives me credit."

"Let me get Maurice."

"No. Don't you dare." She grabbed a silk bathrobe off a chaise longue, slipped it on, and sat down.

"I need to think this out." Her beautiful but remote violet-colored eyes studied me. "DeLane said you two went out last week."

"We had dinner together." With a shaking hand I poured champagne into the two glasses and gave her one. "He wanted to talk with me because I was Colin's wife. Widow. He wanted to know how Colin lived and worked."

"Why?" She crossed her long bare legs. Perfectly manicured toes glistened red.

"I think he was searching for some kind of an example, or a mooring. Some sort of image to hold on to." I took a long swallow of the champagne and avoided DeLane's shocked eyes.

"You mean like a father image?" she asked earnestly.

"More like a male muse. A creative guide in the jungle of Hollywood. He felt his own success was based on sheer guts and ego."

"Isn't everyone's?" Her remote expression became more intent. "Did he talk about me?"

"Yes. He told me he was having an affair with you. His exact words were: 'I'm having an affair with Maurice Hamlin's wife.'"

"But it wasn't enough, was it?"

"He was questioning his relationship to his success. Not his relationship with you," I said carefully, knowing that sex and success were so intermingled in Hollywood that it was difficult to discuss one without the other.

She turned and peered at DeLane. "Why would anybody question success?"

I forced myself to look at him. God, he was so young and such a hack. There was a time when Hollywood turned talented writers into banal, soulless creatures. Now they arrived in town without souls. They arrived schooled in the clichéd and eager to be rewritten.

"He's had three hit movies," I explained. "And he couldn't tell the difference between the first movie and the third movie. He felt that his words had no meaning. No connection to anything or anybody. Most of all they had no connection to himself. Why did you kill him, Robin?"

She didn't answer. I opened a pair of French doors that led out onto a narrow foot balcony. I could see the spinning Ferris wheel and hear the music and the laughter of the guests inside the tent. I took a deep breath and watched Maurice embracing a tree. I looked again. A blue balloon floated out from under a leafy limb. I realized that between him and the tree was the redhead actress, whose chances for making it were looking better. I closed the doors.

"DeLane sneaked up here to give me my birthday gift." Robin gestured toward a stack of leather-bound books piled on the floor near the bed. "The complete works of Ernest Hemingway."

"You killed him because he gave you the complete works of Ernest Hemingway?"

"No. But why give me some macho writer's books?"

"I think he was trying to give his own life some meaning."

"But why give me Hemingway's books? Do you see what I mean? Why me?" Her voice quivered. She stood and began to pace, stopped, thought a moment, then went to her closet and pulled out a yellow dress. She grabbed some pantyhose from a drawer.

"Do you remember who I was having an affair with on my last birthday?" she asked, wiggling into the pantyhose.

"I didn't know you then."

"Philip Vance."

Philip was a featured player. Not a star, not a character actor, but always working and always listed around fifth place in the credits.

"Do you know what he gave me for a present?" Robin pulled open another drawer and took out a rhinestone pin from a small velvet box. The brooch was in the shape of a heart with a ruby arrow piercing it.

"It's cheap but I love it," she said, sounding like a teenage girl.

I knew the pin well. Philip had given me one fifteen years ago. I never wore it. Philip had been giving out these rhinestone pins for twenty years and always with the same line: "I can't afford diamonds but the heart is real." He counted on the expensive taste of his conquests. Knowing his *ladies,* as he called them, would never wear anything so obviously inexpensive, he was free to give the same pin to his next *lady.*

"It's not that I have to have anything expensive," Robin said. "Just something that's sentimental. Something that means I was loved. 'I can't afford diamonds but the heart is real.'" She stared sadly at the pin, then tucked it lovingly back into the drawer.

"Do you remember when we were in acting class together?" she asked, stepping into the yellow dress.

"Yes."

"And Rusty, our teacher, told us to close our eyes and tell him what we saw? What we imagined? Do you remember what you saw?"

"No."

"A bird with a broken wing on a flagstone patio. A man's wrist and the sleeve of his white shirt turned back. Do you remember what I saw?"

"No."

"Nothing. I saw nothing. And then Rusty asked me to describe the nothingness. Remember?"

"Yes?"

"And I asked how can I describe nothing? I mean, you can't. The closest I could come was a sort of a grayish black. Nothing is nothing. Zip me up."

I zipped her up.

"Oh, God, I didn't want to wear this." She turned on DeLane's corpse as if he had commented on her dress. "He made me feel like nothing. I suddenly could see it. Feel it."

"How did he do that, Robin?"

"He just couldn't believe that when all was said and done, he was a writer who was having an affair with his producer's wife. I could handle that. But he couldn't. So he tried to make it more than it was. And he tried to change me. That's when he made me feel like nothing." She put on some lipstick and smoothed her hair.

"Change you into what?"

"He blamed Maurice for everything. He said it was his money and power that kept me from truly knowing who I was. I told him he was crazy, that he was talking about himself. Not me. I told him it was over. That I didn't want to see him anymore." She stared defiantly at herself in the mirror. "I turned forty today and told a man I didn't want him. I didn't need him anymore."

She sat back down on the chaise longue and slipped her feet into bright yellow high heels.

"Then it should've been a great night. Why didn't it just end there?" I poured her another glass of champagne.

"Because as I was leaving to go down to the party he said, 'Please, do us all a favor and don't sing tonight.'"

She tapped her long red nails against the glass, took another sip, and then slowly peered at DeLane.

"Why didn't he want you to sing?" I asked.

"He said people laugh when I sing. I've never heard anybody laugh, Diana. I told him that. He was lying on the bed just like he is now. I was standing by the fireplace. He said it was an uneasy laughter. That if I sang I would remind my guests of how untalented they really are. And how much money they earn for being so untalented. I grabbed the candelabra, turned, and swung it at his head.

Not just once, but a couple of times." Her eyes moved from DeLane to me. "You're going to call the police, aren't you?"

"Yes."

"But not till after I sing. Promise?"

"All right."

She stood, downed the last of her champagne, and walked slowly out of the room.

I poured myself another glass, opened the French doors, and stepped out onto the narrow foot balcony. I looked toward the tree. Maurice and the redhead were gone. Robin appeared on the veranda. She stopped and looked up in my direction and waved. I waved back. The emerald and diamond necklace shone like glass. Guests began to move toward her, surrounding her as if she were a movie star and not just another wife who had turned forty. They all disappeared into the tent.

The caterers wheeled a giant cake out onto the veranda. It blazed like a small brush fire. Christ, Maurice had them put all forty candles on the cake. They lifted it off the cart and carried it into the tent. A hush fell. I could hear applause then guests singing "Happy Birthday." The Ferris wheel went around in a garish blur, its now empty carriages swaying under the cold eye of the moon. There was another hush. Then the sound of a piano. And soon Robin's voice wafted up through the tent into the night sky. I didn't know the song. Some rock ballad. She hit all the right notes, but she had a thin, wavering, unfeeling voice. DeLane was right. She was relentlessly untalented. But not any worse than some others who have made it on just sheer guts and ego. Not any worse than DeLane.

The tent reminded me of an evangelist's tent. A place where people come to be told there is another world. A better world. Where people can believe that Hollywood will save them no matter what they do or how they do it. Her pathetic voice, unintentionally, questioned that belief.

I moved back into the room and again forced myself to look at the body of the young, successful DeLane. I couldn't bear the surprised look in his eyes. After three hit movies his words had finally connected. I pulled the white silk coverlet over his face.

PAT JORDAN

The Mark

FROM *Playboy*

"He sounds different," Bobby said. He downshifted for the
railroad tracks at Dixie. The black SHO bumped over the tracks,
then picked up speed.

"Like how?" Sheila said.

"I don't know. Just different. Not as pissed off as usual." Bobby
turned onto Federal. Two rednecks, a mangy dog lying at their feet,
sat drinking beer in the shade of the Riptide's outdoor bar. A
skinny hooker in a miniskirt that barely covered her ass and dirty
white fringed cowboy boots sashayed past them, looking back over
her shoulder at passing cars while she talked on a cellular phone.

"Poor thing," said Sheila, shaking her head slowly. "It's too hot to
work." The hooker flipped her the finger. Sheila held a cigarette
limp-wristed beside her cheek, her other hand propping up her
elbow in that ladylike way that always amazed Bobby.

"Maybe he's just tired," Sheila said. "He's been working construction, what, the last six months? He's forty-seven, Bobby. A little old
for a career change."

"Not tired like that. Something different. You'll see." As they
passed Fort Lauderdale Airport, a 747, shimmering in the hot
noon sun, was coming in from the ocean.

"He was away two years, Bobby. Maybe doing time didn't agree
with him." The plane passed low overhead, and its shadow, like a
prehistoric bird's, enveloped them for a moment, then moved toward the airport runway. Sheila smiled at Bobby. "It didn't agree
with you."

Bobby liked that in her. She never cut him any slack. Her word.

"You have a tendency to be slack, Robert," she said once in the schoolmistress tone she sometimes took with him. "It's my job to tighten up that slack." She was forty-five, ten years older than Bobby. Ten years smarter, too.

There was nothing slack about Sheila. Trim, tanned, muscled like the fourteen-year-olds who played basketball at Holiday Park. She even had chiseled abs like them. Her hair was bleached platinum and cut so short it stood up like spring grass. It made her look tough in tight jeans or cutoff shorts. She looked sexy, like a high-class hooker, when she wore a black spandex dress and stiletto heels. And when she put on a wig and a business suit, she looked like a lady, maybe a bank president at Centrust. Sheila said there was nothing to it. She had done summer stock for years in New England before she moved to Fort Lauderdale and began to concentrate on TV commercials. "See this face," she would say, smiling her eight-by-ten-glossy smile. "The face that launched a million coffee cups."

Today she wore tight jeans and a black T-shirt with gold writing across her small breasts: BEYOND BITCH! When she had put it on in their apartment, she'd said, "Nice touch, huh? Sol will like it." Bobby hoped so.

Bobby concentrated on Sol. "I mean, he only did two years out of six for smuggling pot. Big deal. A fucking minimum security prison. Club Fed. There's even a chalk line for a fence, like on a football field. But still, it changed him."

"Maybe he's just getting old. They say doing time ages you."

"But it wasn't hard time, for Christ's sake. He gained twenty pounds. No, he lost something. His edge."

Sheila smiled brightly. "Well, baby, we'll just have to find it for him."

Bobby pulled up in front of the Lucky Hotel and parked. "A misnomer," Sheila said. It was an old two-story south Florida building made out of Dade County pine, stuccoed over many times, its mission tiles replaced with a dilapidated tin roof. The second floor was a halfway house for cons serving out the last six months of their sentences while "acclimating" (Sol's word) themselves back into society. They went to work each morning at six and had to be back for supper at six. Today was Sol's last day.

They walked around back. Sol sat at a picnic table under the shade of a gumbo-limbo tree in the scruffy back yard, smoking a cigarette and talking with a woman. Sheila ran over to him. "Sol, baby, we missed you." She bent down and kissed him on the lips. When she straightened up she made a big production of studying him. His bald head was tanned from working in the sun. His Van-dyke beard was neatly trimmed. He was wearing Paul Newman–blue contact lenses and a pressed, long-sleeved, button-down Polo shirt over his big belly. White tennis shorts. Dirty white loafers.

Sheila narrowed her eyes. "You look different, Solly."

"It's the hair," he said, rubbing a hand over his bald head. "I grew it in the slam."

"We *did* miss you, Sol," Sheila said.

"I missed you, too, baby. I like that, the T-shirt."

Sheila turned to Bobby. "See, I told you."

Bobby said, "You ready?"

"I got to check out upstairs." He stood up. Sheila was right. He did look different. There was definitely something missing.

"Where's all your jewelry?" Bobby asked.

"In storage. That's our next stop." Sol seemed almost naked without his Rolex, his gold chains, his diamond pinkie rings, his three beepers. Not to mention the little Seecamp .32 ACP he liked to carry in his front pants pocket.

"Sheila's got the Seecamp," Bobby said. "She likes it."

"Yeah, but I gotta get the jewelry." Nothing could happen to Sol when he wore his jewelry. "And some real fucking cigarettes." He tossed his cigarette in the grass. "Government issue," he said, hold-ing up a pack with BRAND A printed across it. "Brand B's got fil-ters," he said. He crumpled the pack and tossed it, too.

"Aren't you going to introduce us to your friend?" Sheila asked.

The friend looked up at them. She was a tiny, ferret-faced woman with stringy brown hair, baggy sweatshirt, and baggy jeans.

"Sheila, Bobby, this is Connie." She nodded, gave them a sour smile. A con, obviously. Cons never used last names, not real ones, anyway. After five years of friendship, Bobby and Sol still did not know each other's real last names. Sol was Sol Rogers. Bobby was Bobby Squared. Both men had long since distanced themselves from Solomon Bilstein, Brooklyn Jew, and Robert Roberts, né Red-feather, half-breed Cherokee out of the North Carolina mountains. They were now just two business partners in paradise.

*   *   *

Driving back to Fort Lauderdale, Bobby was quiet. So was Sol, sitting beside him. Sheila said, "Connie's an interesting girl, Sol. She said she did three years for fraud."

Sol turned around, grinning, and said, "You never heard of her? Coupon Connie? Was in all the papers. She made millions with coupon fraud. You know what she did in the slam? Corresponded with male cons. They sent her money, she sent them dirty underwear. Broad useta get boxes of underwear every week. Drove the guards nuts trying to figure out what she was doing with it all. If the cons sent her enough money, Connie would send them a dirty letter, too, telling them all the nice things she'd do to them if she could. Whack-off Connie is what she became."

"Good thing none of them saw her," Bobby said.

They passed the Riptide again. The two rednecks and the mangy dog were still there. The hooker was walking back the other way, north now. Sol checked her out. From the back seat, Sheila said, "Solly, want us to stop for her? A welcome-home present?"

Sol shook his head. "I just wanna pick up my jewelry."

Sheila reached under the back of the driver's seat and pulled out Sol's Seecamp. "Here, Sol. This should make you feel better." She handed him the gun. Sol looked at it, then put it in his front pants pocket.

"That's a start," he said.

"We don't have time for the jewelry," Bobby said. Sol looked at him. "We got something more urgent. A little something Sheila and me put together. To ease your way back into things."

"Yeah?"

"Meyer set it up," Bobby said. "A little something to get you spending money, get you on your feet. No risks. A piece of cake, really. Meyer knows this guy runs a limo service. Stretch Lincolns with a bar in back, color TV, cellular phone. Caters only to high rollers, mostly from Europe, some from South America, but we don't want to mess with the spics. You never know with them, could be bad guys. Anyway, these guys fly into MIA, businessmen mostly, maybe a little shady, but that's good, kind of guys like to deal only in cash. They got a wife somewhere, kids, a reputation back home, maybe a little bogus, but still something they got to protect. But they're in south Florida, fucking paradise, with all these beautiful blonde chicks they don't see back home, so after they do some business, they —"

"That's where I come in," said Sheila. She flashed the eight-by-ten-glossy smile. "I'm the fun part."

"Yeah, but not like they think," said Bobby. "What we do is, you pick them up at MIA. We got you a nice black suit, skinny black tie, a chauffeur's cap. You talk to them nice, ask about the wife and kids, look at their pictures. Find out where they're staying, how long, for what, get a feel for how much cash they got, jewelry, you know, easy stuff. Then you start hinting around how much fun paradise can be if you know where to go, who to be with. Maybe hint around you can get them a guide, you know, like at Disney World, someone who can show them a good time. Very pretty, classy, won't embarrass them in public. Someone who they'd be proud to have on their arm."

"Who could that be?" Sol glanced back at Sheila. She smiled again and spread her arms wide, like an actress accepting applause.

"Ta-da!" she said.

"If they bite," said Bobby, "great. If not, we set it up anyway. By accident, Sheila happens to bump into the guy at the hotel, a bar, someplace you know the guy's gonna be."

"How do we know the guy's gonna go for it?"

"Puh-leez, Solly!" Sheila said in mock outrage. "Don't insult me." Sol nodded. "Right. I been away too long."

"So they have a little dinner, some drinks, go back to his room," said Bobby. "I wait in the lobby. Sheila fixes him a drink, makes like Coupon Connie, tells him all the things she's gonna do to him. Boom! Next thing he knows, he's dreamin' what he's doing to Sheila, only he ain't doin' it. We're doing it to him. He wakes up ten hours later, he is cleaned out."

"Yeah, and he don't go to the man to complain?" asked Sol.

"You ain't been listening, Sol. I said the guy's got a wife and kids back home, a rep, he don't wanna be embarrassed, tell anybody he's been had by a broad. Plus, he don't even miss the money, the jewelry, he just wants to finish his business and get out of the country. Which is why we leave him his credit cards. They're just a way to get caught."

"The guy's humiliated," said Sheila. "He just wants to forget the whole thing, get back to the wife and kids, write it off as a lesson."

"It works right," said Bobby, "we can do it over and over. Make ourselves a few grand a week until we put something bigger to-gether."

"What do you think, Sol?" said Sheila.

"I think I wanna get my jewelry."

Bobby said, "After tonight, Solly, you can buy a shitload of jewelry. The guy's coming in from New York, by way of Rome, ten o'clock. Some guinea Ferrari importer who does business with that fancy sports car place out on Sunrise. You remember, with the blonde in the window, sitting behind the antique desk, so everybody passing by can see her nice tits in that low-cut blouse. Real classy-looking."

"Yeah, Bobby," said Sheila. "Very classy, chewing her fucking gum like a cow."

Sol glanced back at Sheila. She smiled at him. He said, "Jesus, Bobby, don't piss her off, ya know."

"Hell hath no fury, Sol," Sheila said, still smiling.

"Tonight, you're gonna pick up the guinea," said Bobby. "Give him the ride of his life."

"No, that's my job, Bobby," said Sheila. Sol and Bobby looked back at her. She flashed the smile. They all laughed, Sol for the first time since they had picked him up.

Sol stood at gate 13 at Miami International Airport, waiting behind a crowd of people who had come to meet passengers off the New York flight, holding up a hand-lettered sign: EXECUTIVE LIMO — ATTN: SIGNORE PAOLO FORTUNATO.

All of the first-class passengers had passed through, heading for baggage claim. Now the coach passengers began to come through the gate, mostly Haitians and Jamaicans. Sol turned around to see if he'd missed the mark. He held the sign over his head. Someone tapped him on the shoulder.

"*Scusi, signore.* Are you, perhaps, looking for me?"

Sol turned around to see a tall, slightly hunched-over guinea in a cheap, wrinkled brown suit. He was carrying a small nylon bag. He smiled at Sol, like one of those comic Italian actors. Shaggy black hair, droopy mustache, dark bulging eyes.

"Signore Fortunato?" Sol said. The man had no jewelry, no watch. Geez, was this the right guy?

"*Si,*" the man said, still smiling.

"Here, let me take that for you, sir."

"No need."

"This way toward baggage claim."

"I have only this," the man said, holding up the little bag. "I travel, how you Americans say, white?"

"Light. Travel light."

Sol eased down State Road 836, through the toll, onto I-95 north to Lauderdale. He passed the time bullshitting with the mark. How was the flight, the food, was he tired, stupid fucking questions Sol didn't give a shit about.

"Fix yourself a drink, sir. From the bar."

"A little scotch, maybe." The mark sat back and sipped his drink.

"Mind if I smoke?" Sol said.

"Certainly not. Only Americans worry about cigarettes."

Sol lit a cigarette, a Camel. It tasted good, no Brand fucking A. He asked the mark what hotel he was staying at, assuming it would be the Marriott Harbor Beach, with the five restaurants and the rock waterfall in the pool.

"The Mark. I am staying at the Mark on the beach. You know it?"

"Yes." Shit, yes, I know it. Fucking nothing motel, secluded, nobody knows about it except wiseguys from New York wanting to lay low, do their business, then split. What is this fucking guy doing at the Mark?

"It is quiet. I like that. No tourists. But first, I have to do some business. I have to check on a delivery tonight. Do you know Paradise Auto Works? It is on Sunset Boulevard."

"Sunrise," Sol said. "Sunset is in L.A."

"Of course." The guy settled back, sipping his scotch, looking at it as if it were the best scotch he'd ever tasted. The way guineas do, holding up the glass, smiling at it, talking about it, like they got half their pleasure from that. They could never just drink it. Jesus, Sol thought, forty fucking years I can't shake the guineas. At fourteen, Sol had had to make a choice — either hang with the Jews and become an orthodontist, or hang with the guineas and become what he was. It was an easy decision to make.

The guinea in the back of the limo was working on his second scotch. "Yes, I love Fort Lauderdale," he said. "The beautiful sun and the water and the palm trees."

"We have some beautiful sights. We call it paradise. Of course, you know, staying at the Mark. The girls on the beach."

"Ah, *si*. Very beautiful. Browned and blonde."

"Mostly exotic dancers. Very young, though. Beautiful but not sophisticated, you know what I mean? Not the kind of woman you can take places. I know such a woman, very beautiful, more mature, classy, could show you things in Lauderdale you've never seen before."

The guinea made believe he didn't understand. Either he was dumb or straight, or faking it. "Yes, that would be wonderful. But I am only here this one night. I fly back to Rome tomorrow night, after my business is completed."

"Too bad," Sol said, thinking, Sheila has her work cut out for her, getting this guinea to stay an extra day.

They got off at the Sunrise exit and headed east through Blacktown, past the Swap Shop with its big circus signs glowing neon in the darkness. They crossed the railroad tracks at Dixie, next to Searstown, then slowed at the car place.

"Turn here," the mark said.

Sol turned down a side street alongside the dealership's showroom window. In the darkness inside, Sol could make out the shapes of exotic cars, hump after hump packed together like a herd of hippopotamuses in a river.

"Park here," the mark said. Sol parked along an eight-foot-high concrete wall topped with razor wire. Geez, for cars? The guinea must have known what Sol was thinking. "Very expensive machines in there," he said. "Ferraris, worth more than $200,000 each. They are works of art, really. You can wait here. I will be only a few minutes."

Sol turned off the engine and waited. The guinea went to an iron gate and rang a buzzer. Sol opened his window. He heard voices. The gate was buzzed open, and the mark went in. Sol heard the sound of cars being moved with the engines shut off. When the mark had been gone five minutes, Sol got out and walked around the wall, looking for an opening. He came to a Dumpster against the side of a seedy mom-and-pop motel, the Royal Palm. Sol looked but couldn't see a palm. The Dumpster was on wheels, so Sol pushed it up against the wall, the wheels creaking from rust. He struggled to climb on top of it, first trying to push himself up with his arms, then trying to swing a leg up, his knee banging against the Dumpster, his big belly stopping him. A light came on in one of the motel rooms. Sol waited a moment, sweating, cursing the twenty pounds he'd put on in the slam. An old woman's face appeared at the window. Sol crouched behind the Dumpster. After a minute, the light went out. He saw a discarded concrete block, carried it over to the Dumpster, and used it to climb on top. He peered over the wall through the razor wire.

A bunch of guys were off-loading Ferraris from a trailer, coasting them down a ramp, then pushing them by hand. There were four cars, low and guinea red, with fat tires. Off to the side, Sol could see the mark talking with a shorter man. They talked while they watched the other guys jack up the cars and take off each wheel, using hand wrenches. They took off each tire and rolled it over to the mark and his friend. A worker took a knife from his back pocket and cut open the sidewall of one of the tires. He reached inside and pulled out a square package. When all the tires had been cut open and emptied, there was a neat pile of packages in front of the mark and his friend, like the beginnings of a block wall. The mark's friend kneeled and cut open a package. He reached in with his knife and took out something on the blade, a powder. He wet his finger, dabbed it on the powder and tasted it with a grimace. He nodded to the mark and waved to his men. They took the packages into the mechanics' bay and closed the door. The last guy out handed two briefcases to the mark and his friend. The friend opened one, and the mark reached in and took out a wad of bills. He flipped through it, then another, and another. He did the same with the second briefcase.

Smack, Sol thought. Maybe 10 kilos a tire, 16 tires, 160 kilos, worth maybe 50 grand a key wholesale, a total 800 large, maybe even a mil. But something was wrong. The mark gestured with his hands at the little guy. The little guy shrugged, turned his hands palm up, as if there were nothing he could do about it. The mark flung the back of his hand at the little guy, grabbed the briefcases, and walked toward the iron gate. Sol jumped off the Dumpster with a whoomph, falling facedown in the dirt. The light in the motel room went on again, and the woman at the window hissed, "Who's there? I have a gun. I have a gun. I have a .357 Magnum, you son of a bitch!"

Sol ran back to the limo. He was sitting in the driver's seat, smoking a cigarette, when the mark came through the gate with the two briefcases.

"We can go to the hotel now," he said.

"Everything all right, sir?"

The mark smiled at Sol. A cool customer, like nothing had happened. "Everything's fine," the mark said. "I might have to stay an extra night to tie up, how do you say, tight ends?"

"Loose ends," Sol said, pulling the limo back onto Sunrise, toward the beach and the Mark.

When Sol dropped him off about two A.M., the guy handed him a c-note and said, "I need maybe your services tomorrow. Will you be available?" Sol handed over his beeper number and the limo's cell-phone number.

"At your service, Signore Fortunato," Sol said.

Sol watched the mark go into the hotel carrying his two briefcases like they held nothing more than dirty laundry. Then he backed the limo onto the street, headed west, and picked up the car phone. "Bobby," he said, "you won't fucking believe it."

Paolo Fortunato sat under the shade of an umbrella at a table on the boardwalk, a few feet from the beach and the aqua water beyond the hotel. He wore a sleeveless, ribbed undershirt, baggy khaki shorts, and sandals. His body was white and hairy, his black hair rumpled from sleep. He sipped American coffee that tasted like urine. He'd asked the waitress for an espresso, but she only smiled and shrugged, "I'm sorry."

The beach was already crowded with sunbathers, young American men and women with beautiful brown bodies. Paolo smelled the sweet coconut oil that made their bodies glisten in the sun. Paolo always wondered about Americans' obsession with blonde hair and perfect bodies and youth. It was a strange preoccupation for a country so sexually repressed. These young women wore thong bathing suits with tiny tops that barely covered their nipples, as if those nipples were a prize to be revealed only after a bargain had been struck. The tiny tops were tied in such a way as to push up their breasts, make them look plumper, more seductive than they would be naked, demystified.

The whole country is a tease, he thought. Boring, really. Americans' pleasure came from the possession of things, never the things themselves. Which was why it was so easy for him to do business with them. He always knew what they wanted. More. Like the car dealer. He could not settle for the profit he and Paolo had agreed on for the product. He had to try to cheat him out of his fair share. Paolo did not care so much about the money. How many chickens could he eat? But he cared about the insult, that this Jewish-American-Israeli-Russian dared to think he could cheat him and that Paolo would just take it and leave. He was a fool, this mongrel American.

Paolo settled back in his chair, lit an American cigarette, and enjoyed the beautiful bodies spread out like ripe fruit before him. He appreciated this beauty, but the limousine driver was right. An older woman would be preferable. Still, he would prefer more than merely commercial sex. Like that woman sitting on her blanket close to the water's edge. Even with her back to him, he could tell she was older, maybe forty, but still exquisitely shaped, if slightly too muscular for his taste. This one I must first hang in the smokehouse to tenderize her, he thought.

He smiled at his little joke just as the woman stood up and walked into the ocean. She wore a hat like those American baseball players, the bill pulled low over her eyes, and a thong bikini, like the younger girls, which exposed her perfectly shaped behind.

He watched her cool off in the ocean, then turn and walk back toward her blanket. She walked past it, directly toward Paolo, the sun at her back, her face and body in shadow except at the edges, her shoulders, the curve of her hips, shooting off little sparks of golden light. She moved curiously, the balls of her feet twisting in the sand as if stomping out cigarettes. The movement made her slim hips swivel in a way Paolo found enticing. She stopped a few feet away from Paolo at the outdoor shower, took off her cap, and tossed it down on the wooden deck, near Paolo's feet. She had short, harsh blonde hair, almost white. She pulled the shower chain and rinsed the salt water off her body without modesty. When she released the chain, she looked for her hat. Paolo picked it up and offered it to her with a smile. She accepted it with a nod and turned to walk back to her blanket.

"Scusi, Signora." She looked at him, with her big blue eyes and a pleasantly lined face without expression. "Would you care to join me? Maybe a cool drink on such a hot day?"

She smiled and stepped up onto the boardwalk. "That would be nice," she said. "Thank you." She sat across from him, her legs crossed so that only a tiny patch of her bathing suit was visible at the crotch.

"Do you mind if I have one of your cigarettes?" she asked.

"Of course not." She took one. Paolo lit it for her as she held his hand to steady the flame. He raised his arm to summon a waitress. "And to drink?" he said.

She thought for a moment. "Vodka collins."

Paolo turned to the waitress behind him. "*Due* vodka collins," he said. Then, "So sorry. I mean two." Before he turned back, he noticed, seated behind him at another table, a tall American cowboy in a flowered shirt and blue jeans and boots. Paolo turned back to the woman.

"You're Roman," she said.

"Yes, I am Italian."

"No. I said Roman. Your accent." He had underestimated this woman. She lessened his embarrassment with a smile. "I've worked in Rome," she said. "Accents are my business."

"You are an actress?"

"Not really. Just television commercials. It pays the rent." She stuck out her hand. "I'm Sheila."

Paolo shook her hand gently, with a slight nod of his head. "I am Paolo Fortunato," he said.

"You're here on business," she said. It was not a question.

"You can tell," he said, looking down at his white body.

"Yes. Businessmen have a certain look at the beach. Discomfort, I think. They feel powerless out of uniform. Do you know what I mean?" He nodded. "Plus, they don't understand what all the fuss is about. The oil and the sand and the heat. It makes no sense to them because there's no profit in it."

"Ah, profit. Yes." He made a gesture toward all the beautiful young bodies. "But for some there is a profit, eh?" He smiled.

"Maybe for some," Sheila said, not smiling. "But not for me. It's just a way to relax."

"Of course." You'd better watch yourself with this woman, Paolo thought. But he liked that. Beautiful, but interesting, too, in a way few American women are.

"What kind of business are you in?" she asked.

"I am an automobile importer."

"Let me guess. Ferraris?" He nodded. "An easy guess. I don't imagine there's much profit in importing Fiats?" They both laughed. "I had a Fiat once," she said. "It rusted right out from under me in this salt air."

"Maybe you should try a Ferrari."

"That would be nice," she said dreamily. "Do you have a spare one you don't need?"

Paolo smiled, shrugged, and tossed up his hands, palms out, in that Italian gesture of mock resignation. "I'm sorry," he said. He tugged on his empty pants pockets until they stuck out like ears. "Nothing at the moment. But maybe I can offer you something else."

The woman studied him briefly, then said, "You spend a lot of time in Florence, too."

He looked surprised. "How do you know?"

"The shrug. Your arms tight to your sides the Florentine way."

Paolo threw back his head and laughed. She stubbed out her cigarette in the ashtray and stood up. "Thank you for the drink," she said.

"Must you leave?"

"Yes. I've had enough sun. There's no profit in it anymore." She smiled at him.

"You must come to dinner with me tonight. Please. I hate to dine alone." He furrowed his eyebrows in a sad, comical way. "Alone in a foreign country."

Now she frowned, mocking him. "Poor man. I should take pity on you?"

"Not pity. A blessing maybe. Eight o'clock? We can have drinks at the bar." He gestured down the walkway, toward the hotel's enclosed bar and restaurant that looked out over the water. "Then we can dine anywhere you wish."

"Well actually," she said, "the Mark's restaurant is quite good. The catch of the day and the ocean sparkling at night. Very romantic." She turned and walked back to her blanket. Paolo followed her with his eyes. Very beautiful, he thought. Very interesting. He paid his bill, reminded himself to leave a tip, the American way, and then walked back toward the hotel, past the American cowboy with the blond ponytail.

Bobby sat in darkness, away from the lights strung along the boardwalk that ran from the Mark's restaurant to the Chickee Bar. It was warm, but a soft breeze drifted in from the ocean. A few people walked along the beach, couples mostly, tourists holding hands. No one else sat on the boardwalk, though there were a few people at the outdoor bar.

When the waitress walked past Bobby, he called out from the darkness. "Honey, could you get me a Coors?"

"Oh! I didn't see you there. Certainly."

She brought the beer and Bobby sipped it, keeping an eye on Sheila in the restaurant to his right. She and the mark were sitting by the window, close to the beach. He could see their faces by the light of the candle on their table. Very romantic, he thought, remembering that Sheila had once done a TV commercial in the same setting. The guy had been older than the mark, handsome, with silver hair and one of those phony actor's voices from deep in his chest. Bobby tried to remember what she was selling in that commercial. A cruise, that was it. Sheila in an off-the-shoulder evening gown, an upswept brown wig and dangling earrings, the guy in a tux, the candle, the waiter in the little white jacket cut at sharp angles at each hip. When Bobby saw the commercial one night, he was shocked at the way Sheila looked into the actor's eyes, how believable she was. So fucking believable, Bobby told her, he wanted to book a cruise that minute. "Yeah, me and my lover," Sheila said, "having a romantic dinner while his fag boyfriend stood off the set watching us like a hawk, afraid maybe I was going to cop his pal's joint if he blinked."

"Well, if anybody could make a fag switch, baby, it's you."

"That would be a challenge," Sheila said. "I don't know if I'm that good an actress."

But she was good tonight, Bobby thought, watching her reel in the mark. Laughing, looking into his eyes, laying her hand on his arm to make a point, touching her wineglass to his in a toast. A toast to what? Eight hundred fucking Gs, that's what. Only the mark didn't know it.

Sheila and the mark stood up from the table, the mark pulling out her chair. He gestured with his hand toward the ceiling, probably asking her if she wanted to go to his room. Sheila shook her head no and pointed outside to the boardwalk. Nice touch, baby, not too anxious. They stepped outside. Bobby pushed his chair farther back into the darkness, onto the walkway between the hotel and the Chickee Bar. He watched as Sheila slid her arm into the mark's. They stopped a few feet from Bobby to look at the moon — two lovers, very fucking romantic. The mark faced her and put his arms round her, pulled her tight against his body, and kissed her. Sheila kissed him passionately, finally pulling back and nodding her head. They turned and walked quickly back to the hotel. Bobby peeked out from the walkway. The mark opened the door for Sheila. She walked through, he glanced one last time at the boardwalk, the beautiful summer night, and then followed her.

Bobby gave them time to get to the room, then went over to the bar for another beer. He changed his mind, asked the waitress for coffee instead, black. Twenty minutes passed. Thirty. An hour. What was taking so long? All she had to do was slip him the mickey and split with the briefcases. Maybe they weren't there and she was looking for them.

"Excuse me," the waitress said. "Are you Mr. Roberts?" Bobby nodded. She handed him the bar phone. "For you."

"Bobby," Sheila said, "get up here. Room 218." And she hung up.

Something wasn't right. Bobby hurried out to the parking lot, got his CZ from under the driver's seat, racked the slide, and stuck it into the back of his jeans. He pulled his Hawaiian shirt out of his pants to cover it and went into the hotel. He passed the elevator and instead took the stairs two steps at a time, went through a door and down a hallway to room 218. He took out the CZ, held it by his ear, turned the doorknob. The door wasn't locked. He pushed it open and stepped through, the gun pointed in front of him.

"*Buono sera,* Signore Squared." The mark was sitting on the sofa, smiling, a drink in his hand. Before Bobby could say anything, the bedroom door opened and Sheila walked into the room, smoking a cigarette.

"Put the piece down, Robert," she said, like he was her student. Then, smiling, she said, "Say hello to Signore Fortunato." The mark stood up like a gentleman and reached out to shake Bobby's hand. Sheila said, "Mr. Fortunato is our new business partner."

At five o'clock on Saturday afternoon, a white stretch Lincoln Continental pulled up in front of the Paradise Auto Works showroom and parked. Two salesmen walked to the showroom window and stared as a chauffeur in a black suit and cap hustled out of the limo and opened the back door. A pair of long, tan legs emerged first. Then a woman's hand, long red fingernails, diamond rings, gold bracelets. The chauffeur helped her out of the limo. She was wearing gold-rimmed Porsche Carrera sunglasses, a black-and-white Chanel suit — the skirt short, but not too short — and a wide-brimmed black straw hat, the brim pulled down over one eye. She carried a square black handbag.

The woman walked to the front door and waited. The chauffeur opened it for her and she went inside to the blonde receptionist seated behind the faux-Oriental, black lacquered desk. The receptionist was reading a paperback novel and chewing gum. She looked up dimly and said, "Can I help you?"

"I'm here to purchase a car," the woman said.

"I'll get you a salesman."

"I don't do business with salesmen. I want to see the owner."

The receptionist shrugged, picked up her telephone and said, "Mr. Kressell, a lady to see you about a car." Then, to the woman, she said, "He'll be with you in a moment."

The woman turned toward the showroom window and looked out at Sunrise Boulevard and the 7-Eleven across the street. She opened her purse, flipped open a gold cigarette case, and withdrew a long brown cigarette. She put it to her lips and waited. The chauffeur flicked open a lighter. The receptionist, lost in her book, wrinkled her nose and looked up. "There's no smoking in here," she said. The woman exhaled and continued to stare out the window. She glanced at the chauffeur, then tossed a head fake toward the receptionist's moving jaws. "I told you," she said.

A salesman came up to her. "Mr. Kressell will see you now," he said. He led her through the showroom, packed tightly with exotic foreign cars, Porsche Speedsters and older Dinos and Gullwing Mercedes. The chauffeur followed them, not bothering to look at the cars but instead looking at the ceiling, the surveillance cameras in each corner of the room, the wires running down to the windows and doors. Burglar alarms.

"Whom should I say is calling?" the salesman said. He had an English accent — no, not English, Australian — and was a handsome man with a neat Princeton cut, an Ivy League suit and a smarmy smile.

"Who," said the woman. "And it's Mrs. Chickie Vantage. From Las Vegas."

She gestured toward the tightly packed cars and added, "It must be difficult to rearrange these when someone wants a test drive."

"We're not in the business of test drives," he said. He opened a door for her, let her pass through and said, "Mr. Kressell, Mrs.

Chickie Vantage to see you. From Las Vegas." The salesman closed the door behind her. The chauffeur waited outside.

She stood in the small office and waited for the little man at the desk to look up. When he finally did he said, "Have a chair, Mrs. . . ."

"Vantage," she said without moving. She stared at him through her sunglasses, at his pockmarked skin, beady eyes, and fat lips, like a troll's. Finally, he sighed, stood up, and gestured toward a chair. She sat down, crossed her legs, and lowered her head a bit to arrange the sand-colored hair pinned under her straw hat. "I'm here to buy one of your cars, Mr. . . . ah . . ."

"Kressell," he said.

"Yes. The beige Silver Spirit convertible you advertised in the *Robb Report*. But I don't see it in the showroom."

"It's in the mechanics' bay out back."

She waited. "Well, could I see it?"

His homely Edward G. Robinson face looked pained. Without interest he said, "If you insist."

"I do." He led her through the back door of his office, down a narrow corridor, and outside to the back parking lot crowded with exotic cars. A concrete wall surrounded the lot on three sides. It had two electronically controlled iron gates, a small one for people and a larger one for cars.

"This way," he said. He led her to the mechanics' bay and pressed a button on the wall. Its doors opened, and there were six cars inside. A Porsche Turbo, the beige Rolls, and four red Ferraris elevated on jacks because they had no tires. Four new sets of racing tires were propped against one wall. They were mounted on magnesium wheels with prancing black horses on the hubs.

"You like Ferraris," he said.

"Oh, no, not really. They're not too practical. But they are such beautiful machines. I can appreciate that."

"Yes. I guess, at $250,000 each. Here's the Silver Spirit. As you can see, it, too, is . . . how did you put it? A beautiful machine." He spoke without passion or interest in the car.

The woman walked around it, looked through the window at its leather seats and burled dashboard. "Yes, it's beautiful. Now, shall we fill out the papers?"

"You haven't asked the price."

"It doesn't matter. I'm buying it." The little man furrowed his brow. The woman smiled at him. "I'm a widow, Mr. Kressell. Three months now. My husband had certain business interests in Las Vegas, very complex, some of it tied up in court, some, to put it honestly, under the scrutiny of the IRS. I'm sure it will all work out. But while it does, I have a little problem. My husband used to keep some money at home, he called it walking-around money, in case of an emergency. Actually, it's what might be called undeclared money, if you know what I mean. If the IRS were to discover it, well, there might be a problem. I'd like to convert that money into something tangible as quickly as possible. So I thought, why not treat myself to a car?"

Kressell looked at her suspiciously. She smiled at him as she thought, Paolo was right. This man has interest in only one thing. She opened her handbag and withdrew a stack of $100 bills. The man's suspicious look vanished. "That's why I'm paying cash for the car. Would a $10,000 deposit be satisfactory?"

Kressell smiled for the first time. "Yes," he said. "More than satisfactory."

"Shall we fill out the papers, then?"

When the woman finished the paperwork, she stood up and laid $10,000 on the desk. "I'll be by tomorrow evening to pick up the car and bring you the rest of the money. Two hundred thousand, am I right?"

The man looked at the money, then at the woman, as if he had a problem. "We're closed Sundays," he said. "It will have to be on Monday."

"That's impossible, Mr. Kressell. I'm leaving for Las Vegas Sunday evening."

"I don't know."

"If it's a problem —" she said, reaching for the money on his desk. He snatched it up before she could get it. She smiled, "All right, then," she said. "Tomorrow at nine P.M." She adjusted her sunglasses with a touch of her nails, then she left.

In the limo, Sol turned to Sheila in the back seat. "Did you see all the fucking security?" he said. "Cameras, alarms, like a fucking prison. I don't like it."

Sheila took off her straw hat, unpinned her hair, lowered her head and gave it a shake. Long sand-colored hair fell around her shoulders. "What do you think, Sol? A nice look?" She arched her neck to catch a glimpse of herself in the mirror.

He shook his head warily. "We should have just rolled the guinea like we planned."

"Not an option, Sol. He'd stashed the briefcases elsewhere before I got to his room. He knew the whole scam. There was nothing we could do. We either walked away or accepted his business proposition. It's not exactly a fucking hardship case, Sol. A hundred thousand each if we pull it off."

Sol shook his head in despair. "Geez, I wish I had my jewelry."

Sheila opened her handbag and withdrew a Rolex, two diamond-encrusted pinkie rings, a diamond bracelet, and a gold chain with a gold camel-shaped pendant. She handed the jewelry to Sol. "The camel is a nice touch, Solly," she said. "Like no one would ever know you're a Jew. Mistake you for maybe Yasir fucking Arafat."

Sol, smiling, examined his jewelry to make sure it was all there. "Where's my Star of David?" he asked, the smile vanishing. Sheila, grinning, handed it to him.

At nine o'clock on Sunday evening the woman stood at the door of Paradise Auto Works and rang the buzzer. Her chauffeur stood by the limousine parked outside the showroom window. The showroom was dark except for a sliver of light under the owner's office door at the far end of the room. The crowded cars looked menacing — dark, humped shapes waiting to spring.

Kressell appeared at the door and buzzed the woman in. He was momentarily confused when she stepped inside. She looked different. No sunglasses. Sand-colored hair halfway down her back. A white silk blouse, tight jeans, and black high-top sneakers. She smiled at him and held up a briefcase.

"Ah, yes," he said. "This way."

Outside, the chauffeur lit a cigarette. He flicked his lighter three times, the flame sparkling off his gold jewelry and rings. From across the street, parked at the 7-Eleven, a U-Haul truck flicked its lights three times, then started up and moved onto Sunrise. It turned down the side street and went past the limo to the end of the concrete wall, next to the electronic gates and the Royal Palm Motel. The driver clicked off the U-Haul's lights but left the engine running.

Inside, the woman sat across from the homely little man in his office. He rustled through some papers on his desk, looking for her contract. The woman put the briefcase on her lap.

"Ah, here it is," Kressell said. He glanced through it, then handed it to her. "Everything's in order."

"I'm sure," she said. She looked at the papers briefly, then returned them to the man. She opened the briefcase and said, "I think I have what you want, Mr. Kressell." He smiled, but his smile disappeared as she took out a CZ-85 semiautomatic pistol. The man's mouth dropped open. The woman aimed the pistol almost casually at him.

"Now, let's go see about some tires, shall we?" she said.

The little man didn't move. She could see him thinking, trying to put it together, this woman with a gun, what she wanted, finally getting it right in his mind. "That dago bastard!" he spluttered. "He sent you!"

"Well, yes, as a matter of fact I am a business partner of Mr. Fortunato's. He sent me to tie up some — how did he put it? — oh, yes, some 'tight ends.' A charming man, really. Now get your ass up."

Kressell sat back in his chair, grinning. "Fuck you," he said. "You're not gonna shoot. The noise will bring every cop in the city. Besides, I got your face on the video camera. How you gonna get away from that?"

Sheila looked around the small office. There were no cameras. With one hand she reached behind her head and pulled off her wig, her spiky blonde hair straight up.

"You may be right about the noise, however," she said. She put the gun back in the briefcase, then reached inside it with her other hand. She withdrew the pistol again, this time with a silencer screwed onto its threaded barrel. She fired one shot over Kressell's shoulder into the wall behind him.

"Jesus fucking Christ!" The little man jumped out of his chair.

"Now for the tires," she said. She followed him out back to the parking lot and the mechanics' bay. He hesitated to buzz open the bay doors until she stuck the CZ into the small of his back and cocked the hammer.

"All right! All right! Jesus! Be careful with that thing." He opened the door and reached for the lights.

"No lights," she said. "Now open the gates outside." The man hesitated again, and felt the barrel of the gun leave his back. He turned to look over his shoulder and saw the woman gripping the gun with both hands, aiming it at him. He buzzed open the gates and saw a U-Haul backing up to the bay. A big guy with a blond ponytail and cowboy boots jumped out from the driver's side, the chauffeur from the passenger side.

"Everything all right, baby?" the cowboy said.

"No problem, baby."

The chauffeur pushed Kressell to the ground, into a puddle of oil. "Jesus, what the fuck you doing?" Kressell said just before the chauffeur taped his mouth shut with duct tape. Then he taped the man's hands behind his back, then taped his feet together.

The cowboy pulled a flashlight from his back pocket and shined it around the bay until it lighted on the four sets of Ferrari tires. He pulled a knife from his belt, a big hunting knife, and sliced open one sidewall. He tugged at the edge of a cellophane package filled with white powder, then turned and smiled. "Bingo!" he said.

"Just like on the fucking reservation, eh, Bobby?" said the chauffeur.

The two men wheeled the tires into the back of the U-Haul while the woman kept the gun on the little man writhing on the floor. "Keep it up," she said, "and you're going to cover yourself with oil." He glared at her.

They buzzed the bay doors shut on Kressell and got into the U-Haul. As they drove through the gates, the truck's lights illuminated an old woman standing in front of the Royal Palm Motel with a nickel-plated .357 Magnum at her side.

"I told you," Sol said. "She's a fucking loony." The woman followed the U-Haul with her eyes and watched it stop at the limo. A man in a dark suit got out, jumped into the limo, and then followed the truck. When the truck and the limo turned the corner onto Sunrise, the woman went back into the motel.

Bobby drove the U-Haul to the enclosed, short-term parking lot at Fort Lauderdale Airport. Sol drove the limo to the Delta baggage claim area and stopped. Bobby parked the truck in a darkened space at the corner of the lot and waited. A figure emerged from the shadows and walked toward them. Sheila raised the CZ to the window.

"*Buona sera, amici.* Everything went well, eh?"

"Everything went well," Sheila said as she and Bobby climbed out of the truck. They opened the back door and showed Paolo the tires. He smiled. "*Grazie,*" he said. "And for you." He handed Sheila a briefcase. She opened it and smiled.

"*Grazie,* Paolo," she said. "This is for you." She gave him the parking ticket and the keys to the U-Haul. "Ciao, baby," she said.

"*Buona notte, cara mia.*" He kissed the back of her hand.

The next morning, Paolo arrived at the airport two hours early for his flight to Rome. He waited until the mechanics at Paradise Auto Works had enough time to find their boss in the bay, then called him.

"Signore Kressell. You have lost something, I hear. I have found it. Now you have something for me, maybe?"

A day later, Bobby, Sheila, and Sol sat at a table under a hot afternoon sun on the boardwalk next to the Mark. Bobby and Sol drank beer, while Sheila sipped a vodka collins and read the morning's *Sun-Sentinel.* Suddenly she began to laugh. Bobby and Sol looked at her.

"You won't believe it," she said. "Listen to this."

"'Almost 160 kilograms of pure heroin, with an estimated street value of $10 million, was seized in an early-morning police raid on Paradise Auto Works. Six people were arrested at the Sunrise Boulevard car dealership. The heroin was concealed in sixteen Ferrari racing tires that were being unloaded from a rented truck when the tactical drug squad arrived.

"'Among those apprehended was dealership owner Sholomo Kressell, a.k.a. Sonny Kresnick, an Israeli national with U.S. citizenship. The police shut down the dealership pending an investigation and confiscated more than $20 million in exotic cars.

"'The police were tipped off to the drug ring by Estelle Townsend, proprietor of the neighboring Royal Palm Motel. She telephoned 911 when she noticed suspicious activity at the dealership at an early morning hour for the third time in five days. Townsend, seventy-six, said, "I knew there were nefarious goings-on there. I could have taken them out twice myself with my Magnum." Townsend owns a Smith & Wesson .357 Magnum revolver. She has a concealed-weapon permit and is a member of the National Rifle Association.

"'The police have put out an all points bulletin for the last member of the ring, a foreigner of undetermined nationality.

"'Also found at the dealership were Kressell's office records, a 9mm bullet lodged in the wall behind his desk, and a woman's light-colored wig.'"

Sheila put down the paper and looked out at the ocean. "I'm glad he got away," she said.

Bobby and Sol glanced at her. Sol said nothing. Bobby said, "I gotta start kissing your hand now, *cara mia*?"

"Oh, Bobby. He was a sweet guy."

"That why you spend a fucking hour in his room, come out of his bedroom smoking a cigarette, with a dreamy look on your face?"

"Baby, I told you once, you've got nothing to be jealous about." She looked into his eyes. Bobby had seen that look before but couldn't remember where. "Don't you know that, baby?" she said.

And Bobby thought, She's so fucking believable.

JONATHAN KELLERMAN

The Things We Do for Love

FROM *Murder for Love*

MASHED SPAGHETTI. Some things you could never prepare for.

It wasn't as if she and Doug were mega-yuppies but they both liked their pasta al dente and they both liked to sleep late.

Then along came Zoe, God bless her.

The *sculptress.*

Karen smiled as Zoe plunged her tiny hands into the sticky, cheesy mound. Three peas sat on top like tiny bits of topiary. The peas promptly rolled off the high chair and landed on the restaurant floor. Zoe looked down and cracked up. Then she pointed and began to fuss.

"Eh-eh! Eh-eh!"

"Okay, sweetie." Karen bent, retrieved the green balls, and put them in front of her own plate.

"Eh-*eh!*"

"No, they're dirty, honey."

"Eh-eh!"

From behind the bar, the fat dark waiter looked over at them. When they'd come in, he hadn't exactly greeted them with open arms. But the place had been empty, so who was he to be choosy? Even now, fifteen minutes later, the only other lunchers were three men in the booth at the far end. First they'd slurped soup loud enough for Karen to hear. Now they were hunched over platters of spaghetti, each one guarding his food as if afraid someone would steal it. *Theirs* was probably al dente. And from the briny aroma drifting over, with clam sauce.

"Eh!"

"No, Zoe, Mommy can't have you eating dirty peas, okay?"

"*Eh!*"

"C'mon, Zoe-puss, yucko-grosso — no, no, honey, don't cry — here, try some carrots, aren't they pretty, nice pretty *orange* carrots — orange is *such* a pretty color, much prettier than those yucky peas — here, look, the carrot is dancing. I'm a dancing carrot, my name is Charlie. . . ."

Karen saw the waiter shake his head and go back through the swinging doors into the kitchen. Let him think she was an idiot, the carrot ploy was working: Zoe's gigantic blue eyes had enlarged and a chubby hand reached out.

Touching the carrot. Fingers the size of thimbles closed over it.

Victory! Let's hear it for distraction.

"Eat it, honey, it's soft."

Zoe turned the carrot and studied it. Then she grinned.

Raised it over her head.

Windup and the pitch: fastball straight to the floor.

"Eh-*eh!*"

"Oh, Zoe."

"*Eh!*"

"Okay, okay."

Time for Mommy to do her four thousandth bend of the morning. Thank God her back was strong but she hoped Zoe got over the hurl-and-whine stage soon. Some of the other mothers at Group complained of serious pain. So far, Karen felt surprisingly fine, despite the lack of sleep. Probably all the years of taking care of herself, aerobics, running with Doug. Now he ran by himself. . . .

"Eh!"

"Try some more spaghetti, honey."

"*Eh!*"

The waiter came out like a man with a mission, bearing plates heaped with meat. He brought them to the three men at the back, bowed, and served. Karen saw one of the three — the thin lizardy one in the center — nod and slip him a bill. The waiter poured wine and bowed again. As he straightened he glanced across the room at Karen and Zoe. Karen smiled but got a glare in return.

Bad attitude, especially for a dinky little place this dead at the height of the lunch hour. Not to mention the musty smell and what passed for decor: worn lace curtains drawn back carelessly from flyspecked windows, dark, dingy wood varnished so many times it looked like plastic. The booths that lined the mustard-colored walls were cracked black leather, the tables covered with your basic cliché checkered oilcloth. Ditto Chianti bottles in straw hanging from the ceiling and those little hexagonal floor tiles that would never be white again. Call *Architectural Digest*.

When she and Zoe had stepped in, the waiter hadn't even come forward, just kept wiping the bartop like some religious rite. When he'd finally looked up, he'd stared at the highchair Karen had dragged along as if he'd never seen one before. Stared at Zoe, too, but not with any kindness. Which told you where he was at, because *everyone* adored Zoe, every single person who laid eyes on her said she was the most adorable little thing they'd ever encountered.

The milky skin — Karen's contribution. The dimples and black curls from Doug.

And not just family. Strangers. People were always stopping Karen on the street just to tell her what a peach Zoe was.

But that was back home. This city was a lot less friendly. She'd be happy to get back.

Let's hear it for business trips. God bless Doug, he did try to be liberated. Agreeing to have all three of them travel together. He'd made a commitment and stuck to it; how many men could you say that about?

The things you do for love.

They'd been together four years. Met on the job, both of them free-lancing, and right away she'd thought he was gorgeous. Maybe too gorgeous, because that type was often unbearably vain. Then to find out he was nice. And bright. *And* a good listener. Pinch me, I'm dreaming.

Within a week they were living together, married a month later. When they'd finally decided to build a family, Doug showed his true colors: true blue. Agreeing to an equal partnership, splitting parenthood right down the middle so they could both take on projects.

It hadn't worked out that way but that was her doing, not his. Karen was a firm believer in the value of careful research and during her pregnancy she read everything she could find about child development. But despite all the books and magazine articles, there was no way she could have known how demanding motherhood would turn out to be. And how it would change her.

Even with that, Doug had done more than his share: convincing her to express milk so he could get up for middle-of-the-night

feedings, changing diapers. *Lots* of diapers; Zoe had a healthy diges-
tive system, God bless her, but Doug wasn't one to worry about
getting his hands dirty.

He'd even offered to cut back on projects and stay home so
Karen could get out more but she found herself wanting to spend
less time on the job, more with Zoe.

What a homebody I've become. Go know.

She touched Zoe's hair, thought of the feel of Zoe's soft little
body, stretched out wiggling and kicking and pink on the changing
table. Then Doug's body, long and muscled . . .

The restaurant had grown quiet.

She realized Zoe was quiet. Elbow-deep in the spaghetti now,
kneading. Little Ms. Rodin. Maybe it was a sign of talent. Karen considered herself artistic, though sculpture wasn't her medium.

Watching Zoe's little hands work the mess of what had once been
linguine with just a little butter and cheese, she laughed to herself.
Pasta. It meant paste and now it really was.

Zoe scooped up a gob, looked at it, threw it onto the floor,
laughing.

"*Eh*-eh."

Bend and stretch, bend and stretch . . . she did miss running with
Doug. The two of them shared so much, had such a special rapport.
Working in the same field helped, of course, but Karen liked to
think the bond went deeper. That their union had produced something greater than the sum of its parts.

And baby makes three . . . Motherhood was much tougher than
anything she'd ever done, but also more rewarding in ways she'd
never expected. Nubby fingers caressing her cheek as she rocked
Zoe to sleep. The first cries of "Mama!" from the remote-control
speaker each morning. Such incredible *need.* Thinking about it
almost made her cry. How could she go back to working full-time
with this little peach needing her so intensely?

Thank God money was no problem. Doug was doing great and
how many people could say that during these hard times. Karen
had learned long ago not to believe in the concept of deservedness,
but if anyone deserved success it was Doug. He was terrific at what
he did, a rock. Once you got a reputation for reliability, clients
came to you.

"*Eh-eh!*"

"Now what, hon?"

Karen's voice rose and one of the three men in the corner glanced over. The thin one, the one who seemed to be the leader. Definitely saurian. Mr. Salamander. He wore a light gray suit and a black shirt open at the neck, the long-point collars spread over wide jacket lapels. His dirty blond hair was slicked back and he wasn't bad looking, if you went for reptiles. Now he was smiling.

But not at Zoe. Zoe's back was to him.

At Karen and not a what-a-cute-baby smile.

Karen turned away, catching the waiter's eye and looking down at her plate. The thin man waved and the waiter went over and disappeared into the kitchen again. The thin man was still looking at her.

Amused. Confident.

Mr. Stud. And her with a baby! Classy place. Time to finish up and get out of here.

But Zoe was busy with something new, little face turning beet-red, hands clenched, eyes bulging.

"Great," said Karen, ignoring the thin man but certain he was still giving her the once-over. Then she softened her tone, not wanting to give Zoe any complexes. "That's fine, honey. Poop to your heart's content, make a nice big one for Mommy."

Moments later the deed was done and Zoe was scooping up pasta again and hurling it.

"That's it, young lady, time to clean you up and go meet Daddy."

"Eh-eh."

"No more eh-eh, change-change." Standing, Karen undid the straps of the high chair and lifted Zoe out, sniffing.

"*Definitely* time to change you."

But Zoe had other ideas and she began to kick and fuss. Holding the baby under one arm like an oversized football, Karen lifted the gigantic denim bag that now took the place of the calf-leather purse Doug had given her and walked over to the bar where the waiter stood polishing glasses and sucking his teeth.

He continued to ignore them even when Karen and Zoe were two feet away.

"Excuse me, sir."

One heavy black eyebrow cocked.

"Where's your ladies' room?"

Wet brown eyes ran over Karen's body like dirty oil, then Zoe's. *Definitely* a creep.

He licked his lips. A crooked thumb indicated the back of the restaurant.

Right past the booth with Lizard and his pals.

Taking a deep breath and staring straight ahead, Karen marched, swinging the big bag. God, it was heavy. All the stuff you had to carry.

The three men stopped talking as she walked by. Someone chuckled.

Lizard cleared his throat and said, "Cute kid," in a nasal voice full of locker-room glee.

More laughter.

Karen pushed through the door.

She emerged a few minutes later, having wrestled Zoe to a three-round decision. In one of Zoe's hands was the cow rattle Karen employed to take Zoe's mind off diaper-changing.

Let's hear it for distraction.

Forced to pass the three men, Karen stared straight ahead but managed to see what they were eating. Double-cut veal chops, bone and gristle and meat spread out over huge plates. Some poor calf had been confined and force-fed and butchered so these three creeps could stuff their faces.

Lizard said, "*Very* cute." The other two laughed and Karen knew he hadn't meant Zoe.

Feeling herself flush, she kept going.

The men started talking.

Zoe shook the rattle.

Karen said, "Eh-eh, huh, Zoe?" and the baby grinned and drew back her hand.

Windup and the pitch.

The rattle sailed toward the back of the restaurant.

Rolling on the tile floor toward the back booth.

Karen ran back, startling the three men. The rattle had landed next to a shiny black loafer.

As she picked it up, the tail end of a sentence faded into silence. A word. A name.

A name from the evening news.

A man, not a nice one, who'd talked about his friends and had been murdered in jail, yesterday, despite police protection.

The man who'd uttered the name was staring at her.

Fear — ice-cube terror — spread across Karen's face, paralyzing it.

Lizard put his knife down. His eyes narrowed to hyphens.

He was still smiling, but differently, very differently.

One of the other men cursed. Lizard shut him up with a blink.

The rattle was in Karen's hand now. Shaking, making ridiculous rattle sounds. Her hand *couldn't* stop shaking.

She began backing away.

"Hey," said Lizard. "Cutie."

Karen kept going.

Lizard looked at Zoe and his smile died.

Karen clutched her baby tight and ran. Past the waiter, forgetting about the high chair, then remembering, but who cared, it was a cheap one, she needed to get out of this place.

She heard chairs scrape the tile floor. "Hey, Cutie, hold on."

She kept going.

The waiter started to move around from behind the bar. Lizard was coming at her too. Moving fast. Taller than he looked sitting down, the gray suit billowing around his lanky frame.

"Hold on!" he shouted.

Karen gripped the door, swung it open, and dashed out, hearing his curses.

Quiet neighborhood, a few people on the sidewalk who looked just like the creeps in the restaurant.

Karen turned right at the corner and ran. Rattling, the heavy denim bag knocking against her thigh.

Zoe was crying.

"It's okay, baby, it's okay, Mommy will keep you safe."

She heard a shout and looked back to see Lizard coming after her, people moving away from him, giving him room. Fear in their faces. He pointed at Karen, went after her.

She picked up her pace. Let's hear it for jogging. But this wasn't like running in shorts and a T-shirt; between Zoe and the heavy bag she felt like a plow horse.

Okay, keep a rhythm, the creep was skinny but he probably wasn't in good shape. Nice and easy with the breathing, pretend this is a

10K and you've carbo-loaded the night before, slept a peaceful eight hours, gotten up when you wanted to. . . .

She made it to another corner. Red light. A taxi sped by and she had to wait. Lizard was gaining on her — running loosely on long legs, his face sharp and pale — not a lizard, a snake. A venomous snake.

Ugly words came out of the snake's mouth. He was pointing at her.

She stepped off the curb. A truck was approaching halfway down the block. She waited until it got closer, bolted, made it stop short. Blocking the snake.

Another block, this one shorter, lined with shabby storefronts. But no corner at the end of this one. Green dead end. A hedge behind high, graffitied stone walls.

A park. The entrance a hundred yards left.

Karen went for it, running even faster, hearing Zoe's cries and the raspy sound of her own breathing.

Plow horse . . .

Steep, cracked steps took her down into the park. A bronze statue besmirched by pigeon dirt, poorly maintained grass, big trees.

She placed a hand behind Zoe's head, making sure not to jolt the supple neck — she'd read that babies could get whiplash without anyone knowing and then years later they'd show signs of brain damage. . . .

Clap clap behind her as Snake's footsteps slapped the steps. Mr. Viper . . . stop thinking stupid thoughts, he was just a man, a creep. Just keep going, she'd find a place to be safe.

The park was empty, the stone path shaded almost black by huge spreading elms.

"*Hey!*" shouted the snake. "Stop, awready . . . what . . . the . . . *fuck!*"

Panting between words. The creep probably never did anything aerobic.

"What . . . fuck . . . problem . . . wanna talk!"

Karen pumped her legs. The path took on an upward slope.

Good, make the creep work harder, she could handle it, though Zoe's cries in her ear were starting to get to her — poor thing, what kind of mother was she, getting her baby into something like this —

"*Jesus!*" From behind. Huff, huff. "Stupid . . . *bitch!*"

More trees, bigger, the pathway even darker. Along the side, occasional benches, graffitied, too, no one on them.

No one to help.

Karen ran even faster. Her chest began to hurt and Zoe hadn't stopped wailing.

"Easy, honey," she managed to gasp. "Easy, Zoe-puff."

The slope grew steeper.

"Fucking bitch!"

Then something appeared on the path. A metal-mesh garbage can. Low enough for her to jump in her jogging days, but not with Zoe. She had to sidestep it and the snake saw her lose footing, stumble, veer off onto the grass, and twist her ankle.

She cried out in pain. Tried to run, stopped.

Zoe's chubby cheeks were soaked with tears.

The snake smiled and walked around the can and toward her.

"Fucking city," he said, kicking the can and whipping out a handkerchief and wiping the sweat from his face. Up close he smelled of too-sweet cologne and raw meat. "No maintenance. No one takes any fucking pride anymore."

Karen started to edge away, looked sharply at her ankle, and winced.

"Poor baby," said the snake. "The big one, I mean. With the little one making all that fucking noise — does she ever shut up?"

"Listen, I —"

"No, *you* listen." A long-fingered hand took hold of Karen's arm. The one she held Zoe with. "You listen, what the fuck you running away like some idiot make-me-chase-you-sweat-up-my-suit?"

"I — my baby."

"Your baby should shut the fuck *up*, understand? Your baby should learn a little discipline, know what I mean? No one learns discipline how's it gonna be?"

Karen didn't answer.

"You know?" said the snake. "How's it gonna be the puppy learns discipline when the bitch don't know it? You tell me that, huh?"

"That's —"

He slapped her face. Not hard enough to sting, just a touch really. Worse than pain.

"You and me," he said, squeezing her arm. "We got things to talk about."

"What?" Panic tightened Karen's voice. "I'm just visiting from —"

"Shut up. And shut the goddamn baby up too —"

"I can't help it if —"

A hard slap rocked Karen's head. "No, bitch. Don't argue. You notice what we were eating back there?"

Karen shook her head.

"Sure you did, I saw you look. What was it?"

"Meat."

"Veal. You know what veal is, sweet-cheeks?"

"Calf."

"'Zactly. Baby cow." Winking. "Something can be young and cute, go bah-bah, moo-moo, but it don't matter shit when people's *needs* are involved, you know what I'm saying?"

He licked his lips. The hand on her arm moved to Zoe's arm. Pulling.

Karen pulled back and managed to free Zoe. He laughed.

Tripping backward, Karen said, "Leave me alone," in a too-weak voice.

"Yeah, sure," said the snake. "All alone."

The long-fingered hands became fists and he inched toward her. Slowly, enjoying it. The park so silent. No one here, dangerous part of town.

Karen kept retreating, Zoe wailing.

The snake advanced.

Raising a fist. Touching his knuckles with the other hand.

Suddenly, Karen was moving faster, as if her ankle had never been injured.

Moving with an athlete's grace. Placing Zoe on the grass gently, she stepped to the left while reaching into the big, heavy denim bag.

All the things you had to carry.

Zoe cried louder, screaming, and the snake's eyes snapped to the baby.

Let's hear it for distraction.

The snake looked back at Karen.

Karen brought something out of the bag, small and shiny.

Reversing direction abruptly, she walked right up to the snake.

His eyes got very wide.

Three handclaps, not that different from the sound of his feet on the steps. Three small black holes appeared on his forehead, like stigmata.

He gaped at her, turned white, fell.

She fired five more shots into him as he lay there. Three in the chest, two in the groin. Per the client's request.

Placing the gun back in the bag, she rushed toward Zoe. But the baby was already up, in Doug's arms. And quiet. Doug always had that effect upon Zoe. The books said that was common, fathers often did.

"Hey," he said, kissing Zoe, then Karen. "You let him hit you. I was almost going to move in."

"It's fine," said Karen, touching her cheek. The skin felt hot and welts were starting to rise. "Nothing some makeup won't handle."

"Still," said Doug. "You know how I love your skin."

"I'm okay, honey."

He kissed her again, nuzzled Zoe. "That was a little intense, no? And poor little kiddie — I really don't think we should take her along on business."

He picked up the denim bag. Karen felt light — not just because her hands were empty. That special sense of lightness that marked the end of a project.

"You're right," said Karen as the three of them began walking out of the park. "She is getting older, we don't want to traumatize her. But I don't think this'll freak her out too bad. The stuff kids see on TV nowadays, right? If she ever asks we'll say it was TV."

"Guess so," said Doug. "You're the mom, but I never liked it."

A bit of sun came down through the thick trees, highlighting his black curls. And Zoe's. One beautiful tiny head tucked into a beautiful big one.

"It worked," said Karen.

Doug laughed. "That it did. Everything go smoothly?"

"As silk." Karen kissed them both again. "Little Peach was great. The only reason she was crying is she was having so much fun throwing food in the restaurant and didn't want to leave. And the eh-eh worked perfectly. She threw the rattle, gave me a perfect chance to get close to the jerk."

Doug nodded and looked over his shoulder at the body lying across the pathway.

"The Viper," he said, laughing softly. "Not exactly big game."

"More like a worm," said Karen.

Doug laughed again, then turned serious. "You're sure he didn't hit you hard? I love your skin."

"I'm fine, baby. Not to worry."

"I always worry, babe. That's why I'm alive."

"Me too. You know that."

"Sometimes I wonder."

"Some gratitude."

"Hey," said Doug. "It's just that I love your skin, right?" A moment passed. "Love you."

"Love you too."

A few steps later, he said, "When I saw him hit you, babe — the second time — I could actually hear it from the bushes. Your head swiveled hard and I thought uh-oh. I was ready to come out and finish it myself. Came this close. But I knew it would tick you off. Still, it was a little . . . anxiety-provoking."

"You did the right thing."

He shrugged. Karen felt so much love for him she wanted to shout it to the world.

"Thanks, babe," she said, touching his earlobe. "For being there and for *not* doing anything."

He nodded again. Then he said it:

"The things we do for love."

"Oh, yeah."

His beautiful face relaxed.

A rock. Thank God he'd let her go all the way by herself. First project since the baby and she'd needed to get back into the swing.

Zoe was sleeping now, fat cheeks pillowing out on Doug's broad shoulder, eyes closed, the black lashes long and curving.

They grew up so fast.

Soon, before you knew it, the little pudding would be in preschool and Karen would have more time on her hands.

Maybe one day they'd have another baby.

But not right away. She had her career to consider.

ANDREW KLAVAN

Lou Monahan, County Prosecutor

FROM *Guilty as Charged*

THE THINGS YOU REMEMBER; the things you regret. Funny,
Monahan thought — they were such little things. That last week of
summer vacation. Rick Ellerbee's bash. It was more than twenty
years ago now. It was the last week before they all went off to
college. The evening had grown cool by the water after the leaden
heat of the day, and he had smelled the edge of September, and he
had smelled the sea. The Sound was a silver ridge out beyond the
white mansion, and the lawn, beryl in the dusk, swept down from
under the house's foundations and swelled beneath his feet and
swept away again. Liveried waiters angled among the clusters of
teenagers. A jazz quartet in white tuxedos neutered the latest hits
beneath the yellow-striped tent. "Jive Talkin'." "Love Will Keep
Us Together." Whatever — it was just a white pudding of noise in
there. All the same, the couples danced to it. And the girls were so
pretty, their necks and arms so fresh in their sleeveless dresses.

For Monahan, to whom Ellerbee had always been kind, the setting was the element, the music the heartbeat, the girls the very
soul of sophistication, wealth, and grace. Ellerbee himself seemed
their presiding genius: his smooth, animated features gracious and
manly and without arrogance; the figure he cut both slender and
solid — and casual, too, in tan chinos and an open-necked shirt;
the way he gestured to the circle of smiles around him as if he were
conjuring the whole occasion out of thin air only to enhance the
comfort and sweetness of their lives. To Monahan, he sparkled, it all
sparkled, and he stood watching them — Ellerbee, all his class-
mates — a little apart, drink in hand, knowing full well that, after

today, they would become strangers to him. In a week, Ellerbee would be starting at Princeton and after that, almost surely, would go on to Harvard Law. Monahan would cram and labor his way through the state school in Westchester and get his law degree at NYU, if he was lucky, if he was very lucky and worked very hard. They would meet during vacations. They would chat on the street and part. There would never be this friendship again, this intimacy, not for him. Not that Monahan was bitter about it — he had never expected more, not even this much — but he couldn't help feeling wistful that last evening. They were charming — his high school friends — and they were charmed; and he knew he was there to say good-bye.

His drink finished, the glass spirited away, Monahan moved across the lawn to the tent, his hands in the pockets of his green suit, his tie stirring in the first breeze off the Sound. He reached the edge of the tent and stepped within the shade of the canvas, stepped up onto the wooden floor. He surveyed the dancers absently, casually tapping his foot to the quartet's thumpingly bland "Behind Closed Doors."

And he saw a girl. Leaning against the far tent pole. Resting her cheek against it dreamily.

She could not possibly have been as beautiful as he remembered her twenty years on. Her skin could not have been so white beneath such thoroughly raven hair. Her figure, lightly pressed against the support, outlined, in her floral dress, against the beryl lawn and the azure sky, so graceful and enchanting — women looked like that in memory, in movies, not in real life. All the same even then, Monahan was made breathless by the sight of her.

And then she raised her eyes to him, saw him watching her. And she smiled at him across the dance floor.

The smile lanced his rib cage; it made his head swim. Only half aware, he began to approach her. He wove slowly through the couples dancing around him. The music, in his woozy state, seemed to shatter into glistering bursts and dabs in the summer air. There was nothing but that music as he moved, and the pulse in his head, and her heartbreaking beauty. Monahan was amazed. He could not believe the sudden possibilities. Everything, he knew, was about to become wonderful.

She straightened from the pole to await him. He neared the edge of the floor. A couple moved between them, cutting her from his view for a moment — just for a moment. Then they passed.

The girl was gone.

Monahan blinked. The pole stood alone. He moved out of the tent and looked over the lawn. There was no sign of her, no sign at all. Monahan was too prosy a fellow to believe that she had vanished — but he didn't go hunting for her, either; he was too unassuming for that. No, he figured he had simply made a mistake. She had not been smiling at him. She'd been smiling at someone else, someone behind him probably. That made more sense; the whole world made a lot more sense that way. He would have made a fool of himself if he'd reached her, if he'd spoken. She would have looked at him blankly. "Excuse me," she would have said, and walked away. He'd been spared that, at least. He should have felt grateful.

Instead, for twenty years, he remembered her, he regretted losing her. There were days — there were nights — when he imagined entire lifetimes with her. Which was funny. Well, it was pretty stupid, really. It wasn't like down-to-earth Lou Monahan at all.

Yet there it was. That memory, that moment. From time to time, out of nowhere after years, it turned up again and melted him, wrung him. The things you remember, the things you regret.

They were there to haunt him in force the night the rock star got his throat cut.

Monahan had never even heard of the guy. What did he know about rock stars nowadays? They were just monstrous images on T-shirts to him — those shirts on the sad little punks he sent to juvenile hall. But this one, Thrust — yes, that was his name — he must've had a fairly sizable following. Because when Monahan pulled the department Chevy into the dead man's driveway, reporters converged on him like black flies.

The prosecutor had never seen so many of them. Not on any case he'd ever caught. As he shut off the car, he had a glimpse through the window of their straining faces. He saw Rorke from the local weekly, and Helen Martin from the county's lone ten-thousand-watt sundowner. But these two, usually the only two to show up anywhere, were quickly jostled out of sight by the swarming others. Flashes went off, spotlights; camera lenses jutted at him; outstretched hands held microphones that chittered against the pane.

And the mikes had big-time logos on them, city call letters, and
the networks', too. Monahan even noticed a few glamorous news-
women out there, women he recognized but couldn't name. How
the hell had they gotten up here so fast?

As he pushed the door open, he tried to look bored and belea-
guered because — well, because that's the way prosecutors always
looked on TV shows. But as the cameras started flashing and the
shouted questions deafened him and the microphones and mini-
cams were pushed into his face, Monahan felt himself going sweaty
and muslin-headed. He had never been through anything remotely
like this before. He had no idea, finally, what he said to them. He
spoke thickly, his tongue swollen, his brain stuporous. All he could
think about was how wrinkled his brown jacket was — and how
brown it was! — and how he had to hold it closed to cover the
coffee stain on his shirt pocket. Then it was over. Investigator Corvo
drew him out of the throng — like being hauled out of quicksand
— and the deputies pushed the reporters back. And then Monahan, still trying to button his jacket, was climbing beside Corvo up
the front path through a spotlit rock garden dotted with bonsai
trees.

"Wow, huh?" said Corvo.

"Jesus," said Monahan. "Who was this guy?"

They approached the long, low front of the ranch house. Corvo
was a small man, short, thin, with a round, squinched face and a
dogged gait. Monahan had to take long strides to keep up with him.

"It's not the guy," Corvo said, "it's the young lady that did him.
Old Thrust was sticking Ginny Reingold. Only it looks like she stuck
him, right?"

Corvo spoke the woman's name with such weight that Monahan
thought he must know it, but there was nothing there. "Who the
hell is Ginny Reingold?"

Corvo snorted. "Who the hell is Ginny Reingold? You know your
wife?"

"Yeah," said Monahan. "I know my wife."

"You know the magazines she reads? You know the face on the
cover? That's Ginny Reingold."

Monahan slowed down, trying to form an image. Corvo kept
walking. "Which magazine?" said Monahan.

"All of them," said Corvo. He reached the door and looked back

at him, gestured at the press in the driveway below. "You better get
used to that shit down there," he said to the prosecutor. "You're
about to become a star."

The body lay half off the bed, and the head lay half off the body.
The blood had spilled over the singer's face and drenched his long
black hair and stained the tan shag under him red. A sheet, also
stained, still covered him to his thighs, and the man's pale, hairy
nakedness, and his gaping mouth and his staring eyes and his blood
and the metallic smell of his blood and the sour smell of his urine
made the murder scene — for all the cameras and glamorous news
babes outside — as dingy and miserable and sordid as every other
Monahan had seen.

"Is everyone done with him?"

"Yeah," said Corvo, "but we thought you'd want a look."

"Thrust? That was his name? Thrust?"

"That's what he called himself. He was lead singer for Fatwa.
Fatwa." Corvo shook his head.

Monahan snorted. "Fatwa and Thrust."

"Born Jerry Finkelstein," said Corvo, and laughed.

Monahan looked around the bedroom casually. "So what about
her?"

Corvo told him what they had while Monahan studied the place.
It was a large room, all shag below, a wall of mirrors facing a wall of
windows open on the September night, a wall of shelves and stereo
equipment connecting them. A crime scene man was dusting the
CD player for prints. Monahan took it all in, and Corvo went on
detailing the evidence against the suspect: the bloodstains, the possible skin traces, the maid who'd sometimes heard them fighting.
Monahan took this in, too. He was the most successful prosecutor
in three counties, and he was known for his unspectacular, sturdy,
determined mastery of every case.

So he took it all in. But a part of his mind was elsewhere. Still
thinking about those reporters outside. Excited about them now.
His first astonishment had passed, and he could feel the chill of
excitement in his chest, the wind of it across his nerve endings.
*Assistant District Attorney Lou Monahan told reporters at the scene that he
would act quickly to secure an indictment . . .* he thought.

Strangely enough, it was just then — not later — that the memory came to him. Rick Ellerbee's end-of-summer bash. The dancers under the tent. The girl, against the tent pole, smiling at him. Standing beside the shabby corpse, he felt a ridiculous surge of yearning and love.

"Why the hell would she do it?" he said sharply, snapping out of it. "The legendary Ginny Reingold."

"Old Thrust," said Corvo, showing a fist. "Boom-boom — tsk-tsk — you know? Hell hath no fury like a woman punched."

Monahan raised his eyebrows. "She said that?"

"Not her. She's not talking till her lawyer gets up from the city. You're gonna be in some very fancy company on this one, my friend."

Monahan lifted his chin, ready for it.

"She's bringing in Richard Ellerbee," said Corvo. "Run for your life."

Wendy Monahan kept saying the same thing. "You were on the eleven o'clock news!"

Monahan kept eating. Wendy kept putting food in front of him. Cold roast beef, string beans, rolls. A dish of coleslaw now. "The eleven o'clock news!" She kept saying the same thing. "I tell you, the phone would *not* stop ringing. I thought Sandy was just going to fall over dead." Usually, if he came home at this hour, Monahan had to forage for himself, scour the back reaches of the refrigerator. Now Wendy fetched him another beer, poured it into his glass for him. He wondered if Rick Ellerbee's wife treated him like this all the time.

"So?" She plunked down in the seat next to him. Peered at him, her chin on her fists, as if he had tales to tell of a Polar expedition. "Did you see her? What does she look like?"

"'What does she look like?'" Monahan sat like Old King Cole, his fists on the table before him, his fork in one, his beer in the other. "She's on every magazine in the house — I can't go to the bathroom without seeing her . . ."

"I mean in real life."

"In real life? In real life, she has a black eye."

Wendy reeled back with a full-volume gasp. "You mean he hit her?" Monahan nodded. "The creep! Well, then he deserved it."

"On television, he deserved it," said Monahan, digging into the slaw. "In court, they tend to consider it an overreaction."

Wendy's blue eyes grew bright, and she leaned in toward him again, making him feel strange: warm; good. "But the court's going to be *on* television," she said. "They have cameras now."

He hadn't actually thought of that. Uncertainly, he said, "Nah. Up here?"

"For this?" said Wendy. "Are you kidding? The trial'll be on every day. You'll be like a show."

He tried to laugh it off. "*Lou Monahan, County Prosecutor,*" he said. But it bounced around inside him. Cameras at the trial every day, like a show.

"I'd watch it," said Wendy. And she stood up, slipped around the edge of the table, and sat on her husband's lap.

Monahan remembered now about Ellerbee's wife. She was some muck-a-muck's daughter — some rich guy's. Monahan had seen a picture of the two of them at some kind of charity function. The wife was very beautiful and posh with wavy black hair.

Wendy nestled against him. She moved her hands gently over the back of his neck, and he put his hands on her bottom. She was a little pudgy now — she hadn't lost all the weight she'd gained before their second son was born — but she still had a cute round girlish face under the short hair she kept blond. She'd look okay standing beside him, he thought. A good wife for a man-of-the-people type. Viewers would see he had a solid family life . . .

She leaned forward and put her lips to his ear. "I married a star," she whispered.

Monahan had a stray thought: maybe the girl at Rick Ellerbee's party would see him on television . . . "You're a goof," he said aloud, and he nuzzled his wife's neck and kissed her.

Prosecutor Lou Monahan today came face to face with the man who was once his friend but has now become his ruthless opponent in the trial of the century, Monahan thought as he ambled down the courthouse hallway to meet with Ginny Reingold and her lawyer. He was careful to amble, casual, his hands in his pockets, his expression thoughtful, distant. In truth, he hadn't been this nervous since the Sunday school Nativity play when his trembling lips had turned "myrrh" into a six-syllable word.

So far, though, things were going pretty well this morning. His performance before the press on the courthouse steps, for instance, had been a big improvement over yesterday's. This time he'd been prepared for them. Wendy had chosen his clothes, so he felt confident and well dressed. He'd rehearsed his statement as he drove to work, and practiced pointing his finger as he spoke and narrowing his eyes forcefully. He'd talked briefly and clearly as the mob of them congealed around him like pork fat. Then he'd turned and marched away from their shouted questions as if he had more important things to do. He hadn't had time to review the film clips yet, but some of the deputies who'd seen them on the ten o'clock report had teased him — "Looking good, Lou!" — so he guessed it had gone okay.

Now, though . . . Now came the meeting he dreaded. His first confrontation with Ellerbee. And even though they would meet in the interview room with no one to see the moment but Corvo and the deputy and the defendant, those cameras, those reporters — they stayed in Monahan's head; he could see the film of himself in his head, he could hear the newsman's narration there. *Prosecutor Lou Monahan strode to the interview room door and nodded grimly to the deputy . . .*

Monahan strode to the interview room door and nodded grimly to the deputy. He had to get this just right, he thought. From the very first, the first greeting. Friendly but not eager; poised; a handshake; a manly nod of recognition. Nothing that suggested how he had revered Ellerbee in youth, how Ellerbee had gone on to become everything Monahan knew he could never be. Film of his inferiority at eleven.

"Jesus," Monahan whispered under his breath as the deputy pushed open the door.

Corvo was already in the room, standing before the table. The deputy, Ellen Brown, was against the wall. Ginny Reingold, the skin over her high cheekbone purple and broken, sat with her hands clasped on the table and stared forward blankly. She was long-haired, long-, silky-, chestnut-haired, wide-eyed, shapely but frail. The "neo-waif look," his wife had told him. Whatever it was, every time Monahan set eyes on her, he felt himself stirred as by some primitive instinct to rise to her defense.

Which was pretty unhelpful under the circumstances. Because there, seated beside her, was her defender in fact.

Jesus, he looks great! Monahan thought. *What a great suit!*

Ellerbee had thickened over these twenty years; he was not the winsome Boy King of the Suburbs he had been. But he was still trim, clearly muscular. His width only gave his figure power and maturity. There was none of Monahan's paunch, nor his widow's peak. And where Monahan felt his own features had spread and blurred with time, Ellerbee's dauntless profile seemed to have solidified, sharpened, the soft lines straighter, the boy's face a man's.

On top of which, it really was a great suit. Sleek and black. Pinstripes so faint, so suggestive, they almost disdained to be there at all.

"Mr. Ellerbee," said Corvo. "Louis Monahan, the ADA on the case."

Monahan shot his hand out a little too quickly. But he hit the correct expression perfectly: a tight half-smile, a narrowed eye, knowing, amused. *So we meet again, old friend.*

Ellerbee stood. He pumped Monahan's hand. His brilliant eyes seemed to drink the prosecutor down in one smooth swallow. "Mr. Monahan," he said. Then he sat again. Then he said, "My client would like to make a statement."

Everyone started moving around Monahan. Ellerbee turned to his client. Ginny Reingold straightened, drew breath. Corvo nodded to Deputy Brown, who stepped to the door and spoke to the deputy outside. Only Monahan himself remained motionless. Frozen. Staring. Gaping at Ellerbee.

He . . . didn't recognize me, he thought. It was his only thought for the moment, the only thought of which he was aware, a neon billboard of a thought, all other thoughts fading in its blaze. *Didn't. Recognize. Me? Me?* Monahan kept standing, kept staring. *But . . . we were in school together. We ran . . . we ran track together. Track. At school. Together. I beat him — I beat him in the fifty-yard dash. And he doesn't recognize . . .*

"Uh . . . Lou?" said Corvo.

"Miss Reingold, this session is now being videotaped," said Monahan smoothly, pulling out the chair across from her, sitting, facing her. "So I'll inform you of your rights again for the record, and then you can begin." *Didn't . . . ? Me? Lou?* he thought. *The fifty-yard dash? I hit the line a yard ahead of you. A yard at least, Freddy Markham was there, he saw it . . .*

"Last night," said Ginny Reingold. She cleared her throat. "Last night, before Jerry died, before he was killed . . ."

That's why you only ran the three hundred after that, thought Monahan sullenly, shaking his head at the Formica tabletop. He was suddenly very depressed.

"We had a fight," Ginny Reingold went on softly. She had the voice of a boy's fantasy, half flute, half whisper. Monahan, drawing his gut up with a breath, forced himself to listen to her. "It wasn't anything big. I just made some joke, you know, about his hair, he needed a haircut, teasing him, you know, but . . . well, his last album didn't do so well, and he's been kind of down about it, you know. And, anyway, he started yelling, and it got out of hand, and he — he hit me. In the face. And see, he never — I told him he could never hit me in the face. I *told* him, you know. I said I'd leave him. But he was just wild. He was crazy. And I got scared, you know. So I ran out. Outside. I got in the car, the tan one, the Mercedes. And I locked all the doors, you know, but . . . I didn't have the key, see. It was in my purse. And Jerry came out, and he was pounding on the windows, screaming. I kept hoping someone would hear, you know, call the police, I even leaned on the horn, but . . . well, there's really only woods around us, and, anyway, I guess people are kind of used to it. Anyway, after a while, he said, you know, that he was going in to get the key. And then he said he was going to come back out and teach me a lesson. And then he — he laughed this kind of maniacal laughter, you know, and . . . he went back inside." Ginny Reingold gulped back tears, glanced at her attorney, her big eyes appealing. Ellerbee reached out and put his strong hand over her thin, white fingers. Monahan watched them touch. *I beat him, you know,* he told Ginny Reingold in his mind. *A solid yard. Freddy Markham saw it. He had to be all noble and sportsmanlike about it. It killed him.* Ginny Reingold swallowed again and went on. "I didn't know what to do. I was afraid to try and run. I just stayed there. But Jerry didn't come back. I was out there over an hour, you know, and then . . . well, it started to get really cold. I didn't have my jacket or anything. So, finally, you know, I got out. And I went around the back. I wanted to . . . peek in at the window, the bedroom window, I was hoping maybe Jerry had gone to sleep. Like, passed out. He'd had a lot of vodka and, and some dope, too, so I thought . . ." She touched the corner of her eye with a fingernail, as if to keep a tear there neatly contained. "So, like, anyway, I kind of crept around to the back, and . . . there was a man. A big . . . I don't know . . . a big fat guy, white guy with, like, real short hair. He was climbing out of the window . . ."

Monahan's mouth opened, but he didn't speak. Suddenly, the heaviness in his belly began to lighten. *Hey,* he thought.

"He was wearing . . . kind of one of those checkered hunting jackets, you know," Ginny Reingold said. "He didn't even see me, he didn't look at me, he just climbed out of the window and . . . started running. He just ran off into the woods in back. And I ran to the window and looked in, and . . . and there was Jerry . . ."

Now she shuddered, covered her mouth with her hands, and her tears spilled over. They coursed over her bruised cheek and her silken hair covered the other side of her face as she leaned toward her attorney. Ellerbee squeezed her shoulder, and she pressed her forehead against his lapel. Investigator Corvo clenched his fist at his side. Ginny Reingold looked like a beaten child.

But Monahan wasn't looking at Ginny Reingold now. By now, his mood had transformed entirely, and he was looking at Richard Ellerbee. Running his gaze over the bold, thin nose, the forthright brow, the whole expert etching of his countenance. Looking at him as one lawyer to another, one savvy courtroom practitioner to another. Excitement, like cold water boiling, was rising up through his chest, into his throat. And he was thinking: *Hey. Hey, what do you know? What do you know, counselor? Her story is crap. Craparoni. And you know it's crap, Mr. Counselor Ellerbee. And the jury will sure as hell know it, too.* He almost let himself laugh out loud. *And I'm going to beat you,* he thought in surprise. *I'm going to beat you blind. On TV. On TV every ding-dong day. For everyone to see every day. For her to see. At your lousy party. I beat you once. At the fifty-yard dash. You arrogant son of a bitch. And I'm going to beat you now. Again. For everyone to see.*

Monahan shoved into his office, riding his confidence. This time, Corvo had to hurry to keep up with him.

"You better find an all-girl jury, boy," Corvo was saying, "'cause there's not a man in the world who'd vote to convict her. Even I wouldn't vote to convict her, and I know she's guilty."

Monahan's desk was covered with pink message slips. Newspapers and TV stations and radio stations had been calling him. People from the Sonny Charleston talk show were calling him. Sonny wanted to have him on.

"They'll convict her," he said. "She's lying. They'll convict her."

He cleared a space at the corner of the desk. He had brought one of the portable JVCs in from the squad room. He hoisted it onto the desk and switched it on. It was almost time for the twelve o'clock report.

"That Ellerbee, he's something, huh," said Corvo. "Nice suit."

"Yeah," said Monahan. "It's a great suit." The picture on the set came up fast. A woman was holding up a box of detergent. She looked a little like Monahan's wife — round-faced, blond — only thinner, prettier, in a crisp, pretty yellow blouse. If Wendy could make herself look a little bit more like that, she'd be perfect, Monahan thought.

"He's actually a really nice guy," Corvo went on, as if he'd met a movie star who'd given him the time of day. "I was talking to him on the way out. He was asking me about the fishing up here. You know, he says he thinks he went to school with you."

"Oh yeah?" said Monahan. "I didn't recognize him."

"What do you think he makes? Like a million a year or something?"

The news came on then. Music like Morse code played on violins. An exciting swoop toward the anchorwoman's desk, the keen beam of her gaze at the camera. And behind her, a glamour shot of Ginny Reingold over the image of a broken guitar.

The anchorwoman's lead was quick, sharp. Revelations today that Thrust had repeatedly battered his supermodel lover. Then they were into the tape, and there was Monahan, pushing up the courthouse steps as the reporters closed around him like the sea.

"Hey — looking good," said Corvo.

But Monahan briefly shook his head. He knew he did not look good. He did not even look like he looked. In real life, he had a candid, intelligent face, more handsome than not. On TV, his features seemed thick and coarse, his hair thin and unkempt. His attempts to speak forcefully, jabbing the air with his finger, seemed ludicrous, stagey and stiff. From a competent, honest, small-county prosecutor, the cameras had somehow transformed him into a bullying, beady-eyed thug of a bureaucrat.

But his new energy, his new confidence, did not falter. He was not experienced in this, that's all. The cameras, the press. It had caught him off-guard. Now, though, now that he knew he could win, he had a plan.

Ellerbee came on. "This case has been mishandled from the start," he said. He spoke quietly but precisely, addressing the reporter, and thus the audience, as a colleague, an equal. "The town police were on the scene before the county sheriff's department, and they wandered all over the property. Contaminated the evidence completely. Obliterated any trace of an intruder. No attempt to find another suspect has been made. And there's been no attempt to trace the ownership of the murder weapon."

"Yeah, those townies," Corvo said.

Monahan didn't hear him. *He's slick,* he was thinking. Ellerbee's approach to the camera was practiced, slick. He included the audience in his thoughts as if they were all lawyers trying the case together. Monahan nodded, thinking, *But this is my county, counselor, my track. And the jury will come from here.*

This was his plan. Monahan was going to change. Now, right away, before the reporters had time to notice. He was going to become a local boy. He'd lived here long enough; he knew just how to do it. *Well, that Mr. Ellerbee, he sure is one fine city lawyer,* he was going to tell the reporters. *I guess a small-county prosecutor doesn't have much chance against him in court,* he would say, *so I'll just have to tell folks the truth and hope they'll listen.* Monahan, staring at the TV, smiled without knowing it. It would work. He knew it would work. Even the fact that they had gone to school together would play right into it, sharpen the clash of personalities. Every day, the people would see it. Small-county David against big-city Goliath. The cameras would be on them. In the courtroom, every day. Just like a show. And he would amble back and forth before the witness stand, one hand in his pants pocket, the other scratching at his head, his shirt rumpled, his tie undone. The Honest Bumpkin, Shrewder than He Looked, Justice on His Side — that would be him — Alone Against All the Power of the Rich and Famous. The jury would love it. And he would win. On TV. The whole country — maybe even the whole world — would be watching it. *Lou Monahan, County Prosecutor.*

"What're *you* thinking?" said Corvo with a laugh. "With that look on your face — what're you thinking about?"

"I'm thinking about a blouse I'm gonna buy for my wife," said Monahan. "Yellow." And he picked up the phone to call the Sonny Charleston show.

* * *

Lou Monahan, County Prosecutor, looked at the murder scene in the fading light, Monahan thought. He looked at the murder scene in the fading light. He was standing in back of the ranch house, out of sight of the deputy guarding the front. He was standing in the grass with his hands in his pockets. A cool breeze full of dusk and autumn traveled up the gentle slope of the hill from the woods below.

He had wanted to come and inspect the place again, get a sense of it. Supply himself with ammunition against Ellerbee's charges that the scene had been contaminated. *Well, now,* he would tell Sonny Charleston, *that Mr. Ellerbee has some real fancy ideas, but I had a look-see at the place myself, and, well, if there was any sign of an intruder* . . . He smiled as he turned to look down at the trees below him. He was going on the TV program tomorrow. The Lou Monahan show would begin its run tomorrow. Everything, he knew, was about to become wonderful.

The leaves in the forest rustled faintly. He could smell them beginning to die. And suddenly his soul was in the past, and he was full of yearning. Walking across the dance floor to where she stood. The girl so achingly near and youth so achingly near again that he nearly groaned aloud in his desire to touch them both.

He had been wrong, he thought. Wrong all this time. She *had* been smiling at him. Beckoning him. He should have searched for her, found her, spoken to her. Everything would have been different. He would have been . . . something. Something else. He didn't know what. Some gleaming thing he could now only hanker for blindly.

Monahan began to walk toward the woods, down the slope of the lawn. He thought he was still examining the scene, but really he was just walking, feeling himself walk, as he had walked twenty years ago beneath the tent. He was wandering toward the woods and the source of the wind, and toward that smell of summer's end that he remembered. He was approaching the forest shadows and their sense of mystery as if he hoped to wander there right through the veil and into the un-happened thing.

But he slowed, stopped, right at the tree line. Gazed into the deeper darkness wryly, because he knew it was only the darkness after all. There was no going back, of course not. There were no alternative histories. Everything had to be as it was. His time had not been then. But his time was coming now.

He drew his gaze back to the front rank of trees and was about to turn away. But then he noticed something.

Lou Monahan, County Prosecutor, stepped forward, his eyes narrowing. He looked down at a young maple growing at the forest's edge, its lower branches. On one of them there was a small puff of color trembling in the air. Red and black among the leaves that were still green. He leaned closer to it, and he knew exactly what it was. It was a trace of fabric, a few threads. Pulled from one of those checkered hunting jackets. Like the jacket Ginny Reingold said had been worn by the murderous intruder.

Something in Monahan greeted the sight without surprise, as if he had known all along it would be there. Just as he had known, somehow, that the girl at the edge of the dance floor would be gone by the time he reached her. This made sense to him, too. That Ginny Reingold was innocent. That she would not go to trial. That there would be no trial. Some drug-crazed drifter would be busted for the murder and would confess. The model would leave the county, and Ellerbee would leave, and the cameras would leave. *Lou Monahan, County Prosecutor* would be canceled before it even premiered. It did not surprise him at all. The world made much more sense to him that way. It always had.

And yet . . . thought Monahan dreamily. *And yet . . .*

He reached out and pinched the little scrap of cloth between his thumb and finger. He tugged it, and it came free from the snag of the branch on which it hung. He held it up, a little above his eyes, as if to examine it in the darkling. The breeze blew up to him from its mysterious source in the woods. And he opened his fingers.

And the little scrap of cloth blew away.

ELMORE LEONARD

Karen Makes Out

FROM *Murder for Love*

THEY DANCED UNTIL Karen said she had to be up early tomorrow. No argument, he walked with her through the crowd outside
Monaco, then along Ocean Drive in the dark to her car. He said,
"Lady, you wore me out." He was in his forties, weathered but
young-acting, natural, didn't come on with any singles-bar bullshit
buying her a drink, or comment when she said thank you, she'd
have Jim Beam on the rocks. They had cooled off by the time they
reached her Honda and he took her hand and gave her a peck on
the cheek saying he hoped to see her again. In no hurry to make
something happen. That was fine with Karen. He said "Ciao," and
walked off.

Two nights later they left Monaco, came out of that pounding
sound to a sidewalk café and drinks and he became Carl Tillman,
skipper of a charter deep-sea fishing boat out of American Marina,
Bahia Mar. He was single, married seven years and divorced, no
children; he lived in a ground-floor two-bedroom apartment in
North Miami — one of the bedrooms full of fishing gear he didn't
know where else to store. Carl said his boat was out of the water,
getting ready to move it to Haulover Dock, closer to where he
lived.

Karen liked his weathered, kind of shaggy look, the crow's-feet
when he smiled. She liked his soft brown eyes that looked right at
her talking about making his living on the ocean, about hurricanes,
the trendy scene here on South Beach, movies. He went to the
movies every week and told Karen — raising his eyebrows in a
vague, kind of stoned way — his favorite actor was Jack Nicholson.
Karen asked him if that was his Nicholson impression or was he

doing Christian Slater doing Nicholson? He told her she had a
keen eye; but couldn't understand why she thought Dennis Quaid
was a hunk. That was okay.

He said, "You're a social worker."

Karen said, "A *social* worker —"

"A teacher."

"What kind of teacher?"

"You teach Psychology. College level."

She shook her head.

"English Lit."

"I'm not a teacher."

"Then why'd you ask what kind I thought you were?"

She said, "You want me to tell you what I do?"

"You're a lawyer. Wait. The Honda — you're a public defender."
Karen shook her head and he said, "Don't tell me, I want to guess,
even if it takes a while." He said, "If that's okay with you."

Fine. Some guys, she'd tell them what she did and they were
turned off by it. Or they'd act surprised and then self-conscious and
start asking dumb questions. "But how can a girl do that?" Assholes.

That night in the bathroom brushing her teeth Karen stared at
her reflection. She liked to look at herself in mirrors: touch her
short blond hair, check out her fanny in profile, long legs in a
straight skirt above her knees, Karen still a size six approaching
thirty. She didn't think she looked like a social worker or a school-
teacher, even college level. A lawyer maybe, but not a public defender. Karen was low-key high style. She could wear her favorite
Calvin Klein suit, the black one her dad had given her for Christmas, her Sig Sauer .38 for evening wear snug against the small of
her back, and no one would think for a moment she was packing.

Her new boyfriend called and stopped by her house in Coral
Gables Friday evening in a white BMW convertible. They went to a
movie and had supper and when he brought her home they kissed
in the doorway, arms slipping around each other, holding, Karen
thanking God he was a good kisser, comfortable with him, but not
quite ready to take her clothes off. When she turned to the door he
said, "I can wait. You think it'll be long?"

Karen said, "What're you doing Sunday?"

They kissed the moment he walked in and made love in the
afternoon, sunlight flat on the window shades, the bed stripped
down to a fresh white sheet. They made love in a hurry because

they couldn't wait, had at each other and lay perspiring after. When they made love again, Karen holding his lean body between her legs and not wanting to let go, it lasted and lasted and got them smiling at each other, saying things like "Wow," and "Oh, my God," it was so good, serious business but really fun. They went out for a while, came back to her yellow stucco bungalow in Coral Gables, and made love on the living room floor.

Carl said, "We could try it again in the morning."

"I have to be dressed and out of here by six."

"You're a flight attendant."

She said, "Keep guessing."

Monday morning Karen Sisco was outside the federal courthouse in Miami with a pump-action shotgun on her hip. Karen's right hand gripped the neck of the stock, the barrel extending above her head. Several more U.S. deputy marshals were out here with her, while inside, three Colombian nationals were being charged in District Court with the possession of cocaine in excess of five hundred kilograms. One of the marshals said he hoped the scudders liked Atlanta as they'd be doing thirty to life there pretty soon. He said, "Hey, Karen, you want to go with me, drop 'em off? I know a nice ho-tel we could stay at."

She looked over at the good-ole-boy marshals grinning, shuffling their feet, waiting for her reply. Karen said, "Gary, I'd go with you in a minute if it wasn't a mortal sin." They liked that. It was funny, she'd been standing here thinking she'd gone to bed with four different boyfriends in her life: an Eric at Florida Atlantic, a Bill right after she graduated, then a Greg, three years of going to bed with Greg, and now Carl. Only four in her whole life, but two more than the national average for women in the U.S. according to *Time* magazine, their report of a recent sex survey. The average woman had two partners in her lifetime, the average man, six. Karen had thought everybody was getting laid with a lot more different ones than that.

She saw her boss now, Milt Dancey, an old-time marshal in charge of court support, come out of the building to stand looking around, a pack of cigarettes in his hand. Milt looked this way and gave Karen a nod, but paused to light a cigarette before coming over. A guy from the Miami FBI office was with him.

Milt said, "Karen, you know Daniel Burdon?"

Not Dan, not Danny, Daniel. Karen knew him, one of the younger black guys over there, tall and good looking, confident, known to brag about how many women he'd had of all kinds and color. He'd flashed his smile at Karen one time, hitting on her. Karen turned him down saying, "You have two reasons you want to go out with me." Daniel, smiling, said he knew of one reason, what was the other one? Karen said, "So you can tell your buddies you banged a marshal." Daniel said, "Yeah, but you could use it, too, girl. Brag on getting *me* in the sack." See? That's the kind of guy he was.

Milt said, "He wants to ask you about a Carl Tillman."

No flashing smile this time, Daniel Burdon had on a serious, sort of innocent expression, saying to her, "You know the man, Karen? Guy in his forties, sandy hair, goes about five-ten, one-sixty?"

Karen said, "What's this, a test? Do I *know* him?"

Milt reached for her shotgun. "Here, Karen, lemme take that while you're talking."

She turned a shoulder saying, "It's okay, I'm not gonna shoot him," her fist tight on the neck of the twelve-gauge. She said to Daniel, "You have Carl under surveillance?"

"Since last Monday."

"You've seen us together — so what's this do-I-know-him shit? You playing a game with me?"

"What I meant to ask, Karen, was how long have you known him?"

"We met last week, Tuesday."

"And you saw him Thursday, Friday, spent Sunday with him, went to the beach, came back to your place . . . What's he think about you being with the marshals' service?"

"I haven't told him."

"How come?"

"He wants to guess what I do."

"Still working on it, huh? What you think, he a nice guy? Has a sporty car, has money, huh? He a pretty big spender?"

"Look," Karen said, "why don't you quit dickin' around and tell me what this is about, okay?"

"See, Karen, the situation's so unusual," Daniel said, still with the innocent expression, "I don't know how to put it, you know, delicately. Find out a U.S. marshal's fucking a bank robber."

* * *

Milt Dancey thought Karen was going to swing at Daniel with the shotgun. He took it from her this time and told the Bureau man to behave himself, watch his mouth if he wanted cooperation here. Stick to the facts. This Carl Tillman was a *suspect* in a bank robbery, a possible suspect in a half-dozen more, all the robberies, judging from the bank videos, committed by the same guy. The FBI referred to him as "Slick," having nicknames for all their perps. They had prints off a teller's counter might be the guy's, but no match in their files and not enough evidence on Carl Edward Tillman — the name on his driver's license and car registration — to bring him in. He appeared to be most recently cherry, just getting into a career of crime. His motivation, pissed off at banks because Florida Southern foreclosed on his note and sold his forty-eight-foot Hatteras for nonpayment.

It stopped Karen for a moment. He might've lied about his boat, telling her he was moving it to Haulover; but that didn't make him a bank robber. She said, "What've you got, a video picture, a teller identified him?"

Daniel said, "Since you mentioned it," taking a Bureau wanted flyer from his inside coat pocket, the sheet folded once down the middle. He opened it and Karen was looking at four photos taken from bank video cameras of robberies in progress, the bandits framed in teller windows, three black guys, one white.

Karen said, "Which one?" and Daniel gave her a look before pointing to the white guy: a man with slicked-back hair, an earring, a full mustache, and dark sunglasses. She said, "That's not Carl Tillman," and felt instant relief. There was no resemblance.

"Look at it good."

"What can I tell you? It's not him."

"Look at the nose."

"You serious?"

"That's your friend Carl's nose."

It was. Carl's slender, rather elegant nose. Or like his. Karen said, "You're going with a nose ID, that's all you've got?"

"A witness," Daniel said, "believes she saw this man — right after what would be the first robbery he pulled — run from the bank to a strip mall up the street and drive off in a white BMW convertible. The witness got a partial on the license number and that brought us to your friend Carl."

Karen said, "You ran his name and date of birth . . ."

"Looked him up in NCIC, FCIC, and Warrant Information, drew a blank. That's why I think he's just getting his feet wet. Managed to pull off a few, two three grand each, and found himself a new profession."

"What do you want me to do," Karen said, "get his prints on a beer can?"

Daniel raised his eyebrows. "That would be a start. Might even be all we need. What I'd like you to do, Karen, is snuggle up to the man and find out his secrets. You know what I'm saying — intimate things, like did he ever use another name. . . ."

"Be your snitch," Karen said, knowing it was a mistake as soon as the words were out of her mouth.

It got Daniel's eyebrows raised again. He said, "That what it sounds like to you? I thought you were a federal agent, Karen. Maybe you're too close to him — is that it? Don't want the man to think ill of you?"

Milt said, "That's enough of that shit," standing up for Karen as he would any of his people, not because she was a woman; he had learned not to open doors for her. The only time she wanted to be first through the door was on a fugitive warrant, this girl who scored higher with a handgun, more times than not, than any marshal in the Southern District of Florida.

Daniel was saying, "Man, I need to use her. Is she on our side or not?"

Milt handed Karen her shotgun. "Here, you want to shoot him, go ahead."

"Look," Daniel said, "Karen can get me a close read on the man, where he's lived before, if he ever went by other names, if he has any identifying marks on his body, scars, maybe a gunshot wound, tattoos, things only lovely Karen would see when the man has his clothes off."

Karen took a moment. She said, "There is one thing I noticed."

"Yeah? What's that?"

"He's got the letters f-u-o-n tattooed on his penis."

Daniel frowned at her. "Foo-on?"

"That's when it's, you might say, limp. When he has a hard-on it says Fuck the Federal Bureau of Investigation."

Daniel Burdon grinned at Karen. He said, "Girl, you and I have to get together. I mean it."

*   *   *

Karen could handle "girl." Go either way. Girl, looking at herself in a mirror applying blush-on. Woman, well, that's what she was. Though until just a few years ago she only thought of women old enough to be her mother as women. Women getting together to form organizations of women, saying, Look, we're different from men. Isolating themselves in these groups instead of mixing it up with men and beating them at their own men's games. Men in general were stronger physically than women. Some men were stronger than other men and Karen was stronger than some too; so what did that prove? If she had to put a man on the ground, no matter how big or strong he was, she'd do it. One way or another. Up front, in his face. What she couldn't see herself playing was this sneaky role. Trying to get the stuff on Carl, a guy she liked, a lot, would think of with tender feelings and miss him during the day and want to be with him. Shit . . . Okay, she'd play the game, but not undercover. She'd first let him know she was a federal officer and see what he thought about it.

Could Carl be a bank robber?

She'd reserve judgment. Assume almost anyone could at one time or another and go from there.

What Karen did, she came home and put a pot roast in the oven and left her bag on the kitchen table, open, the grip of a Beretta nine sticking out in plain sight.

Carl arrived, they kissed in the living room, Karen feeling it but barely looking at him. When he smelled the pot roast cooking Karen said, "Come on, you can make the drinks while I put the potatoes on." In the kitchen, then, she stood with the refrigerator door open, her back to Carl, giving him time to notice the pistol. Finally he said, "Jesus, you're a cop."

She had rehearsed this moment. The idea: turn saying, "You guessed," sounding surprised; then look at the pistol and say something like "Nuts, I gave it away." But she didn't. He said, "Jesus, you're a cop," and she turned from the refrigerator with an ice tray and said, "Federal. I'm a U.S. marshal."

"I would never've guessed," Carl said, "not in a million years."

Thinking about it before, she didn't know if he'd wig out or what. She looked at him now, and he seemed to be taking it okay, smiling a little.

He said, "But why?"

"Why what?"

"Are you a marshal?"

"Well, first of all, my dad has a company, Marshall Sisco Investigations. . . ."

"You mean because of his name, Marshall?"

"What I am — they're not spelled the same. No, but as soon as I learned to drive I started doing surveillance jobs for him. Like following some guy who was trying to screw his insurance company, a phony claim. I got the idea of going into law enforcement. So after a couple of years at Miami I transferred to Florida Atlantic and got in their Criminal Justice program."

"I mean why not FBI, if you're gonna do it, or DEA?"

"Well, for one thing, I liked to smoke grass when I was younger, so DEA didn't appeal to me at all. Secret Service guys I met were so fucking secretive, you ask them a question, they'd go, 'You'll have to check with Washington on that.' See, different federal agents would come to school to give talks. I got to know a couple of marshals — we'd go out after, have a few beers, and I liked them. They're nice guys, condescending at first, naturally; but after a few years they got over it."

Carl was making drinks now, Early Times for Karen, Dewar's in his glass, both with a splash. Standing at the sink, letting the faucet run, he said, "What do you do?"

"I'm on court security this week. My regular assignment is warrants. We go after fugitives, most of them parole violators."

Carl handed her a drink. "Murderers?"

"If they were involved in a federal crime when they did it. Usually drugs."

"Bank robbery, that's federal, isn't it?"

"Yeah, some guys come out of corrections and go right back to work."

"You catch many?"

"Bank robbers?" Karen said, "Nine out of ten," looking right at him.

Carl raised his glass. "Cheers."

While they were having dinner at the kitchen table he said, "You're quiet this evening."

"I'm tired, I was on my feet all day, with a shotgun."

"I can't picture that," Carl said. "You don't look like a U.S. marshal, or any kind of cop."

"What do I look like?"

"A knockout. You're the best-looking girl I've ever been this close to. I got a pretty close look at Mary Elizabeth Mastrantonio, when they were here shooting *Scarface*? But you're a lot better looking. I like your freckles."

"I used to be loaded with them."

"You have some gravy on your chin. Right here."

Karen touched it with her napkin. She said, "I'd like to see your boat."

He was chewing pot roast and had to wait before saying, "I told you it was out of the water?"

"Yeah?"

"I don't have the boat anymore. It was repossessed when I fell behind in my payments."

"The bank sold it?"

"Yeah, Florida Southern. I didn't want to tell you when we first met. Get off to a shaky start."

"But now that you can tell me I've got gravy on my chin . . ."

"I didn't want you to think I was some kind of loser."

"What've you been doing since?"

"Working as a mate, up at Haulover."

"You still have your place, your apartment?"

"Yeah, I get paid, I can swing that, no problem."

"I have a friend in the marshals lives in North Miami, on Alamanda off a Hundred and twenty-fifth."

Carl nodded. "That's not far from me."

"You want to go out after?"

"I thought you were tired."

"I am."

"Then why don't we stay home?" Carl smiled. "What do you think?"

"Fine."

They made love in the dark. He wanted to turn the lamp on, but Karen said, no, leave it off.

Geraldine Regal, the first teller at Sun Federal on Kendall Drive, watched a man with slicked-back hair and sunglasses fishing in his inside coat pocket as he approached her window. It was 9:40, Tuesday morning. At first she thought the guy was Latin. Kind of cool, except that up close his hair looked shellacked, almost metallic. She wanted to ask him if it hurt. He brought papers, deposit slips, and a blank check from the pocket saying, "I'm gonna make this out for four thousand." Began filling out the check and said, "You hear about the woman trapeze artist, her husband's divorcing her?"

Geraldine said she didn't think so, smiling, because it was a little weird, a customer she'd never seen before telling her a joke.

"They're in court. The husband's lawyer asks her, 'Isn't it true that on Monday, March the fifth, hanging from the trapeze upside down, without a net, you had sex with the ringmaster, the lion tamer, two clowns, and a dwarf?'"

Geraldine waited. The man paused, head down as he finished making out the check. Now he looked up.

"The woman trapeze artist thinks for a minute and says, 'What was that date again?'"

Geraldine was laughing as he handed her the check, smiling as she saw it was a note written on a blank check, neatly printed in block letters, that said:

> THIS IS NO JOKE
> IT'S A STICKUP!
> I WANT $4,000 *NOW!*

Geraldine stopped smiling. The guy with the metallic hair was telling her he wanted it in hundreds, fifties, and twenties, loose, no bank straps or rubber bands, no bait money, no dye packs, no bills off the bottom of the drawer, and he wanted his note back. Now.

"The teller didn't have four grand in her drawer," Daniel Burdon said, "so the guy settled for twenty-eight hundred and was out of there. Slick changing his style — we *know* it's the same guy, with the shiny hair? Only now he's the Joker. The trouble is, see, I ain't Batman."

Daniel and Karen Sisco were in the hallway outside the central courtroom on the second floor, Daniel resting his long frame against the railing, where you could look below at the atrium, with its fountain and potted palms.

"No witness to see him hop in his BMW this time. The man coming to realize that was dumb, using his own car."

Karen said, "Or it's not Carl Tillman."

"You see him last night?"

"He came over."

"Yeah, how was it?"

Karen looked up at Daniel's deadpan expression. "I told him I was a federal agent and he didn't freak."

"So he's cool, huh?"

"He's a nice guy."

"Cordial. Tells jokes robbing banks. I talked to the people at Florida Southern, where he had his boat loan? Found out he was seeing one of the tellers. Not at the main office, one of their branches, girl named Kathy Lopez. Big brown eyes, cute as a puppy, just started working there. She's out with Tillman she tells him about her job, what she does, how she's counting money all day. I asked was Tillman interested, want to know anything in particular? Oh, yeah, he wanted to know what she was supposed to do if the bank ever got robbed. So she tells him about dye packs, how they work, how she gets a two-hundred-dollar bonus if she's ever robbed and can slip one in with the loot. The next time he's in, cute little Kathy Lopez shows him one, explains how you walk out the door with a pack of fake twenties? A half minute later the tear gas blows and you have that red shit all over you and the money you stole. I checked the reports on the other robberies he pulled? Every one of them he said to the teller, no dye packs or that bait money with the registered serial numbers."

"Making conversation," Karen said, trying hard to maintain her composure. "People like to talk about what they do."

Daniel smiled.

And Karen said, "Carl's not your man."

"Tell me why you're so sure."

"I know him. He's a good guy."

"Karen, you hear yourself? You're telling me what you feel, not what you know. Tell me about *him* — you like the way he dances, what?"

Karen didn't answer that one. She wanted Daniel to leave her alone.

He said, "Okay, you want to put a wager on it, you say Tillman's clean?"

That brought her back, hooked her, and she said, "How much?"

"You lose, you go out dancing with me."

"Great. And if I'm right, what do I get?"

"My undying respect," Daniel said.

As soon as Karen got home she called her dad at Marshall Sisco Investigations and told him about Carl Tillman, the robbery suspect in her life, and about Daniel Burdon's confident, condescending, smart-ass, irritating attitude.

Her dad said, "Is this guy colored?"

"Daniel?"

"I *know* he is. Friends of mine at Metro-Dade call him the white man's Burdon, on account of he gets on their nerves always being right. I mean your guy. There's a running back in the NFL named Tillman. I forget who he's with."

Karen said, "You're not helping any."

"The Tillman in the pros is colored — the reason I asked. I think he's with the Bears."

"Carl's white."

"Okay, and you say you're crazy about him?"

"I like him, a lot."

"But you aren't sure he isn't doing the banks."

"I said I can't believe he is."

"Why don't you ask him?"

"Come on — if he is he's not gonna tell me."

"How do you know?"

She didn't say anything and after a few moments her dad asked if she was still there.

"He's coming over tonight," Karen said.

"You want me to talk to him?"

"You're not serious."

"Then what'd you call me for?"

"I'm not sure what to do."

"Let the FBI work it."

"I'm supposed to be helping them."

"Yeah, but what good are you? You want to believe the guy's clean. Honey, the only way to find out if he is, you have to assume he isn't. You know what I'm saying? Why does a person rob banks? For money, yeah. But you have to be dumb, too, considering the odds against you, the security, cameras taking your picture. . . . So another reason could be the risk involved, it turns him on. The same reason he's playing around with you. . . ."

"He isn't playing around."

"I'm glad I didn't say, 'Sucking up to get information, see what you know.'"

"He's never mentioned banks." Karen paused. "Well, he might've once."

"You could bring it up, see how he reacts. He gets sweaty, call for backup. Look, whether he's playing around or loves you with all his heart, he's still risking twenty years. He doesn't know if you're on to him or not and that heightens the risk. It's like he thinks he's Cary Grant stealing jewels from the broad's home where he's having dinner, in his tux. But your guy's still dumb if he robs banks. You know all that. Your frame of mind, you just don't want to accept it."

"You think I should draw him out. See if I can set him up."

"Actually," her dad said, "I think you should find another boyfriend."

Karen remembered Christopher Walken in *The Dogs of War* placing his gun on a table in the front hall — the doorbell ringing — and laying a newspaper over the gun before he opened the door. She remembered it because at one time she was in love with Christopher Walken, not even caring that he wore his pants so high.

Carl reminded her some of Christopher Walken, the way he smiled with his eyes. He came a little after seven. Karen had on khaki shorts and a T-shirt, tennis shoes without socks.

"I thought we were going out."

They kissed and she touched his face, moving her hand lightly over his skin, smelling his after-shave, feeling the spot where his right earlobe was pierced.

"I'm making drinks," Karen said. "Let's have one and then I'll get ready." She started for the kitchen.

"Can I help?"

"You've been working all day. Sit down, relax."

It took her a couple of minutes. Karen returned to the living room with a drink in each hand, her leather bag hanging from her shoulder. "This one's yours." Carl took it and she dipped her shoulder to let the bag slip off and drop to the coffee table. Carl grinned.

"What've you got in there, a gun?"

"Two pounds of heavy metal. How was your day?"

They sat on the sofa and he told how it took almost four hours to land an eight-foot marlin, the leader wound around its bill. Carl said he worked his tail off hauling the fish aboard and the guy decided he didn't want it.

Karen said, "After you got back from Kendall?"

It gave him pause.

"Why do you think I was in Kendall?"

Carl had to wait while she sipped her drink.

"Didn't you stop by Florida Southern and withdraw twenty-eight hundred?"

That got him staring at her, but with no expression to speak of. Karen thinking, Tell me you were somewhere else and can prove it.

But he didn't; he kept staring.

"No dye packs, no bait money. Are you still seeing Kathy Lopez?"

Carl hunched over to put his drink on the coffee table and sat like that, leaning on his thighs, not looking at her now as Karen studied his profile, his elegant nose. She looked at his glass, his prints all over it, and felt sorry for him.

"Carl, you blew it."

He turned his head to look at her past his shoulder. He said, "I'm leaving," pushed up from the sofa and said, "If this is what you think of me . . ."

Karen said, "Carl, cut the shit," and put her drink down. Now, if he picked up her bag, that would cancel out any remaining doubts. She watched him pick up her bag. He got the Beretta out and let the bag drop.

"Carl, sit down. Will you, please?"

"I'm leaving. I'm walking out and you'll never see me again. But first . . ." He made her get a knife from the kitchen and cut the phone line in there and in the bedroom.

He *was* pretty dumb. In the living room again he said, "You know something? We could've made it."

Jesus. And he had seemed like such a cool guy. Karen watched him go to the front door and open it before turning to her again.

"How about letting me have five minutes? For old times' sake."

It was becoming embarrassing, sad. She said, "Carl, don't you understand? You're under arrest."

He said, "I don't want to hurt you, Karen, so don't try to stop me." He went out the door.

Karen walked over to the chest where she dropped her car keys and mail coming in the house: a bombé chest by the front door, the door still open. She laid aside the folded copy of the *Herald* she'd placed there over her Sig Sauer .38, picked up the pistol, and went out to the front stoop, into the yellow glow of the porch light. She saw Carl at his car now, its white shape pale against the dark street, only about forty feet away.

"Carl, don't make it hard, okay?"

He had the car door open and half turned to look back. "I said I don't want to hurt you."

Karen said, "Yeah, well . . . ," raised the pistol to rack the slide, and cupped her left hand under the grip. She said, "You move to get in the car, I'll shoot."

Carl turned his head again with a sad, wistful expression. "No you won't, sweetheart."

Don't say ciao, Karen thought. Please.

Carl said, "Ciao," turned to get in the car, and she shot him. Fired a single round at his left thigh and hit him where she'd aimed, in the fleshy part just below his butt. Carl howled and slumped inside against the seat and the steering wheel, his leg extended straight out, his hand gripping it, his eyes raised with a bewildered frown as Karen approached. The poor dumb guy looking at twenty years, and maybe a limp.

Karen felt she should say something. After all, for a few days there they were as intimate as two people can get. She thought about it for several moments, Carl staring up at her with rheumy eyes. Finally Karen said, "Carl, I want you to know I had a pretty good time, considering."

It was the best she could do.

MICHAEL MALONE

Red Clay

FROM *Murder for Love*

UP ON ITS short slope the columned front of our courthouse was
wavy in the August sun, like a courthouse in lake water. The leaves
hung from maples, and the flag of North Carolina wilted flat
against its metal pole. Heat sat sodden over Devereux County week
by relentless week; they called the weather "dog days," after the star,
Sirius, but none of us knew that. We thought they meant no dog
would leave shade for street on such days — no dog except a mad
one. I was ten that late August in 1959; I remembered the summer
because of the long heat wave, and because of Stella Doyle.

When they pushed open the doors, the policemen and lawyers
flung their arms up to their faces to block the sun and stopped
there in the doorway as if the hot light were shoving them back
inside. Stella Doyle came out last, a deputy on either side to walk
her down to where the patrol car, orange as Halloween candles,
waited to take her away until the jury could make up its mind about
what had happened two months earlier out at Red Hills. It was the
only house in the county big enough to have a name. It was where
Stella Doyle had, maybe, shot her husband, Hugh Doyle, to death.

Excitement over Doyle's murder had swarmed through the town
and stung us alive. No thrill would replace it until the assassination
of John F. Kennedy. Outside the courthouse, sidewalk heat steaming up through our shoes, we stood patiently waiting to hear Mrs.
Doyle found guilty. The news stood waiting, too, for she was, after
all, not merely the murderer of the wealthiest man we knew; she
was Stella Doyle. She was the movie star.

Papa's hand squeezed down on my shoulder and there was a

tight line to his mouth as he pulled me into the crowd and said, "Listen now, Buddy, if anybody ever asks you, when you're grown, 'Did you ever see the most beautiful woman God made in your lifetime,' son, you say 'Yes, I had that luck, and her name was Stella Dora Doyle.'" His voice got louder, right there in the crowd for everybody to hear. "You tell them how her beauty was so bright, it burned back the shame they tried to heap on her head, burned it right on back to scorch their faces."

Papa spoke these strange words looking up the steps at the almost plump woman in black the deputies were holding. His arms were folded over his seersucker vest, his fingers tight on the sleeves of his shirt. People around us had turned to stare and somebody snickered.

Embarrassed for him, I whispered, "Oh, Papa, she's nothing but an old murderer. Everybody knows how she got drunk and killed Mr. Doyle. She shot him right through the head with a gun."

Papa frowned. "You don't know that."

I kept on. "Everybody says she was so bad and drunk all the time, she wouldn't let folks even live in the same house with her. She made him throw out his own mama and papa."

Papa shook his head at me. "I don't like to hear ugly gossip coming out of your mouth, all right, Buddy?"

"Yes, sir."

"She didn't kill Hugh Doyle."

"Yes, sir."

His frown scared me; it was so rare. I stepped closer and took his hand, took his stand against the rest. I had no loyalty to this woman Papa thought so beautiful. I just could never bear to be cut loose from the safety of his good opinion. I suppose that from that moment on, I felt toward Stella Doyle something of what my father felt, though in the end perhaps she meant less to me, and stood for more. Papa never had my habit of symbolizing.

The courthouse steps were wide, uneven stone slabs. As Mrs. Doyle came down, the buzzing of the crowd hushed. All together, like trained dancers, people stepped back to clear a half-circle around the orange patrol car. Newsmen shoved their cameras to the front. She was rushed down so fast that her shoe caught in the crumbling stone and she fell against one of the deputies.

"She's drunk!" hooted a woman near me, a country woman in a flowered dress belted with a strip of painted rope. She and the child she jiggled against her shoulder were puffy with the fat of poverty. "Look'it her" — the woman pointed — "look at that dress. She thinks she's still out there in Hollywood." The woman beside her nodded, squinting out from under a visor of the kind of hat pier fishermen wear. "I went and killed my husband, wouldn't no rich lawyers come running to weasel me out of the law." She slapped at a fly's buzz.

Then they were quiet and everybody else was quiet and our circle of sun-stunned eyes fixed on the woman in black, stared at the wonder of one as high as Mrs. Doyle about to be brought so low.

Holding to the stiff, tan arm of the young deputy, Mrs. Doyle reached down to check the heel of her shoe. Black shoes, black suit and purse, wide black hat — they all sinned against us by their fashionableness, blazing wealth as well as death. She stood there, arrested a moment in the hot immobility of the air, then she hurried down, rushing the two big deputies down with her, to the open door of the orange patrol car. Papa stepped forward so quickly that the gap filled with people before I could follow him. I squeezed through, fighting with my elbows, and I saw that he was holding his straw hat in one hand and offering the other hand out to the murderer. "Stella, how are you? Clayton Hayes."

As she turned, I saw the strawberry-gold hair beneath the hat; then her hand, bright with a big diamond, took away the dark glasses. I saw what Papa meant. She was beautiful. Her eyes were the color of lilacs, but darker than lilacs. And her skin held the light like the inside of a shell. She was not like other pretty women, because the difference was not one of degree. I have never seen anyone else of her kind.

"Why, Clayton! God Almighty, it's been years."

"Well, yes, a long time now, I guess," he said, and shook her hand.

She took the hand in both of hers. "You look the same as ever. Is this your boy?" she said. The violet eyes turned to me.

"Yes, this is Buddy. Ada and I have six so far, three of each."

"Six? Are we that old, Clayton?" She smiled. "They said you'd married Ada Hackney."

A deputy cleared his throat. "Sorry, Clayton, we're going to have to get going."

"Just a minute, Lonnie. Listen, Stella, I just wanted you to know I'm sorry as I can be about your losing Hugh."

Tears welled in her eyes. "He did it himself, Clayton," she said.

"I know that. I know you didn't do this." Papa nodded slowly again and again, the way he did when he was listening. "I know that. Good luck to you."

She swatted tears away. "Thank you."

"I'm telling everybody I'm sure of that."

"Clayton, thank you."

Papa nodded again, then tilted his head back to give her his slow, peaceful smile. "You call Ada and me if there's ever something we can do to help you, you hear?" She kissed his cheek and he stepped back with me into the crowd of hostile, avid faces as she entered the police car. It moved slow as the sun through the sightseers. Cameras pushed against its windows.

A sallow man biting a pipe skipped down the steps to join some other reporters next to us. "Jury sent out for food," he told them. "No telling with these yokels. Could go either way." He pulled off his jacket and balled it under his arm. "Jesus, it's hot."

A younger reporter with thin, wet hair disagreed. "They all think Hollywood's Babylon and she's the whore. Hugh Doyle was the local prince, his daddy kept the mills open in the bad times, quote unquote half the rednecks in the county. They'll fry her. For that hat if nothing else."

"Could go either way," grinned the man with the pipe. "She was born in a shack six miles from here. Hat or no hat, that makes her one of them. So what if she did shoot the guy, he was dying of cancer anyhow, for Christ's sake. Well, she never could act worth the price of a bag of popcorn, but Jesus damn she was something to look at!"

Now that Stella Doyle was gone, people felt the heat again and went back to where they could sit still in the shade until the evening breeze and wait for the jury's decision. Papa and I walked back down Main Street to our furniture store. Papa owned a butcher shop, too, but he didn't like the meat business and wasn't very good at it, so my oldest brother ran it while Papa sat among the mahogany bedroom suites and red maple dining room sets in a big rocking chair and read, or talked to friends who dropped by. The rocker was actually for sale but he had sat in it for so long now that it was just Papa's chair. Three ceiling fans stirred against the quiet, shady air while he answered my questions about Stella Doyle.

He said that she grew up Stella Dora Hibble on Route 19, in a

three-room, tin-roofed little house propped off the red clay by concrete blocks — the kind of saggy-porched, pinewood house whose
owners leave on display in their dirt yard, like sculptures, the broken artifacts of their aspirations and the debris of their unmend-
able lives: the doorless refrigerator and the rusting car, the pyre of
metal and plastic that tells drivers along the highway "Dreams don't
last."

Stella's mother, Dora Hibble, had believed in dreams anyhow.
Dora had been a pretty girl who'd married a farmer and worked
harder than she had the health for, because hard work was necessary just to keep from going under. But in the evenings Mrs. Hibble
had looked at movie magazines. She had believed the romance was
out there and she wanted it, if not for her, for her children. At
twenty-seven, Dora Hibble died during her fifth labor. Stella was
eight when she watched from the door of the bedroom as they covered her mother's face with a thin blanket. When Stella was fourteen, her father died when a machine jammed at Doyle Mills. When
Stella was sixteen, Hugh Doyle, Jr., who was her age, my father's
age, fell in love with her.

"Did you love her, too, Papa?"

"Oh, yes. All us boys in town were crazy about Stella Dora, one
time or another. I had my attack of it, same as the rest. We were
sweethearts in seventh grade. I bought a big-size Whitman's Sam-
pler on Valentine's. I remember it cost every cent I had."

"Why were y'all crazy about her?"

"I guess you'd have to worry you'd missed out on being alive if
you didn't feel that way about Stella, one time or another."

I was feeling a terrible emotion I later defined as jealousy. "But
didn't you love Mama?"

"Well, now, this was before it was my luck to meet your mama."

"And you met her coming to town along the railroad track and
you told your friends 'That's the girl for me and I'm going to marry
her,' didn't you?"

"Yes, sir, and I was right on both counts." Papa rocked back in the
big chair, his hands peaceful on the armrests.

"Was Stella Dora still crazy about you after you met Mama?"

His face crinkled into the lines of his reply laughter. "No, sir, she
wasn't. She loved Hugh Doyle, minute she laid eyes on him, and he
felt the same. But Stella had this notion about going off to get to be

somebody in the movies. And Hugh couldn't hold her back, and I guess she couldn't get him to see what it was made her want to go off so bad either."

"What was it made her want to go?"

Papa smiled at me. "Well, I don't know, son. What makes you want to go off so bad? You're always saying you're going here, and there, 'cross the world, up to the moon. I reckon you're more like Stella than I am."

"Do you think she was wrong to want to go be in the movies?"

"No."

"You don't think she killed him?"

"No, sir, I don't."

"Somebody killed him."

"Well, Buddy, sometimes people lose hope and heart and feel like they can't go on living."

"Yeah, I know. Suicide."

Papa's shoes tapped the floor as the rocker creaked back and forth. "That's right. Now you tell me, why're you sitting in here? Why don't you ride your bike on over to the ballpark and see who's there?"

"I want to hear about Stella Doyle."

"You want to hear. Well. Let's go get us a Coca-Cola, then. I don't guess somebody's planning to show up in this heat to buy a chest of drawers they got to haul home."

"You ought to sell air conditioners, Papa. People would buy air conditioners."

"I guess so."

So Papa told me the story. Or at least his version of it. He said Hugh and Stella were meant for each other. From the beginning it seemed to the whole town a fact as natural as harvest that so much money and so much beauty belonged together, and only Hugh Doyle with his long, free, easy stride was rich enough to match the looks of Stella Dora. But even Hugh Doyle couldn't hold her. He was only halfway through the state university, where his father had told him he'd have to go before he married Stella, if he wanted a home to bring her to, when she quit her job at Coldsteam's beauty parlor and took the bus to California. She was out there for six years before Hugh broke down and went after her.

By then every girl in the county was cutting Stella's pictures out of the movie magazines and reading how she got her lucky break, how she married a big director and divorced him, and married a big star, and how that marriage broke up even quicker. Photographers traveled all the way to Thermopylae to take pictures of where she was born. People tried to tell them her house was gone, had fallen down and had been used for firewood, but they just took photographs of Reverend Ballister's house instead and said Stella had grown up in it. Before long, even local girls would go stand in front of the Ballister house like a shrine, sometimes they'd steal flowers out of the yard. The year that *Fever*, her best movie, came to the Grand Theater on Main Street, Hugh Doyle flew out to Los Angeles and won her back. He took her down to Mexico to divorce the baseball player she'd married after the big star. Then Hugh married her himself and put her on an ocean liner and took her all over the world. For a whole two years, they didn't come home to Thermopylae. Everybody in the county talked about this two-year honeymoon, and Hugh's father confessed to some friends that he was disgusted by his son's way of life.

But when the couple did come home, Hugh walked right into the mills and turned a profit. His father confessed to the same friends that he was flabbergasted Hugh had it in him. But after the father died Hugh started drinking and Stella joined him. The parties got a little wild. The fights got loud. People talked. They said he had other women. They said Stella'd been locked up in a sanatorium. They said the Doyles were breaking up.

And then one June day a maid at Red Hills, walking to work before the morning heat, fell over something that lay across a path to the stables. And it was Hugh Doyle in riding clothes with a hole torn in the side of his head. Not far from his gloved hand, the police found Stella's pistol, already too hot from the sun to touch. The cook testified that the Doyles had been fighting like cats and dogs all night long the night before, and Hugh's mother testified that he wanted to divorce Stella but she wouldn't let him, and so Stella was arrested. She said she was innocent, but it was her gun, she was his heir, and she had no alibi. Her trial lasted almost as long as that August heat wave.

A neighbor strolled past the porch, where we sat out the evening heat, waiting for the air to lift. "Jury's still out," he said. Mama waved her hand at him. She pushed herself and me in the big green wood swing that hung from two chains to the porch roof, and answered my questions about Stella Doyle. She said, "Oh, yes, they all said Stella was 'specially pretty. I never knew her to talk to myself."

"But if Papa liked her so much, why didn't y'all get invited out to their house and everything?"

"Her and your papa just went to school together, that's all. That was a long time back. The Doyles wouldn't ask folks like us over to Red Hills."

"Why not? Papa's family used to have a *whole* lot of money. That's what you said. And Papa went right up to Mrs. Doyle at the courthouse today, right in front of everybody. He told her, You let us know if there's anything we can do."

Mama chuckled the way she always did about Papa, a low ripple like a pigeon nesting, a little exasperated at having to sit still so long. "You know your papa'd offer to help out anybody he figured might be in trouble, white or black. That's just him; that's not any Stella Dora Doyle. Your papa's just a good man. You remember that, Buddy."

Goodness was Papa's stock-in-trade; it was what he had instead of money or ambition, and Mama often reminded us of it. In him she kept safe all the kindness she had never felt she could afford for herself. She, who could neither read nor write, who had stood all day in a cigarette factory from the age of nine until the morning Papa married her, was a fighter. She wanted her children to go farther than Papa had. Still, for years after he died, she would carry down from the attic the yellow mildewed ledgers where his value was recorded in more than $75,000 of out-of-date bills he had been unwilling to force people in trouble to pay. Running her sun-spotted finger down the brown wisps of names and the money they'd owed, she would sigh that proud, exasperated ripple, and shake her head over foolish, generous Papa.

Through the front parlor window I could hear my sisters practicing the theme from *The Apartment* on the piano. Someone across the street turned on a light. Then we heard the sound of Papa's shoes coming a little faster than usual down the sidewalk. He turned at the hedge, carrying the package of shiny butcher's paper in which he brought meat home every evening. "Verdict just came in!" he called out happily. "Not guilty! Jury came back about forty minutes ago. They already took her home."

Mama took the package and sat Papa down in the swing next to her. "Well, well," she said. "They let her off."

"Never ought to have come up for trial in the first place, Ada, like I told everybody all along. It's like her lawyers showed. Hugh went down to Atlanta, saw that doctor, found out he had cancer, and he took his own life. Stella never even knew he was sick."

Mama patted his knee. "Not guilty; well, well."

Papa made a noise of disgust. "Can you believe some folks out on Main Street tonight are all fired up *because* Stella got off! Adele Simpson acted downright indignant!"

Mama said, "And you're surprised?" And she shook her head with me at Papa's innocence.

Talking of the trial, my parents made one shadow along the wood floor of the porch, while inside my sisters played endless variations of "Chopsticks," the notes handed down by ghostly creators long passed away.

A few weeks later, Papa was invited to Red Hills, and he let me come along; we brought a basket of sausage biscuits Mama had made for Mrs. Doyle.

As soon as Papa drove past the wide white gate, I learned how money could change even weather. It was cooler at Red Hills, and the grass was the greenest grass in the country. A black man in a black suit let us into the house, then led us down a wide hallway of pale yellow wood into a big room shuttered against the heat. She was there in an armchair almost the color of her eyes. She wore loose-legged pants and was pouring whiskey from a bottle into a glass.

"Clayton, thanks for coming. Hello there, little Buddy. Look, I hope I didn't drag you from business."

Papa laughed. "Stella, I could stay gone a week and never miss a customer." It embarrassed me to hear him admit such failure to her.

She said she could tell I liked books, so maybe I wouldn't mind if they left me there to read while she borrowed my daddy for a little bit. There were white shelves in the room, full of books. I said I didn't mind but I did; I wanted to keep on seeing her. Even with the loose shirt soiled and rumpled over a waist she tried to hide, even with her face swollen from heat and drink and grief, she was something you wanted to look at as long as possible.

They left me alone. On the white piano were dozens of photographs of Stella Doyle in silver frames. From a big painting over the

mantelpiece her remarkable eyes followed me around the room. I
looked at that painting as sun deepened across it, until finally she
and Papa came back. She had a tissue to her nose, a new drink in
her hand. "I'm sorry, honey," she said to me. "Your daddy's been
sweet letting me run on. I just needed somebody to talk to for a
while about what happened to me." She kissed the top of my head
and I could feel her warm lips at the part in my hair.

We followed her down the wide hall out onto the porch. "Clayton, you'll forgive a fat old souse talking your ear off and bawling
like a jackass."

"No such thing, Stella."

"And you *never* thought I killed him, even when you first heard.
My God, thank you."

Papa took her hand again. "You take care now," he said.

Then suddenly she was hugging herself, rocking from side to
side. Words burst from her like a door flung open by wind. "I could
kick him in the ass, that bastard! Why didn't he tell me? To quit, to
quit, and use *my* gun, and just about get me strapped in the gas
chamber, that goddamn bastard, and never say a word!" Her pro-
fanity must have shocked Papa as much as it did me. He never used
it, much less ever heard it from a woman.

But he nodded and said, "Well, good-bye, I guess, Stella. Probably
won't be seeing you again."

"Oh, Lord, Clayton, I'll be back. The world's so goddamn little."

She stood at the top of the porch, tears wet in those violet eyes
that the movie magazines had loved to talk about. On her cheek a
mosquito bite flamed like a slap. Holding to the big white column,
she waved as we drove off into the dusty heat. Ice flew from the glass
in her hand like diamonds.

Papa was right; they never met again. Papa lost his legs from diabetes, but he'd never gone much of anywhere even before that. And
afterward, he was one of two places — home or the store. He'd sit
in his big wood wheelchair in the furniture store, with his hands
peaceful on the armrests, talking with whoever came by.

I did see Stella Doyle again; the first time in Belgium, twelve years
later. I went farther than Papa.

In Bruges there are small restaurants that lean like elegant elbows on the canals and glance down at passing pleasure boats.
Stella Doyle was sitting, one evening, at a table in the crook of the

elbow of one of them, against an iron railing that curved its reflection in the water. She was alone there when I saw her. She stood, leaned over the rail, and slipped the ice cubes from her glass into the canal. I was in a motor launch full of tourists passing below. She waved with a smile at us and we waved back. It had been a lot of years since her last picture, but probably she waved out of habit. For the tourists motoring past, Stella in white against the dark restaurant was another snapshot of Bruges. For me, she was home and memory. I craned to look back as long as I could, and leapt from the boat at the next possible stop.

When I found the restaurant, she was yelling at a well-dressed young man who was leaning across the table, trying to soothe her in French. They appeared to be quarreling over his late arrival. All at once she hit him, her diamond flashing into his face. He filled the air with angry gestures, then turned and left, a white napkin to his cheek. I was made very shy by what I'd seen — the young man was scarcely older than I was. I stood unable to speak until her staring at me jarred me forward. I said, "Mrs. Doyle? I'm Buddy Hayes. I came out to see you at Red Hills with my father, Clayton Hayes, one time. You let me look at your books."

She sat back down and poured herself a glass of wine. "You're *that* little boy? God Almighty, how old am I? Am I a hundred yet?" Her laugh had been loosened by the wine. "Well, a Red Clay rambler, like me. How 'bout that. Sit down. What are *you* doing over here?"

I told her, as nonchalantly as I could manage, that I was traveling on college prize money, a journalism award. I wrote a prize essay about a murder trial.

"Mine?" she asked, and laughed.

A waiter, plump and flushed in his neat black suit, trotted to her side. He shook his head at the untouched plates of food. "Madame, your friend has left, then?"

Stella said, "Mister, I helped him along. And turns out, he was no friend."

The waiter then turned his eyes, sad and reproachful, to the trout on the plate.

"How about another bottle of that wine and a great big bucket of ice?" Stella asked.

The waiter kept flapping his fat quick hands around his head, entreating us to come inside. *"Les moustiques, madame!"*

"I just let them bite," she said. He went away grieved.

She was slender now, and elegantly dressed. And while her hands and throat were older, the eyes hadn't changed, nor the red-gold hair. She was still the most beautiful woman God had made in my lifetime, the woman of whom my father had said that any man who had not desired her had missed out on being alive, the one for whose honor my father had turned his back on the whole town of Thermopylae. Because of Papa, I had entered my adolescence day-dreaming about fighting for Stella Doyle's honor; we had starred together in a dozen of her movies: I dazzled her jury; I cured Hugh Doyle while hiding my own noble love for his wife. And now here I sat drinking wine with her on a veranda in Bruges; me, the first Hayes ever to win a college prize, ever to get to college. Here I sat with a movie star.

She finished her cigarette, dropped it spinning down into the black canal. "You look like him," she said. "Your papa. I'm sorry to hear that about the diabetes."

"I look like him, but I don't think like him," I told her.

She tipped the wine bottle upside down in the bucket. "You want the world," she said. "Go get it, honey."

"That's what my father doesn't understand."

"He's a good man," she answered. She stood up slowly. "And I think Clayton would want me to get you to your hotel."

All the fenders of her Mercedes were crushed. She said, "When I've had a few drinks, I need a strong car between me and the rest of the cockeyed world."

The big car bounced over the moon-white street. "You know what, Buddy? Hugh Doyle gave me my first Mercedes, one morning in Paris. At breakfast. He held the keys out in his hand like a damn daffodil he'd picked in the yard. He gave me *this* goddamn thing." She waved her finger with its huge diamond. "This damn thing was tied to my big toe one Christmas morning!" And she smiled up at the stars as if Hugh Doyle were up there tying diamonds on them. "He had a beautiful grin, Buddy, but he was a son of a bitch."

The car bumped to a stop on the curb outside my little hotel. "Don't miss your train tomorrow," she said. "And you listen to me, don't go back home; go on to Rome."

"I'm not sure I have time."

She looked at me. "*Take* time. Just take it. Don't get scared, honey."

Then she put her hand in my jacket pocket and the moon came around her hair, and my heart panicked crazily, thudding against my shirt, thinking she might kiss me. But her hand went away, and all she said was, "Say hi to Clayton when you get home, all right? Even losing his legs and all, your daddy's lucky, you know that?"

I said, "I don't see how."

"Oh, I didn't either till I was a lot older than you. And had my damn in-laws trying to throw me into the gas chamber. Go to bed. So long, Red Clay."

Her silver car floated away. In my pocket, I found a large wad of French money, enough to take me to Rome, and a little ribboned box, clearly a gift she had decided not to give the angry young man in the beautiful suit who'd arrived too late. On black velvet lay a man's wristwatch, reddish gold.

It's an extremely handsome watch, and it still tells me the time.

I only went home to Thermopylae for the funerals. It was the worst of the August dog days when Papa died in the hospital bed they'd set up next to his and Mama's big four poster in their bedroom. At his grave, the clots of red clay had already dried to a dusty dull color by the time we shoveled them down upon him, friend after friend taking a turn at the shovel. The petals that fell from roses fell limp to the red earth, wilted like the crowd who stood by the grave while Reverend Ballister told us that Clayton Hayes was "a good man." Behind a cluster of Mama's family, I saw a woman in black turn away and walk down the grassy incline to a car, a Mercedes.

After the services I went driving, but I couldn't outtravel Papa in Devereux County. The man at the gas pump listed Papa's virtues as he cleaned my windshield. The woman who sold me the bottle of bourbon said she'd owed Papa $215.00 since 1944, and when she'd paid him back in 1966 he'd forgotten all about it. I drove along the highway where the foundations of tin-roofed shacks were covered now by the parking lots of minimalls; beneath the asphalt, somewhere, was Stella Doyle's birthplace. Stella Dora Hibble, Papa's first love.

Past the white gates, the Red Hills lawn was as parched as the rest of the county. Paint blistered and peeled on the big white columns. I waited a long time before the elderly black man I'd met twenty years before opened the door irritably.

I heard her voice from the shadowy hall yelling, "Jonas! Let him in."

On the white shelves the books were the same. The photos on the piano as young as ever. She frowned so strangely when I came into the room. I thought she must have been expecting someone else and didn't recognize me.

"I'm Buddy Hayes, Clayton's —"

"I know who you are."

"I saw you leaving the cemetery. . . ."

"I know you did."

I held out the bottle.

Together we finished the bourbon in memory of Papa, while shutters beat back the sun, hid some of the dirty glasses scattered on the floor, hid Stella Doyle in her lilac armchair. Cigarette burns scarred the armrests, left their marks on the oak floor. Behind her the big portrait showed Time up for the heartless bastard he is. Her hair was cropped short, and gray. Only the color of her eyes had stayed the same; they looked as remarkable as ever in the swollen face.

"I came out here to bring you something."

"What?"

I gave her the thin, cheap, yellowed envelope I'd found in Papa's desk with his special letters and papers. It was addressed in neat, cursive pencil to "Clayton." Inside was a silly Valentine card. Betty Boop popping bonbons into her pouty lips, exclaiming "Ooooh, I'm sweet on you." It was childish and lascivious at the same time, and it was signed with a lipstick blot, now brown with age, and with the name "Stella," surrounded by a heart.

I said, "He must have kept this since the seventh grade."

She nodded. "Clayton was a good man." Her cigarette fell from her ashtray onto the floor. When I came over to pick it up, she said, "Goodness is luck; like money, like looks. Clayton was lucky that way." She went to the piano and took more ice from the bucket there; one piece she rubbed around the back of her neck then dropped into her glass. She turned, the eyes wet, like lilac stars. "You know, in Hollywood, they said, '*Hibble*?! What kind of hick name is that, we can't use that!' So I said, 'Use Doyle, then.' I mean, I took Hugh's name six years before he ever came out to get me. Because I knew he'd come. The day I left Thermopylae he kept yelling at me, 'You can't have both!' He kept yelling it while the bus was pulling out. 'You can't have me and it both!' He wanted to rip my heart out for leaving, for *wanting* to go." Stella moved along the curve of the white piano to a photograph of Hugh Doyle in a white open shirt, grinning straight out at the sun. She said, "But I could have both. There were only two things I *had* to have in this little world, and one was the lead in a movie called *Fever,* and the other one was Hugh Doyle." She put the photograph down carefully. "I didn't know about the cancer till my lawyers found out he'd been to see that doctor in Atlanta. Then it was easy to get the jury to go for suicide." She smiled at me. "Well, not easy. But we turned them around. I think your papa was the only man in town who *never* thought I was guilty."

It took me a while to take it in. "Well, he sure convinced me," I said.

"I expect he convinced a lot of people. Everybody thought so much of Clayton."

"You killed your husband."

We looked at each other. I shook my head. "Why?"

She shrugged. "We had a fight. We were drunk. He was sleeping with my fucking maid. I was crazy. Lots of reasons, no reason. I sure didn't plan it."

"You sure didn't confess it either."

"What good would that have done? Hugh was dead. I wasn't about to let his snooty-assed mother shove me in the gas chamber and pocket the money."

I shook my head. "Jesus. And you've never felt a day's guilt, have you?"

Her head tilted back, smoothing her throat. The shuttered sun had fallen down the room onto the floor, and evening light did a movie fade and turned Stella Doyle into the star in the painting behind her. "Ah, baby, don't believe it," she said. The room stayed quiet.

I stood up and dropped the empty bottle in the wastebasket. I said, "Papa told me how he was in love with you."

Her laugh came warmly through the shuttered dusk. "Yes, and I guess I was sweet on him, too, boop boop dedoo."

"Yeah, Papa said no man could say he'd been alive if he'd seen you and not felt that way. I just wanted to tell you I know what he meant." I raised my hand to wave good-bye.

"Come over here," she said, and I went to her chair and she

reached up and brought my head down to her and kissed me full and long on the mouth. "So long, Buddy." Slowly her hand moved down my face, the huge diamond radiant.

News came over the wire. The tabloids played with it for a few days on back pages. They had some pictures. They dug up the Hugh Doyle trial photos to put beside the old studio glossies. The dramatic death of an old movie star was worth sending a news camera down to Thermopylae, North Carolina, to get a shot of the charred ruin that had once been Red Hills. A shot of the funeral parlor and the flowers on the casket.

My sister phoned me that there was even a crowd at the coroner's inquest at the courthouse. They said Stella Doyle had died in her sleep after a cigarette set fire to her mattress. But rumors started that her body had been found at the foot of the stairs, as if she'd been trying to escape the fire but had fallen. They said she was drunk. They buried her beside Hugh Doyle in the family plot, the fanciest tomb in the Methodist cemetery, not far from where my parents were buried. Not long after she died, one of the cable networks did a night of her movies. I stayed up to watch *Fever* again.

My wife said, "Buddy, I'm sorry, but this is the biggest bunch of sentimental slop I ever saw. The whore'll sell her jewels and get the medicine and they'll beat the epidemic but she'll die to pay for her past and then the town'll see she was really a saint. Am I right?"

"You're right."

She sat down to watch awhile. "You know, I can't decide if she's a really lousy actress or a really good one. It's weird."

I said, "Actually, I think she was a much better actress than anyone gave her credit for."

My wife went to bed, but I watched through the night. I sat in Papa's old rocking chair that I'd brought north with me after his death. Finally, at dawn I turned off the set, and Stella's face disappeared into a star, and went out. The reception was awful and the screen too small. Besides, the last movie was in black and white; I couldn't see her eyes as well as I could remember the shock of their color, when she first turned toward me at the foot of the courthouse steps, that hot August day when I was ten, when my father stepped forward out of the crowd to take her hand, when her eyes were lilacs turned up to his face, and his straw hat in the summer sun was shining like a knight's helmet.

MABEL MANEY

Mrs. Feeley Is Quite Mad

FROM *Out for More Blood: Tales of Malice and Retaliation by Women*

For Miss Tinkham and Mrs. Rasmussen

MONDAY, FEBRUARY 5, Mrs. Feeley, of 37 Badger Avenue, did her wash, as usual. It was a gray day. Mrs. Feeley, as usual, first soaked Mr. Feeley's shirts in a concentrate of Duz detergent, thirty-nine cents for the large-size box *that week only* at the new Piggly-Wiggly. Then she scrubbed the collars and cuffs with a little scrub brush, five cents from the five-and-dime, put the shirts through the hand wringer, and hung them on the clothesline out back to dry. There were storm clouds in the eastern sky, so Mrs. Feeley clipped Mr. Feeley's wet shirts to a makeshift line in the basement, something she knew would annoy Mr. Feeley terribly but couldn't be helped.

"There's a place for everything, and everything in its place," Mr. Feeley had scolded Mrs. Feeley once when he had come home early and found his good shirts hanging in the dark cellar. If they had a telephone, Mr. Feeley could notify Mrs. Feeley that he was coming home at an unexpected hour, but a private telephone was a luxury the Feeleys could ill afford.

Mr. Feeley had put up the clothesline in the back yard himself, thus saving a tidy sum, and so rightly preferred Mrs. Feeley use it as it was meant to be used and not as a resting place for the chickadees and sparrows that came around looking for bird seed, three cents a pound at Smith's Hardware, paid for by Mrs. Feeley out of her personal allowance with which she purchased stockings, facial powder, and other female fripperies.

Mr. Feeley, who was good with money and other important things, kept track of Mrs. Feeley's expenditures since it was clear that Mrs. Feeley, who had no head for numbers, would give the coat off her back to anyone with a hard-luck story and a sad smile. The coat was a perfectly good red wool, three-quarter-length overcoat with a smart squirrel collar that was only a little worn in places and with care would see Mrs. Feeley through many more harsh winters.

Mrs. Feeley had never worked in her entire life and so didn't know the true cost of things. Some women like poor Mrs. Bederhoeffer from the Rotary Club had learned this lesson the hard way. Mr. Bederhoeffer had gone hunting one day and never returned, and was later spotted in Chicago with his secretary, Miss Dithers. Mrs. Bederhoeffer would die old and alone in a little room at her sister's. Thank goodness for Mr. Feeley, who was as loyal as the day was long.

Tuesday, after Mrs. Feeley had finished the breakfast dishes, she took Mr. Feeley's shirts from the line and sprinkled them with water from a 7-Up bottle with tiny holes punched through the cap. She had made it herself using a number-two sewing needle and a hammer. Making things yourself saves you money. Mrs. Feeley had driven the needle through her nail only once and that had stopped bleeding by the time Mr. Feeley had returned home for supper. Mr. Feeley had been quick to point out that what little Mrs. Feeley had saved she had wasted in bandages for her finger. Mrs. Feeley was to remember that most accidents happen in the home, Mr. Feeley told her.

After Mr. Feeley's shirts were sufficiently dampened, Mrs. Feeley rolled them into tight bundles, squeezed them into plastic bread wrappers, and stacked them in an orderly fashion in the giant stainless-steel deep-freeze in the cellar, a gift from Mr. Feeley on the occasion of her sixtieth birthday, almost exactly one year ago. Mrs. Feeley had secretly wished for a modern freezer like her best friend Myra Meeks's, which was pink and went so well with her white-and-gold Formica kitchen set, but Mr. Feeley said the large commercial freezer was more economical. Mr. Feeley could bring home entire cows bought wholesale, and Mrs. Feeley could carve them with a large cleaver Mr. Feeley kept razor sharp. Mrs. Feeley often felt faint as she sawed through muscle and flesh, but she knew the savings were great and so never complained.

Mr. Feeley had gotten the idea from their next-door neighbor, Mrs. Mertz, a retired home economics teacher who ran her household as tight as a battleship. Since Mrs. Mertz was a widow, Mr. Feeley helped her with difficult chores. Not only was he a good neighbor, he picked up many helpful household tips for Mrs. Feeley.

The bottom of the freezer was lined with tidy bundles of meat, wrapped in white butcher paper and marked with a big black grease pencil. Flank. Rump. Tongue. Liver. A dozen smaller bundles occupied a corner of the deep-freeze. It was venison Mr. Feeley brought home every week, gifts from the men at work who appreciated Mr. Feeley's careful handling of their money, Mr. Feeley being a loan officer at the biggest bank in town. Some of the meat had been there for a whole year now, but Mr. Feeley had instructed Mrs. Feeley to leave it be. Mrs. Feeley figured the meat was gamy to begin with; otherwise, it would have found its way to the supper table long ago, as theirs was a frugal household.

Mr. Feeley was simply too nice to hurt anyone's feelings by turning down their gift. Besides, the freezer was so big there was plenty of room for the casseroles and vegetables Mrs. Feeley spent her afternoons putting up, not to mention Mr. Feeley's shirts. The freezer was big enough to hold a body, Myra had once pointed out, with a little laugh. It gave Mrs. Feeley the shivers every time she went downstairs.

The freezer had belonged to a butcher driven out of business by the Piggly-Wiggly supermarket and was just a tiny bit stained inside with blood. The prices were better at the Piggly-Wiggly so Mrs. Feeley shopped there now, from a list Mr. Feeley prepared for her before he went to work. It kept her from acting impulsively.

Mrs. Feeley always felt like a traitor when she walked past the small shops owned by people who had always seemed genuinely interested in her well-being. Mrs. Pringle from the bakery had even gifted Mrs. Feeley with a little pink birthday cake on her sixtieth, and everyone in the store had sung "Happy Birthday," but once Mr. Feeley had made up his mind, there was no arguing with him.

"There's a place for everything and everything in its place," Mr. Feeley had said. Clothes belonged on the clothesline, birds in the sky, and money in the bank.

Mrs. Feeley's birthday was Friday, her regular shopping day, and this year she wasn't at all looking forward to it. Last year Myra had given her a lovely rayon housecoat and matching slippers that were far too elegant for someone like Mrs. Feeley. This year Myra was at her daughter's in Cleveland helping with a new baby, a girl, so there would be no one to sing to Mrs. Feeley. Friday night was Mr. Feeley's night out with the boys. Soon Mr. Feeley would retire and be home all day, every day.

Wednesday Mrs. Feeley took Mr. Feeley's stiff, icy shirts from the freezer and, after they thawed, pressed them good and flat with an old iron heated on the gas range. The results were almost as good as a professional presser at no cost whatsoever. Mrs. Feeley sometimes felt as though she would snap in two from the effort.

Mrs. Feeley decided she would ask Mr. Feeley that very night if they could purchase a lightweight electric iron with temperature controls and a durable safety cord. It would be her birthday gift. An advertisement in *Good Housekeeping* magazine promised it would make her ironing day a breeze. A photograph of skating star Sonja Henie illustrated this point. Mrs. Feeley's iron would glide over the cold, hard mountain of shirts like a lady skater gliding over the ice.

Myra had been a wonderful skater as a girl, so Mrs. Feeley had carefully cut out the photograph and put it in the top drawer of her sewing chest to show her later.

As she ironed, Mrs. Feeley began to smile. She imagined herself perched on gleaming white skates doing figure-eights while the ladies from the Rotary Club applauded politely. Then she imagined she was skating with Myra, her best friend in the world, and almost burned Mr. Feeley's favorite shirt!

Now that Myra was a widow and long out of mourning, she went on glamorous trips to faraway places, often inviting Mrs. Feeley along, free of charge. Short leisure trips interrupted household duties and caused havoc to Mr. Feeley, who relied on Mrs. Feeley to keep the home-fires burning while Mr. Feeley worked hard to ensure them a future in an unstable world. Just that morning Mrs. Feeley had received a postcard from the Snow Carnival in Cleveland, which only reminded Mrs. Feeley again of the electric iron she so badly wanted.

That night when Mrs. Feeley tried to bring up the subject of the iron she got confused and, to her horror, found herself telling Mr. Feeley that she wished to become a figure skater! Mr. Feeley looked alarmed but said nothing. After a while he asked Mrs. Feeley to pass the mashed potatoes. Later, while in the cellar getting sausage for the next day's breakfast, Mrs. Feeley convinced herself that Mr. Feeley hadn't heard her at all. Mrs. Feeley was awfully relieved. Many of the women in Mrs. Feeley's family had lived long, unhappy lives with no one to care for them. Mrs. Feeley was fortunate. She and Mr. Feeley would be together until death.

Thursday, as Mrs. Feeley mended the frayed cuffs of Mr. Feeley's shirts and replaced chipped buttons, she got the surprise of her life. The afternoon mail brought with it a bus ticket and a note from Myra begging her to spend her birthday in Cleveland. In her excitement, Mrs. Feeley, who hadn't gone anywhere since her honeymoon, almost forgot about the prunes stewing on the stove. The bus would leave Friday after breakfast and, after a stopover in Chicago, would arrive in Cleveland at noon. Mrs. Feeley would return first thing Monday morning, leaving plenty of time to start her wash.

Confident that Mr. Feeley would never miss her, Mrs. Feeley packed her suitcase, the same one she had taken on her honeymoon, laid the dinner dishes on the dining room table, and waited for Mr. Feeley. She spent the afternoon rehearsing her conversation with Mr. Feeley.

But before she could finish telling Mr. Feeley about the free ticket, Mr. Feeley announced that he had news of his own. He was going hunting. He would leave right after work tomorrow and be gone the entire weekend. Mr. Feeley would need his hunting clothes, sandwiches, and beer. While he spent the evening cleaning his rifle, Mrs. Feeley must run to the supermarket before it closed and get some of that tasty spiced ham in a can, for sandwiches. Mr. Feeley didn't intend to come home after work tomorrow. He would take his things with him.

Mrs. Feeley threw on her worn red coat with the squirrel collar and practically ran to the Piggly-Wiggly. Success was assured, for even Mr. Feeley would see how practical it was for her to go away at the same time. She told everyone, even the sour store manager who never smiled at her, that Mr. Feeley was going hunting. The man who sold her the spiced ham stared at her just like Mr. Feeley did when Mrs. Feeley prattled on too long about insignificant things, as she was wont to do.

Mrs. Feeley realized with a start that she had run out of the house without her coupons, and spiced ham was on sale that week, six cans for one dollar *with coupon only*. The store manager promised she could bring her coupon tomorrow and he would give her the extra two cans, but tonight she could only have four. Mrs. Feeley ran home praying Mr. Feeley wouldn't want more than four sandwiches, only to find a startling scene in her kitchen. Her most private things, including the lovely rayon housecoat and matching slippers from Myra, were heaped in a pile on the worn linoleum kitchen floor and her suitcase was nowhere to be found.

Had Mrs. Feeley been robbed?

Mrs. Feeley jumped when she heard something lumbering about in the cellar. Mrs. Feeley tiptoed down the stairs and was surprised to see Mr. Feeley standing near the stainless-steel deep-freeze, a package of that old venison from the boys at work in his hand. Mr. Feeley was a big man with hands like hams who moved clumsily through the world. Mr. Feeley had blurted out an abrupt proposal of marriage just weeks after his mother's death. No one else had wanted Mrs. Feeley. No one else had even asked.

Her suitcase, the one she had had long before she married Mr. Feeley, lay open nearby, packed with neat bundles of meat. Luckily, Mrs. Feeley's maiden name had also begun with an F, and so she hadn't had to get any new luggage when she married.

Mrs. Feeley cringed. The meat would thaw overnight and ruin her only suitcase! Mrs. Feeley plopped down heavily on the creaky wooden stairs and tried to stop the fluttering in her chest. How could she go to Cleveland now?

"Mr. Feeley, have you lost your mind?" Mrs. Feeley surprised herself by crying out. After thirty-five years of marriage, she knew full well that Mr. Feeley hated to converse after a hard day at work.

Mr. Feeley placed another neat bundle of meat into the suitcase, then turned to look at Mrs. Feeley.

"Mrs. Feeley," he said, running his hand over his faded brown hair, or what was left of it, "Mrs. Feeley, I'm leaving you." He said it in the same tone of voice one might have used when reporting the weather. *Showers are expected for this evening, but look for sunshine tomorrow.*

"You are going hunting." Mrs. Feeley felt confused and flushed. She clutched the paper sack containing four cans of spiced ham to her bosom.

"I am going away," Mr. Feeley corrected her, talking slowly and deliberately as if speaking to a daft child. "You'll find the mortgage papers in my top desk drawer, although they'll be of little use to you when the bank comes to collect its due."

Mrs. Feeley took off her eyeglasses and wiped them on the hem of her cotton housecoat. It was long past time for Mrs. Feeley to get stronger lenses, but she could see Mr. Feeley clear enough. A little drop of saliva clung to his bottom lip, a lip so thin and stretched it looked like an angry red mark in his large, meaty face. Mrs. Feeley must be hearing things, like that girl from Menasha who said a voice told her to jump off the Wanamukka Bridge and so she did.

"You can go live with your brother and his wife," Mr. Feeley added helpfully. "You can have all the furniture and your clothes." He took a freshly starched handkerchief from his back pocket and wiped his high, shiny forehead with it. Bending over the deep-freeze had caused Mr. Feeley to exert himself unduly.

Mrs. Feeley realized she wasn't dreaming. "But why should I go live somewhere else?" Mrs. Feeley cried aloud. "This is my home."

Mr. Feeley ignored her frightful outburst. Mrs. Feeley obviously didn't understand the ways of the world. Mr. Feeley had done his best to protect her, but there was only so much one could do.

Mr. Feeley threw the last bundle of venison into Mrs. Feeley's suitcase. The bundle broke open, and, to Mrs. Feeley's surprise, a thick stack of hundred-dollar bills spilled out. Mr. Feeley hurriedly swooped up the money and stuffed it into the suitcase. He snapped the lid shut, tied a double length of rope around it, and secured it with a square knot.

"Don't say a word to the police about the money," Mr. Feeley hissed. "It's mine free and clear. By the time the bank misses it, I'll be long gone. They'll never trace it, and they'll never find me," he boasted. "All you know is, I went hunting and failed to return as scheduled. Do you understand?"

Mrs. Feeley understood. Mr. Feeley, it seemed, was a thief. She opened her mouth to speak but nothing came out. Mrs. Feeley sat there in her old red coat, her mouth hanging open like a marionette waiting for someone to supply the voice.

A look of relief spread over Mr. Feeley's doughy face. Mrs. Feeley would let him go without a fight.

Mrs. Feeley felt scared. She had to say something.

"I got four cans of ham," Mrs. Feeley blurted out. "They're six for one dollar but I forgot my coupon, but the manager, who's usually so rude but was quite pleasant tonight, told me I could bring back the coupon tomorrow and he'll let me have the other two cans." For as mute as she was a minute earlier, now she couldn't make herself stop talking. Mrs. Feeley talked on and on, about Myra and the Snow Carnival, the little baby girl, and how last year on her birthday Mrs. Pringle from the bakery had made her a cake, and how much she *really* wanted that new iron. Mr. Feeley looked alarmed, but didn't try to stop her. Excitement welled in Mrs. Feeley's chest. She feared she would be sick all over herself. She felt quite mad. She couldn't make herself stop talking.

"He isn't going to give you two perfectly good cans of ham for nothing. He was lying to get you to shut up," Mr. Feeley finally interrupted angrily. "You probably scared the other customers. You are quite insane, Mrs. Feeley."

"Yes, I know," Mrs. Feeley replied softly. "I am mad."

Mr. Feeley seemed a little startled by this admission. Then he smiled his false little banker's smile. He was done here and wanted business to move along. "Suppose you go upstairs and make sandwiches for my trip. There's no use letting good food go to waste," he suggested.

Mrs. Feeley, to her astonishment, didn't move. She sat still as a lamb, feeling the *thump thump thump* of her heart as it beat under the worn wool of her one good coat. She flushed with embarrassment when she realized Mr. Feeley was right about the store manager. She shook her head. "I *am* mad," she said aloud, more to herself than to Mr. Feeley.

Mr. Feeley chortled triumphantly. "Mrs. Feeley," he said, "you have no common sense. God knows what's going to happen to you when I'm gone." Mrs. Feeley took a good look at Mr. Feeley. His forehead was glistening with sweat, much like the fat on a strip of bacon as it sizzled in Mrs. Feeley's griddle. Mr. Feeley liked bacon; he liked it a lot.

"You mustn't believe everything everyone tells you," he added in a friendly tone that showed he was full of concern for Mrs. Feeley's welfare. Mr. Feeley prided himself on his ability to steer people in the right direction. It was his job.

Mrs. Feeley smiled. A small smile. "I won't," she assured Mr. Feeley. Then she reached into the paper sack and took out a can of

spiced ham, Mr. Feeley's favorite sandwich spread on sale now at
the Piggly-Wiggly, six cans for one dollar, and held it in her hand.
Mrs. Feeley had never noticed before how closely Mr. Feeley resembled the cartoon pig on the label. She must remember to mention
it to Myra someday.

Mrs. Feeley pitched her hand back and hurled the can right at
Mr. Feeley, striking him right between his small, watery, blue, close-
set eyes.

Mr. Feeley stood there, stunned. A trickle of blood ran down his
bulbous red nose. Mrs. Feeley had surprisingly strong arms for such
a tiny woman. All that ironing.

Mr. Feeley's thin lips fell apart, making a perfect "O," but no
sound emerged. Mr. Feeley looked just like a goldfish, Mrs. Feeley
decided. She had never really liked fish, they seemed so cold and
slimy. A friendly little dog would suit her much better.

Mrs. Feeley plucked another can of spiced ham from the bag and
pitched it right at Mr. Feeley's rather large head. Mr. Feeley stumbled backward, lost his footing, and fell heavily against the sharp
side of the stainless-steel deep-freeze, striking his head with a loud
crack.

Mrs. Feeley sat frozen to the step. After a while, Mr. Feeley's low
moans turned to gurgles and his shallow breathing stopped. A bad
smell wafted toward Mrs. Feeley. It was the smell of death. Mrs.
Feeley was well acquainted with that odor, having spent many hours
in that dark cellar wielding a sharp cleaver over some poor beast
destined for the deep-freeze.

Mrs. Feeley sighed. She had never wanted this enormous appli-
ance in her house, but Mr. Feeley had said she must live with it and
so she had.

Friday, Mrs. Feeley, of 37 Badger Avenue, boarded the bus for
Cleveland. This was her first trip since her honeymoon, when she
and Mr. Feeley had stayed in his cousin's cabin at nearby Bear Lake.
This time Mrs. Feeley might never come back. There was no law
against it, after all. By Tuesday, maybe Wednesday, Mr. Feeley's
absence from the bank would be cause for concern. A bank official would come to the house and find it deserted. Mr. Feeley, it
seemed, had gone on a hunting trip and had never come home.
His theft would surface eventually, but by then it would be too late.
Mr. Feeley would be long gone.

The house would be sold to pay the back taxes. The threadbare furnishings would be hauled away by the junk man. Mrs. Mertz, who had taught home economics for thirty-five years and so knew all there was to know about spoilt food, would keep the rump roast Mrs. Feeley had wrapped for the deep-freeze only last week but would know to throw away the large quantity of three-year-old pork, marked in Mrs. Feeley's tidy hand. Mrs. Mertz would think Mrs. Feeley had fallen down on her duty as a homemaker, keeping old meat like that around, but it couldn't be helped.

Mrs. Mertz would find four empty cans stacked neatly on the drainer, but no other sign of the Feeleys. While it would come as a shock that Mr. Feeley was a thief, it would surprise no one that Mrs. Feeley had disappeared along with him. She always was such a devoted wife.

Mrs. Feeley smoothed the skirt of her one good suit, a light-weight black crepe she took out of mothballs only for weddings and funerals, and tucked her shoes out of sight under her seat. They were so worn the leather was paper-thin and cracked in places. She had had no room for any of her clothes as her only suitcase had already been packed, by Mr. Feeley. The suitcase was at her feet where she could keep an eye on it, although the chances of anyone stealing a worn pasteboard box with a rope holding it together seemed slim.

In a paper sack on her lap was the lovely rayon housecoat and matching slippers from Myra and four tasty spiced-ham sandwiches, wrapped in wax paper. Mrs. Feeley had been too excited to eat a proper breakfast, and there was no telling when the driver would stop for a snack. Besides, there was no sense letting food go to waste.

Will You Always Love Me?

FROM *Story*

WHEN HARRY STEINHART introduced himself to Andrea Mc-Clure that evening, at the crowded reception in the atrium of Kress, Inc., he allowed her to assume that she was encountering him for the first time. Yet, in fact, Harry had been well aware of the young woman for months, since she'd come to work at Kress, Inc., the investment firm for which he was a market analyst. She was not a beautiful woman exactly, but rather odd-looking, with an asymmetrical face, sharp cheekbones, large liquid-dark quick-darting eyes that nonetheless failed to absorb much of their surroundings. Her hair was a fine fawn-brown streaked prematurely with gray. She was in her early thirties, with a habit of crinkling her forehead, a quizzical half-smile. There are women who preserve their faces by denying such expressions of emotion (Harry had known such women, well) and there are women so indifferent to their faces as to seem reckless, even profligate. Maybe that was why Harry found himself so attracted to her: a lack of guile?

Once, Harry had ridden alone with her in a swiftly rising elevator for twenty-two floors but she'd been so distracted by a sheath of papers she was carrying, she hadn't noticed him at all. (And he was a man accustomed to being noticed by women, especially at Kress, Inc.) Another time, sighting her in a local park where, one misty-bright April morning, she was running alone on a jogging trail, Harry found himself following her, at a discreet distance; he'd unobtrusively crossed a rocky strip where the trail doubled back and the young woman would have to pass him a second time. He'd been strangely excited, watching her. Watching her and not being seen. The small-boned woman with the prematurely graying hair, legs in loose-fitting white shorts slenderly muscular, small fists clenched. She wasn't a natural runner: Her arms swung stiffly at her sides, not quite rhythmically. She was frowning, crinkling her forehead, her mouth working as if, silently, she was arguing with someone. Harry climbed up onto an outcropping of rock, to stand in full view in the sun, in order not to be misunderstood (truly, he wasn't the kind of man to spy on a woman in a lonely place), but still the woman seemed oblivious of him. Possibly, as she ran past, her eyes brushed over him, but only for an instant.

Harry stared after her, amazed. It was not that he'd been re-buffed — he hadn't even been noticed. His *maleness* had not been acknowledged, let alone contemplated. Yet he'd felt not annoyed, but oddly amused. And protective of the woman.

After that, he'd avoided the park at that hour, to spare himself the temptation of seeking her out, watching her, again.

And now she was smiling up at him, saying, "Why do I like to act? — because I feel comforted by the stage."

An amateur actress! Harry was intrigued.

Andrea McClure spoke with a curious bright impersonality, as if discussing a third person. Her deep-socketed eyes took on a tawny light, the dark iris rimmed with hazel as, with her peculiar intensity, she responded to a casual question of Harry's. Even in high-heeled shoes she was much shorter than Harry, so she had to peer up at him — which he liked. As he liked her frankness, how within min-utes of shaking hands, exchanging names, she spoke with such warmth. "I played Irina in Chekhov's *Three Sisters,* a few years ago. Irina is the youngest of the sisters, the most naive and the most hopeful. Now I'd like to play Masha — 'in mourning for my life,' Masha says. I love the stage because emotions, there, are always justified — even self-pity. Even despair. At Kress, Inc., I'm one of hundreds of employees — I'm an 'editor,' I'm reasonably well paid — but the job is interchangeable with a thousand others, I feel no emotional commitment to it, and the company certainly feels no commitment to me. But when I'm on the stage, I know exactly who I am. I'm in another person's imagination, not my own. I can't say —" and here she began to act, with exaggerated "feminine" man-nerisms, to make Harry smile, "— 'Look, please, I'm not impor-tant, that any of you should care about me! — pay attention to me!' No, I'm an integral part of the production. It's a family, and I'm a member. Whatever a play *is,* it's a family."

How moved Harry was by the young woman's warm response. By the end of the evening, he'd forgotten his first impression of her, as a woman who took little notice of her surroundings, and of him.

They began to see each other in the evenings and on weekends, and through that spring and early summer Andrea's mysteriousness in Harry's eyes deepened — that vexation, almost sometimes like a physical chafing, of the *not-known:* the sexually provocative. Harry had been confident that they would soon become lovers, and was surprised that they did not; their relations were sociable, and warm — to a point. He was hurt, baffled, somewhat resentful, not at Andrea exactly but at the situation. Didn't she like him? Wasn't she attracted to him? Was there something wrong with him? (He was thirty-six years old, long ago married, and divorced. That part of his life belonged to the eighties, as if to another man.) Yet Andrea seemed to him so strangely oblivious, innocent. Even when she spoke with apparent artlessness, baring her soul.

"You really should find someone normal, Harry!" Andrea joked after kissing him, and stiffening in his embrace. So she acknowledged the tension between them, even as, by her manner, and the searching way she looked at him, she seemed to suggest there was nothing to be done.

Harry said, smiling, "Yes, but, Andy — I'm crazy about *you.*"

This, too, in a mildly jokey manner. The first evening they'd met, she'd told him, "My name is Andrea McClure and no one ever calls me 'Andy.'" Which Harry interpreted not as a warning but as a request.

When finally, in late summer, they made love, it was in silence, in the semi-darkness of Andrea's bedroom into which one night, impulsively, she'd led Harry by the hand as if declaring to herself *Now! now or never!* Andrea's bedroom was on the ninth floor of a white-brick apartment building overlooking a narrow strip of green, her window open to a curious humming-vibrating sound of traffic from the interstate a mile away. Penetrating this wash of sound through the night (Harry stayed the night) were distant sirens, mysterious cries, wails. Harry whispered, "You're so beautiful! I love you!" — the words torn from him, always for the first time.

It would be their custom, then, to make love in virtual silence, by night and not by day. By day, there was too much of the other to see and to respond to; by day, Harry felt himself too visible, and in lovemaking as opposed to mere sexual intercourse, it's preferable to be invisible. So Harry thought.

They were lovers, yet sporadically. They were not a couple.

So far as Harry knew, Andrea was not seeing other men; nor did she seem to have close women friends. Unlike the women he'd known intimately, including the woman who'd been, for six years, his wife, Andrea was the one who never inquired about his previous love affairs — how tactful she was, or how indifferent! *She doesn't want you to ask any questions of her,* Harry thought.

Harry told Andrea he'd been married and divorced and his ex-wife now lived in London and they were on "amicable" terms though they rarely communicated. He said, as if presenting her with a gift, the gift of himself, "It's over completely, emotionally, on both sides — luckily, we didn't have any children."

Andrea said, frowning, "That's too bad."

What was *not-known* in her. Which not even lovemaking could penetrate, after all.

Once lifting her eyes swiftly to his, startled as if he'd asked a question — "I'll need to trust you." This was not a statement but a question of her own. Harry said quickly, "Of course, darling. Trust me how?" And she looked at him searchingly, her smooth forehead suddenly creased, her mouth working. There was something ugly about the way, Harry thought, Andrea's mouth moved in an anguished sort of silence. He repeated, "Trust me how? What is it?"

Andrea stood and walked out of the room. (That evening, they were in Harry's apartment. He'd served an elaborate Italian meal, chosen special Italian wines — preparing meals for women had long been a crucial part of his ritual of seduction which perhaps he'd come to love for its own sake.) He followed Andrea, concerned she might leave, for the expression in her face was not one he recognized, a drawn, sallow, embittered look, as of a young girl biting her lips to keep from crying, but there she stood in a doorway weakly pressing her forehead against the doorframe, her eyes tightly shut and her thin shoulders trembling. "Andy, what is it?" Harry took her in his arms. He felt a sharp, simple happiness as if he was taking the *not-known* into his arms — and how easy it was, after all.

I will protect you: Trust me!

Later, when she'd recovered, calmed and softened and sleepy by several glasses of wine, Andrea confessed to Harry she'd thought he'd asked her something. She knew he hadn't, but thought she'd heard the words. When Harry asked, what were the words, Andrea said she didn't know. Her forehead, no longer creased with worry, kept the trace of thin horizontal lines.

Harry thought: We're drawn to the mystery of others' secrets, and not to those secrets. Do I really want to *know*?

In fact, Andrea would probably never have told him. For what would have been the occasion? — he could imagine none.

But: One day in March a telephone call came for Andrea which she took in her bedroom, where Harry heard her raised voice, and her sudden crying — Andrea, whom he'd never heard cry before. He did not know what to do — comfort her, or stay away. Listening to her cry tore at his heart. He felt he could not bear it. Thinking, too, *Now I'll know — now it will come out!* Yet he respected her privacy. In truth, he was a little frightened of her. (They were virtually living together now though hardly as a conventional couple. There was no sense of playing at marriage, domestic permanency as there usually is in such arrangements. Most of Harry's things remained in his apartment several miles away, to which he retreated frequently; sometimes, depending upon the needs of his work or Andrea's schedule or whether Harry might be booked for an early air flight in the morning, he spent the night in his own bed.)

Harry entered Andrea's bedroom but stopped short, seeing the look on her face which wasn't grief but fury, a knotted contorted fury, of a kind he's never seen in any woman's face before. And what are her incredulous, choked words into the receiver — "What do you mean? What are you saying? Who are you? I can't believe this! Parole hearing? He was sentenced to life! That filthy *murderer was sentenced to life!*"

Later, Harry came to understand how the dead sister had been an invisible third party in his relationship with Andrea. He recalled certain curiously insistent remarks she'd made about having been lonely growing up as an "only child" — her remoteness from her mother even as, with an edge of anxiety, she telephoned her mother every Sunday evening. She refused to read newspaper articles about violent crimes and asked Harry please to alert her so she could skip those pages. She refused to watch television except for cultural programs and there were few movies she consented to see with Harry — "I distrust the things a camera might pick up."

In a way, it was a relief of sorts, for Harry to learn that the *not-known* in Andrea's life had nothing to do with a previous lover, a disastrous marriage, a lost child, or, what was most likely of all, an abortion. He had no male rival to contend with!

This much, Harry learned: In the early evening of April 13, 1973, Andrea's nineteen-year-old sister Frannie, visiting their widowed grandmother in Wakana Beach, Florida, was assaulted while walking in a deserted area of the beach — beaten, raped, strangled with her shorts. Her body was dragged into a culvert where it was discovered within an hour by a couple walking their dog, before the grandmother would have had reason to report her missing. Naked from the waist down, her face so badly battered with a rock that her left eye dangled from its socket, the cartilage of her nose was smashed, and teeth broken — Frannie McClure was hardly recognizable. It would be discovered that her vagina and anus had been viciously lacerated and much of her pubic hair torn out. Rape may have occurred after her death.

The victim had died at about eight o'clock. By eleven, Wakana Beach police had in custody a twenty-seven-year-old motorcyclist-drifter named Albert Jefferson Rooke, Caucasian, with a record of drug arrests, petty thefts, and misdemeanors in Tallahassee, Tampa, and his hometown, Carbondale, Illinois, where he'd spent time in a facility for disturbed adolescent boys. When Rooke was arrested he was reported as drunk on malt liquor and high on amphetamines; he was disheveled, with long scraggly hair and filthy clothes, and violently resisted police officers. Several witnesses would report having seen a man who resembled him in the vicinity of the beach where the murdered girl's body was found, and a drug-addicted teenaged girl traveling with Rooke gave damaging testimony about his ravings of having "committed evil." In the Wakana Beach police station, with no lawyer present, Rooke confessed to the crime, his confession was taped, and by two o'clock of the morning of April 14, 1973, police had their man. Rooke had relinquished his right to an attorney. He was booked for first-degree murder, among other charges, held in detention, and placed on suicide watch.

Months later, Rooke would retract his confession, claiming it was coerced, that police had beaten him and threatened to kill him. He was drugged-out, spaced-out, didn't know what he'd said. But he hadn't confessed voluntarily. He knew nothing of the rape and murder of Frannie McClure — he'd never seen Frannie McClure. His lawyer, a public defender, entered a plea of not guilty to all charges but at his trial Rooke did so poorly on the witness stand that the lawyer requested a recess and conferred with Rooke and convinced him that he should plead guilty, so the case wouldn't go to the jurors, who were sure to convict him and send him to the electric chair; Rooke could then take his case to the state court of appeals, on the grounds that his confession had been coerced, and he was innocent.

So Rooke waived his right to a jury trial, pleaded guilty, and was sentenced to life in prison. But the strategy misfired when, reversing his plea another time to not guilty and claiming that his confession was invalid, his case was summarily rejected by the court of appeals. That was in 1975. Now, in spring 1993, Rooke was eligible for parole, and the county attorney who contacted Andrea's mother under the auspices of the Florida Victim/Witness Program, and was directed by Andrea's mother to contact her, reported that Rooke seemed to have been a "model prisoner" for the past twelve years — there was a bulging file of supportive letters from prison guards, therapists, counselors, literacy volunteers, a Catholic chaplain. The Victim/Witness Program allowed for the testimony to parole boards of victims and family members related to victims, and so Andrea McClure was invited to address Rooke's parole board when his hearing came up in April. If she wanted to be involved, if she had anything to say.

Her mother was too upset to be involved. She'd broken down, just discussing it on the phone with Andrea.

Except for a representative from the Wakana County Attorney's Office, everyone who gave testimony at Albert Jefferson Rooke's parole hearing, if Andrea didn't attend, would be speaking on behalf of the prisoner.

Andrea said, wiping at her eyes, "If that man is freed, I swear I will kill him myself."

* * *

"I was fourteen years old at the time Frannie died," Andrea said. "I was supposed to fly down with her to visit Grandma, at Easter, but I didn't want to go, and Frannie went alone, and if I'd gone with Frannie she'd be alive today, wouldn't she? I mean, it's a simple statement of fact. It isn't anything but a simple statement of fact."

Harry said, hesitantly, "Yes, but —" trying to think what to say, knowing that Andrea had made this accusation against herself continuously over the past twenty years, "— a fact can distort. Facts need to be interpreted in context."

Andrea smiled impatiently. She was looking, not at Harry, but at something beyond Harry's shoulder. "You're either alive, or you're not alive. That's the only context."

Where in the past Andrea had kept the secret of her murdered sister wholly to herself, now, suddenly, she began to talk openly, in a rapid nervous voice, about what had happened. Frannie, and how her death had affected the family, and how, after the trial, they'd assumed it was over — "He *was* sentenced to life in prison. Instead of the electric chair. Doesn't that mean anything?"

Harry said, "There's always the possibility of parole, unless the judge sets the sentence otherwise. You must have known that."

Andrea seemed not to hear. Or, hearing, not to absorb.

Now she brought out of a closet a scrapbook. Showing Harry snapshots of the dead girl — pretty, thin-faced, with large expressive dark eyes like Andrea's own. Sifting through family snapshots, Andrea would have skipped over her own and seemed surprised that Harry would want to look at them. There were postcards and letters of Frannie's, clippings from a Roanoke paper — Frances McClure the recipient of a scholarship to Middlebury, Frances McClure embarked upon a six-week work-study program in Peru. (No clippings — none — pertaining to the crime.) Andrea answered at length, with warmth and animation, Harry's questions; in the midst of other conversations, or silence, she'd begin suddenly to speak of Frannie as if, all along, she and Harry had been discussing her.

Harry thought, It must be like a dream. An underground stream. Never ceasing.

"For years," Andrea confessed, "I wouldn't think of Frannie. After the trial, we were exhausted and we never talked about her. I truly don't believe it's what psychiatry calls 'denial' — there was nothing more to say. The dead don't change, do they? The dead don't get any older, they don't get any less dead. It's funny how Frannie was so old to me, so mature, now I see these pictures and I see she was so young, only nineteen, and now I'm thirty-four and I'd be so old to *her.* I almost wish I could say that Frannie and I didn't get along but we did — I loved her. She was older than I was by just enough, five years, so we never competed in anything, *she* was the one, everybody loved her, you would have loved her, she had such a quick, warm way of laughing, she was so *alive.* Her roommate at Middlebury would say how weird it was, that Frannie wasn't *alive* because Frannie was the most *alive* person of anybody and that doesn't change. But we stopped talking about her because it was too awful. I was lonely for her but I stopped thinking about her. I went to a different high school, my parents moved to a different part of Roanoke, it was possible to think different thoughts. I dream about Frannie now and it's been twenty years but I really don't think I was dreaming about her then. Except sometimes when I was alone, especially if I was shopping, and this is true now, because Frannie used to take me shopping when I was young, I'd seem to be with another person, I'd sort of be talking to, listening to, another person — but not really. I mean, it wasn't Frannie. Sometimes I get scared and think I've forgotten what she looks like exactly — my memory is bleaching out. But I'll never forget. I'm all she has. The memory of her — it's in my trust. She had a boyfriend, actually, but he's long gone from my life — he's married, has kids. If he walked up to me on the street, if he turned up at work, if he turned up as my supervisor someday — I wouldn't know him. I'd look right through him.

"I look through my mother sometimes, and I can see she looks through me. Because we're thinking of Frannie but we don't acknowledge it because we can't talk about it. But if she's thinking of Frannie, and at the moment I'm not, that's when she really *will* look through me. My father died of liver cancer and it was obviously from what Frannie's murderer did to us. We never said his name, and we never thought his name. We were at the trial and we saw him and I remember how relieved I was — I don't know about Mom and Dad, but I know I was — to see he truly was depraved. His face was all broken out in pimples. His eyes were bloodshot. He was always pretending to be trying to commit suicide, to get sympathy, or to make out he was crazy, so they had him drugged, and the drugs did something to his motor coordination. Also, he was pretending. *He* was an actor. But the act didn't work — he's in prison for life. I can't believe any parole board would take his case seriously. I know it's routine. The more I think about it, of course it's routine. They won't let him out. But I have to make sure of that because if I don't, and they let him out, I'll be to blame. It will all be on my head. I told you, didn't I? — I was supposed to go to Grandma's with Frannie, but I didn't. I was fourteen, I had my friends, I didn't want to go to Wakana Beach exactly then. If I'd gone with Frannie, she'd be alive today. That's a simple, neutral fact. It isn't an accusation, just a fact. My parents never blamed me, or anyway never spoke of it. They're good people, they're Christians I guess you could say. They must have wished I'd gone in Frannie's place but I can't say I blame them."

Harry wasn't sure he'd heard correctly. "Your parents must have — what? Wished you'd died in your sister's place? Are you serious?"

Andrea had been speaking breathlessly. Now she stared at Harry, the skin between her eyebrows puckered.

She said, "I didn't say that. You must have misunderstood."

Harry said, "I must have — all right."

"You must have heard wrong. What did I say?"

At such times Andrea would become agitated, running her hands through her hair so it stood in affrighted comical tufts; her mouth would tremble and twist. "It's all right, Andy," Harry would say, "— hey c'mon. It's fine." He would stop her hands and maybe kiss them, the moist palms. Or slide his arms around her playful and husbandly. How small Andrea was, how small an adult woman can be, bones you could fracture by squeezing, so be careful. Harry's heart seemed to hurt, in sympathy. "Don't think about it anymore today, Andy, okay? I love you."

And Andrea might say, vague, wondering, as if she were making this observation for the first time, which in fact she was not, "— The only other person who ever called me 'Andy' was Frannie. Did you know?"

He'd been trained as a lawyer. Not criminal law but corporate law. But he came to wonder if possibly Andrea had been attracted to him originally, that evening, because he had a law degree. When he'd mentioned law school, at Yale, her attention had quickened.

Unless he was imagining this? Human memory is notoriously unreliable, like film fading in amnesiac patches.

Memory: Frannie McClure now exists only in memory.

That's what's so terrible about being dead, Harry thought wryly. You depend for your existence as a historic fact upon the memories of others. Failing, finite, mortal themselves.

Though they'd never discussed it in such abstract terms, for Andrea seemed to shrink from speaking of her sister in anything but the most particular way, Harry understood that her anxiety was not simply that Albert Jefferson Rooke might be released on parole after having served only twenty years of a life sentence but that, if he was, Frannie McClure's claim to permanent, tragic significance would be challenged.

Also: For Frannie McClure to continue to exist as a historic fact, the memories that preserve her as a specific individual — not a mere name, a sexual assault statistic — court case must continue to exist. These were still, after twenty years, fairly numerous, for as an American girl who'd gone to a large public high school and had just about completed two years of college, she'd known, and been known by, hundreds of people; but the number was naturally decreasing year by year. Andrea could count them on the fingers of both hands — relatives, neighbors who'd known Frannie from the time of her birth to the time of her death. The grandmother who'd lived in a splendid beachfront condominium overlooking Apalachee Bay of the Gulf of Mexico had been dead since 1979. She'd never recovered from the shock and grief, of course. And there was Andrea's father, dead since 1981. And Andrea's mother, whom Harry had yet to meet, and whom Andrea spoke of with purposeful vagueness as a "difficult" woman, living now in a retirement community in Roanoke, never spoke of her murdered daughter to anyone. So it was impossible to gauge to what extent the mother's memory did in fact preserve the dead girl.

Sometimes, when Andrea was out of the apartment, Harry contemplated the snapshots of Frannie McClure by himself. There was one of her dated Christmas 1969, she'd been fifteen at the time, hugging her ten-year-old sister Andy and clowning for the camera, a beautiful girl, in an oversized sweater and jeans, her brown eyes given an eerie red-maroon glisten by the camera's flash. Behind the girls, a seven-foot Christmas tree, resplendent with useless ornamentation.

Harry noted: When he and Andrea made love it was nearly always in complete silence except for Andrea's murmured incoherent words, her soft cries, muffled sobs. You could credit such sounds to love, passion. But essentially there was silence, a qualitatively different silence from what Harry recalled from their early nights together. Harry understood that Andrea was thinking of Frannie's struggling body as it, too, was penetrated by a man's penis; this excited Harry enormously but made him cautious about being gentle, not allowing his weight to rest so heavily upon Andrea. The challenge for Harry as a lover was to shake Andrea free of her trance and force her into concentrating on *him*. If Harry could involve Andrea in physical sensation, in actual passion, he would have succeeded. At the same time Harry had to concentrate on Andrea, exclusively upon Andrea, and not allow his mind to swerve to the mysterious doomed girl of the snapshots.

The call from the Victim/Witness Program advocate came for Andrea in late March. Giving her only twenty-six days to prepare, emotionally and otherwise, for the hearing on April 20, in Tallahassee. Andrea mentioned to Harry that it was only a coincidence, of course — the first parole hearing for Rooke had been scheduled for a Tuesday, which was a week and two days following Easter, and it was 12:10 A.M. of the Tuesday following Easter 1973 that the call came from Wakana Beach notifying the McClures of Frannie's death.

Andrea went on, wiping at her eyes, "It wasn't clear from that first call just how Frannie had died. What he'd done to her. She was dead, that was the fact. They said it was an 'assault' and they'd arrested the man but they didn't go into details over the telephone — of course. Not that kind of details. I suppose it's procedure. Notifying families when someone's been killed — that requires procedure. When they called Grandma, to make the identification, that night, *that* must have been difficult. She'd collapsed, she didn't remember much about it afterward. My mother and father had to make the identification, too. I suppose it was only Frannie's face?

— but her face was so damaged. I didn't see, and the casket was closed, so I don't know. I shouldn't be talking about something I don't know, should I? I shouldn't be involving you in this, should I? So I'll stop."

"Of course I want to be involved, honey," Harry said. "I'm going with you. I'll help you all I can."

"No, really, you don't have to. Please don't feel that you have to."

"Of course I'm going with you to that goddamned hearing," Harry said. "I wouldn't let you go through something so terrible alone."

"But I could do it," Andrea said. "Don't you think I could? I'm not fourteen years old now. I'm all grown up."

Except: Harry heard Andrea crying when he woke and discovered she was gone from bed, several nights in succession hearing her in the bathroom with the fan running to muffle her sobs. Or was it Andrea talking to herself in a low, rapid voice. Rehearsing her testimony for the parole board. She'd been told it was best not to read a prepared statement, nor give the impression that she was repeating a prepared statement. So in the night locked in the bathroom with the fan running to muffle her words which were punctuated with sobs, or curses, Andrea practiced her role as Harry lay sleepless wondering, *Am I strong enough? What is required of me?*

This, without telling Andrea: A few days before they were scheduled to fly to Tallahassee, Harry drove to the Georgetown Law School library and looked up the transcript of the December 1975 appeal of the verdict of guilty in the *People of the State of Florida* v. *Albert Jefferson Rooke* of September 1973. He'd only begun reading Rooke's confession when he realized there was something wrong with it.

That night I got a feeling I wanted to do it . . . hurt one of them real bad . . . so I went out to find her . . . a girl or a woman . . . I hate them . . . I really hate them . . . I get a kick out of hurting people . . . I get a kick out of putting something over on you guys . . . so I saw this girl on the beach . . . I'd never seen her before . . . I jumped her and she started to scream and that pissed me off and I got real mad . . . and so on through twenty-three pages of a rambling monologue Harry believed he'd read before, or something very like it; its Wakana Beach, Florida, details specific but its essence, its tone familiar.

What was Albert Jefferson Rooke's "confession" but standard

boilerplate said to have been used until recently in certain parts of the United States by police who have arrested a vulnerable, highly suspicious subject? A stranger in a community, so drunk or stoned or so marginal and despicable a human being witnesses take one look at him and say *He's the one!* cops take one look at him *He's the one!* and if the poor bastard hadn't committed this crime you can assume he's committed any number of other crimes he's never been caught for so let's help him remember, let's give him a little assistance. Harry could imagine it: This straggly-haired hippie-punk brought handcuffed to police headquarters raving and disoriented not knowing where the hell he is, waives his right to call an attorney or maybe they don't even read him the Miranda statement, he's eager to cooperate with these cops so they stop beating his head against the wall and won't "restrain" him with a chokehold when he "resists" for it's self-evident to these professionals as eventually to a jury that this is exactly the kind of sick degenerate pervert who rapes, mutilates, murders. Sure we know "Albert Jefferson Rooke," he's our man.

Harry sat in the law library for a long time staring into space. He felt weak, sick. Can it be? *Is* it possible?

Andrea said, "Please don't feel you should care about this — obsession of mine. You have your own work, and you have your own life. It isn't —" and here she paused, her mouth working, "— as if we're married."

"What has that got to do with it?" Harry saw how the quickened light in Andrea's eyes for him, at his approach, had gone dead; she was shrinking from him. He'd come home from the law library and he'd told her just that he'd been reading about the Rooke trial and would she like to discuss it in strictly legal terms and she'd turned to him this waxy dead-white face, these pinched eyes, as if he'd confessed being unfaithful to her. "That isn't an issue."

"I shouldn't have told you about Frannie. It was selfish of me. You're the only person in my life now who knows and it was a mistake for me to tell you and I'm *sorry*."

She walked blindly out of the room. This was the kind of apology that masks bitter resentment. Harry knew the tone, Harry had been there before.

Still, Harry followed Andrea, into another room, and to a win-

dow where she stood trembling, refusing to look at him, saying in a
low rapid voice as if to herself how she shouldn't have involved him,
he had never known her sister, what a burden to place upon him, a
stranger to the family, how shortsighted she'd been, that night the
call had come for her she should have asked him please to go
home, this was a private matter — and Harry listened, couldn't
bring himself to interrupt, he loved this woman didn't he, in any
case he can't hurt her, not now. She was saying, "I'm not a vengeful
person, it's justice I want for Frannie. Her memory is in my trust —
I'm all she has, now."

Harry said, carefully, "Andy, it's all right. We can discuss it some
other time." On the plane to Tallahassee, maybe? They were leaving
in the morning.

Andrea said, "We don't have to discuss it at all! I'm not a vengeful
person."

"No one has said you're a vengeful person. Who's said that?"

"You didn't know Frannie and maybe you don't know me. I'm
not always sure who I am. But I know what I have to *do*."

"That's the important thing, then. That's the —" Harry was
searching for the absolutely right, the perfect word, which eluded
him, unless, "— moral thing, then. Of course."

The moral thing, then. Of course. On the plane to Tallahassee,
he'd tell her.

But that night Andrea slept poorly. And in the early morning,
Harry believed he heard her being sick in the bathroom. And on
their way to the airport and on the plane south Andrea's eyes were
unnaturally bright, glistening and the pupils dilated and she was al-
ternately silent and nervously loquacious, gripping his hand much
of the time and how could he tell her, for what did he *know*, he *knew*
something, only suspected, it was up to Rooke's defense attorney to
raise such issues, how could he interfere, he could not.

Andrea said, her forehead creased like a chamois cloth that's
been crumpled, "It's so strange: I keep seeing *his* face, *he's* my
audience. I'm brought into this room that's darkened and at the
front the parole board is sitting and the lights are on them and *he's*
there — he hasn't changed in twenty years. As soon as he sees me,
he knows. He sees, not me, of course not me, he wouldn't remember me, but Frannie. He sees Frannie. I've been reading these doc-

uments they've sent me, you know, and the most outrageous, the really obscene thing is, Rooke claims he doesn't remember Frannie's name, even! He claims he never saw her and he never raped her and he never tortured her and he never strangled her, he never knew her, and now, after twenty years, he's saying he wouldn't remember her name if he isn't told it!" Andrea looked at Harry, to see if he was sharing her outrage. "But when he sees me, he'll see Frannie, and he'll remember everything. And he'll know. He'll know he's going back to prison for the rest of his life. Because Frannie wouldn't want revenge, she wasn't that kind of person, but she *would* want justice."

Harry considered: Is the truth worth it? — even if we can know the truth.

In the end, in the State Justice Building in Tallahassee, it wasn't clear whether Albert Jefferson Rooke was on the premises when Andrea spoke with the parole board; and Andrea made no inquiries. In a blind, blinking daze she was escorted into a room by a young woman attorney from the Victim/Witness Program and Harry Steinhart was allowed to accompany her as a friend of the McClure family, though not a witness. *At last,* Harry thought. *It will be over, something will be decided.*

The interview lasted one hour and forty minutes during which time Andrea held the undivided attention of the seven middle-aged Caucasian men who constituted the board — she'd brought along her cherished snapshots of her murdered sister, she read from letters written to her by Frannie, and by former teachers, friends, and acquaintances mourning Frannie's death in such a way as to make you realize (even Harry, as if for the first time, his eyes brimming with tears) that a young woman named Frances McClure did live, and that her loss to the world is a tragedy. The room in which Andrea spoke was windowless, on the eleventh floor of a sleekly modern building, not at all the room Andrea seemed to have envisioned but one brightly lit by recessed fluorescent lighting. No shadows here. The positioning of the chair in which Andrea sat, facing at an angle the long table where the seven men sat, suggested a minimal, stylized stage. Andrea wore a dark-blue linen suit and a creamy silk blouse and her slender legs were nearly hidden beneath the suit's fashionably long, flared skirt. Her face was pale, and her forehead finely crossed with the evidence of grief, her voice now and then trembling but overall she remained composed, speaking calmly, looking each of the parole board members in the eye, each in turn; answering their courteous questions unhesitatingly, with feeling, as if they were all companions involved in a single moral cause. *It's people like us against people like him.* By the end of the interview Andrea was beginning to crack, her voice not quite so composed and her eyes spilling tears but still she managed to speak steadily, softly, each word enunciated with care. "No one can ever undo what Albert Jefferson Rooke did to my sister — even if the State of Florida imprisons him for all his life, as he'd been sentenced. He escaped the electric chair by changing his plea and then he changed his plea again so we know how he values the truth and he's never expressed the slightest remorse for his crime so we know he's the same man who killed my sister, he can't have changed in twenty years. He hasn't come to terms with his crime, or his sickness. We know that violent sex offenders rarely change even with therapy, and this man has not had therapy relating to his sickness because he has always denied his sickness. So he'll rape and kill again. He'll take his revenge on the first young girl he can, the way he did with my sister — he can always pretend he doesn't remember any of it afterward. He's claiming now he doesn't even remember my sister's name but her name is Frances McClure and others remember. He claims he wants to be free on parole so he can 'begin again.' What is a man like that going to 'begin again'? I see he's collected a file of letters from well-intentioned, fair-minded people he's deceived the way he hopes to deceive you gentlemen — you know what prison inmates call this strategy, it's a vulgar word I hesitate to say: 'bullshitting.' They learn to 'bullshit' the prison guards and the therapists and the social workers and the chaplains and, yes, the parole boards. Sometimes they claim they're sorry for their crimes and won't ever do such things again — they're 're-morseful.' But in this killer's case, there isn't even 'remorse.' He just wants to get out of prison to 'begin again.' I seem to know how he probably talked to you, tried to convince you it doesn't matter what he did twenty years ago this Easter because he's reformed *now,* no more drugs and no more crime *now.* He'll get a job, he's eager to work. I seem to know how you want to believe him, because we want to believe people when they speak like this. It's a Christian

impulse. It's a humane impulse. It makes us feel good about ourselves — we can be 'charitable.' But a prisoner's word for this strategy is 'bullshitting' and that's what we need to keep in mind. This
killer has appealed to you to release him on parole — to 'bullshit'
you into believing him. But I've come to speak the truth. I'm here
on my sister's behalf. She'd say, she'd plead — don't release this
vicious, sick, murderous man back into society, to commit more
crimes! Don't be the well-intentioned parties whose 'charity' will
lead to another innocent girl being brutally raped and murdered.
It's too late for me, Frannie would say, but potential victims — they
can be spared."

Only a half-hour later, Andrea was informed that the parole board
voted unanimously against releasing Albert Jefferson Rooke. She
asked could she thank the board members and she was escorted
back into the room and Harry waited for her, smiling in relief as she
shook their hands one by one. Now she did burst into tears but it
was all right. Telling Harry afterward, in their hotel room, "Every
one of those men thanked *me*. They thanked *me*. One of them said,
'If it wasn't for you, Miss McClure, we might've made a bad mistake.'"

Harry said, in a neutral voice, "It was a real triumph, then, wasn't
it? You exerted your will, and you triumphed."

Andrea looked at him, puzzled. She was removing her linen
jacket and hanging it carefully on a pink silk hanger. Her face was
soft, that soft brimming of her eyes, soft curve of her mouth, the
woman's most intimate look, the look Harry sees in her face after
love. Yet there's a clarity to her voice, almost a sharpness. "Oh, no
— it wasn't my will. It was Frannie's. I spoke for her and I told the
truth for her and that was all. Now it's over."

That evening Andrea is too exhausted to eat anywhere except in
their hotel room and midway through the dinner she's too exhausted to finish it and then too exhausted to undress herself, to
take a bath, to climb into the enormous king-sized canopied bed
without Harry's help. He's exhausted, too. And he's been drinking.
Since that afternoon foreseeing with calm, impersonal horror how,
like clockwork, every several years Albert Jefferson Rooke will present himself to the parole board and Andrea will fly to Tallahassee

to present herself in opposition to the man she believes to be her sister's murderer; and so it will go through the years, and Rooke might die one day in prison, and this would release them both, or Rooke might be freed on parole, finally — of that, Harry doesn't want to think. Not right now.

In the ridiculous elevated bed, the lights out; a murmurous indefinable sound that might be the air-conditioning, or someone in an adjacent room quietly and drunkenly arguing; the feverish damp warmth of Andrea's body, her mouth hungry against his, her slender arms around his neck. Naively, childishly, in a voice Harry has never heard before, as if this is, of all Andrea's several voices, the one truly her own, she asks, "Do you love me, Harry? Will you always love me?" and he kisses her mouth, her breasts, her warm flat belly, bunching her nightgown in his fists, he whispers, "Yes."

GEORGE PELECANOS

When You're Hungry

FROM *Unusual Suspects*

THE WOMAN IN THE aisle seat to the right of John Moreno tapped him on the shoulder. Moreno swallowed the last of his Skol pilsner to wash down the food in his mouth. He laid his fork across the segmented plastic plate in front of him on a fold-down tray.

"Yes?" he said, taking her in fully for the first time. She was attractive, though one had to look for it, past the thick black eyebrows and the too-wide mouth painted a pale peach color that did no favor to her complexion.

"I don't mean to be rude," she said, in heavily accented English. "But you've been making a lot of noise with your food. Is everything all right?"

Moreno grinned, more to himself than to her. "Yes, I'm fine. You have to excuse me. I rushed out of the house this morning without breakfast, and then this flight was delayed. I suppose I didn't realize how hungry I was."

"No bother," she said, smiling now, waving the manicured fingers of her long brown hand. "I'm not complaining. I'm a doctor, and I thought that something might be wrong."

"Nothing that some food couldn't take care of." They looked each other over. Then he said, "You're a doctor in what city?"

"A pediatrician," she said. "In Bahia Salvador. Are you going to Bahia?"

Moreno shook his head. "Recife."

So they would not meet again. Just as well. Moreno preferred to pay for his companionship while under contract.

"Recife is lovely," the woman said, breathing out with a kind of

relief, the suspense between them now broken. "Are you on a holiday?"

"Yes," he said. "A holiday."

"Illiana," she said, extending her hand across the armrest.

"John Moreno." He shook her hand, and took pleasure in the
touch.

The stewardess came, a round woman with rigid red hair, and
took their plates. Moreno locked the tray in place. He retrieved his
guidebook from the knapsack under the seat, and read.

> Brazil is a land of great natural beauty, and a country unparalleled in its
> ideal of racial democracy. . . .

Moreno flipped past the rhetoric of the guidebook, went directly
to the meat: currency, food and drink, and body language. Not that
Brazil would pose any sort of problem for him; in his fifteen-odd
years in the business, there were very few places in the world where
he had not quickly adapted. This adaptability made him one of the
most marketable independents in his field. And it was why, one
week earlier, on the first Tuesday of September, he had been called
to the downtown Miami office of Mr. Carlos Garcia, vice president
of claims, United Casualty and Life.

Garcia was a trim man with closely cropped, tightly curled hair.
He wore a wide-lapelled suit of charcoal gray, a somber color for
Miami, and a gray and maroon tie with an orderly geometric design. A phone sat on his lacquered desk, along with a blank note-
pad, upon which rested a silver Cross pen.

Moreno sat in a leather chair with chrome arms across from
Garcia's desk. Garcia's secretary served coffee, and after a few sips
and the necessary exchange of pleasantries, Moreno asked Garcia
to describe the business at hand.

Garcia told him about Guzman, a man in his fifties who had
made and then lost some boom-years money in South Florida real
estate. Guzman had taken his pleasure boat out of Key Largo one
day in the summer of 1992. Two days later his wife reported him
missing, and a week after that the remains of his boat were found,
along with a body, two miles out to sea. Guzman and his vessel had
been the victims of an unexplained explosion on board.

"Any crew?" asked Moreno.

"Just Guzman."

"A positive identification on the body?"

"Well. The body was badly burned. Horribly burned. And most of what was left went to the fish."

"How about his teeth?"

"Guzman wore dentures." Garcia smiled wanly. "Interesting, no?"

The death benefits of Guzman's term policy, a two-million-dollar payoff, went to the widow. United's attorneys fought it to a point, but the effort from the outset was perfunctory. The company absorbed the loss.

Then, a year later, a neighbor of the Guzmans was vacationing in Recife, a city and resort on the northeast coast of Brazil, and spotted who she thought was Guzman. She saw this man twice in one week, on the same beach. By the time she returned to the States, she had convinced herself that she had in fact seen Guzman. She went with her suspicions to the widow, who seemed strangely unconcerned. Then she went to the police.

"And the police kicked it to you," Moreno said.

"They don't have the jurisdiction, or the time. We have a man on the force who keeps us informed in situations like this."

"So the widow wasn't too shook up by the news."

"No," Garcia said. "But that doesn't prove or even indicate any kind of complicity. We see many different kinds of emotions in this business upon the death of a spouse. The most common emotion that we see is relief."

Moreno folded one leg over the other and tented his hands in his lap. "What have you done so far?"

"We sent a man down to Brazil, an investigator named Roberto Silva."

"And?"

"Silva became very drunk one night. He left his apartment in Recife to buy a pack of cigarettes, stepped into an open elevator shaft, and fell eight stories to his death. He was found the next morning with a broken neck."

"Accidents happen."

Garcia spread his hands. "Silva was a good operative. I sent him because he was fluent in Portuguese, and because he had a history of success. But I knew that he had a very bad problem with alcohol. I had seen him fall down myself, on more than one occasion. This time, he simply fell a very long way."

Moreno stared through the window at the Miami skyline. After a while he said, "This looks to be a fairly simple case. There is a man in a particular area of Recife who either is or is not Guzman. I will bring you this man's fingerprints. It should take no more than two weeks."

"What do you require?"

"I get four hundred a day, plus expenses."

"Your terms are reasonable," Garcia said.

"There's more," Moreno said, holding up his hand. "My expenses are unlimited, and not to be questioned. I fly first class, and require an apartment with a live-in maid to cook and to clean my clothes. And, I get two and one half percent of the amount recovered."

"That's fifty thousand dollars."

"Correct," Moreno said, standing out of his seat. "I'll need a half-dozen wallet-sized photographs of Guzman, taken as close to his death date as possible. You can send them along with my contract and travel arrangements to my home address."

John Moreno shook Garcia's hand, and walked away from the desk.

Garcia said to Moreno's back, "It used to be 'Juan,' didn't it? Funny how the simple change of a name can open so many doors in this country."

"I can leave for Brazil at any time," Moreno said. "You know where to reach me."

Moreno opened Mr. Garcia's door and walked from the office. The next morning, a package was messengered to John Moreno's home address.

And now Moreno's plane neared the Brasilia airport. He closed the guidebook he had been reading, and turned to Illiana.

"I have a question for you, Doctor," Moreno said. "A friend married a first-generation American of Brazilian descent. Their children, both of them, were born with blue-black spots above their buttocks."

Illiana smiled. "Brazil is a land whose people come from many colors," she said, sounding very much like the voice of the guidebook. "Black, white, brown, and many colors in between. Those spots that you saw" — and here Illiana winked — "it was simply the nigger in them."

So much for the ideal of Racial Democracy, Moreno thought, as the plane began its descent.

Moreno caught a ride from the airport with a man named Eduardo who divided his time as an importer/exporter between Brasilia and Miami. They had struck up a conversation as they waited in line to use the plane's lavatory during the flight. They were met at the airport by someone named Val, who Eduardo introduced as his attorney, a title which Moreno doubted, as Val was a giggly and rather silly young man. Still, he accepted a lift in Val's VW Santana, and after a seventy-mile-per-hour ride through the flat treeless landscape that was Brasilia, Moreno was dropped at the Hotel Dos Nachos, a place Eduardo had described with enthusiasm as "two and one half stars."

The lobby of the Hotel Dos Nachos contained several potted plants and four high-backed chairs occupied by two taxicab drivers, an aging tout in a shiny gray suit, and a bearded man smoking a meerschaum pipe. A drunken businessman accompanied by a mulatto hooker in a red leather skirt entered the lobby and walked up the stairs while Moreno negotiated the room rate. The hotel bellman stood sleeping against the wall. Moreno carried his own bags through the elevator doors.

Moreno opened the windows of his small brown room and stuck his head out. Below, in an empty lot, a man sat beneath a Pepsi-Cola billboard with his face buried in his hands, a mangy dog asleep at his feet. Moreno closed the window to a crack, stripped to his shorts, did four sets of fifty pushups, showered, and went to bed.

The next morning he caught an early flight to Recife. At the airport he hailed a taxi. Several foul-smelling children begged Moreno for change as he sat in the passenger seat of the cab, waiting for the driver to stow his bags. Moreno stared straight ahead as the children reached in his window, rubbing their thumbs and forefingers together in front of his face. Before the cab pulled away, one of the children, a dark boy with matted blond hair, cursed under his breath and dropped one American penny in Moreno's lap.

Moreno had the cab driver pass through Boa Viagem, Recife's resort center, to get his bearings. When Moreno had a general idea of the layout, the driver dropped him at his *apartamento* in the nine hundred block of Rua Setubal, one street back from the beach. A

uniformed guard stood behind the glassed-in gatehouse at the ten-
story condominium; Moreno tipped him straight off, and carried
his own bags through the patio of hibiscus and standing palm to the
small lift.

Moreno's *apartamento* was on the ninth floor, a serviceable ar-
rangement of one large living and dining room, two bedrooms, two
baths, a dimly lit kitchen, and a windowless sleeper porch on the
west wall where clothes were hung to dry in the afternoon sun. The
east wall consisted of sliding glass doors that opened to a concrete
balcony finished in green tile. The balcony gave to an unobstructed
view of the beach and the aquamarine and emerald swells of the
south Atlantic, and to the north and south the palm-lined beach
road, Avenida Boa Viagem. The sliding glass doors were kept open
at all times: a tropical breeze blew constantly through the *apartamento,* and the breeze ensured the absence of bugs.

For the first few days Moreno stayed close to his condominium,
spending his mornings at the beach working on his local's tan,
watching impromptu games of soccer, and practicing his Portuguese on the vendors selling oysters, nuts, and straw hats. At one
o'clock his maid, a pleasant but silent woman named Sonya, prepared him huge lunches, black beans and rice, salad, mashed potatoes, and pork roasted and seasoned with *tiempero,* a popular spice.
In the evenings Moreno would visit a no-name, roofless café, where
a photograph of Madonna was taped over the bar. He would sit
beneath a coconut palm and eat a wonderfully prepared filet of
fish, washed down with a cold Brahma beer, sometimes with a shot
of aguardente, the national rotgut that tasted of rail tequila but had
a nice warm kick. After dinner he would stop at the Kiosk, a kind of
bakery and convenience market, and buy a bottle of Brazilian cabernet, have a glass or two of that on the balcony of his *apartamento*
before going off to bed. The crow of a nearby rooster woke him
every morning through his open window at dawn.

Sometimes Moreno passed the time leaning on the tile rim of his
balcony, looking down on the activity in the street below. There
were high walls of brick and cinderblock around all the neighboring condominiums and estates, and it seemed as if these walls were
in a constant state of repair or decay. Occasionally an old white
mare, unaccompanied by cart or harness, would clomp down the
street, stopping to graze on the patches of grass that sprouted along
the edges of the sidewalk. And directly below his balcony, through

the leaves of the black curaçao that grew in front of his building, Moreno saw children crawl into the gray canvas Dumpster that sat by the curb, and root through the garbage in search of something to eat.

Moreno watched these children with a curious but detached eye. He had known poverty himself, but he had no sympathy for those who chose to remain within its grasp. If one was hungry, one worked. To be sure, there were different degrees of dignity in what one did to get by. But there was always work.

As the son of migrant workers raised in various Tex/Mex border towns, Juan Moreno had vowed early on to escape the shackles of his own lowly, inherited status. He left his parents at sixteen to work for a man in Austin, so that he could attend the region's best high school. By sticking to his schedule of classes during the day and studying and working diligently at night, he was able, with the help of government loans, to gain entrance to a moderately prestigious university in New England, where he quickly learned the value of lineage and presentation. He changed his name to John.

Already fluent in Spanish, John Moreno became degreed in both French and criminology. After graduation he moved south, briefly joining the Dade County sheriff's office. Never one for violence and not particularly interested in carrying or using a firearm, Moreno took a job for a relatively prestigious firm specializing in international retrievals. Two years later, having made the necessary connections and something of a reputation for himself, he struck out on his own.

John Moreno liked his work. Most of all, whenever his plane left the runway and he settled into his first-class seat, he felt a kind of illusion, as if he were leaving the dust and squalor of his early years a thousand miles behind. Each new destination was another permanent move, one step farther away.

> The Brazilians are a touching people. Often men will hug for minutes on end, and women will walk arm and arm in the street.

Moreno put down his guidebook on the morning of the fourth day, did his four sets of fifty pushups, showered, and changed into a swimsuit. He packed his knapsack with some American dollars, ten dollars worth of Brazilian cruzeiros, his long-lensed Canon AE-I, and the Guzman photographs, and left the *apartamento*.

Moreno was a lean man a shade under six feet, with wavy black hair and a thick black mustache. His vaguely Latin appearance passed for both South American and southern Mediterranean, and with his newly enriched tan he received scarcely a look as he moved along the Avenida Boa Viagem toward the center of the resort, the area where Guzman had been spotted. The beach crowd grew denser, women in thong bathing suits and men in their Speedos, vendors, hustlers, and shills.

Moreno claimed a striped folding chair near the beach wall, signaled a man behind a cooler who brought him a tall Antarctica beer served in a Styrofoam thermos. He finished that one and had two more, drinking very slowly to pass away the afternoon. He was not watching for Guzman. Instead he watched the crowd, and the few men who sat alone and unmoving on its periphery. By the end of the day he had chosen two of those men: a brown Rasta with sun-bleached dreadlocks who sat by the vendors but did not appear to have goods to sell, and an old man with the leathery, angular face of an Indian who had not moved from his seat at the edge of the market across the street.

As the sun dropped behind the condominiums and the beach draped in shadow, Moreno walked over to the Rasta on the wall and handed him a photograph of Guzman. The Rasta smiled a mouthful of stained teeth and rubbed two fingers together. Moreno gave him ten American dollars, holding out another ten immediately and quickly replacing it in his own pocket. He touched the photograph, then pointed to the striped folding chair near the wall to let the Rasta know where he could find him. The Rasta nodded, then smiled again, making a "V" with his fingers and touching his lips, blowing out with an exaggerated exhale.

"Fumo?" the Rasta said.

"Não fumo," Moreno said, jabbing his finger at the photograph once more before he left.

Moreno crossed the road and found the old man at the edge of the market. He replayed the same proposition with the man. The man never looked at Moreno, though he accepted the ten and slid it and the photograph into the breast pocket of his eggplant-colored shirt. Moreno could not read a thing in the man's black pupils in the dying afternoon light.

As Moreno turned to cross the street, the old man said in Portuguese, "You will return?"

Moreno said, *"Amanhã,"* and walked away.

On the way back to his place Moreno stopped at a food stand — little more than a screened-in shack on the beach road — and drank a cold Brahma beer. Afterward he walked back along the beach, now lit by streetlamps in the dusk. A girl of less than twenty with a lovely mouth smiled as she passed his way, her hair fanning out in the wind. Moreno felt a brief pulse in his breastbone, remembering just then that he had not been with a woman for a very long time.

It was this forgotten need for a woman, Moreno decided, as he watched his maid Sonya prepare breakfast the next morning in her surf shorts and T-shirt, that had thrown off his rhythms in Brazil. He would have to remedy that, while of course expending as little energy as possible in the hunt. First things first, which was to check on his informants in the center of Boa Viagem.

He was there within the hour, seated on his striped folding chair, on a day when the sun came through high, rapidly moving clouds. His men were there too, the Rasta on the wall and the old man at the edge of the market. Moreno had an active swim in the warm Atlantic early in the afternoon, going out beyond the reef, then returned to his seat and ordered a beer. By the time the vendor served it the old man with the Indian features was moving across the sand toward Moreno's chair.

"*Boa tarde,*" Moreno said, squinting up in the sun.

The old man pointed across the road, toward an outdoor café that led to an enclosed bar and restaurant. A middle-aged man and a young woman were walking across the patio toward the open glass doors of the bar.

"*Bom,*" Moreno said, handing the old man the promised ten from his knapsack. He left one hundred and twenty thousand cruzeiros beneath the full bottle of beer, gestured to the old man to sit and drink it, put his knapsack over his shoulder, and took the stone steps from the beach up to the street. The old man sat in the striped folding chair without a word.

Moreno crossed the street with caution, looking back to catch a glimpse of the brown Rasta sitting on the wall. The Rasta stared unsmiling at Moreno, knowing he had lost. Moreno was secretly glad it had been the old man, who had reminded him of his own father. Moreno had not thought of his long-dead father or even seen him in his dreams for some time.

Moreno entered the restaurant. There were few patrons, and all of them, including the middle-aged man and his woman, sat at a long mahogany bar. Moreno took a chair near an open window. He leaned his elbow on the ledge of the window and drummed his fingers against wood to the florid music coming from the restaurant. The bartender, a stocky man with a great belly that plunged over the belt of his trousers, came from behind the bar and walked towards Moreno's table.

"Cervejas," Moreno said, holding up three fingers pressed together to signify a tall one. The bartender stopped in his tracks, turned, and headed back behind the bar.

Moreno drank his beer slowly, studying the couple seated at the bar. He considered taking some photographs, seeing that this could be done easily, but he decided that it was not necessary, as he was certain now that he had found Guzman. The man had ordered his second drink, a Teacher's rocks, in English, drinking his first hurriedly and without apparent pleasure. He was tanned and seemed fit, with a full head of silvery hair and the natural girth of age. The woman was in her twenties, quite beautiful in a lush way, with the stone perfect but bloodless look of a photograph in a magazine. She wore a bathing suit top, two triangles of red cloth really, with a brightly dyed sarong wrapped around the bottoms. Occasionally the man would nod in response to something she had said; on those occasions, the two of them did not look in each other's eyes.

Eventually the other patrons finished their drinks and left, and for a while it was just the stocky bartender, the man and his woman, and Moreno. A very tall, lanky young man with long curly hair walked into the bar and with wide strides went directly to the man and whispered in his ear. The man finished his drink in one gulp, tossed bills on the bar, and got off his stool. He, the woman, and the young man walked from the establishment without even a glance in Moreno's direction. Moreno knew he had been made but in a practical sense did not care. He opened his knapsack, rose from his seat, and headed for the bar.

Moreno stopped in the area where the party had been seated and ordered another beer. As the bartender turned his back to reach into a cooler, Moreno grabbed some bar napkins, wrapped them around the base of Guzman's empty glass, and began to place the glass in his knapsack.

A hand grabbed Moreno's wrist.

The hand gripped him firmly. Moreno smelled perspiration, partly masked by a rather obvious men's cologne. He turned his head. It was the lanky young man, who had reentered the bar.

"You shouldn't do that," the young man said in accented English. "My friend João here might think you are trying to steal his glass."

Moreno placed the glass back on the bar. The young man spoke rapidly in Portuguese, and João the bartender took the glass and ran it over the brush in the soap sink. Then João served Moreno the beer that he had ordered, along with a clean glass. Moreno took a sip. The young man did not look more than twenty. His skin had the color of coffee beans, with hard bright eyes the color of the skin. Moreno put down his glass.

"You've been following my boss," the young man said.

"Really," Moreno said.

"Yes, really." The young man grinned. "Your Rastaman friend, the one you showed the pictures to. He don't like you so good no more."

Moreno looked out at the road through the open glass doors. "What now?"

"Maybe me and a couple of my friends," the young man said, "now we're going to kick your ass."

Moreno studied the young man's face, went past the theatrical menace, found light play in the dark brown eyes. "I don't think so. There's no buck in it for you, that way."

The young man laughed shortly, pointed at Moreno. "That's right!" His expression grew earnest again. "Listen, I tell you what. We've had plenty excitement today, plenty enough. How about you and me, we sleep on top of things, think it over, see what we're going to do. Okay?"

"Sure," Moreno said.

"I'll pick you up in the morning, we'll go for a ride, away from here, where we can talk. Sound good?"

Moreno wrote his address on a bar napkin. The young man took it, and extended his hand.

"Guilherme," he said. "Gil."

"Moreno."

They shook hands, and Gil began to walk away.

"You speak good American," Moreno said.

Gil stopped at the doors, grinned, and held up two fingers. "New York," he said. "Astoria. Two years." And then he was out the door.

Moreno finished his beer, left money on the bar. He walked back to his *apartamento* in the gathering darkness.

Moreno stood drinking coffee on his balcony the next morning, waiting for Gil to arrive. He realized that this involvement with the young man was going to cost him money, but it would speed things along. And he was not surprised that Guzman had been located with such ease. In his experience those who fled their old lives merely settled for an equally monotonous one in a different place, and rarely moved after that. The beachfront hut in Pago Pago becomes as stifling as the center hall colonial in Bridgeport.

Gil pulled over to the curb in his blue sedan. He got out and greeted the guard at the gate, a man Moreno had come to know as Sergio, who buzzed Gil through. Sergio left the glassed-in guard-house then and approached Gil on the patio. Sergio broke suddenly into some sort of cartwheel, and Gil stepped away from his spinning feet, moved around Sergio fluidly and got him into a headlock. They were doing some sort of local martial art, which Moreno had seen practiced widely by young men on the beach. Sergio and Gil broke away laughing, Gil giving Sergio the thumbs-up before looking up toward Moreno's balcony and catching his eye. Moreno shouted that he'd be down in a minute, handing his coffee cup to Sonya. Moreno liked this kid Gil, though he was not sure why.

They drove out of Boa Viagem in Gil's Chevrolet Monsa, into downtown Recife, where the breeze stopped and the temperature rose an abrupt ten degrees. Then they were along a sewage canal near the docks, and across the canal a kind of shantytown of tar-paper, fallen cinderblock, and chicken wire, where Moreno could make out a sampling of the residents: horribly poor families, morning drunks, two-dollar prostitutes, men with murderous eyes, criminals festering inside of children.

"It's pretty bad here now," Gil said, "though not so bad like in Rio. In Rio they cut your hand off just to get your watch. Not even think about it."

"The *Miami Herald* says your government kills street kids in Rio."

Gil chuckled. "You Americans are so righteous."

"Self-righteous," Moreno said.

"Yes, self-righteous. I lived in New York City, remember? I've seen the blacks and the Latins, the things that are kept from them.

There are many ways for a government to kill the children it does not want, no?"

"I suppose so."

Gil studied Moreno at the stoplight as the stench of raw sewage rode in on the heat through their open windows. "Moreno, eh? You're some sort of Latino, aren't you?"

"I'm an American."

"Sure, American. Maybe you want to forget." Gil jerked his thumb across the canal, toward the shantytown. "Me, I don't forget. I come from a *favela* just like that, in the south. Still, I don't believe in being poor. There is always a way to get out, if one works. You know?"

Moreno knew now why he liked this kid Gil.

They drove over a bridge that spanned the inlet to the ocean, then took a gradual rise to the old city of Olinda, settled and burned by the Dutch in the fifteenth century. Gil parked on cobblestone near a row of shops and vendors, where Moreno bought a piece of local art carved from wood for his mother. Moreno would send the gift along to her in Nogales, a custom that made him feel generous, despite the fact that he rarely phoned her, and it had been three Christmases since he had seen her last. Afterward Moreno visited a bleached church, five hundred years old, and was greeted at the door by an old nun dressed completely in white. Moreno left cruzeiros near the simple altar, then absently did his cross. He was not a religious man, but he was a superstitious one, a remnant of his youth spent in Mexico, though he would deny all that.

Gil and Moreno took a table shaded by palms near a grille set on a patio across from the church. They ordered one tall beer and two plastic cups. A boy approached them selling spices, and Gil dismissed him, shouting something as an afterthought to his back. The boy returned with one cigarette, which he lit on the embers of the grille before handing it to Gil. Gil gave the boy some coins and waved him away.

"So," Gil said, "what are we going to talk about today?"

"The name of your boss," Moreno said. "It's Guzman, isn't it?"

Gil dragged on his cigarette, exhaled slowly. "His name, it's not important. But if you want to call him Guzman, it's okay."

"What do you do for him?"

"I'm his driver, and his interpreter. This is what I do in Recife. I hang around Boa Viagem and I watch for the wealthy tourists having trouble with the money and the language. The Americans, they have the most trouble of all. Then, I make my pitch. Sometimes it works out for me pretty good."

"You learned English in New York?"

"Yeah. A friend brought me over, got me a job as a driver for this limo service he worked for. You know, the guys who stand at the airport, holding signs. I learned the language fast, and real good. The business, too. In one year I showed the man how to cut his costs by thirty percent. The man put me in charge. I even had to fire my friend, too. Anyway, the man finally offered me half the company to run it all the way. I turned him down, you know? His offer, it was too low. That's when I came back to Brazil."

Moreno watched the palm shadows wave dreamily across Gil's face. "What about Guzman's woman?"

"She's some kinda woman, no?"

"Yes," Moreno said. "When I was a child I spotted a coral snake and thought it was the most beautiful thing I had ever seen. I started to follow it into the brush when my mother slapped me very hard across the face."

"So now you are careful around pretty things." Gil took some smoke from his cigarette. "It's a good story. But this woman is not a poisonous snake. She is just a woman." Gil shrugged. "Anyway, I don't know her. So she cannot help us."

Moreno said, "Can you get me Guzman's fingerprints?"

"Sure," Gil said. "It's not a problem. But what you are going to get me?"

"Go ahead and call it," Moreno said.

"I was thinking, fifty-fifty, what you get."

Moreno frowned. "For two weeks, you know, I'm only going to make a couple thousand dollars. But I'll tell you what — you get me Guzman's fingerprints, and I'll give you one thousand American."

Gil wrinkled his forehead. "It's not much, you know?"

"For this country, I think that it's a lot."

"And," Gil continued quickly, "you got to consider. You, or the people you work for, maybe they're going to come down and take my boss and his money away. And then Gil, he's going to be out of a job."

Moreno sat back and had a swig of beer and let Gil chew things over. After a while Gil leaned forward.

"Okay," Gil said. "So let me ask you something. Have you reported back to your people that you think you have spotted this man Guzman?"

"No," Moreno said. "It's not the way I work. Why?"

"I was thinking. Maybe my boss, it's worth a lot of money to him that you don't go home and tell anyone you saw him down here. So I'm going to talk to him, you know? And then I'm going to call you tomorrow morning. Okay?"

Moreno nodded slowly. "Okay."

Gil touched his plastic cup to Moreno's and drank. "I guess now," Gil said, "I work for you too."

"I guess you do."

"So anything I can get you, Boss?"

Moreno thought about it, and smiled. "Yes," he said. "There is one thing."

They drove back down from Olinda into Recife where the heat and Gil's cologne briefly nauseated Moreno, then on into Boa Viagem where things were cooler and brighter and the people looked healthy and there were not so many poor. Gil parked the Monsa a few miles north of the center, near a playground set directly on the beach.

"There is one," Gil said, pointing to a woman, young and lovely in denim shorts, pushing a child on a swing. "And there is another." This time he pointed to the beach, where a plainer woman, brown and finely figured in her thong bathing suit, shook her blanket out on the sand.

Moreno wiped some sweat from his brow and nodded his chin toward the woman in the bathing suit. "That's the one I want," he said, as the woman bent over to smooth out her towel. "And that's the way I want her."

Gil made the arrangements with the woman, then dropped Moreno at his *apartamento* on the Rue Setubal. After that he met some friends on the beach for a game of soccer, and when the game was done he bathed in the ocean. He let the sun dry him, then drove to Guzman's place, an exclusive condominium called Des Viennes on the Avenida Boa Viagem. Gil knew the guard on duty, who buzzed him through.

Ten minutes later he sat in Guzman's living room overlooking the Atlantic where today a group of sailboats tacked back and forth while a helicopter from a television station circled overhead. Guzman and Gil sat facing each other in heavily cushioned armchairs, while Guzman's woman sat in an identical armchair but facing out toward the ocean. Guzman's maid served them three aguardentes with fresh lime and sugar over crushed ice. Guzman and Gil touched glasses and drank.

"It's too much sugar and not enough lime," Guzman said to no one in particular.

"No," Gil said. "I think it's okay."

Guzman set down his drink on a marble table whose centerpiece was a marble obelisk. "How did it go this morning with the American?"

But Gil was now talking in Portuguese to Guzman's woman, who answered him contemptuously without turning her head. Gil laughed sharply and sipped from his drink.

"She's beautiful," Guzman said. "But I don't think you can afford her."

"She is not my woman," Gil said cheerfully. "And anyway, the beach is very wide." Gil's smile turned down and he said to Guzman, "Dismiss her. Okay, Boss?"

Guzman put the words together in butchered Portuguese, and the woman got out of her seat and walked glacially from the room.

Guzman stood from his own seat and went to the end of the living room where the balcony began. He had the look of a man who is falling to sleep with the certain knowledge that his dreams will not be good.

"Tell me about the American," Guzman said.

"His name is Moreno," Gil said. "I think we need to talk."

Moreno went down to the condominium patio after dark and waited for the woman on the beach to arrive. A shirtless boy with kinky brown hair walked by pushing a wooden cart, stopped, and put his hand through the iron bars. Moreno ignored him, practicing his Portuguese instead with Sergio, who was on duty that night behind the glass guardhouse. The shirtless boy left without complaint and climbed into the canvas Dumpster that sat by the curb, where he found a few scraps of wet garbage that he could chew and swallow and perhaps keep down. The woman from the beach ar-

rived in a taxi, and Moreno paid the driver and received a wink
from Sergio before he led the woman up to his *apartamento*.

Moreno's maid, Sonya, served a meal of whole roasted chicken,
black beans and rice, and salad, with a side of shrimp sautéed in
coconut milk and spice. Moreno sent Sonya home with extra cruzeiros, and uncorked the wine, a Brazilian cabernet, himself. He
poured the wine and before he drank asked the woman her name.
She touched a finger to a button on her blouse and said, "Claudia."

Moreno knew the dinner was unnecessary but it pleased him to
sit across the table from a woman and share a meal. Her rather flat,
wide features did nothing to excite him, but the memory of her
fullness on the beach kept his interest, and she laughed easily
and seemed to enjoy the food, especially the chicken, which she
cleaned to the bone.

After dinner Moreno reached across the table and undid the top
two buttons of the woman's blouse, and as she took the cue and
began to undress he pointed her to the open glass doors that led to
the balcony. He extinguished the lights and stepped out of his
trousers as she walked naked across the room to the edge of the
doors and stood with her palms pressed against the glass. He came
behind her and moistened her with his fingers, then entered her,
and kissed her cheek near the edge of her mouth, faintly tasting the
grease that lingered from the chicken. The breeze came off the
ocean and whipped her hair across his face. He closed his eyes.

Moreno fell to sleep that night alone, hearing from someplace
very far away a woman's voice, singing mournfully in Spanish.

Moreno met Gil the following morning at the screened-in food
shack on the beach road. They sat at a cable-spool table, splitting a
beer near a group of teenagers listening to accordion-drive *ferro*
music from a transistor radio. The teenagers were drinking beer.
Gil had come straight from the beach, his long curly hair still damp
and touching his thin bare shoulders.

"So," Gil said, tapping his index finger once on the wood of the
table. "I think I got it all arranged."

"You talked to Guzman?"

"Yes. I don't know if he's going to make a deal. But he has agreed
to meet with you and talk."

Moreno looked through the screen at the clouds and around the
clouds the brilliant blue of the sky. "When and where?"

"Tonight," Gil said. "Around nine o'clock. There's a place off your street, Setubal, where it meets the commercial district. There are many fruit stands there —"

"I know the place."

"Good. Behind the largest stand is an alley. The alley will take you to a bar that is not marked."

"An alley."

"Don't worry," Gil said, waving his hand. "Some friends of mine will be waiting for you to show you to the bar. I'll bring Guzman, and we will meet you there."

"Why that place?"

"I know the man, very well, who runs the bar. He will make sure that Guzman leaves his fingerprints for you. Just in case he doesn't want to play football."

"Play ball," Moreno said.

"Yes. So either way we don't lose."

Moreno drank off the rest of his beer, placed the plastic cup on the cable-spool table. "Okay," he said to Gil. "Your plan sounds pretty good."

In the evening Moreno did four sets of fifty pushups, showered, and dressed in a black polo shirt tucked into jeans. He left his *apartamento* and took the lift down to the patio, where he waved to a guard he did not recognize before exiting the grounds of his condominium and hitting the street.

He walked north on Setubal at a brisk pace, avoiding the large holes in the sidewalk and sidestepping the stacks of brick and cinderblock used to repair the walls surrounding the estates. He passed his no-name café, where a rat crossed his path and dropped into the black slots of a sewer grate. He walked by people who did not meet his eyes and bums who held out their hands but did not speak.

After about a mile he could see through the darkness to the lights of the commercial district, and then he was near the fruit stands. In the shadows he could see men sitting, quietly talking and laughing. He walked behind the largest of the stands. In the mouth of an alley a boy stood leaning on a homemade crutch, one badly polioed leg twisted at the shin, the callused toes of that leg pointed down and brushing the concrete. The boy looked up at Moreno and rubbed his fingers together, and Moreno fumbled in his pock-

ets for some change, nervously dropping some bills to the sidewalk.
Moreno stooped to pick up the bills, handing them to the boy, then
he entered the alley. He could hear *ferro* music playing up ahead.

He looked behind him, and saw that the crippled boy was following him into the alley. Moreno quickened his step, passing vendors'
carts and brick walls whitewashed and covered with graffiti. He saw
an arrow painted on a wall, and beneath the arrow the names of
some boys, and an anarchy symbol, and to the right of that the
words "Sonic Youth." He followed the direction of the arrow, the
music growing louder with each step.

Then he was in a wide open area that was no longer an alley
because it had ended with walls on three sides. There were four
men waiting for him there.

One of the men was short and very dark and held a machete at
his side. The crippled boy was leaning against one of the walls.
Moreno said something with a stutter and tried to smile. He did not
know if he had said it in Portuguese or in English, or if it mattered,
as the *ferro* music playing from a boombox on the cobblestones was
very loud.

Moreno felt a wetness on his thigh and knew that this wetness was
his own urine. The thing to do was to simply turn and run. But for
the first time he saw that one of the men was Sergio, the guard at his
condominium, who he had not recognized out of his uniform.

Moreno laughed, and then all of the men laughed, including
Sergio, who walked toward Moreno with open arms to greet him.

The Brazilians are a touching people. Often men will hug for minutes
on end, and women will walk arm and arm in the street.

Moreno allowed Sergio to give him the hug. He felt the big muscled arms around him, and caught the stench of cheap wine on
Sergio's breath. Sergio smiled an unfamiliar smile, and Moreno
tried to step back, but Sergio did not release him. Then the other
men were laughing again, the man with the machete and the crippled boy too. Their laughter rode on the sound of the crazy music
blaring in the alley.

Sergio released Moreno.

A forearm from behind locked across Moreno's neck. There was
a hand on the back of his head, pressure, and a violent movement,
then a sudden, unbelievable pain, a white pain but without light.

For a brief moment Moreno imagined that he was looking at his own chest from a very odd angle.

If John Moreno could have spoken later on, he would have told you that the arm that killed him smelled heavily of perspiration and cheap cologne.

Gil knocked on Guzman's door late that night. The maid offered him a drink. He asked for aguardente straight up. She returned with it and served it in the living room, where Gil sat facing Guzman, and then she walked back to the kitchen to wash the dishes before she went to bed.

Guzman had his own drink, a Teacher's over ice, on the marble table in front of him. He ran his fingers slowly through his lion's head of silver hair.

"Where is your woman?" Gil said.

"She took a walk," Guzman said. "Is it over?"

"Yes," Gil said. "It is done."

"All this killing," Guzman said softly.

"You killed a man yourself. The one who took your place on the boat."

"I had him killed. He was just a rummy from the boatyard."

"It's all the same," Gil said. "But maybe you have told yourself that it is not."

Guzman took his scotch and walked to the open glass doors near the balcony, where it was cooler and there was not the smell that was coming off Gil.

"You broke his neck, I take it. Like the other one."

"He has no neck," Gil said. "We cut his head off and threw it in the garbage. The rest of him we cut to pieces."

Guzman closed his eyes. "But they'll come now. Two of their people have disappeared."

"Yes," Gil said. "They'll come. You have maybe a week. Argentina would be good for you, I think. I could get you a new passport, make the arrangements —"

"For a price."

"Of course."

Guzman turned and stared at the lanky young man. Then he said, "I'll get your money."

When he returned, Gil was downing the last of his drink. Guzman handed him five banded stacks of American fifties. Gil slipped them into his trousers after a careless count.

"Twenty-five thousand," Guzman said. "Now you've taken fifty thousand of my money."

"You split the two million with your wife. And there have been many others to pay." Gil shrugged. "It costs a lot to become a new man, you know? Anyway, I'll see you later."

Gil headed for the door, and Guzman stopped him.

"I'm curious," Guzman said. "Why did this Moreno die, instead of me?"

"His bid was very low," Gil said. "Goodnight, Boss."

Gil walked from the room.

Down on the Avenida Boa Viagem, Gil walked to his Chevrolet Monsa and got behind the wheel. Guzman's woman, who was called Elena, was in the passenger seat, waiting for Gil to arrive. She leaned across the center console and kissed Gil on the lips, holding the kiss for a very long while. It was Gil who finally broke away.

"Did you get the money?" Elena said.

"Yes," Gil said. "I got it." He spoke without emotion. He looked up through the windshield to the yellow light spilling onto Guzman's balcony.

"We are rich," Elena said, forcing herself to smile and pinching Gil's arm.

"There's more up there," Gil said. "You know?"

Elena said, "You scare me a little bit, Gil."

She went into her purse, found a cigarette, and fired the cigarette off the lighter from the dash. After a couple of drags she passed the cigarette to Gil.

"What was it like?" Elena said.

"What's that?"

"When you killed this one," she said. "When you broke his neck. Did it make a sound?"

Gil dragged on the cigarette, squinted against the smoke that rose off the ash.

"You know how it is when you eat a chicken," he said. "You have to break many bones if you want to get the meat. But you don't hear the sound, you know?

"You don't hear it," Gil said, looking up at Guzman's balcony, "when you're hungry."

S. J. ROZAN

Hoops

FROM *Ellery Queen's Mystery Magazine*

A COLD WIND was pulling sharp waves from the Hudson as I
drove north, out of town. The waves would strain for height, pushing forward, reaching; but then they'd fall back with small, violent
crashes, never high enough, never breaking free.

I was heading to Yonkers, a tired, shabby city caught between
New York and the real suburbs. I'd been there over the years as
cases had taken me, but I'd never had a client from there before.
I'd never had a client who was just eighteen, either. But it was a
week since I'd closed my last case. Money was a little tight, I was
getting antsy, and working was better than not working, always.

Even working for a relative of Curtis's. I'd been surprised when
he'd called me. The ring of the telephone had burst into a practice
session where a Beethoven sonata I'd thought I had in my fingers
was falling apart, where rhythm, color, texture, everything was off. I
usually don't like being interrupted at the piano, but this time I
jumped at it.

Until I heard who it was, and what he wanted.

"A nephew of yours?" I said into the phone. "I didn't know scum
like you had relatives, Curtis."

"Now, you got no call to be insulting," Curtis's smooth voice gave
back. "Though it ain't surprising. I told the boy I could get him a
investigator do a good job for him, but he gonna have to put up
with a lot of attitude."

"What's he done?" I asked shortly.

"Ain't done nothing. A friend of his got hisself killed. Raymond
think someone should be paying attention."

"When people get killed the cops usually pay attention."

"Unless you some black kid drug dealer in Yonkers, and you the suicide half of a murder-suicide."

He had a point. "Tell me about it."

He told me. An eighteen-year-old high school senior named Charles Lomax had been found in a park where the kids go at night. His pregnant girlfriend, beside him, had a bullet in her heart. Lomax had a bullet through his head and the gun in his hand.

The bodies had been discovered by the basketball coach, who said he'd gone out looking after Lomax hadn't shown up for practice. He hadn't shown up for class, either, but apparently that wasn't unusual enough for his classroom teachers to be bothered about. Lomax had been a point guard with a C average. He'd been expected to graduate, which distinguished him from about half the kids at Yonkers West. He'd been in trouble with the police all his life, which distinguished him from nobody. There was nothing else interesting about him, except that he'd been a friend of Raymond Coe, and Raymond wasn't happy with the official verdict: murder-suicide, case closed.

"What's Raymond's theory?" I asked Curtis, shouldering the phone so I could close the piano and stack my music.

"Let me put it to you this way," Curtis oozed. "I ain't suggested the boy hire hisself a honky detective because I admire the way you people dance."

I pulled slowly around the corner, coasted past the cracked asphalt playground I'd been told to find. The late-day air was mean with the wind's cold edge, but six black kids in sweats and high-tech sneakers crowded the concrete half-court. Their game was fast, loud, and physical, elbows thrown and no fouls called. One kid, tall and meaty, had a game on a level the others couldn't match: Faster and smarter both, he muscled his man when he couldn't finesse him. But it didn't stop the rest. No one hung back, no one gave in. Slam dunks and three-pointers flew through the netless rim. They didn't seem to be keeping score.

A kid fell, rolled, jumped up shaking his hand against the sting of a scrape. Without missing a beat he was back in the game. I parked across the street and watched. One of those kids was Raymond; I didn't know which. Right now I knew nothing about any of them, except for what I could see: strength, focus, a wild joy in pushing themselves. I finished a cigarette. In a minute I'd become part of their world. This moment of possibility would end. Knowledge can't be shaken off. And knowledge is always limiting.

The game faltered and then stopped as I walked to the break in the chain-link fence. They all watched me approach, silent. A chunky kid in a hooded sweatshirt shifted the ball from one hand to the other. To the one who'd fallen he said, "Yo, Ray. This your man?"

"Don't know." Raising his voice as though he suspected I spoke a different language, the kid said, "You Smith?"

I nodded. "Raymond Coe?"

"Yeah." He jerked his head at the others. "These my homeboys."

I glanced at the tight, silent group. "They in on this?"

"You got a problem with that?"

"Should I?"

"Maybe you don't like working for a bunch of niggers."

I stared into his dark eyes. It seemed to me they were softer than he might have wanted them to be. "Maybe I don't like having to pass an exam to get a case." I shrugged, turned to go.

"Yo," Raymond said, behind me.

I turned back.

"Curtis say you good."

"I don't like Curtis," I told him. "He doesn't like me. But we're useful to each other from time to time."

Surprisingly, he grinned. His face seemed, for a moment, to fit with what I'd seen in his eyes. "Curtis tell me you was gonna say that."

"What else did he tell you?"

"That you the man could find out about my man C."

"What's in it for you?"

A couple of the other kids scowled at that, and one started to speak, but Raymond silenced him with a look. "Nothing in it for me," he said.

"I cost money," I pressed. "Forty an hour, plus expenses. Two days up front. Why's it worth it to you?"

The chunky kid slammed the ball to the pavement, snatched it back. "Come on, Ray. You don't need this bull."

Raymond ignored him, looked steadily at me. "C was my main

man, my homie. No way he done what they say he done. Somebody
burned him. I ain't gonna let that pass."

"Why me?" I asked. "Curtis knows every piece of black slime that
ever walked the earth, but he sent you a white detective. Why?"

"'Cause the slime we looking for," Raymond said steadily, "I don't
believe they black."

Raymond, his homies, and I made our way to the end of the block,
to the pizza place. The day had gone and a tired gray evening was
coming in, studded with yellow streetlights and blinking neon. The
homies gave me their names: Ash, Caesar, Skin. Tyrell, the one who
could really play. The chunky one, Halftime. None of them offered
to shake my hand.

Inside, where the air swirled with garlic and oregano, we crowded
around a booth, hauling chairs to the end of the table. Halftime
went to order a pizza. He came back distributing Cokes and Sprites,
and he brought me coffee. Across the room, from the jukebox, a
rap song began, complicated rhythm under complex rhyme, music
with no melody. I drank some coffee. "Well?"

Everyone glanced at everyone else, but they all came back to
Raymond. Raymond looked only at me. "My man C," he started.
"Someone done him, make it look like suicide."

"People kill themselves," I said.

Some heads shook; Tyrell muttered, "Damn."

"You don't know him," Raymond said. "C don't never give up on
nothing. And he had no reason. He was gonna graduate, he was
gonna have a kid. The season was just starting."

"The season?" I left the rest for later.

"Hoops," Raymond told me, though it was clear I was straining
the patience of the others. "My man a guard. Tyrell, Ash, and me,
we on the squad too." Tyrell and Ash, a round-faced quiet kid,
nodded in acknowledgment. "The rest of them," Raymond's sudden, unexpected grin flashed again, "they keep us on our game."

"So you're telling me if Lomax was going to kill himself he would
have waited until after the season?" I lit a cigarette, shook the match
into the tin ashtray.

"Man, I am telling you no way he did that." Raymond's voice was
emphatic. "C don't have no reason to want out. Plus, Ayisha. Ain't
no way he gonna do her like that, the mother of his baby."

"He wanted the baby?"

Halftime grinned, poked at something on the table. Raymond said, "He already buying it things. Toys and stuff. Bought one of them fuzzy baby basketballs, you know? It was gonna be a boy."

"How was he planning to support a family?"

Raymond shrugged. "Some way. Ayisha, she bragging like he gonna get tapped to play for some big school and they gonna be rich, but she don't believe it neither."

"It wasn't true?"

"Nah." Raymond shook his head. "Only dude around here got that kind of chance be my man Tyrell. He gonna make us famous. Put us on the map."

I turned to Tyrell, who was polishing off his second Coke in the corner of the booth. "I watched you play," I told him. "You're smart and fast. You have offers?"

Tyrell stared at me for a moment before he answered. "Coach say scouts coming this season." His voice was deep, resonant, and slow. "He been talking to them."

Halftime's name rang out; he went to the counter for the pizza. I looked around at the others, at their hard faces and at their eyes. Seventeen, eighteen: They should have been on the verge of something, at the beginning. But these boys had no futures and they knew it; and I could see it, in their eyes.

I didn't ask where the money was coming from to pay me. I didn't want to know. I didn't ask what would happen to Tyrell if he didn't get a college offer, or whether the others, the ones who weren't on the squad, were still in school. So what if they were? Where would it get them?

I asked a more practical question. "Who'd want to kill Lomax?"

Raymond shrugged, looked at his homeboys. "Everybody got enemies."

"Who were his?"

"Nobody I know about," he said. "Except the cops."

"Cops?" I looked at Raymond, at the other grim faces. "That's what this is about? You think this was a cop job?"

Halftime came back, with a pizza and a pile of paper plates. Everyone reached for a slice but me; Raymond made the offer but I shook my head.

Raymond didn't answer my question, gave Tyrell a look. Tyrell's deep voice picked it up. "C and me was in a little trouble last year. Gas-station holdup. It was bull. Charges was dropped."

"But them mothers didn't let up," Raymond said impatiently. "Tyrell, nobody care, but C been a pain in the cops' butt for years. You know, up in their face, trash-talking. I tell him, man, back off, you leave them alone and they leave you alone. But he don't never stop. C like to win. Also he like to make sure you know you lose. Cops was all over him after he get out."

"And?"

"And nothing. They couldn't get nothing else on him."

"And?" I said again, knowing what was coming.

"I figure they get tired waiting for him to make a mistake and make it for him."

I pulled on my cigarette. There was nothing left; I stubbed it out. I wanted to tell them they were wrong, they were crazy, that kind of stuff doesn't really go on. But that would be pointless. They might be wrong, in this case, but they weren't crazy and we all knew it.

"Anyone in particular?" I asked.

Raymond shook his head. "Cops around here, they run in packs," he said. "Could be anyone."

Two slices were left on the tray. Without discussion, and seemingly by general consent, Raymond and Tyrell reached for them.

"Okay," I said. "Tell me about her."

Tyrell looked away, as though other things in the room were more interesting than I was.

"Ayisha?" Raymond asked. He seemed to think about my question as he ate. "He can't get enough of her," he finally said.

"But you didn't like her?"

"Nah, she okay." He flipped a piece of crust onto the tray, sat back, and popped the top of a Sprite. "She sorta — you know. She got a smart mouth. And she been around."

A couple of the other guys snickered. I wondered whom she'd been around with.

"She have enemies?"

"I don't know. But like I say, everybody got them. Can't always tell what you done to get them, but everybody got them."

I left, trading phone numbers with Raymond. I took the homies' numbers too, though I was less than certain that getting in touch with any of them would be as easy as a phone call. But I might want to talk to some of them, separately, later. Now, I wanted to talk to a few other people.

The first, from a phone booth down the street, was Lewis Farlow, the basketball coach who'd found the bodies. I called him at the high school, to find a time he'd be available. Half an hour, he told me. He knew about me; he'd been expecting my call.

Next I called the Yonkers P.D., to find the detective on the Lomax case. Might as well get the party line.

He was a high-voiced Irish sergeant named Sweeney. He wasn't impressed with my name or my mission, and he wasn't helpful.

"What's to investigate?" he wanted to know. "That case has already been investigated. By real detectives."

"My client's not sure it was suicide," I said calmly.

"Yeah? Who are you working for?"

"Friend of the family."

"Don't be cute, Smith."

"I'm just asking for the results of the official investigation, Sweeney."

The grim pleasure in Sweeney's voice was palpable. "The official results are, the kid killed the girlfriend. Blam! Then he blew his own brains out. Happy?"

Start out with an easy one. "Whose was the gun?"

"The Pope's."

"You couldn't trace it?"

"No, Smith, we couldn't trace it. Numbers were filed off, inside and out. That a new one on you?"

"Seems like a lot of trouble to go to for a suicide weapon."

"Maybe suicide wasn't on his mind when he got it."

"Why'd he do it?"

"How the hell do I know why he did it? You suppose it had anything to do with her being pregnant?"

"And what, his reputation would be ruined? Anyway, his friends say he wanted the baby."

"Yeah, sure. Da-da." Sweeney made baby noises into the phone.

"Sweeney —"

"Yeah. So maybe he did. And then maybe he finds out it isn't his. You like that for a motive? It's yours."

"You have any proof of that?"

"No. Matter of fact, I just thought it up. I'll let you in on something, Smith. I got better things to do than bust my hump to prove a kid with his brains in the dirt and the gun in his hand pulled the trigger."

"I understand you guys knew this kid."

"We know them all. Most of them have been our guests for short stays in our spacious accommodations."

"I hear you couldn't hold on to this one."

"What, for that gas-station job?" He didn't rise to the bait. "Way I look at it, it's just as well. If we could hold them all as long as they deserve, the streets would be clean and I'd be out of a job."

"Come on, Sweeney. Didn't it steam you just a little when the kid walked? I hear it wasn't the first time."

"Matter of fact, it wasn't."

"Matter of fact, I hear there were cops who had this kid on a special list. Was he on your list, Sweeney?"

"Now just hold it, Smith. What are you getting at? I killed him because I couldn't keep his ass in jail where it belonged?"

I'd made him mad. Good; angry men make mistakes.

"Not necessarily you, Sweeney. It's just that I'll bet there weren't a lot of tears in the department when Lomax bought it."

"Oh," he said slowly, his voice dangerously soft. "I get it. You're looking for a lawsuit, right?"

"Wrong."

"Crap. The family wants to milk it. You find a hole in the police work, they sue the department. The city settles out of court; it's got no backbone with these people. You drive off in your Porsche and I get pushed out early on half my stinking pension. That's it, right?"

"No, Sweeney, that's not it. I'm interested in what really happened to this kid. That's what any good cop would be interested in, too."

"You know what, Smith? You're lucky I don't know your face. Here's some advice for free: Don't let me see it."

The phone slammed down; that was that.

Yonkers West High School filled the entire block, a sulking brick-and-concrete monster whose windows were covered with a tight wire mesh. I asked the security guard at the door the way to the gym. "I'm here to see Coach Farlow," I said.

"You a scout?" he asked after me, as I started down the hall.

"No. You have something worth scouting?"

The guard grinned. "Come back tomorrow, at practice," he said. "You'll see."

I found Lewis Farlow behind his desk in his Athletic Department office, a windowless, cramped, concrete-block space that smelled of liniment, mildew, and sweat. Dusty trophies shared the top of the filing cabinets with papers and old coffee cups. Here and there a towel huddled on the floor, as though too exhausted to make it back through the connecting door to the locker room.

I knocked, checked Farlow out while I waited for him to look up from his paperwork. He was a thin white man, smaller than his players, with deep creases in the sagging skin of his face and sparse, colorless hair that might once have been red.

"Yeah." Farlow lifted his head, glanced over me swiftly with blue eyes that were bright and sharp.

"Smith," I said.

"Oh, yeah. About Lomax, right? Sit down." He gestured to a chair.

"The guard at the door asked me if I was a scout," I said as I moved into the room, trying to avoid the boxes of ropes and balls that should have been somewhere else, if there'd been somewhere else for them to be. "He meant that big guy? Tyrell?"

Farlow nodded. "Tyrell Drum," he said. "Best thing we've had here in years. Everybody's just waiting for him to catch fire. You seen him play?" He looked at me quizzically.

"He was with Raymond Coe just now," I explained. "You have scouts coming down?"

"I already had some stringers early last season. Liked what they saw, but the big guns didn't get a chance to get here while Drum was still playing."

"He didn't play the whole season?"

"Sat it out." One corner of Farlow's mouth turned up in a smile that wasn't a smile.

"Hurt?"

"In jail."

"Oh," I said. "The gas-station job?"

"You heard about that?"

"He told me. It was him and Lomax, right?"

"They say it wasn't either of them. Charges were eventually dropped, but the season was over by then."

"Did he do it?"

"Who the hell knows? If he didn't, he will soon. Or something like it. Unless he gets an offer. Unless he gets out of here. Look, Smith: about this Lomax thing."

Farlow stopped, turned a pencil over in his fingers as though looking for a way to say what he wanted. I waited.

"The guys are pretty upset," Farlow said. "Especially Coe; he and Lomax were pretty tight. Coe's got this half-assed idea that the cops killed Lomax. He's sold it to the rest of them. They told me they were going to hire a private eye to prove it."

"How come they told you?"

"I'm the coach. High school, that's like a father confessor. Wasn't it that way when you were there?"

"The high school I went to, all the kids were white."

"You surprised they talk to me? They gotta talk to someone." He shrugged. "I'm on their side and they know it. I go to bat for them when they're in trouble. I bully them into staying in school. Coe wouldn't be graduating if it weren't for me."

He threw the pencil down on the desk, slumped back in his chair. "Not that I know why I bother. They stay in school, so what? They end up fry cooks at McDonald's." Farlow paused, rubbed a hand across his square chin; I got the feeling he was only half talking to me. "Eighteen years in this hole," he went on, "watching kids go down the drain. No way out. Except every now and then, a kid like Drum comes along. Someone you could actually do something for. Someone with a chance. And the stupid sonuvabitch spends half his junior year in jail."

He looked at me. The half-grin came back. "Sorry, Smith. I get like this. The old coach, feeling sorry for himself. Let's get back to Lomax. Where the hell was I?"

"The guys came to you," I said. "They told you they wanted a P.I."

"Yeah. So I told them to go ahead. Coe's like Lomax was, a stubborn bastard. Easier to agree with than to cross. So I said go ahead, call you. He probably thinks I think he's right, that there's something fishy here. But I don't."

"What do you think?"

"I think the simple answer is the best. Sometimes it's hard, but it's the best. Lomax killed the girl and he killed himself."

"Why?"

"Some beef, I don't know. Old days, he'd have knocked her around, then gone someplace to cool off. Today, they all have guns. You get mad, someone's dead before you know it. By the time he realizes what he's done it's over. Then? She's dead, the baby's dead, what's he gonna do? He's still got the gun."

He reached for the pencil again, turned it in his hand, and watched it turn.

"A guy's best friend turns up dead," he said in a quiet voice, "he wants to do something. Hiring you makes them feel better. Okay." He looked up. "So what I'm asking you is, go through the motions. You gotta do that; they're gonna pay you for it. But try to wrap it up fast. The sooner they put this behind them the better off they'll be."

I had my own doubts about how easy it ever was to put a friend's death behind you, but that didn't make Farlow wrong.

"If there's nothing to find, I'll know that soon enough," I said.

Farlow nodded, as though we'd reached an agreement. I asked him, "You found the bodies?"

"Yeah." He threw the pencil down again.

"What did it look like?"

"Look like?"

"Tell me what you saw."

Farlow's bright eyes fixed me. He paused, but if he had a question he didn't ask it.

"She's lying on her back. Just this little spot of blood on her chest; but God, her eyes are open." He stopped, licked his dry lips. "Him, he's maybe six feet away. Side of his head blown off. Right side; gun's in his right hand. What do you need this for?"

"It's the motions," I said. "What kind of gun?"

"Automatic. Didn't the police report tell you?"

"They won't let me see it."

"Jesus, don't tell Coe that. Is that normal?"

"Actually, yes. Usually you can get someone to tell you what's in it, but I rubbed the detective on the case the wrong way."

"Jim Sweeney? Everything rubs him the wrong way."

"How about Lomax?"

"You mean, Coe's theory? There's not a cop in Yonkers who wouldn't have thrown a party if they could make something stick to Lomax. Backing off wasn't something he knew how to do. They all hated him. But I don't think Sweeney any more than anyone else."

"Tell me about Lomax. Was he good?"

"Good?" Farlow looked puzzled; then he caught on. "Basketball, you mean? He was okay. He could wear better guys out, is what he could do. He'd get up for balls he couldn't reach and shoot shots he couldn't make, even after the bell. He was everywhere, both ends of the floor. Bastard never gave up."

"Did he have a future in the game?"

"Lomax? No." There was no doubt in Farlow's voice. "Eighteen years in this place, I've only seen two or three that could. Drum is the best. An NCAA school could make something out of him. Right school could get him to the NBA. Even the wrong school would get him out of here." I thought back to the concrete playground, to the eyes of the boys around the pizza-parlor table. Here, I had to admit, was a good place to get out of. "But Lomax? No."

"About the girlfriend," I said. "Had you heard anything about trouble between them?"

"No. She had a rep, you know. But all the guys seemed to think she'd quieted down since she took up with Lomax."

"Who'd she been with before?"

"Don't know."

"Do you know anyone with a reason to kill Lomax, or the girl?"

He sighed. "Look," he said. "These kids, they talk big, they look bad, but these are the ones who're trying. Coe, Drum, even Lomax — still in school, still trying. Like something could work out for them." He spread his hands wide, showing me the shabby office, the defeated building, the dead-end lives. "But me, all my life I've been a sucker. My job, the way I figure, is to do my damnedest to help, whenever it looks like something might. That's your job too, Smith. You're here because it makes Coe feel like a man, avenging his buddy. That helps. But you're not going to find anything. There's nothing to find."

"Okay." I stood. I was warm; the air felt stuffy, old. I wanted to be outside; where the air moved, even with a cold edge. I wanted to be where everything wasn't already over. "Thanks. I'll come back if I need anything else."

"Sure," he answered. "And come see Drum play Saturday."

Seeing the family is always hard. People have a thousand different ways of responding to loss, of adjusting to their grief and the sudden new pattern of their lives. A prying stranger on a questionable mission is never welcome; there's no reason he should be.

Charles Lomax's family lived in a tan concrete project about half a mile from the high school. There were no corridors. The elevators went to outdoor walkways; the apartments opened off them. The door downstairs should have been locked, but the lock was broken, so I rode up to the third floor, picked my way through kids' bikes and folding beach chairs to the apartment at the end.

The wind and the air were cold as I waited for someone to answer my ring, but the view was good, and the apartments' front doors were painted cheerful colors. Here and there beyond the doors I could hear kids' voices yelling and the thump of music.

"Yes, can I help you?" The woman who opened the door was thin, tired-looking. She wore no makeup, and her wrists and collarbone were knobby under her shapeless sweater. Her hair, pulled back into a knot, was streaked with gray. It wasn't until I heard her clear soft voice that I realized she was probably younger than I was.

Electronic sirens came from the TV in the room behind her. She turned her head, raised her voice. "Darian, you turn that down."

The noise dropped a notch. The woman's eyes came back to me.

"Mrs. Lomax?" I said. "I'm Smith. Raymond Coe said you'd be expecting me."

"Raymond." She nodded slightly. "Come in."

She closed the door behind me. Warm cooking smells replaced the cold wind as we moved into the living room, where a boy of maybe ten and a girl a few years older were flopped on the sofa in front of the TV. An open door to the left led into a darkened bedroom. On the wall I glimpsed a basketball poster, Magic Johnson calling the play.

Charles Lomax's mother led me to a paper-strewn table in one corner of the living room, offered me a chair. "Claudine," she called to the girl on the sofa, "come and get your homework. Don't you leave your things around like that." The girl pushed herself reluctantly off the pillows. She looked me over with the dispassionate curiosity of children; then, fanning herself with her papers, she flopped onto the floor in front of the TV.

Sitting, Mrs. Lomax turned to me and waited, with the tired patience of a woman who's used to waiting.

"I'm sorry to bother you," I began. "But Raymond said you might answer some questions for me."

"What kind of questions?"

I looked over at the children, trying to judge whether the TV was loud enough to keep this discussion private. "Raymond doesn't think Charles killed himself, Mrs. Lomax."

"I know," she said simply. "He told me that. I think he just don't want to think it."

"Then you don't agree with him?"

She also looked to the children before she answered. "Raymond knew my boy better than I did. If he says someone else had more reason to kill Charles than Charles had, might be he's right. But I don't know." She shook her head slowly.

"Mrs. Lomax, did Charles have a gun?"

"I never saw one. I guess that don't mean he didn't have one."

A sudden sense of being watched made me glance toward the sofa again. My eyes caught the boy's; the girl was intent on the TV. The boy turned quickly back to the set, but not before Mrs. Lomax lifted her chin, straightened her shoulders. "Darian!" The boy didn't respond. "Darian," she said again, "you come over here."

Darian sullenly slipped off the sofa, came over, eyes watching the floor. His sister remained intent on the car chase on TV.

"Darian," his mother said, "Mr. Smith asked a question. Did you hear him?"

Hands in the pockets of his oversized jeans, the boy scowled and shrugged.

"He asked did your brother have a gun."

The boy shrugged again.

"Darian, if you know something you ain't saying, you're about to be in some serious kind of trouble. Did you ever see your brother with a gun?"

Darian kicked at a stray pencil, sent it rolling across the floor. "Yeah, I seen him."

I looked at Mrs. Lomax, then back to the boy. "Darian," I said, "do you know where he kept it?"

Without looking at me, Darian shook his head.

"You sure?" said his mother sharply.

"'Course I'm sure."

Mrs. Lomax looked closely at him. "Darian, you know anything else you ain't saying?"

"No, 'course not," Darian growled.

"If I find you do . . ." she warned. "Okay, you go back and sit down."

Darian spun around, deposited himself on the sofa, arms hugging his knees.

I turned back to Mrs. Lomax. "Can I ask you about Ayisha?"

She shrugged.

"Did you like her?"

"Started out I did. She was smart to her friends, but she was polite to me. I remember her when she was small, too. Bright little thing. . . . But after I found out what she did, no, I didn't like her no more."

"Do you mean getting pregnant?" I asked.

She frowned, as though I were speaking a foreign language she was having trouble following. "Not the baby," she said. "The baby wasn't the problem. Though she didn't have no right to go and do that, after she knew. You got to see I blame her. She killed my son."

"Mrs. Lomax, I don't understand. According to the police, your son killed *her*, and himself."

"Oh, well, he pulled the trigger. But they was both already dead. And that innocent baby, too."

"I don't get it."

"Raymond didn't tell you?" Her eyes, fixed on mine, hardened with sudden understanding, and the realization that she was going to have to tell me herself. "She gave him AIDS."

Back on the winter street, I dropped a quarter in a pay phone, watched a newspaper skid down the walk, and waited for Raymond.

"Your buddy Charles was HIV positive," I said when he came on. "Did you know that?"

A short pause, then Raymond's voice, belligerent around the edges. "Yeah, I knew it."

"And his girlfriend, too."

"Uh-huh."

"Why didn't you tell me?"

"What difference do it make?"

"Sounds like a motive to me."

"What you talking about?"

"Hopelessness," I told him. "Fear. Not wanting to wait around to die. Not wanting to watch his son die."

"Oh, man!" Raymond snorted a laugh. "C didn't care. He say he never feel better. He tell me it gonna be years before he get sick. Not even gonna stop playing or nothing, even if it so piss Coach off. Just 'cause you got the virus don't mean you sick, you know," he pointed out with a touch of contempt. "You as ignorant as some of them 'round here."

"What does that mean?"

"Some of the homies, they nervous 'round C when they find out he got the virus. Talking about he shouldn't be coming 'round. Like Ash, don't want to play if C stay on the squad. I had to talk to that brother. But C just laugh. Say, some people ignorant. Don't pay them no mind, do what you be doing. Maybe someday I get sick, he say, but by then they have a cure."

"Goddamn, Raymond," I breathed. I stuck a cigarette in my mouth, lit it to keep from saying all the angry things I was thinking, things about youth, strength, arrogance not lasting, about consequences, about decisions closing doors behind you. I took a deep drag; it cleared my head. Not your business, Smith. Stick to what Raymond hired you for. "All right: Ayisha," I said. "Who else was she with?"

"Ayisha? She been with a lot of guys." Raymond paused. "You thinking some jealous dude gonna come after C and Ayisha 'cause they together?"

"It happens."

"Oh, man! Ain't no homie done this. Black man do it, it be straight up. Coming with this suicide bull, this some crazy white man. That why you here. See," he said, unexpectedly patient, trying to explain something to me, "C and me and the crew, we tight. Like . . ." He paused, reaching for an analogy I'd understand. "Like, you on a squad, maybe you don't like a brother, but you ain't gonna trip him when he got the ball. You got something to say to him, you go up in his face. You do what you gotta do, and you take what you gotta take."

Uh-huh, I thought. If life were like that.

"Okay, Raymond. I'll call you."

"Yeah, man. Later."

I turned up the collar of my jacket; the wind was blowing harder now, off the river. You could smell the water here, the openness of it, the movement and the distance. To me there had always been an offer in that, and a promise: Elsewhere, things are different. Somewhere, not here, lives are better; and the water connects that place and this.

That offer, that promise, probably didn't mean much to Raymond and his buddies. This was what they had, and, with a clear-eyed understanding I couldn't argue with, they knew what it meant.

Except Tyrell Drum, of course. "Offer" meant something different to him, but maybe not all that different: a chance to start again, to climb out of this and be somewhere else.

I started back to my car. I was cold and hungry, and down. I'd been buying into Raymond's theory. A conspiracy, the Power bringing down a black kid because they couldn't get him legally and they knew they could get away with it. I'd bought into it because I'd wanted to. Wanted to what, Smith? Be the righteous white man, the one on their side? The part of the Power working for them? Offering them justice, this once, so the world wouldn't look so bad to them? Or so it wouldn't look so bad to you? So you could sleep at night, having done your bit for the oppressed. Terrific.

But now it was different. Lomax had a motive, and a good one, if you asked me. Teenage swagger can plunge into despair fast. One bad blood test, one scary story about how it feels to die of AIDS: Something like that could have been enough. Especially if he really loved Ayisha. Especially if he already loved his son.

Running footsteps on the pavement behind me made me spin around, ready. The electricity in my skin subsided when I saw who it was.

"Mister, wait." The voice was small and breathless. Jacket open, pink backpack heavy over her arm, Claudine Lomax stopped on the sidewalk, caught her breath. She regarded me with suspicion.

"Zip your jacket," I said. "You'll freeze."

She glanced down, then did as she was told, pulling up her hood and tucking in her braids. She narrowed her eyes at me. "Mister, you a cop?"

"No," I said. "I'm a private detective."

"Why you come around asking questions like that?"

I thought for a moment. "Raymond asked me to. There were some things about Charles he wanted to know."

She bit her lower lip. "You know Raymond?"

"I'm working for him."

"Raymond was Charles's friend."

"I know."

She nodded; that seemed to decide something for her. Looking me in the eye, she said, "You was asking Mama about Charles's gun."

"That's right. I was asking where he kept it. Do you know?"

"Yeah. And so do Darian. He gonna kill me when he find out it gone. But he just a *kid*. I been crazy worried about this ever since Charles . . ." She trailed off, looking away; then she lifted her head and straightened her shoulders, her mother's gesture. Putting her backpack on the ground with exaggerated care, she pulled a paper bag from it, thrust it at me. "Here."

"What's this?" It was heavy and hard and before I looked inside I knew the answer.

"I don't want it in the house. Mama don't know nothing about it. I don't want it where Darian can get it. He think he stepping like a man, gonna take care of business. Make me laugh, but he got this. Boys like that all the time, huh?"

"Yeah," I said. "Boys are like that all the time."

"I thought Charles took it with him. Meeting some guy at night like that. But he must have — he must have had another one, huh?"

"Maybe," I said carefully. "Claudine, what do you mean 'meeting some guy at night'?"

"Charles don't like to go do his business without his piece. But maybe it wasn't business," she said thoughtfully. "'Cause usually he tell Ayisha stay home when he taking care of business."

I asked her, "What guy was Charles meeting? Do you know?"

"Uh-uh. He just say he gotta go meet some guy, and Ayisha say she want to come. So Charles say okay, she could keep him company. Then he tell me I better be in bed when he get back, 'cause I got a math test the next day and he gonna beat my butt if I don't pass." In a small voice she added, "I passed, too."

I opened the bag, looked without taking the gun out. It was a long-barreled .32. "Claudine, how long had Charles had this?"

"About a year."

"How did you know he had it?"

"I hear him and Tyrell hiking on each other when he got it. Tyrell say it a old-fashioned, dumb kind of piece, slow as shit. Oh." She covered her mouth with her hand. "Sorry. But that what Tyrell say."

"It's okay, Claudine. What did Charles say?"

"He laugh. He say, by the time Tyrell get his fancy piece working, he gonna find out some guy with a old-fashioned dumb piece already blowed his head off, every time."

She stared at me under the yellow streetlights, a skinny twelve-year-old kid in a jacket not warm enough for a night like this.

"Claudine," I said, "did Charles and Tyrell argue a lot?"

"I hear them trash-talking all the time," she answered. "But I don't think nothing of it. Boys do that, don't they?"

"Yeah," I said. "They do."

Tyrell, then. Claudine told me where to go; I drove over. Tyrell Drum lived with his family in a run-down wood-frame house with a view of the river in the distance and the abandoned GM plant closer in. Towels were stuffed around the places where the warped windows wouldn't shut. The peeling paint had faded to a dull gray.

My knock was answered by a young boy with hooded eyes who left me to shut the door behind myself as I followed him in. From the room to the left I heard the canned laughter of a TV game show; from upstairs, the floor-shaking boom of a stereo. "Tyrell be in the basement," the boy told me, pointing without interest to a door under the stairs.

"Who's that?" a woman's voice called from above as I opened that door, headed down.

"Man to see Tyrell," the boy answered, and the household went about its business.

The basement was a weight room. The boiler and hot-water tank had been partitioned off into dimness. On this side of the partition were bright fluorescent lights, mats, weights, jump ropes. The smell of damp concrete mixed with the smell of sweat; the hum of the water heater was punctuated by grunts. Tyrell was on the bench, working his left biceps with what looked like sixty pounds. He lifted his eyes to me when I came down, but he didn't move his head out of position, and he finished his set. He was shirtless. His muscles were mounds under his glinting skin.

When he was done, he clanked the weights to the floor, ran a towel over his face.

"Yeah?" he said. He took in air in deep, controlled breaths.

"I want to talk about Ayisha," I said. "And Lomax."

"Go ahead." He kept his eyes on me for a few moments. Then,

straightening, he picked up the weights with the other hand, started pumping. "Talk."

"She was your girl once, wasn't she?"

He smiled, didn't break his rhythm. "She been everyone's girl once."

"Maybe everyone didn't care."

"Maybe not." Nineteen, twenty. He put the weights down, left the bench, moved over to a Universal machine. He loaded it to 210, positioned himself, started working the big muscles in his thighs.

"But you did."

He stopped, looked at me. He held the weights in position while he spoke. "Yeah. I cared. I was so glad to get rid of her and C at the same time I coulda went to Disney World." Slowly, in total control, he released the weights. He relaxed but didn't leave the seat, getting ready for his next set.

"What does that mean, get rid of them?"

Either he really had no idea what I was getting at or he was a terrific actor. "Didn't have no time for her." Pump, breathe. "For him neither. C always got something going, some idea." Hold. Release, relax. "Always talking at you. Get me confused. Lost my whole last season because of him."

"The gas-station job was his idea?"

He gave me a sly grin. "Charges was dropped." He strained against the weights again. "C talking about, only way to make it be stealin' and dealin'." Pump, release, pump. "I try that, ain't no good at it. Now Coach be telling me —" pump, breathe "— say, I got a chance, a real chance. But I ain't got all the time in the world. Got to do it now, you understand?"

He looked at me. I didn't respond.

"C, he don't never shut up. Don't give a man no chance to think." Hold, release, relax. He swung his legs off the machine, picked up the towel again, wiped his face. "C don't like to think. Don't like it quiet. Dude get nervous if horns ain't honking and sirens going by." He laughed. "Surprise me him and Ayisha end up where they do."

"Meaning?"

"C don't never go to the park. They got nothing there but trees and birds, he say. What I'm gonna do with them?"

"His sister says he was going to meet someone that night."

Tyrell shrugged. He put his legs back in position, started another set.

"And that was it?" I said. "You were through with Lomax and his ideas? You weren't helping him take care of business anymore?"

This time he ran the set straight through before he answered. When he was done, he looked at me, breathing deeply.

"Coach be talking at me, I'm seeing college, the NBA, hotels and honeys and dudes carrying my suitcase. C up in my face, I'm looking at the inside of Rikers. Now what you think I'm gonna do?"

"And that was what you thought of when Lomax took up with Ayisha?"

"Damn sure. They both out my face now, I can take care my business."

"Your business," I mused. "You have a gun, right? An automatic. Can I see it?"

"What the hell for?"

"Lomax was a revolver man, wasn't he?" I asked conversationally. "He had a .32."

Tyrell shook his head in mild disbelief. "Man, Wyatt Earp coulda carried that piece."

"Why do you carry yours, Tyrell?"

"Now why the hell you think I carry mine?" He scowled. "You some kind of detective, can't figure out why a man got to be strapped 'round here?"

"Is it like that around here?" I asked softly. "A man has to have a gun?"

"God*damn!*" Tyrell exploded. "You think I like that? Watching my back just whenever I'm walking? Can't be going here, can't be going there, you got beef or your homies got beef and someone out to get you for it, go to school, everybody packing, just in case. You think I like that?" A sharp pulse throbbed in his temples; his eyes were shining and bitter. "Man, you can forget about it! I'm gonna make it, man. I'm gonna be all that. C, he got this idea, that idea, don't never think about what come next, what gonna happen 'cause of what he do. I tell him, you got Ayisha, now get out my face, leave me be. I got things to do."

His hard eyes locked on mine. The stereo, two floors up, sent down a pounding, recurring shudder that surrounded us.

"Tyrell," I said, "I'd like to see your gun."

For a moment, no reaction. Then a slow smile. He sauntered over to a padlocked steel box on the other side of the room. He ran the combination, creaked the top open, lifted out a .357 Coonan automatic. Wordlessly he handed it to me.

"How long have you had this?" I asked.

"Maybe a year."

"You sure you didn't just get it?"

He looked at me without an answer. Then, climbing the stairs to where he could reach the door, he opened it and yelled, "Shaun!" He paused; then again, "Shaun! Haul your ragged ass down here!"

The boy with the hooded eyes appeared in the doorway. "You calling me, Tyrell?" he asked tentatively.

Tyrell moved aside, motioned him downstairs. The boy, with an unsure look at me, started down. He walked like someone trying not to take up too much room.

"Shaun, this my piece?"

The boy looked at the gun I held out. "Yeah," he said. "I guess."

"Don't be guessing," Tyrell said. "This my piece or ain't it?"

The boy gave Tyrell a nervous look, then peered more closely at the gun, still without touching it. "Yeah," he said. "It got that thing, here."

"What thing?" I asked. I looked where the boy pointed. A wide scrape marred the shiny stock.

Tyrell said, "Shaun, where that come from?"

Shaun answered without looking at Tyrell. "I dropped it."

"When?"

"Day you got it."

"What happen?"

"You mean, what you do?"

"Yeah."

The kid swallowed. "You be cursing at me and you smack me."

"Broke your nose, didn't I?"

The kid nodded.

"So you remember that day pretty good, huh?"

"Yeah."

"When was that?"

"About last year."

"You touched it since?"

"No, Tyrell." The kid looked up quickly.

"Good. Now get the hell out of here."

Shaun scuttled up the stairs and closed the door behind him.

"See?" Tyrell, smiling, took the gun from me. "My heat. Had it a year. How about that?"

"That's great, Tyrell," I said. "It must be great to be so tough. Two more questions. Where were you the night Lomax and Ayisha died?"

"Me?" Tyrell answered, still smiling, looking at the gun in his hand. "I was here."

"Can you prove that?"

"Depends. You could see if my two cousins remember. I went to bed early. Coach say discipline make the difference. You got to be able to do what need to be done, whether you want to or not."

"Uh-huh. You're a model citizen, Tyrell. One more thing. Did you know Lomax was HIV positive?"

Tyrell shrugged, locked his gun back in the box.

"Did it bother you? Friend of yours, with a disease like that?"

"Uh-uh," he said. "Don't got no time to worry about C. He got his troubles, I got mine."

I drove south, found Broadway, stopped at a tavern near the Bronx line. It was a half-empty place, the kind where dispirited old-timers nurse watery drinks and old grudges. In a scarred booth I lit a cigarette, worked on a Bud. I thought about Raymond, about the simple desire to do something, to try to help. About wanting justice, wanting what's right.

Of course, that meant so many things. To Sweeney it could mean taking a taunting, slippery drug dealer out of the picture. To Tyrell Drum it could mean getting rid of a smooth-talking, dangerous distraction. To Lomax himself, it might have meant having the last laugh: not cheating death, but choosing it, choosing your time and your way and your pain. None of these kids had ever had a lot of choices. This was one Lomax could have given himself.

But I didn't like it.

I had a couple of reasons, but the biggest was what Raymond had instinctively felt: Lomax wasn't the type.

I hadn't known Lomax, but the picture I'd gotten of him was consistent, no matter where it came from. Suicide is for when you give up. Lomax never gave up. Taunting cops. Trying to fast-talk

Tyrell into his kind of life. Going up for balls he couldn't reach and shooting shots he couldn't make. That's what the coach said.

Even after the bell.

I lit another cigarette, seeing in my mind the asphalt playground in the fading light, watching the kids charge and jump, hearing the sound of the pounding ball and of their shouts. I saw one fall — I knew now it was Raymond — roll to his feet, try to shake off the sting of the scrape on his hand. Then, immediately, he was back in the game.

Even after the bell.

Suddenly I was cold. Suddenly I knew.

Wanting justice, wanting to help.

There was something else that could mean.

The next day, late afternoon again. The same gray river, the same cold wind.

It would have been pointless to go earlier. I would have been guessing, then, where to look; at this hour, I knew.

I'd made one phone call, to Sweeney, just to check what I already was sure of. He gave me what I wanted, and then he gave me a warning.

"I'm giving you this because I know you'll get it one way or another. But listen to me, Smith: Whatever road you're heading down, it's a dead end. The first complaint I hear, you'll get a look up close and personal at the smallest cell I can find. Do I make myself clear?"

I thanked him. The rest of the day I worked on the Beethoven. It was getting better, slowly, slowly.

Yonkers West loomed darker, bigger, more hostile than before. At the front door I greeted the guard.

"You were here yesterday." He grinned. "Go on, tell me you're not a scout."

"Practice in session?" I asked.

"Uh-huh. Go on ahead. I'm sure Coach won't mind."

I wasn't. But I went.

The gym echoed with the thump of the basketball on the maple. The whole team, starters and bench, was out on the floor practicing a complicated high-low post play. They were rotating through it, changing roles so that each man would understand it in his gut, know how each position felt; but in play, the point would be to get the ball to the big man. To Tyrell. As many times as the play was called, that's how it would end up. Tyrell shooting, Tyrell carrying the team's chances, carrying everyone's hopes.

Coach Farlow was standing on the sideline. He watched the play as they practiced it, following everyone's moves, but especially Tyrell's. I walked the short aisle between the bleachers, came and stood next to him.

He glanced at me, then turned his eyes back to his players. "Hi," he said. "Come to watch practice?"

"No," I said. "I came to talk."

He looked over at me again, then blew the whistle hanging around his neck. "All right, you guys!" The sweating players stopped, stood wiping their faces with their shirts, catching their breath. He rattled off two lists of names. Four guys headed for the sidelines; two teams formed on the court. Raymond, on one end of the floor, caught my eye. I nodded noncommittally. The others looked my way, curious, but snapped their attention back to Farlow when he shouted again.

"Okay, let's go," he called. "Hawkins, take the tip. You and Ford call it."

One of the guys who'd been on his way off the court chased down the ball. Another trotted over to take the coach's whistle. The ball was tossed up in the center of the circle; the game began.

"You let them call games often?" I asked Farlow as he stood beside me, following their movements with his sharp blue eyes.

"It's good for them. Forces them to see what's going on. Makes them take responsibility. Most of them get pretty good at it."

I said, "I'll bet Lomax wasn't."

"Lomax? He used to tick them all off. He'd call fouls on everyone, right and left. Just to throw his weight around."

"Did you stop him?"

Farlow watched Raymond go for a lay-up and miss it. Tyrell snatched the rebound, sank it easily. Farlow said, "The point is for them to find out what they're made of. What each other's made of. Doesn't help if I stop them."

"Besides," I said, "you couldn't stop Lomax, could you?"

This time his attention turned to me, stayed there. "What do you mean?"

"No one could ever stop Lomax from doing whatever he wanted. No matter how dangerous it was, to him or anyone else. He wouldn't stop playing, would he?"

"What?"

"That was it, wasn't it? He had AIDS and he wouldn't stop playing."

A whistle blew. Silence, then the slap of sneakers on wood, the thump of the ball as the game went on. Farlow's eyes stayed on me.

"You couldn't talk him out of it," I said. "You couldn't drop him because he was too good. You'd have had to explain why, and the law protects people from that kind of thing. He'd have been back on the court and you'd have been out of a job.

"But you couldn't let him keep playing. That could have ruined everything."

Shouts came from the far end of the court as Tyrell stole a pass, broke down the floor, and dunked it before anyone from either team got near him.

"Could have ruined what?" Farlow asked in a tight, quiet voice.

"You're going through the motions," I said. "You know I have it. But all right, if you want to do that."

I watched the game, not Farlow, as I continued. "If Lomax had stayed on the team there might have been no season. Some of his own buddies didn't want to play with him. Guys get hurt in this game. They bleed, they spit, they sweat. The other guys were afraid.

"That's what happened to Magic Johnson: He couldn't keep playing after everyone knew he had AIDS because guys on other teams were afraid to play against him. Magic had class. He didn't force it. He retired.

"But that wasn't Lomax's way, was it? Lomax felt fine and he was going to play. And if it got out he had AIDS his own teammates might have rebelled. So would the teams you play against. The whole season would have collapsed.

"That's what you were afraid of. Losing the season. Losing Drum's last chance."

We stared together down the court, to where a kid was getting set to take a foul shot.

"Lomax killed himself," Farlow said, harshly and slowly. "He took his gun and shot his girl and shot himself."

I said, "I have his gun."

"He had more than one. He bragged about it."

"Maybe," I said. "Maybe not. But the one I have is a revolver. Guys who like revolvers — I'm one — like them because they're dependable. You can bury a revolver in the mud for a month and it'll fire when you pull it out. Lomax was like that about this gun. There've been times when I've had to carry an automatic, and it always makes me nervous. Even if I owned one, it's not the gun I'd take if I were going out to shoot myself."

Farlow said nothing, watching his kids, watching the game.

"Then there are the guys who like automatics," I said. "They're fast. They're powerful. That's what you have, isn't it?"

"Me?" Farlow tried to laugh. "You're kidding. A gun?"

"An automatic," I said. "Same make and model as the one that killed Lomax and Ayisha. Drum got me thinking about it. He said everyone around here was packing. I started to wonder who 'everyone' was. I checked your permit with Sweeney. He told me about it, and said if I harassed you he'd throw me in jail. Does he know?"

The ball was knocked out of bounds, near us. The officials and players organized themselves, resumed the game. The ball flew out again almost immediately. Another whistle blew, play began again.

"No," Farlow said quietly.

We watched together in silence for a while. Some of the ball handling was sloppy, but the plays were smart, and every player played flat out, giving the game everything he had.

"Not every coach can get this from his players," I said.

Farlow asked, "How did you know?"

"Little things. They all clicked together. The gun. The fact that Lomax didn't like the park."

"Didn't like the park?" Farlow said. "A guy might pick a place he doesn't like, to die in."

"Sure. But his coach wouldn't think to go looking for him there, unless he had some reason to think he might be there."

Farlow didn't answer. He glanced at the clock on the gym wall; then he stepped onto the court, clapped his hands, and bellowed, "All right, you guys! Looking good. Showers! Stay and wait. I'll talk to you afterwards."

The kid with the whistle brought it back to the coach; the kid with the ball sent it Farlow's way with a bounce pass. Raymond raised his eyebrows as he went by on his way to the locker room. I shook my head.

Farlow watched them go. When the door swung shut behind

them he stayed unmoving, as though he were still watching, still seeing something.

"One kid," he said, not talking to me. "One chance. Year after year, you tear your heart out for these kids and they end up in the gutter. Then you get one kid with a way out, one chance. Drum's ready, but he's weak. Not physically. But he can't keep his head in the game. If he loses this season, too, there'll be nothing left. He'll hold up another damn gas station, or something. It has to be now."

"Lomax was eighteen," I said. "Ayisha was seventeen. She was pregnant."

"They were dead!" The coach's eyes flashed. "They were dead already. How many years do you think they were going to have? Baby born with AIDS, it wouldn't live through Drum's pro career."

"You did them a favor?"

He flinched. "No." His voice dropped. "That's not what I mean. But Drum — so many people are waiting for this, Smith. And they were already dead."

I needed a cigarette. I lit one up; the coach didn't try to stop me.

"You asked him to meet you at the park?"

He nodded. "In this weather there's no one there. I knew he didn't like it there, but . . ." He didn't finish.

"But you're the coach."

"I knew Lomax. He'd never let me see he was nervous. Afraid. It never occurred to me he'd bring her along."

"For company," I told him. "That's what his little sister said."

"I almost didn't — didn't do it, when I saw she was there. I tried one more time to talk him out of it. Told him I'd get his academic grades raised so he'd be sure to graduate. Told him I'd get him a job. Told him Drum needed him to quit."

"What did he say?"

The coach looked across the gym. "He said if scouts were coming down to look at Drum, maybe they were interested in point guards, too."

He brought his eyes back to me. "It was the only way, Smith."

"No," I said.

I smoked my cigarette. Farlow looked down at his hands, tough with years of balls and blackboards.

"What are you going to do?" he asked. "Will you tell Sweeney?"

"Sweeney won't hear it. I have no hard evidence. To him this case is closed."

"Then what?" he asked. His eyes lit faintly with something like hope.

I looked toward the door the players had disappeared through. "I have a client," I said.

"You'll tell Coe?"

I crushed the cigarette against the stands, dropped the butt back in the pack. "Or you will."

We stood together, wordless. "You know what's the worst part?" he finally said.

"What?"

"Coe's twice the man the rest of them are. Drum's a bully, Lomax was a creep. Ash is a coward. But Coe, he's tough but not mean. He can tell right from wrong and he doesn't let his ego get in the way. But there's nothing I can do for him. I can't help him, Smith. But I can help Drum."

"Yesterday," I said, "you told me I was here because avenging his buddy made Raymond feel like a man. And that helped."

He stared at me. He made a motion toward the door where the players had gone, but he stopped.

"I'll wait for Raymond to call me," I said. "I'll give him a few days. Then I'll call him."

I looked once more around the gym, then walked the short aisle between the stands, leaving the coach behind.

I was at the piano the next afternoon when Raymond called. No small talk: "Coach told me," he said.

I shut the keyboard, pulled a cigarette from my pocket. "What did you do?"

"First, I couldn't believe it. Stared at him like an idiot. Coach, man! You know?"

I did know; I said nothing.

"Then I feel like killing him."

I held my breath. "But?"

"But I hear C in my head," Raymond said. "Laughing. 'What so damn funny, homie?' I ask him. 'This the guy burned you.' C keep laughing, in my head. He say, 'For Tyrell, brother? This about the funniest thing ever.' Just laughing and laughing."

"What did you do?"

"Slammed out of there, to go and think. See, I was stuck. What you gonna do, Ray, I be asking myself. Go to the cops? Give me a break."

"If you want to do that," I said, "I'll see it through with you."

"No," he said. "Ain't my way. Another thing, I could do Coach myself; but that ain't my way neither. So what I'm gonna do, just let him walk away? He done my main man; got to pay for that. Got to pay. But in my head, C just laughing. 'For Tyrell, man?' And then I know what he mean. And I know I don't got to do nothing."

"Why not?" I asked.

"'Cause Tyrell, he been with Ayisha before C."

It took a second, then it hit.

"Jesus," I said.

"Yeah," Raymond agreed. "What Coach done, he done to get Tyrell his shot. But Tyrell ain't gonna have no shot."

No shot. No pro career, no college years. Two murders. A lifetime of hard-won trust, everything thrown away for nothing. Tyrell might be able to avoid going public, might be able to keep his mouth shut the way Lomax hadn't; people might not know, at first. But the virus was inexorable. It would get Tyrell before Tyrell had a chance to make everyone's dreams come true.

"Raymond," I said, "I'm sorry."

"Man," he said, "so am I."

There wasn't anything more. I told Raymond to keep in touch; he laughed shortly and we both knew why. When we hung up I stood at the window for a while. After the sky turned from purple to gray, after the promise faded, I pulled on my jacket, went over to the Fourth Street courts, and watched the kids play basketball under the lights.

ALLEN STEELE

Doblin's Lecture

FROM *Pirate Writings*

A CRISP AUTUMN NIGHT on a midwestern university campus. A cool breeze, redolent of pine cones and coming winter, softly rustles bare trees and whisks dead leaves to scurry across the walkways leading to the main hall. Lights glow from within Gothic windows as a last handful of students and faculty members hurry toward the front entrance. There is to be a famous guest speaker tonight; no one wants to be late.

A handful of students picket in the plaza outside the hall; some carry protest signs, others try to hand fliers to anyone who will take them. The yellow photocopies are taken and briefly read, then shoved into pockets or wadded up and tossed into waste cans; the signs are glanced at, but largely ignored.

A poster taped above the open double-doors states that absolutely no cameras, camcorders, or tape recorders are permitted inside. Just inside the doors, the crowd is funneled through a security cordon of off-duty police officers hired for the evening. They check campus IDs, open daypacks, run chirping hand-held metal detectors across chests, arms, and legs. Anyone carrying metal objects larger or less innocent than keyrings, eyeglasses, or ballpoint pens is sent back outside. A trash can behind the guards is half-filled with penknives, bottle openers, cigarette lighters, and tear-gas dispensers, discarded by those who would rather part with them than rush them back to dorm rooms or cars and thereby risk missing the lecture. Seating is limited, and it's been announced that no one will be allowed to stand or sit in the aisles.

Two students, protesters from the campus organization opposed to tonight's presentation, are caught with cloth banners concealed under their jackets. They're escorted out the door by the cops, who dump their banners in the trash without reading them.

The auditorium holds 1,800 seats, and each one has been claimed. The stage is empty save for a podium off to one side and a stiff-backed oak armchair in its center. The chair's legs are securely bolted to the floor, its armrests equipped with metal shackles; loose belts dangle from its sides. Its vague resemblance to a prison electric chair is lost on no one.

Four state troopers stand quietly in the wings on either side of the stage. Several more are positioned in the back of the hall, their arms folded across their chests or their thumbs tucked into service belts carrying revolvers, tasers, and Mace canisters. More than a few people quietly remark that this is the first time in a long while that the auditorium has been filled to capacity without anyone smelling marijuana.

At ten minutes after eight, the house lights dim and the room goes dark save for a pair of spotlights focused on the stage. The drone of voices fades away as the dean of the sociology department — a distinguished-looking academician in his early fifties, thin gray hair and humorless eyes — steps from behind the curtain on stage left and quickly strides past the cops to the lectern.

The dean peeks at the index cards in his hand as he introduces himself, then spends a few moments informing the audience that tonight's speaker has been invited to the university not to provide entertainment, but primarily as a guest lecturer for Sociology 450, Sociology 510, and Sociology 525. His students, occupying treasured seats in the first six rows, try not to preen too much as they open their notebooks and click their pens. They're the chosen few, the ones who are here to learn something; the professor squelches their newfound self-importance by reminding them that their papers on tonight's lecture are due Tuesday by ten o'clock. The professor then tells the audience that no comments or questions will be permitted during the guest speaker's opening remarks, and that anyone who interrupts the lecture in any way will be escorted from the hall and possibly be placed under arrest. This causes a minor stir in the audience, which the dean smoothly placates by adding that a short question-and-answer session will be held later, during which members of the audience may be allowed to ask questions, if time and circumstances permit.

Now the dean looks uncomfortable. He glances uneasily at his cards as if it's faculty poker night and he's been dealt a bad hand. After the guest speaker has made his remarks, he adds (a little more softly now, and with no little hesitancy), and once the Q&A session is over, there may be a special demonstration. If time and circumstances permit.

The background noise rises again. Murmurs, whispers, a couple of muted laughs; quick sidelong glances, raised or furrowed eyebrows, dark frowns, a few smiles hastily covered by hands. The cops on stage remain stoical, but one can detect random shifts of eyes darting this way and that.

The dean knows that he doesn't need to introduce the guest speaker, for his reputation has preceded him and any further remarks he might make would be trivial at best, foolish at worst. Instead, he simply turns and starts to walk off the stage.

Then he stops. For the briefest instant there is a look of bafflement — and indeed, naked fear — on his face as he catches a glimpse of something just past the curtains in the left wing. Then he turns and walks, more quickly now, the opposite way until he disappears past the two police officers on stage right.

A moment of dead silence. Then Charles Gregory Doblin walks out on stage.

He's a big man — six feet and a couple of inches, with the solid build of someone who has spent most of his life doing heavy labor and only recently has put on weight — but his face, though brutal at first sight, is nonetheless kindly and oddly adolescent, like that of a grownup who never let go of some part of his childhood. The sort of person one could easily imagine dressing up as Santa on Christmas Eve to take toys to a homeless shelter and would delight in playing horsey for the kids, or on any day would help jump-start your car or assist an elderly neighbor with her groceries. Indeed, when he was arrested several years ago in another city and charged with the murders of nineteen young black men, the people who lived around him in their white middle-class neighborhood believed that the police had made a serious mistake.

That was until FBI agents found the severed ears of his victims preserved in Mason jars in his basement, and his confession led them to nineteen unmarked graves.

Now here he is: Charles Gregory Doblin, walking slowly across the stage, a manila file folder tucked under his arm.

He wears a blue prison jump suit and is followed closely by a state trooper holding a riot stick, but otherwise he could be a sports hero, a noted scientist, a best-selling author. A few people automatically begin to clap, then apparently realize that this is one time when applause is not warranted and let their hands fall back into their laps. Some frat boys in the back whistle their approval, and one of them yells something about killing niggers before three police officers — two of whom, not coincidentally, are black — descend on them. They've been led out the door even before Charles Gregory Doblin has taken his seat; if the killer has heard them, there is nothing in his face to show it.

Indeed, there is nothing in his face at all. If the audience had expected the dark gaze that had met a news photographer's camera when he was led into a federal courthouse on the day of his arraignment four years ago — a shot engraved in collective memory, deranged Eyes of a Killer — they don't see it. If they had anticipated the beatific look of the self-described born-again Christian interviewed on *60 Minutes* and *PrimeTime Live* in the last year, they don't see that either.

The killer's face is without expression. A sheet of blank paper. A calm and empty sea. A black hole in the center of a distant galaxy. Void. Cold. Vacant.

The killer takes his seat in the hard wooden chair. The state trooper hands him a cordless microphone before taking his position behind the chair. The arm restraints are left unfastened; the belts remain limp. Long moments pass as he opens the manila folder in his lap, then Charles Gregory Doblin — there is no way anyone here can think of him as Charlie Doblin, as his neighbors once did, or Chuck, as his late parents called him, or as Mr. Dobbs, as nineteen teenagers did in their last hours of life; it's the full name, as written in countless newspaper stories, or nothing else — Charles Gregory Doblin begins to speak.

His voice is very soft; it holds a slightly grating Northeastern accent, high-pitched now with barely concealed nervousness, but otherwise it's quite pleasant. A voice for bedtime stories or even pillow talk with a lover, although by all accounts Charles Gregory Doblin had remained a virgin during the thirty-six years he spent as a free man. He quietly thanks the university for inviting him here to

speak this evening, and even earns a chuckle from the audience
when he praises the cafeteria staff for the bowl of chili and the
grilled cheese sandwich he had for dinner backstage. He doesn't
know that the university cafeteria is infamous for its food, and he
could not possibly be aware that three cooks spat in his chili just
before it was delivered to the auditorium.

Then he begins to read aloud from the six sheets of single-spaced
typewritten paper in his lap. It's a fairly long speech, the delivery
slightly monotone, but his diction is practiced and nearly perfect.
He tells of childhood in an abusive family: an alcoholic mother who
commonly referred to him as a little shit and a racist father who
beat him for no reason. He tells of having often eaten canned dog
food, heated in a pan on a hibachi in the bathroom, for dinner
because his parents could afford nothing better, and of going to
school in a slum neighborhood where other kids made fun of him
because of his size and the adolescent lisp that he didn't completely
overcome until he was well into adulthood.

He describes the afternoon when he was attacked by three black
teenagers who beat him without mercy only because he was a big
dumb white kid who had the misfortune of shortcutting through
their alley on the way home from school. His voice remains steady
as he relates how his father gave him another even more savage
beating that same evening, because he had allowed two niggers to
get the better of him.

Charles Gregory Doblin tells of a lifelong hatred for black people
that became ever more obsessive as he became an adult: the brief
involvement with the Klan and the Brotherhood of Aryan Nations
before bailing out of the white supremacy movement in the belief
that they were all rhetoric and no action; learning how some soldiers in Vietnam used to collect the ears of the gooks they had
killed; the night nine years ago when, on impulse, he pulled over
on his way home from work at an electronics factory to give a lift to
a sixteen-year-old black kid thumbing a ride home.

Now the audience stirs. Legs are uncrossed, crossed again over
the other knee. Hands guide pens across paper. Eighteen hundred
pairs of eyes peer through the darkness at the man on the stage.

The auditorium is dead silent as the killer reads the names of the
nineteen teenagers that he murdered during the course of five
years. Besides being black and living in black neighborhoods scattered across the same major city, there are few common denomina-

tors among his victims. Some were street punks, one was a sidewalk
crack dealer, and two were homeless kids looking for handouts, but
he also murdered a high school basketball star, a National Merit
Scholarship winner recently accepted by Yale, a rapper wannabe
who sang in his church choir, an aspiring comic book artist, and a
fifteen-year-old boy supporting his family by working two jobs after
school. All had the misfortune of meeting and getting into a conversation with an easygoing white dude who had money for dope,
beer, or pizza; they had followed him into an alley or a parked car
or some other out-of-the-way place, then made the mistake of letting Mr. Dobbs step behind them for one brief, fatal moment . . .
until the night one kid managed to escape.

The audience listens as he says that he is sorry for the evil he has
done, as he explains that he was criminally insane at the time and
didn't know what he was doing. They allow him to quote from the
Bible, and some even bow their heads as he offers a prayer for the
souls of those he has murdered.

Charles Gregory Doblin then closes the folder and sits quietly,
hands folded across his stomach, ankles crossed, head slightly
bowed with his eyes in shadow. After a few moments, the dean
comes back out on stage; taking his position behind the lectern, he
announces that it is now time for the Q&A session.

The first question comes from a nervous young girl in the third
row center: She timidly raises her hand and, after the dean acknowl-
edges her, asks the killer if he has any remorse for his crimes. Yes,
he says. She waits for him to continue; when he doesn't, she sits
down again.

The next question is from a black student farther back in the
audience. He stands and asks Charles Gregory Doblin if he killed
those nineteen kids primarily because they were black, or simply
because they reminded him of the teenagers who had assaulted
him. Again, Charles Gregory Doblin only says yes. The student asks
the killer if he would have murdered him because he is black, and
Charles Gregory Doblin replies that, yes, he probably would have.
Would you kill me now? No, I would not. The student sits down and
scribbles a few notes.

More hands rise from the audience; one by one, the dean lets
students pose their questions. Has he seen the made-for-TV movie
based on his crimes? No, he hasn't; there isn't a television in the

maximum security ward of the prison, and he wasn't told about the movie until after it was aired. Did he read the book? No, he hasn't, but he's been told that it was a bestseller. Has he met any members of the families of his victims? Not personally, aside from spotting them in the courtroom during his trial. Has any of them attempted to contact him? He has received a few letters, but aside from the one from the mother who sent him a Bible, he hasn't been allowed to read any correspondence from the families. What does he do in prison? Read the Bible he was sent, paint, and pray. What does he paint? Landscapes, birds, the inside of his cell. If he could live his life all over again, what would he do differently? Become a truck driver, maybe a priest. Is he receiving a lecture fee from this visit? Yes, but most of it goes into a trust fund for the families of his victims, with the rest going to the state for travel expenses.

All this time, his gaze remains centered on a space between his knees, as if he is reading from an invisible Teleprompter. It is not until an athletic-looking young man in the tenth row asks him, in a rather arch voice, whether he received any homoerotic gratification when he committed the murders — an erection, perhaps? perhaps a fleeting vision of his father? — that Charles Gregory Doblin raises his eyes to meet those of his questioner. He stares silently at the pale young man for a long, long time, but says nothing until the student sits down again.

An uncomfortable hush follows this final question; no more hands are raised. The dean breaks the silence by announcing that the Q&A session is now over. He then glances at one of the guards standing in the wings, who gives him a slight nod. There will be a brief fifteen-minute intermission, the dean continues, then the program will resume.

He hesitates, then adds that since it will include a demonstration that may be offensive to members of the audience, this might be a good time for those people to leave.

Charles Gregory Doblin rises from his chair. Still refraining from looking directly at the crowd, he lets the state trooper escort him offstage. A few people in the auditorium clap self-consciously, then seldom-used gray curtains slide across the stage.

When the curtains part again fifteen minutes later, only a handful of seats in the auditorium are vacant. The one in the center of the stage is not.

A tall, skinny young black man is seated in the chair that Charles Gregory Doblin has kept warm for him. He wears a prison jump suit similar to the one worn by his predecessor, and his arms are shackled to the armrests, his body secured to the chair frame by the leather belts that had hung slack earlier. The same state trooper stands behind him, but this time his riot stick is in plain view, grasped in both hands before him.

The prisoner's eyes are cold searchlights that sweep across the audience. No one can meet his gaze without feeling revulsion. He catches sight of the young woman in the third row who had asked a question earlier in the evening; their eyes meet for a few seconds and the prisoner's lips curl upward in a predatory smile. He starts to mutter an obscenity, but shuts up when the state trooper places the end of his stick on his shoulder. The girl squirms in her seat and looks away.

The dean returns to the lectern and introduces the young black man. His name is Curtis Henry Blum; he is twenty-two years old, born and raised in this same city. Blum committed his first felony offense when he was twelve years old, when he was arrested for selling crack in the school playground; he was already a gang member by then. Since then he has been in and out of juvenile detention centers, halfway houses, and medium security prisons, and has been busted for mugging, narcotics, carjacking, breaking and entering, armed robbery, rape, attempted murder. Sometimes he was convicted and sent to one house of corrections or another; sometimes he was sentenced on lesser charges and served a shorter term; sometimes he was just let go for lack of evidence. Each occasion he was sent up, he spent no more than eighteen months before being paroled or furloughed and thrown back on the street.

Nineteen months ago, Curtis Blum held up a convenience store on the city's north side, one owned and operated by a South Korean immigrant family. Blum held mother, father, and teenage daughter at gunpoint while he cleaned out the cash register and tucked two bottles of wine into his pockets. The family knelt on the floor and begged him to be merciful and just leave, but he shot them anyway, along with an eleven-year-old kid from the 'hood who had been sent out by his mother to buy some cat food and beer and had the misfortune of walking through the door just as Blum was going out. He didn't want to leave any witnesses, or maybe he simply felt like killing people that night.

A police SWAT team found Blum at his grandmother's house two days later. He wasn't hard to find; although by then he had bragged to everyone he knew about how he had capped three slants the night before, it was his grandmother who had called the cops. She also testified at her grandson's trial six months later, saying that he regularly robbed and beat her.

Curtis Blum was convicted on four counts of second-degree murder. This time, he faced a judge who didn't believe in second chances; he sentenced Blum to death. Since then, he has been filling in time on death row in the state's maximum security prison.

The dean steps from behind the lectern and walks over to where the prisoner is seated. He asks Blum if he has any questions. Blum asks him if the girl in the third row wants to fuck.

The dean says nothing. He simply turns and walks away, vanishing once again behind the curtains on stage left.

Curtis laughs out loud, then looks again at the woman in the third row and asks her directly if she wants to fuck. She starts to get up to leave, which Blum misinterprets as willingness to conjugate; even as he assails her with more obscenities, though, another female student grasps her arm and whispers something to her.

The girl stops, glances again at the stage, and then sits back down. This time, she has a slight smile on her face, for now she sees something that Blum doesn't.

Curtis is about to shout something else at the girl when a shadow falls over him. He looks up, and finds himself looking into the face of Charles Gregory Doblin.

Killing a man is actually a very easy thing to do, if you know how. There's several simple ways that this can be accomplished that don't require knives or guns, or even garrotte wires or sharp objects. You don't even have to be very strong.

All you need are your bare hands, and a little bit of hate.

The dry crack of Curtis Blum's neck being snapped follows the students as they shuffle out of the auditorium. It's a cold wind, harsher than the one that blows dry leaves across the plaza outside the main hall, that drives them back to dormitories and apartments.

No one will sleep very well tonight. More than a few will waken from nightmares to find their sheets clammy with sweat, the sound of Blum's final scream still resonating in their ears. Wherever they may go for the rest of their lives, whatever they may do, they will never forget what they have witnessed this evening.

Fifteen years later, a sociology post-grad student at this same university, in the course of researching her doctoral thesis, will discover an interesting fact. Upon tracking down the students who were present at Charles Gregory Doblin's lecture and interviewing them or their surviving relatives, she will find that virtually none of them was ever arrested on a felony offense, and not one was ever investigated or charged with spousal or child abuse, statistics far below the national average for a population of similar age and social background.

Yet that is still in the future. This is the present:

In a small dressing room behind the stage, Charlie Doblin — no longer Charles Gregory Doblin, but simply Charlie Doblin, Inmate #7891 — sits in a chair before a makeup counter, hunched over the dog-eared Bible the mother of one of his victims sent him several years ago. His lips move soundlessly as he reads words he does not fully comprehend, but which help to give his life some meaning.

Behind him, a couple of state troopers smoke cigarettes and quietly discuss tonight's lecture. Their guns and batons are holstered and ignored, for they know that the man in the room is utterly harmless. They wonder aloud how much vomit will have to be cleaned off the auditorium floor, and whether the girl in the third row will later remember what she yelled when the big moment came. She sounded kinda happy, one cop says, and the other one shakes his head. No, he replies, I think she was pissed because she missed out on a great date.

They both chuckle, then notice that Charlie Doblin is silently peering over his shoulder at them. Shut up, asshole, one of them says, and Doblin returns his attention to his Bible.

A radio crackles. A trooper plucks the handset off his jacket epaulet, murmurs into it, listens for a moment. The van is waiting out back, the local cops are ready to escort them to the interstate. He nods to his companion, who turns to tell Charlie that it's time to go. The killer nods his head; he carefully marks his place in the Bible, then picks it up along with the speech that he read tonight.

He didn't write this speech, but he has dutifully read it many times already, and will read it again tomorrow night in another college auditorium, to a different audience in a different city. And, as always, he will end his lecture by becoming a public executioner.

Somewhere else tonight, another death-row inmate unwittingly awaits judgment for his crimes. He sits alone in his cell, playing solitaire or watching a sitcom on a TV on the other side of the bars, and perhaps smiles at the notion that, this time tomorrow, he will be taken out of the prison to some college campus to make a speech to a bunch of kids, unaware that what awaits him are the eyes and hands of Charles Gregory Doblin.

It's a role that Charlie Doblin once savored, then found morally repugnant, and finally accepted as predestination. He has no say over what he does; this is his fate, and indeed it could be said that this is his true calling. He is very good at what he does, and his services are always in demand.

He has become a teacher.

Charles Gregory Doblin scoots back his chair, stands up and turns around, and lets the state troopers attach manacles to his wrists and ankles. Then he lets them take him to the van, and his next lesson.

BRAD WATSON

Kindred Spirits

FROM *Last Days of the Dog-Men*

ON THE LONG GREEN LAWN that led down to the lake, Bailey's boy tumbled with their two chocolate Labs, Buddy and Junior. The seven of us sat on Bailey's veranda sipping bourbon and watching the boy and his dogs, watching partly because of what Bailey had just told us about the younger dog, Buddy's progeny, a fat brute and a bully. Bailey had chosen Buddy's mate carefully, but the union had produced a pure idiot. A little genetic imbalance, Bailey said, hard to avoid with these popular breeds.

Watching Junior you could see that this dog was aggressively stupid. A reckless, lumbering beast with no light in his eyes, floundering onto old Buddy's back, slamming into the boy and knocking him down. The boy is about ten or eleven and named Ulysses though they call him Lee (sort of a joke), thin as a tenpenny nail, with spectacles like his mama. He was eating it up, rolling in the grass and laughing like a lord-god woodpecker, Junior rooting at him like a hog.

"I hate that dog," Bailey said. "But Lee won't let me get rid of him."

The slow motions of cumulus splayed light across the lawn and lake in soft golden spars, the effect upon me narcotic. My weight pressed into the Adirondack chair as if I were paralyzed from the chest down. Bailey planned this place to be like an old-fashioned lake house, long and low with a railed porch all around. Jack McAdams, with us this day, landscaped the slope to the water, then laid St. Augustine around the dogwoods, redbuds, and a thick American beech, its smooth trunk marked with tumorous carvings. Three sycamores and a sweet gum lined the shore down toward the woods. The water's surface was only slightly disturbed, like the old glass panes Bailey bought and put in his windows.

Russell took our glasses and served us frosty mint juleps from a silver tray. Silent Russell. The color and texture of Cameroon tobacco leaf, wearing his black slacks and white serving jacket. I am curious about him to the point of self-consciousness. I try not to stare, but want to gaze upon his face through a one-sided mirror. I see things in it that may or may not be there and I'm convinced of one thing, this role of the servant is merely that: Russell walks among us as the ghost of a lost civilization.

Bailey says Russell's family has been with his since the latter's post–Civil War Brazilian exile, when Bailey's great-great-grandfather fled to hack a new plantation out of the rain forest. Ten years later he returned with a new fortune and workforce, a band of wild Amazonians that jealous neighbors said he treated like kings. Only Russell's small clan lingers.

I looked at Russell and nodded to him.

"Russell," I said.

He looked at me a long moment and nodded his old gray head.

"Yah," he said, followed in his way with the barely audible "sah." After he'd handed drinks out all around, he eased back inside the house.

"Russell makes the best goddamn mint julep in the world," said Bailey, his low voice grumbly in the quiet afternoon, late summer, the first thin traces of fall in the air.

I could see two other men of Russell's exact coloring working at the barbecue pit down in the grove that led to the boathouse. Russell's boys. They'd had coals under the meat all night, Bailey said, and now we could see them stripping the seared, smoked pork into galvanized tubs. Beyond them, visible as occasional blurred slashing shadows between the trunks and limbs and leaves of small-growth hardwoods, were Bailey's penned and compromised wild pigs, deballed and meat sweetening in the lakeside air. He looked to be building up a winter meatstock, product of several hunting trips to the north Florida swamps with Skeet Bagwell and Titus Smith, who were seated next to me on Bailey's side. It seemed an unusual sport, to catch and castrate violent swine and pen them until their meat mellowed with enforced domesticity, and then to slit

their throats. Russell's boys partially covered the rectangular cooking pit with sheets of roofing tin and carried the tubs of meat
around back of the house to the kitchen. Along the veranda we
drank our mint juleps — McAdams, Bill Burton, Hoyt Williams,
Titus, Skeet, Bailey, and me — arranged in a brief curving line in
Bailey's brand-new Adirondack chairs. Russell came out with more
mint juleps, nodded, and slipped away.

"Here's to love," Bailey said, raising his silver cup. He smiled as if
about to hurt someone. Probably himself. A malignant smile. Here
we go, I said to myself, I don't want to hear it. I didn't want to hear
his story any more than I wanted to take his case. He'd called the
day before and invited me to the barbecue with these men, his best
friends, and said he wanted me to represent him "in this business
with Maryella." Bailey, I'd said, I've never handled divorces and I
don't intend to change — as criminal as some of those cases may
be. I suggested he call Larry Weeks, who's done very well with big
divorce cases in this town. No, Bailey, said, you come on out, come
on. We'll talk about it. I supposed at the time it was because we've
known each other since the first grade, though in the way of those
who live parallel lives without ever really touching.

So here we were. There were no women around, apparently,
none of these men's wives. I began to feel a familiar pain in my
heart, as if it were filling with fluid, and it seemed I had to think
about breathing in order to breathe. Even what little I knew about
Bailey's problem at the time forced me into places I didn't want to
go. So his wife has left him for his partner, I thought — so what?
What else is new in the world? We all know something of that pain,
to one degree or another.

Ten years ago I defended a man accused of pushing his brother
off a famous outcropping in the Smoky Mountains in order to get
his brother's inheritance, set for some reason at a percentage much
greater than his own. It was an odd case. There'd been several
other people at the lookout, where in those days a single rail kept
visitors from succumbing to vertigo and tumbling down the craggy
face of the cliff. My client's hand had rested in the small of his
brother's back as they leaned over the railing to look down when
the brother — like a fledgling tumbling from the nest, one witness
said — pitched over the edge and disappeared.

It was considered an accident until my client's cousin, who had never liked or trusted him, who in fact claimed he had once dangled her by her wrists from the treehouse behind their grandmother's home until she agreed to give him her share of their cache of Bazooka bubble gum, hired a private investigator who was able to plant the seeds of doubt in the minds of enough witnesses to bring the case before a grand jury in Knoxville. Incredibly, the guy was indicted for murder one. I thought it so outrageous that when he called I immediately took over his case, even though it meant spending time traveling back and forth across the state line.

I liked the man. While he and I prepared for trial, my wife, Dorothy, and I had him out to dinner a few times and twice even took him to my family's old shanty on the Gulf Coast for the weekend. He and Dorothy hit it off well. Each was a lover of classical music (Doro had studied piano at the university until she gave up her hope of composing and switched to music history), and he was a tolerable pianist. They discussed the usual figures, Schubert and Brahms and Mozart, etc., as well as names I'd never heard of. They sat at the piano to study a particular phrase. They retired to the den to play old LPs Doro had brought to our marriage but which had gathered dust during the years I'd built my practice, never having had the energy to listen with her after dragging in at near midnight with a satchel full of work for the next morning. I often awoke at one or two in the morning, tie twisted and cinched against my throat, the dregs of a scotch and water in the glass in my lap, while the stereo needle scratched at the label of a recording long done easing strains of Sibelius from its grooves. In the bedroom I'd find Doro turned into the covers, her arms tossed over a pillow that covered her head, as was her sleeping habit, as if she were trying to smother herself.

I can look back now and see things. I pursued her when she didn't necessarily want to be pursued. The law school was just two blocks from the music school, and I would wander down the boulevard and into the resonant halls of the studios and to the room where she practiced and composed. I would stand outside the door, looking in through the narrow window no wider than half my face, until she looked up, would have to look up, with her dark eyes as open upon mine as an animal's in the woods when it discovers you standing still and watching it, and it is watching your eyes to see if you are something alive. I did not do this every day, but only when my blood was up too high to sit at the law library desk and, thinking of the last time we had been together, I had to see her. One day when she looked up, I knew that she had not wanted to but for some reason had been unable not to, and when she did look up she knew that was it, she was mine. It was the moment when one is captured by love in spite of one's misgivings and is lost.

But light bends to greater forces, and so does fate, in time. I should not have been so stricken when she left with my client after the trial, but of course I was. An overweight man who eats bacon, drinks heavily, smokes, and never exercises should expect a heart attack, too, and does, but is nevertheless surprised when it comes and he is certainly stricken. I'd given my all to the case, I'd fought for the man. Work had become my life, after all. I'd exposed the cousin as a bankrupt, scheming bitch, read letters between the brothers that were full of fraternal endearments, and I borrowed and brought into court an expensive, full-size oil copy of Durand's famous painting, *Kindred Spirits,* depicting the painter Thomas Cole and the poet William Bryant standing on an outcropping in the Catskills, a spot less lofty than the scene of my client's alleged crime, but more beautiful in its romantic, cloistering light, and I asked them how a brother, in a setting such as this, and with witnesses less than ten feet away, could do something so *unnatural* as pitch his own flesh and blood to a bloody end. It was a stroke of brilliance. No one sees that painting without being moved to sentimental associations. Rosenbaum, the D.A., was furious I got away with it. My client also had a noble face: a straight nose, strong brow, high forehead, strong jaw and chin, clear brown eyes that declared a forthright nature. But in the end, after the hung jury and the judge's bitter words, my client and my wife moved to Tennessee, of all places, where he would set himself up in the insurance business. And here is my point, I suppose, or what makes the story worth telling.

When she began to call me three years later, in secret, explaining how he had become a cold and manipulative man, she told me he had admitted to her while drunk that he had indeed pushed his brother off the lookout, and he'd said that only I had any evidence of this, in a statement I'd taken wherein he slipped up and said the one thing that could have convicted him had the D.A. gotten his hands on it. I could hear the ghosted voices of other, garbled conversations drifting into our line. What one thing is that? I said. I don't know, she said. He wouldn't tell me. There was a pause on the line, and then she said, You could find it, Paul.

But I have never opened the file to search for the incriminating words. Moreover, although I have acquired an almost tape-recorder memory of the utterances of people in trouble, I have not bothered to prod that little pocket in my brain. I have detoured around it as easily as I swerve around a sawhorsed manhole in the street. I protected my client, as any good attorney would. I've moved on.

We walked down into the grove, past the thin smoking curtain of heat at the edge of the pit, its buckled tin, and up to the heavy-gauge wire fencing that surrounded about a half-acre of wooded area bordering the cove. Here there was no grass, and the moist leaves were matted on the rich, grub- and worm-turned earth. Through the rectangular grid of the fencing we saw small pockets of ground broken up as if by the steel blades of a tiller where the pigs had rooted, and slashes and gouges in tree trunks where they'd sharpened their tusks.

I looked over at Bailey swirling the crushed ice in his cup, the righteous tendons in his jaw hardening into lumpy bands of iron. He was seething with his own maudlin story. But before he could start up, we heard a rustling followed by a low grunt, and a wild hog shot out of the undergrowth and charged. We all jumped back but Bailey as the hog skidded to a stop just short of the wire, strangely dainty feet on scraggly legs absurdly spindly beneath its massive head. Its broad shoulders tapered along its mohawkish spinal ridge to the hips of a running back and to its silly poodlish tail. The pig stood there, head lowered, small-eyed, snorting every few breaths or so, watching Bailey from beneath its thick brow. Bailey looked back at the beast, impassive, as if its appearance had eased his mind for a moment. And the boar grew even more still, staring at Bailey.

The spell was broken by the loud clanging of a bell. Russell, clanging the authentic antique triangle for our meal. The pig walked away from us then, indifferent, stiff-legged, as if mounted on little hairy stilts.

We made our way back to the porch. Russell and one of the men who'd been tending the pit came out with a broad tray of meat already sauced, and a woman (no doubt one of Russell's daughters

or granddaughters) came out and set down on the table a stack of
heavy plates, a pile of white bread, an iron pot full of baked beans,
and we all got up to serve ourselves. When we sat back down, Bill
Burton, who'd dug into his food before anybody else, made a noise
like someone singing falsetto and looked up, astonished.

"By God, that's good barbecue," he said through a mouthful of
meat. Burton was a plumbing contractor who'd done the plumbing
for Bailey's house. He said to Skeet Bagwell, "Say you shot this pig?"

"Well," Skeet said, "let me tell you about that pig." Like me, Skeet
is a lawyer, but we aren't much alike. He rarely takes a criminal case,
but goes for the money, and loves party politics and the country
club and hunting trips and all that basically extended fraternity
business, never makes a phone call his secretary can make for him,
and needless to say he loves to tell big lies. His compadre Titus built
shopping malls during the 1980s and doesn't do much of anything
now.

"Titus and I *captured* that pig," Skeet said, "down in the Florida
swamps. Ain't that right, Titus?"

"I wouldn't say, not exactly captured," Titus said. "In a way, or
briefly, perhaps, we captured that pig, but then we killed it. It may
be a mite gamy."

"Unh-uh," voices managed. "Not a bit!"

Skeet said, "You ain't had your blood stirred till you crossing a
clearing in the swamp and hear a bunch of pigs rooting and grunting, you don't know where they are, and then you see their shapes,
just these big, low, broad, hulking shadows, inside the bushes on
the other side, and then they smell you and disappear, just disappear. It's eerie." Skeet took a mouthful of the barbecue, sopped up
some sauce with a piece of bread, and chewed. We waited on him to
swallow, sitting there on the veranda. Down on the lawn the boy,
(Ulysses) Lee, ran screaming from the bounding dogs.

Skeet said it was exciting to see the pigs slip out of the woods and
light out across a clearing, and the dogs' absolute joy in headlong
pursuit. They were hunting these pigs with the local method, he
said. You didn't shoot them. You used your dogs to capture them.

"We had this dog, part Catahoula Cur — you ever heard of
them?"

"State dog of Louisiana," Hoyt said.

"Looks kind of prehistoric," Skeet said. "They breed them over in

the Catahoula Swamp in Louisiana. Well, this dog was a cross between a Catahoula Cur and a pit bull, and that's the best pig dog
they is. Like a compact Doberman. They can run like a deer dog
and they're tough and strong as a pit bull. And they got that streak
of meanness they need, because a boar is just mean as hell." Skeet
said he'd seen an African boar fight a whole pack of lions on TV
one night, did we see that? Lions tore the boar to bits, but he fought
the whole time. "I mean you couldn't hardly see the boar for all the
lion asses stuck up in the air over him, tails swishing, ripping him
up, twenty lions or more," Skeet said. They had pieces of him
scattered around the savanna in seconds, but there was his old
head, tusking blindly even as one of the lions licked at his heart.
Skeet took another bite of barbecue and chewed, looking off down
the grassy slope at the tussling boy and dogs.

"This dog Titus and I had, we bought him off a fellow down there
said he was the best dog he'd ever seen for catching a hog, and he
was right." Titus nodded in agreement. "We got out in the swamp
with him, and *bim,* he was off on a trail, and ran us all over that
swamp for about an hour, and never quit until he run down that
hog.

"We come up on him out in this little clearing, and he's got
this big old hog by the snout, holding his head down on the
ground, hog snorting and grunting and his eyes leaking bile. I
mean, that dog had him. But then we come to find out how we got
this wonder dog at such a bargain."

"I had a preacher sell me a blind dog one time," Hoyt said. "Said
how hot he was for a rabbit, and cheap. Sumbitch when I let loose
the leash took off flying after a rabbit and run right into an oak
tree, knocked hisself cold."

Everybody laughed at that.

"Preacher said, 'I never said he wasn't blind,'" Hoyt said.

"Well, this dog wasn't blind," Skeet said, "Not *literally,* but you
might could say he had a blind spot. He would run the hog down,
like he's supposed to do, then take it by the snout and hold its old
head down, so you can go up and hog-tie him and take him in. Way
they do down there, like Bailey's doing here, they castrate them and
pen them up, let the meat sweeten awhile before they kill 'em.

"But this dog, once you grabbed the hog by the hind legs and
begun to tie him, thought his job was done, and he lets go."

Skeet paused here, looking around at us. "So there was old Titus, gentlemen, playing wheelbarrow with a wild pig that's trying to twist around and rip his nuts off with one of them tusks. I mean that son of a bitch is mean, eyes all bloodshot, foaming at the mouth. That meat ain't too tough, is it?"

Everyone mumbled in the negative.

"Ain't gamy, is it?"

Naw, unh-uh.

"So finally Titus jumped around close to a tree, lets go of the hog, and hops up into it, and I'm already behind one and peeping out, and the hog jabbed his tuskers at the tree Titus was in for a minute and then shot out through the woods again, and the dog — he'd been jumping around and barking and growling and nipping at the hog — took out after him again. So Titus climbed down and we ran after them."

"Dog was good at *catching* the hog," Titus said.

"That's right," Skeet said. "Just didn't understand the seriousness of the situation, once he'd done it. Actually, the way I see it, the dog figured that once the man touched the hog, then he had taken *possession* of the hog, see, and his job — the dog's — was over.

"Anyway, you can imagine, Titus wasn't going near that hog held by that dog again, so one of these fellows we're with tries it, and the same thing happens, two more times: As soon as the man *touched the hog,* the dog let go. And it was starting to get dark. But this fellow, name was Beauregard or something —"

"Beaucarte," Titus said.

"— he comes up with a plan. And the next time the dog has the hog down, he manages with some kind of knot to hog-tie the hog without actually touching the hog, and the dog's watching his every move, you know, and looking into his eyes every now and then, thinking, Why the hell ain't he taking hold of this hog, but he holds on just fine till it's done. But then when the guy starts to drag the hog over to this pole we go'n carry him out on, the dog — since the man hasn't actually *touched* the hog at all with his hands, now — he's *still hanging on,* and pulling backwards and growling like a pup holding on to a sock. Damn hog is squawling in pain and starting to buck."

Skeet stopped here a minute to chow down on his barbecue before it got cold, and we waited on him. Bailey seemed distant, looking out over the lake, sitting still, not eating any barbecue himself.

"So the guy stops and looks back at that dog, and you could see him thinking about it. Just standing there looking at that dog. And we were tired, boy, I mean we'd been running through that damn swamp all day, and we was give out. And I could see the guy thinking about it, thinking all he had to do was reach down and touch that hog one time, and the dog would let go. And you could see the dog looking at him, still chomped down on the hog's nose, looking up at the guy as if to say, Well, you go'n touch the hog or ain't you? And that's when the guy pulls his .44 Redhawk out, cocks it, and blows the son of a bitch away."

"The hog?" says Jack McAdams, sounding hopeful. Skeet shakes his head.

"The dog," he says.

"*Your* dog?" Hoyt says.

"That's right," Skeet said. "All in all, I guess he was doing me a favor."

Everybody stopped eating, looking at Skeet, who finished up the little bit of barbecue on his plate and sopped up the sauce and grease with a piece of white bread. He rattled the ice chips and water in the bottom of his cup and drained the sugar-whiskey water, and I saw Russell note this and slip back into the house for more drinks.

"I guess he let go then," Bailey said quietly, sunk deeply into his Adirondack. "The dog."

"*No,*" Skeet said, "*he didn't.*"

"He was a mess, head all blown way, but his jaws still clamped on that nose in a death grip. He was rigor-mortised onto that hog. You can imagine the state of mind of the hog right then, that .44 laid down the ridge of his nose and going *boom,* shooting blue flame, and that dog's head opening up, blood and brains and bone all over him, dog teeth clamping down even more on his nose. Hog went crazy. He jumped up and thrashed his head around, screaming in pain, shook the ropes almost free, and started hobbling and belly-crawling around this little clearing we were in. And he was dragging the dog around, flopping it around, and it wadn't anything now but a set of teeth attached to a carcass, just a body and jaws.

"Meanwhile old Beaucarte's feet had gotten tangled in the ropes and so there they all were, thrashing around in the near-dark, stinking swamp with a wild hog, a dead dog, and this damn cracker trying to aim his hand-cannon at the hog just to make it all stop, and finally he shot it, the hog. By then it was almost dark, and everything was still as the eye of a hurricane and the air smelled of gunpowder smoke and blood and something strange like sulfur, with the swamp rot and the gore and the sinking feeling we all had with a hunt gone wrong, and a good dog with just one flaw now dead, and everybody felt bad about it, especially this long, skinny Beaucarte.

"We dragged the hog and the dog back to the truck in the dark, tossed them in back and drove on back to the camphouse, and told these two swamp idiots on the porch, a couple of beady-eyed brothers, to take care of the hog, and then we drank some whiskey and went to bed. The next day, when we were leaving, one of the swamp idiots, name was Benny, had this old cheap pipe stuck in the corner of his mouth, brings out a big ice chest full of meat wrapped in butcher paper. And he says, 'We goin' on into town, now. Me and Fredrick put yo meat in this icebox, now Daddy'n them took some of the meat from the big'un.'"

Here Skeet stopped talking and let silence hang there a moment and sipped from a fresh drink Russell had set down on the arm of his Adirondack. Hoyt gestured to his plate.

"So you saying this might be hog, might be dog."

"Tastes mighty sweet to be dog," Bill Burton said.

"Some of it's sweeter than the rest," Skeet allowed.

Everybody had a laugh over that, sitting there picking their teeth with minty toothpick wedges Russell had passed around from a little silver box. He freshened the drinks. The afternoon seemed to slide pleasantly, almost imperceptibly, along the equinoctial groove toward autumn.

"I tell you something," Bailey said then. "I got a story to tell, too. Skeet's story brings me to mind of it."

The immediate shift in mood was as palpable as if someone had walked up and slapped each one of us in the mouth. We sat in our Adirondacks, sunken, silent, and trying to focus on the boy on the lake bank tossing the ball to his dogs swimming the shallows. Holding our breath this wouldn't be the old epic of Bailey's yawping grief.

"You know this fellow, my erstwhile friend and partner, Reid Covert."

"Bailey, ain't you got any dessert to go with this fine barbecue?" Skeet said.

Bailey held his hand up. "No, now, hear me out," he said, his eyes fixed somewhere out over the lake. He made a visible effort to relax. "It's a good story, it's all in fun."

All right, someone mumbled, let him tell it.

"But that's not saying it ain't *true*," Bailey said, and turns to us with such a devilish grin that we're all a little won over by it. It was a storyteller's smile. A liar's smile.

All right, everybody said, easing up, go ahead on.

"Y'all didn't know a thing about this," he said, "but I whipped that sorry sapsucker's ass three times before I finally got rid of him."

Three times! we said.

"Kicked his ass."

No! we said. We had fresh mint juleps in our hands. Russell stood to one side in his white serving jacket, looking out over the lake. Out in the yard, the boy chased the Labs down to the water. He had a blue rubber-looking ball in his hand and he stopped at the bank, holding the ball up, and the dogs leaped into the air around him. Junior knocked the boy all over the place, trying to get his chops on the ball. He knocked off the boy's glasses and then grabbed the ball when the boy got down on his knees to retrieve them.

"The first time I heard about it I went into his office and confronted him," Bailey said. "He denied it. But, hell, I knew he was lying. It was after five. The nurses had gone, receptionist gone, insurance clerk gone. No patients. I told him, 'You're lying, Reid.' He just sat there then, looking stupid, and I knew I was right. I went over and slapped him. My own partner. Friend since elementary school. Went through med school together. Slapped shit out of him. 'How long has it been going on?' I said. He just sat there. I told him to get up but he wouldn't. So I slapped him again. He still just sat there. I tried to pick him up out of his chair by his shirt but he held on to the goddamn armrests, so I slapped him again. 'Stop it, Bailey,' he says then. 'Stop it, hell,' I said. I said, 'Get up, you son of a bitch.' And he says, 'Stop it, Bailey.' And so I said, 'You son of a bitch, I want you out of this office, you and I are through.' And I walked out."

We were all quiet again then. It was as bad as we'd thought it would be. Bailey hadn't worked in weeks. All his patients had to go to Birmingham. Reid Covert had taken off somewhere, and Bailey's wife, Maryella, had gone off, too. Everybody figured they were together. And I was thinking, I guess he'll ask me to help him divide his and Reid's business, too.

"Well," Bailey went on then, "Maryella wouldn't talk to me about it, and I kept hearing they were still seeing each other. So I drove over to his house one day and pulled up as he was trying to leave. I cut off his car with mine, got out, went over, and pulled him out of his goddamn Jeep Cherokee. He didn't even get the thing into park, it rolled over and ran into a pine tree. And I mean I pummeled him, right there in his own goddamn front yard. Berry, she came out into the yard yelling at me, went back in to call the police, and old Reid, I'm beating the shit out of him, his nose is bloody, and he's holding out his arm toward Berry and saying, No, don't call the police. I let go of him and watched him limp after her, then I got back into my car and came out here. When I got here Maryella passed me in the driveway, zooming out onto the road, dust flying. Hell, Berry must've called her instead of the cops. Hell, she left Lee out in the goddamn yard with the dogs and went to her mother's house, didn't come home for two days, and when she did I had her suitcase packed and told her to get the hell out."

All this — all the detail, anyway — was new, we had not heard it from the various sources. Lee was throwing the blue ball into the water now and the dogs were swimming out to get it, then swimming back in, whereupon the one without it, usually the boorish Junior, would chase the one who had it, Buddy, and get it away from him. Whereupon the boy would chase down Junior, get the ball, and throw it back out into the lake.

"Look at that," Bailey said. "I tell you it was Reid's bitch Lab we mated Buddy with to get that sorry Junior? I should've drowned the goddamn dog."

A couple of us, Hoyt and me, got up for barbecue seconds. Dog or hog, it was good, and Bailey's story was eating at my stomach in a bad way. I needed something more in it.

"Y'all eat up," Bailey said. "What's left belongs to the niggers." Old Russell, standing off to one side of the barbecue table, sort of shifted his weight and blinked, still looking out over the lake. Bailey saw this and pulled his lips tight over his teeth. "Sorry, Russell," he mumbled. Russell, his eyes fixed on the lake's far shore, appeared unfazed. Bailey got up, went inside, and came back out with the bottle of Knob Creek. He poured some into his mint julep cup and drank it.

"Well, finally, I followed him one day, and I watched him meet her in the parking lot of the Yacht Club, and I followed them way out here, down to the Deer Lick landing. I'd cut my lights, and I parked up the road, and then I walked down. I had my .38 pistol with me, but I wasn't going to kill them. I had me some blanks, and I'd screwed a little sealing wax into that little depression at the end of the blanks. You ever noticed that, that little depression? When I got down there they weren't in the car. I looked around and saw a couple standing down on the beach, just shadows in that darkness, so I walked down there. They looked around when I walked up to them, and when they realized it was me it scared them pretty bad, me showing up. I stepped up to him and said, 'I told you to give it up, Reid,' and that's when he hit me, almost knocked me down. I guess he wanted to get the first lick in, for once. I went back at him, and it was a real street fight, pulling hair and wrestling and kicking and throwing a punch every now and then, and hell, Maryella might have been in on it for all I know. I finally threw him down onto the sand, and his shirt ripped off in my hands. Maryella was standing with her feet in the water, with her hands over her face, and I was standing there over Reid, out of breath and worn out. And he looked up then and said, 'You're going to have to kill me to get rid of me, Bailey. I love her.' So I pulled out the pistol from my pocket and said, 'All right.' And I shot him. All five rounds."

We were all quiet as ghosts. The squeals from the boy and the playful growling of Junior and the good-natured barking of Buddy all wafted up from the lake. The ball arced out over the water, and the dogs leapt after it with big splashes.

"Well, he hollered like he was dying," Bailey said. "I imagine it hurt, wax or not, and scared the holy shit out of him. It was loud as hell. I saw these dark blotches blossom on his skin. You know Reid always was a pale motherfucker. When he saw the blood, his head fell back onto the beach sand.

"Maryella said, 'You killed him.' By God, I thought I had, too. I thought, Jesus Christ, I am so addled I forgot to use the blanks, I have shot the son of a bitch with real bullets. I jumped down there and took a look, and in a minute I could see that I hadn't done that.

The pieces of wax had pierced the skin, though, and he was bleeding from these superficial wounds. He'd fainted.

"And Maryella panicked then. She started to run away. I tackled her and dragged her back to Reid to show her he was all right, but she wouldn't quit slapping at me and screaming, 'You killed him, you killed him!' over and over again. She said she loved him, and she'd never loved me. I shoved her head under the shallow water there at the beach, but when I pulled her up again she just took a deep breath and started screaming the same thing again, 'You killed him, I hate you!' And that's when Reid jumped onto my back and shoved me forward. I still had a hold on Maryella's neck, see, and my arms were held out stiff, like this," and he held his arms out, his hands at the end of them held in a horseshoe shape, the way they would be if they were around a neck. Bailey looked at his hands held out there, like that.

"I felt her neck crack beneath my hands," he said. "Beneath our weight, mine and Reid's." He didn't say anything for a minute. I heard his boy, Lee, calling him from down at the lake. No one answered him or looked up. We were all staring at Bailey, who wasn't looking at anything in particular. He looked tired, almost bored.

"Anyway," he said then, "I couldn't let Reid get away with causing that to happen. I found the gun and hit him over the head with it. And then I held him under until he drowned."

Bailey swirled what was left in his mint julep cup, looking down into the dregs. He turned it up and sucked at the bits of ice and mint and the soggy sugar in the bottom. Then he sat back in his chair, poured more bourbon into the cup, and said in a voice that was chilling to me, because I recognized the method of manipulation behind it, taking the shocked imagination and diverting it to the absurd: "So when I brought them back here, that's when Russell's boys skinned 'em up and put 'em over the coals."

There was silence for a long moment, and then McAdams, Bill Burton, Hoyt, Titus, and Skeet broke into a kind of forced, polite laughter.

"Shit, Bailey," McAdams said. "You just about tell it too good for me."

"So gimme some more of that human barbecue, Russell," Titus said.

"'Long pig' is the Polynesian term, I believe," Skeet said.

Their laughter came more easily now.

The boy, Lee, came running up to the porch steps.

"Daddy," he said. He was crying, his voice high and quailing. Bailey turned his darkened face to the boy as if to an executioner.

"Daddy, Junior's trying to hurt old Buddy."

We looked up. Out in the lake, Buddy swam with the ball in his mouth. Junior was trying to climb up onto Buddy's back. Both dogs looked tired, their heads barely clearing the surface. Junior mounted Buddy from behind, and as he climbed Buddy's back, the older dog, his nose held straight up and the ball still in his teeth, went under.

He didn't come back up. We all of us stood up out of our chairs. Junior swam around for a minute. He swam in a circle one way, then reversed himself, and then struck out in another direction with what seemed a renewed vigor, after something. It was the blue ball, floating away. He nabbed it off the surface and swam in. He set the ball down on the bank and shook himself, then looked up toward all of us on the veranda. He started trotting up the bank toward the boy standing stricken in the yard.

Bailey had gone into the house and come out with what looked like an old Browning shotgun. He yanked it to his shoulder, sighted, and fired it just over the boy's head at the dog. The boy ducked down flat onto the grass. The dog stopped still, in a point, looking at Bailey holding the gun. He was out of effective range.

"Bailey!" Skeet shouted. "You'll hit the boy!"

Bailey's face was purplish and puffed with rage. His eyes darted all over the lawn. He saw his boy Lee lying down in the grass with an empty, terrified look in his eyes. He lowered the barrel and drew a bead on the boy. The boy, and I tell you he looked just like his mama, was looking right into his daddy's eyes. He will never be just a boy again. There was a small strangled noise down in Bailey's chest, and he swung the gun up over the grove and fired it off, *boom*, the shot racing out almost visibly over the trees. The sound caromed across the outer bank and echoed back to us, diminished. Junior took off running for the road, tail between his legs. The boy lay in the grass looking up at his father. Titus stepped up and took the shotgun away, and Bailey sat down on the pinewood floor of the veranda as if exhausted.

"Well," he said after a minute. His voice was deep and hoarse and croaky. "Well." He shook with a gentle, silent laughter. "I wonder what I ought to do." He cleared his throat. "I don't know who else to ask but you boys." He struggled up and tottered drunkenly to the barbecue table, put together a sandwich of white bread and meat, and began to devour it like a starving man. He snatched large bites and swallowed them whole, then stuck his fingers into his mouth, sucking off the grease and sauce. He gave that up and wiped his hands on his khakis, up and down, as if stropping a razor. "Russell," he said, looking around, seeming unable to focus on him, "get another round, some of that Mexican beer, maybe. We need something light to wash down this meal." He ran his fingers through his hair.

Old Russell glided up like a shadow then, taking plates, stacking them in one broad hand, smiling with his mouth but his eyes as empty and blank as the sky, "Heah, sah," he said, "let me take your plate. Let me help you with that. Let one of my boys bring your car around. Mr. Paul," he said to me. "I guess you'll be wanting to stay."

There was little more to say, after that. We formalized the transfer of deed for the old place in Brazil, along with the title to Bailey's Winnebago, to Russell. By nightfall he and his clan had eased away on their long journey to the old country, stocked with barbecue and beer and staples. The women left the kitchen agleam. Bailey and I sat by the fire in the den. They'd lain Reid Covert and Maryella on the hickory pyre that, reduced to pure embers, had eventually roasted our afternoon meal. There was nothing much left there to speak of, the coals having worked them down to fine ash in the blackened earth. I could hear a piece of music, though the sound system was hidden, nowhere to be seen. It sounded like Schubert, one of those haunting sonatas that seem made for the end of the day. In his hand Bailey held a little bundle of cloth, a tiny palm-sized knapsack that Russell had given him before he left. A little piece of the liver, sah, to keep the bad souls from haunting your dreams. A little patch of this man's forehead, who steal his own best friend's wife. This light sap from her eyes, Mr. Bailey, you hardly see it, where the witch of beauty live in her, them eyes that could not lie to you. You take it, eat, and you don't be afraid. He eased carefully out the front door and disappeared. Bailey placed the little knapsack on the glowing coals in the hearth, watched the piece of cloth begin to blacken and burn, and the bits of flesh curl and shrink into ash. He was calm now, his boy asleep fully clothed and exhausted up in his room.

In the last moments out on the porch, before we'd drifted inside in a dream of dusk, the afternoon had ticked down and shadows had deepened on the lake's far bank. The other men, dazed, had shuffled away. Russell's two younger sons had stood on the shore and tossed ropes with grappling hooks to retrieve old Buddy. Bailey's boy stood on the bank hugging himself against some chill, watching them swing the hooks back over their shoulders and sling them, the long ropes trailing out over the lake, where the hooks landed with a little splash of silver water. A momentarily delayed report reached us, softly percussive, from across the water and the lawn. Bailey stood on the steps and watched them, his hands on top of his head.

"Look at that," he whispered, the grief and regret of his life in the words. "Old Buddy."

They brought the old dog out of the water. The boy, Lee, fell to his knees. Russell's sons stood off to one side like pallbearers. Above the trees across the lake, a sky like torn orange pulp began to fade. Light seeped away as if extracted, and grainy dusk rose up from the earth. For a long while none of us moved. I listened to the dying sounds of birds out over the water and in the trees, and the faint clattering of small sharp tusks against steel fencing out in the grove, a sound that seemed to come from my own heart.

JOHN WEISMAN

There Are Monsterim

FROM *Unusual Suspects*

Jerusalem, July 1977

LIZ'S FIFTH BIRTHDAY was on Saturday, and so Terry, the perfect father, took her to Nahariya on Wednesday for a long weekend at the beach. Sainted mother Maggie let them go without her.

They'd first thought of celebrating the kid's premier half-decade in Haifa, in a big room at the Dan Carmel where, from the terrace, they could look down on the bustling port and eat dinner at the perpetually crowded Romanian restaurant on the edge of the farmer's market. But while Terry had already telexed his "Summer Travel in the Holy Land" piece to the *New York Times* Tuesday, Maggie was still tied up polishing a profile of Foreign Minister Moshe Dayan that was due at *Woman's Day*. She wouldn't shake free until Friday night.

Besides, they decided, the Dan was expensive and he'd have to pay for a double room all five nights. Besides, they rationalized, Liz wasn't a big fan of Haifa anyway, preferring the construction of sand castles, wallowing in the surf, and the scarfing of fast food to romantic harbor views and Romanian steaks slathered with — in Liz's words — "Eecch, garlic."

So, after a brief parental discussion about four-year-olds' eating habits, family finances, and the fact that he'd be carless in Haifa until Maggie arrived, they chose to go farther north and stay at a modest pension they knew in Nahariya, chockablock to a dozen falafel and shashlik stands, fifty yards from the water and, as it happened, one-fifth the price of the Dan.

Terry packed a duffel for himself and Liz, carefully stowed Liz's teddy bear, Shmulik, right on top of the bags, and then they all piled into the beat-up Renault 4 and Maggie dropped them at the taxi stand on Luntz Street, where they caught one of the Israeli communal jitney cabs known as a sherut to Haifa. The big gray Mercedes diesel car was just about to pull out. Maggie gave them quick pecks on the cheek and shooed them on their way. They shared the two-hour ride with a Hasid who smoked incessantly, a middle-aged yenta who fell asleep just after the turnoff to Abu Gosh and snored contentedly for the rest of the trip, and two Israeli Army girls on leave.

Liz, too, slept most of the way to Haifa, waking only briefly when the sherut stopped at the Herzliyah interchange to take on a passenger, then dropping back into full snooze, her knees curled fetally, head on Terry's lap.

He, the conscientious parent, developed lock-joint in his knees by the time they pulled into Haifa, his long legs having been frozen uncomfortably in one position for forty-four kilometers.

In Haifa they switched to an aged Egged bus that chugged and wheezed, Lizzie insisted, like the Little Engine That Could, gears grating and the red-faced driver, a cigarette clenched between tight lips, cursing the autos that had the audacity to pass on the narrow, two-lane highway north of Akko. Terry watched Liz as she kneeled, nose pressed to filthy window glass, remarking on every olive grove, banana tree, hitching soldier, donkey, and tractor in the fields as the bus lurched inexorably northward.

Four-year-olds, the father thought, were incredible. He never stopped marveling at the creature he and Maggie had created: he took pleasure in watching Liz sleep; doted on her when she was awake; snapped endless pictures of her antics, her poses, her wide-eyed grins.

He sometimes wondered whether this perpetual enchantment with his daughter was the result of his becoming a father so late in life, or whether it was based on his own middle-aged fears of mortality and the deep-rooted, primordial need to procreate in order to see one's self reflected in another human being. Those were two possible answers, of course. But more basically, he simply loved his daughter with a love so total, absolute, and all-consuming that, from time to time, the enormity of that love frightened the hell out of him.

He reached over and caressed Liz's cheek tenderly with the back
of his hand. She'd gotten herself all dolled up for the trip north,
declining Maggie's practical suggestions of jeans or shorts with a
maverick shake of golden hair and insisting instead on wearing a
bright pink and white plaid "Mommy dress," as she called it, accompanied by a quartet of plastic sparkle bangle bracelets, a necklace of
fluorescent green beads, and a rhinestone barrette carefully placed
askew atop her head.

"Etonnant!" Maggie'd exclaimed as she coolly perused the defiant combination of colors, then giggled and swept the child into
her arms to rearrange the barrette. "You are your mother's daughter."

Even after her sherut nap, Terry realized, the kid was tired by the
time they reached Nahariya in midafternoon, and so instead of
going down to the beach immediately they shared a pair of greasy
falafels spiked with piquant tomato sauce and a couple of grape-
fruit sodas swigged from the bottle at a kiosk near the bus stop.
Then Terry swung the duffel bag over his left shoulder, swept up
Liz with his free arm, lugged the two bundles three blocks, and
checked into a first-floor room at the Pension Har Zion that had
a three-by-six-foot balcony overlooking an alley and lots of other
three-by-six-foot balconies, and the two of them lay down for an
hour on squeaky camp cots.

They woke at six-thirty, sweaty and grungy. Terry turned on the
shower (it wasn't much of a shower but it was wet) and put Liz into
it first, then dried her off and while she dressed herself he rinsed
off the travel grime, shampooing his red hair twice and lathering
quickly with the hard hotel soap as the water temperature dropped
precariously fast. Wrapped in a towel he stepped back in the room
to find his daughter singing to Shmulik, whom she held cradled in
small arms.

He started to speak but she put a finger to her lips.

"Quiet, Daddy. Shmulik's tired from the long trip and he's afraid
because it's a different bed and I'm singing him to sleep." So he
followed orders and watched silent as Liz, who'd put her T-shirt on
inside out, rocked the steady teddy, three days younger than she
was, and sang an incredible melange of English and Hebrew nonsense syllables as the creature stared up at her lovingly with button
eyes.

She was a bright child. Precocious, Terry thought proudly; always the coquette. Her habit (just like her mother) was to stand, legs slightly apart, feet planted firmly, hands on her hips, and, well, command. She'd spoken words at nine months, sentences at sixteen, and after having lived in Israel more than half her life she could make do in Hebrew almost as well as either of her parents, learning the language by osmosis from Orli, the Yemenite maid who came daily to clean and watch her while Terry and Maggie pursued their writing chores. Bright, hell, she was a pistol. Take Shmulik the bear. Originally his name had been Bar-Bar, which was short for bear-bear. But seven or eight months after they'd arrived in Israel Liz announced that the teddy had been rechristened.

"Shmulik," she said, oozing the syllables. "Shmu-u-u-ulik." And Shmulik he'd been ever since.

They'd come to Israel three years before, moving from Rome in the fall of 1974. The nomadic, vaguely newlywed American Family Robinson on a Great New Adventure. Maggie was the one with the job: an associate producer for a U.S. television network whose news panjandrums decided to expand Middle East coverage by opening a minibureau in Jerusalem.

Terry, who made his living freelance writing and occasionally editing English-language texts, had lived overseas for two decades, a confirmed bachelor well into his late thirties, until he'd met the beautiful, auburn-haired Maggie Ross on a blind date in Rome, wooed her for sixteen months with flowers, white Italian truffles, and weekends in Tuscany, and finally — finally — convinced her, twelve years his junior and ambitious as hell, that marriage to a struggling journalist entering early middle age was the fate to which she'd been doomed.

Eleven months after they set up housekeeping in a small but comfortable house with a huge garden in Jerusalem's German Colony, Maggie's network got a new vice president for news and a new set of budget priorities, which did not include a Jerusalem minibureau. So, twenty-six weeks' severance pay in their pockets, the network American Express card cut in two and express-mailed to New York, they were suddenly on their own in the Promised Land, evicted from the expense-account Eden of network news. They thought about going back to Rome, but they'd rented out the five-room flat Terry owned in Parioli — a four-year lease to an American diplomatic couple. Besides, they rationalized, Rome was expensive, while the house in Jerusalem cost a mere $350 a month and Israel's living costs were lower than anywhere in Western Europe except Portugal. The country was beautiful, the people were friendly. Moving would be a hassle. They decided to stay on, as long as they could make ends meet.

Maggie, a natural scrambler, got work as a freelance producer whenever Barbara Walters or Walter Cronkite or some other network luminary came to town and needed extra hands. She also pitched article ideas about many of the Israeli political contacts she'd made to every American magazine she could think of — and a few paid off. The *Woman's Day* profile of Dayan was her first big-time assignment and she fretted over each comma and semicolon.

If the magazine bought and published it, it would be a breakthrough — not to mention the $3,500 fee, enough to keep them going for four months if they were cautious about how they spent it.

There was other money, of course. The net income from Terry's apartment was a thousand a month. His freelance articles brought in four to six thousand a year. A one-day-a-week editing stint at the *Jerusalem Post*'s International Edition was good for another fifteen hundred per annum. And if things got really rough there was the account in Switzerland, a numbered account containing just under five hundred and fifty thousand U.S. dollars in Swiss francs, Terry Robinson's accumulated pay as an NOC — Non-Official-Cover — contract agent for the Central Intelligence Agency, for which he'd worked on and off since graduating from Brown University twenty-three years before.

He wasn't one of those gun-toting cowboys of suspense fiction. Not his style, although he'd qualified with a handgun during a training session back in the States a decade earlier. Nor was he an expert on ciphers and satellite transmissions.

Terence Robinson was an information gatherer, an evaluator, a shrewd judge of others. He was adept at recruiting and setting up networks of agents, running them, and protecting his people. His cover was perfect: as a freelance journalist, a writer of ephemeral articles on travel (and, very occasionally, Euro-politics), he got to see a lot of things and meet a lot of people.

Much of the information he gleaned he passed on to Langley through a series of case officers. In Italy he spent his time writing about tourism, even publishing a paperback on Tuscany. He wrote occasionally about the labor movement for the *Wall Street Journal* and a somewhat overdramatic, he thought at the time, piece on the rise of domestic Italian terror for *Playboy*. But for the most part, Terry Robinson stayed clear of controversial themes. They were dangerous because they pegged you one way or another, and his entire existence depended on his not being pegged as anything but a nondescript freelancer, a generic American expatriate.

Maggie knew what he did of course.

Johnny T, Terry's case officer when he'd gotten married, had encouraged him to tell Maggie the truth.

"There are secrets and there are secrets," Johnny had said, long fingers drumming idly on a Formica table at a nondescript trattoria just off the crowded Piazza Farnese. "If Maggie doesn't know, it could be worse for you in the long run." Besides, Johnny'd explained, the Agency was leery of agents who couldn't share one of the most basic facets of their existence with their wives.

So, shortly after their marriage he'd taken Maggie to San Gimignano for the weekend on the pretext of researching a piece on some of the small wineries in the area. They stayed at a simple hotel in Pancole, a few kilometers outside the town, and over wine, crusty peasant bruschetta, salad made of wild greens, and thick grilled veal chops, he quietly explained to his bride just what he did for a living.

"You're kidding," she said, her hand clapped to her mouth. When he didn't smile, she dropped her hand and said, genuinely shocked, "You're not."

And then, perceptive reporter that she was, she cut to the heart of the matter: "Why, Terry?"

He played with his wineglass. "Because there are bad guys out here, and the only way to keep them from winning is to do everything you can to be one of the good guys."

She frowned. "Everything you can?"

"All I can — the best I can."

She shook her head. "But history —"

"Nobody really understands history. Not really. Not all the way."

She nodded in agreement. "Okay — let's leave history out of it.

What makes me so afraid right now, is the 'everything you can' thing. If you do *everything* you can stop the world's bad guys, don't you end up committing the same kind of crimes you most want to prevent?"

"Sometimes. If you let yourself," Terry said evenly. He looked at her, his face dead serious. "But I'll never let myself."

Her eyes told him she wasn't sure about that.

"Believe me, Maggie," he said, "I could never become the same thing I'm fighting against." He took a sip of wine and returned her stare. "Because if you do that, you stop being political — you simply become a criminal. I know — I've seen it happen. And I don't like it."

He saw she had tears in her eyes. "What's the problem?"

"I love you so much," she said.

And so they agreed to a truce. He was never totally explicit with her about the details of his covert existence. There were clandestine meetings that he went to, and trips he took suddenly. But the specifics were never discussed between them. She had insisted on that, and he honored her request. Unlike Terry, who used his writing as a cover and considered himself a dilettante, Maggie's appointed role in life was professional journalist, and sometimes she felt torn between the ideals she had learned as a student at Northwestern University's Medill Graduate School of Journalism and the hard-edged economic, political, and social realities with which she now came in contact on a daily basis.

She had been twenty-six when she'd met Terry; less than three years out of grad school, the Midwest patina of her childhood in Lakewood, Ohio, barely scrubbed away. She had known from the age of twelve she would be a journalist, and she had worked hard to achieve that goal, waitressing her way through Ohio State University, winning a scholarship to Medill, and, following her graduation, moving to New York and a greenhorn's slot on the assignment desk of NBC News. She was vibrant and energetic and filled with the righteous indignation common to young practitioners of the journalist's craft. Her job, she argued (often passionately), was to comfort the afflicted and afflict the comfortable.

It took her some months to reconcile what she did with what Terry did. She was a child of the sixties blessed (or cursed) with the antagonism toward government common to most of her generation. And yet she respected, albeit somewhat grudgingly, what

Terry did. He supported the system and was willing to put himself on the line for his beliefs. And so, despite Maggie's negative feelings about such things as the war in Vietnam, Nixon's presidency, and the way Henry Kissinger ran U.S. foreign policy, she understood Terry's commitment (perhaps it was her conservative Lakewood upbringing) to his agency and to their Nation.

Not that she didn't experience emotional conflicts. She approved of what her husband did. But she also realized the disasters that could befall them if her friends and colleagues from Rome's American journalistic community ever found out about Terry's covert activities. Like it or not, Maggie was drawn inside the double-edged existence shared by all spies' families: the cover stories and outright lies that have to be told in order to survive. Lying to her friends and colleagues did not sit easily with her. And yet she did what she had to do, because her husband's safety depended on her constancy and consistency.

She'd experienced more of those conflicts in Italy than she did in Israel. Italy in the mid-seventies was fertile turf for Terry's clandestine operations. The Red Brigades were active. The Libyans, rich with petrodollars and vehemently anti-American, bought their way into foundering Italian corporations. The Communist Party controlled newspapers, labor unions, and thousands of local politicians. In Italy there was a lot for Terry to do — and he worked continually on Agency business while Maggie produced infrequent two-minute news stories about the Pope, earthquakes, and the anarchy of Neapolitan society, all the time fretting quietly about her husband's safety.

In Israel things were different. Liz made the biggest change in their lives, of course. The kid had been unplanned, the result of a trip to Venice. Terry had asked her to come along with him at the last minute, she'd forgotten to pack her diaphragm, and the rest was history. Maggie had always sworn to herself she wouldn't have a child until she had won her first Emmy. The day Liz was born she'd realized what a real award she'd been given. Not that she was any less ambitious, it was simply that her ambitions now had two objectives: a terrific daughter and great news stories. After her layoff, she found herself less and less inclined toward the eighteen-hour days she'd willingly put in as a network producer, preferring to spend time with Liz and putter in the garden between writing assignments.

Their move from Italy, she noticed, had affected Terry as well. Israel was an ally, a friendly oasis in a hostile environment. If Terry were operating in Jerusalem, he showed no sign of it, working on freelance journalism and his part-time job at the *Post*'s grimy Romema headquarters and most every day coming home for lunch, a nap, and a couple of hours' playtime with Liz. He'd told her that Israel would be a virtual vacation for him, and that seemed to be the case.

"Friends don't spy on each other," he'd insisted. "I'm an expert on Communist labor unions, not the Histadrut."

And the PLO?

"Geez, Mag, the Israelis have those guys cold. I couldn't find out one thousandth of what the Shin Bet's got on Arab terrorists even if I were fluent in Arabic and had Yasir Arafat his bloody self on my payroll."

Still, he'd developed professional contacts — Maggie was sure of it — among the left-wing members of Israel's parliament, the Knesset. And he went out of his way to cultivate a few of the more moderate West Bank Palestinian Arabs.

Israel was not Italy. There were no late-night assignations, no dead drops or one-time cipher books. There were no calls to Maggie from pay phones that went, "I gotta see a man about a horse, darlin'," his way of letting her know he might not be home for a few hours or a few days. There was none of the perpetual, gnawing, unspoken dread Terry Robinson had come to know in his gut, the brickbat pain that hit him like an ulcer when he worked the streets alone and unprotected. He'd felt those twinges for twenty years, in Rome, Paris, Amsterdam, and London.

No, Israel was different. Strange for him, a Christian in a Jewish homeland, that he felt so comfortable in this rough country of olives and orange groves and scrub-brush wadis, this raw, unsophisticated place with its boy soldiers and bearded Hasids and break-neck drivers. He loved Israel's vitality, took pleasure in its adolescent chauvinism, its matter-of-fact fatalism, its almost professional irreverence. He'd come to feel safe walking Israel's crowded streets and visiting its historic sites.

He watched as Liz laid the bear on her cot, fussing, tucking it under the covers tightly, its nappy head right in the middle of the pillow.

She turned to him, bright-eyed, her index finger touching

pursed lips, the bracelets up around her elbow. "Okay, Daddy, we can go. But we have to leave the light on because Shmulik is scared by the monsterim."

"Monsterim?" He was amazed. She'd fixed a Hebrew plural suffix onto an English word.

Hands on her hips, she glared up at him, her face serious, and stage-whispered, "You know — monsters."

He nodded sagely. "Any special kind of monsters?"

"Big ones. With teeth —" She spread her hands two feet apart.

"I've seen those big monsters before," he said. "I know all about them. But Shmulik doesn't have to worry."

"Why not?"

"Because." He scanned the room quickly. It was Spartan: paneled walls, a single bare-bulb lamp with clip-on shade for light, an armoire where they'd hung their clothes, and, hidden by the panels' vertical joints, a spring-closed storage closet where the extra bedding and a third cot were kept. Terry went to the section of panel where the faint outline of the storage closet could just be seen and pressed the hidden door. It sprung open. He gestured. "See? All Shmulik has to do is run in there and close the door and he'll be safe."

Liz scampered over and looked inside, wrinkling her face disapprovingly. "Eecch, Daddy, it's smelly. I'd rather leave the lights on."

He laughed. "Okay, okay. Shmulik gets the lights."

They walked hand in hand through the crowded streets, marveling at the electric lanterns that were strung above their heads. On the beachfront Terry headed toward a restaurant he remembered from their last trip, and after obtaining Liz's approval they commandeered a table facing the water, and the attention of an overworked waiter. Terry ordered a Gold Star beer; Liz decided on Coke. Solemnly, they poured the drinks into streaked glasses and touched rims.

"Cheers, my birthday girl."

"Daddy — it's not till Saturday."

"Well, it's soon enough to say cheers."

She shook her head. "No it isn't. You can only say 'Cheers, my birthday girl' when it's my birthday."

She was so literal. Just like her father, he thought. "Okay," he improvised, "cheers, my non-birthday girl."

"You're silly, Daddy."

"Of course I'm silly. I'm a daddy. You know what you are?"

She shook her head.

"You," he paused, waiting for the desired effect, "are an imp."

Reaction achieved. "Am not. There's no such real word like *imp*."

"Oh yes there is. I can show it to you in the dictionary when we get home. Or we can call your mother and ask her to look it up."

Inquisitive: "What does imp mean?"

"It means Liz Robinson."

Defiant: "No it doesn't."

"It means Liz-who-wears-dresses-on-the-bus-and-tucks-in-her-teddy-Robinson."

Petulant: "No it doesn't."

"It means Liz-who-likes-Coca-Cola-because-it-makes-her-nose-wrinkle-Robinson."

"It means what you're doing, Daddy. Being mischiev . . . mis-chievoonieous."

Where the hell did she come up with the damn words? He laughed. He agreed. "When I was your age I was an imp."

Triumphant: "You are an imp, too, Daddy." She took her glass in two hands and slurped contentedly on Coke. "We are *impim*!"

They dined royally, so far as Liz was concerned, on kebab sand-wiches and French fries drowned in ketchup. Terry had two more Gold Stars, Liz another Coke.

After he paid the bill they walked down the beach and Liz took off her sandals and scampered down to the water. Terry rolled his trouser legs, shed his Top-Siders, and followed. Then they went for ice cream, *glida* in Hebrew; coconut ice cream in a sugar cone that had, to Terry's dismay, a bad leak. He wiped at Liz's chin and the top of her T-shirt with an inefficient, wax-coated napkin then gave up and swabbed wholeheartedly with his pocket handkerchief.

By nine-thirty Liz was feeling tired again so they abandoned the streets for their hotel room. He peeled Liz out of her clothes, sent her to the bathroom, and waited as she brushed her teeth, then dumped her playfully into her bed, Shmulik resting comfortably in the crook of her arm.

"Daddy?"

He kissed her forehead. "What, Liz?"

"Would you stay here with me?"

"Sure, honey. Why?"

"This bed is lumpy and I'm not sure I can get right to sleep but I'm tired and I want to sleep and I —"

He cut her off. "Not to worry, imp. Daddy's here." He slipped onto the narrow bed and cradled his daughter. He kissed her cheeks and her forehead and held the child to him. "Not to worry. Daddy's here."

He was still on Liz's bed, lying fully clothed and dreaming when the shots woke him. He didn't know what time it was and his head was foggy with sleep but the shots were unmistakable: automatic weapons fire coming from close by.

Instinctively he rolled out of the bed. Liz, too, was awake and she started, startled, to go with him but he pushed her head gently back onto the pillow and looked her straight in the face. "Stay here, baby, stay here."

He moved quickly to the door of the balcony, cracked it open and peered outside, wincing as the firing grew closer, bullets whining ricochets off nearby stone. There were shouts, cries, and then an explosion from somewhere down below. He looked back at the bed where Liz lay frightened. He called to her: "Lizzie, hit the deck. Get down on the floor and stay there."

"Daddy —"

"Liz — do exactly what I say. Now!"

He couldn't tell where the firing was coming from, or from whom, or —

More shots. Closer. Now from inside the hotel. Down the stairs. Down the hall. Were they coming — they — terrorists? Soldiers? He crawled toward the door and pressed his ear against it. *Shouting.*

But not Hebrew shouting. Arabic shouting.

Terrorists. Oh, goddamn to hell terrorists. Liz. Terrorists. His heart raced. They were trapped. A twenty-foot drop to hard pavement outside and maybe the goddamn terrorists were waiting for them there, too. He tried to ease his racing heart. Okay. Think. You are a goddamn professional. You are supposed to know what to do.

He went on automatic pilot. Light? No light. Dark room. Dark equals safety. He rolled to the desk and reached up ("Oh, damn, Lizzie," as he heard the adjacent door splinter) and smashed the bulb.

Now — shelter. His mind worked in milliseconds debating the

possibilities. Under the bed. No protection. Bathroom. No protection. Closet.

Closet: dark room; closet hidden. Grab Liz. Stay quiet. Wait. Roll to the left. Take Liz.

Her eyes were frightened, panicked saucers. She began to cry out and he realized that she was reflecting his own state. He forced himself to calm down. Whispered shushing noises in her ear as he held her and crawled to the paneled wall, found the hidden door, pulled the two of them inside and then, fingers searching desperately for an exposed piece of wood, clicked the door closed. Exhausted, he lay panting in the small black space, his body wrapped around the child.

He found her ear and kissed it. "Lizzie — there are bad men outside. Very bad. We have to lie here very, very still until we hear them go away."

The child began to sob uncontrollably. He covered her mouth and whispered in her ear again. "Can't do that, Lizzie. Can't cry or talk or anything because if they find us they'll hurt us." His mind raced. All his training; all his experience — nothing to show for it. Lying in a dark place waiting to be killed. Waiting for the child to be killed. Take me — leave Liz. Hostages. Gunshot wounds. Grenades. Knives in Liz's throat. Liz's head severed.

Liz cried. He held her mouth tighter. "No, no, no, baby. No crying. Can't cry."

"Shmulik," she gargled. "Shmulik —" and she clawed at the wood door, trying to push it open in the suffocating blackness.

Terry held her down, wrestling his body atop hers, his eyes wide in the stifling, airless hidey-hole.

"No-no-no-no," he wheezed, his hands tightening on the child's mouth and nose. Hurting her, he knew, but he had to, to protect her. "Shmulik's okay, Liz. He's okay right where he is. He's a big bear. He can take care of himself."

The outside door splintered. Terry could hear the wood give way and he cringed as automatic weapons raked the place. Loud voices. Arabic. Screams. Liz echoed them, or tried to — Terry held her down as she struggled. More shots. More screams. From . . . somewhere, a drum beat loudly, incessantly, against his ear. He realized it was the pulse in his wrist. He tried to still it. Took the knuckle of his index finger and put it in his mouth. Bit down hard. The pain would kill the noise. Under him, Liz calmed down, her sobbing stopped. Now the loudest noise in the black was his own heartbeat.

Other voices. Gunshots. Distant voices. How long had they lain there? Minutes? Hours? His eyes closed in the darkness, Terry waited, waited, waited.

Other voices closer now. Hebrew or Arabic? He bit on his finger until tears came to his eyes. Quiet, Lizzie, or they'll hear us. The monsterim. Big teeth. Sharp knives.

Lights outside their hiding place. Oh, God, we're found out . . . be killed. Voices. Shots. Hebrew. English. English English English: "Mr. Robinson — Mr. Robinson, this is the Army."

Pounding. Sudden brilliant light. His eyes couldn't take it.

Wincing, he saw a lethal silhouette, a helmeted face, a hand holding an Uzi submachine gun.

Arms dragged him and Liz into the room.

Hands lifted him. Quick frisk then onto the bed. God it was cold. A body was sprawled on the floor, red-and-white keffiyeh splotched with blood covering the head. Nearby, two grenades and an AK-47 rifle with long, curved ammo clips taped back to back. The corpse was reaching for the weapons with a stone-dead hand.

He tried to find his daughter. "Liz? Liz? You okay, kiddo? We made it, Lizzie. The Army's here. The bad men are all gone (They are gone, aren't they? You killed the sons of bitches, didn't you?) Don't worry, Liz, the bad men all gone."

Where the hell's the bear? Where's Shmulik? Lizzie wants Shmulik. She'd cried for Shmulik. Where's the goddamn bear?

"Sit up Mr. Robinson," said a voice. "Please sit up."

He obeyed, his eyes still unaccustomed to the brightness of the room. "Liz — where's Liz?"

The commando had her. The hooded commando in black SWAT clothing, dripping state-of-the-art ordnance, looking like a character out of a Ninja fantasy, had Liz in his arms and he was KISSING HER? KISSING HER ON THE LIPS? Terry launched himself across the room but strong arms held him back.

The commando's eyes raised toward Terry but his mouth never left Liz's lips. He lowered the child onto the floor, pushing on her chest, muttering a cadence in Hebrew, "Echad, shtyim, shilosh, arba, shesh . . ." then blowing in her mouth.

The commando's eyes locked with his own. Dead gray eyes, Terry would recall much, much later. Dead gray eyes peering through holes in the black balaclava hood.

There was a lot of muted conversation carried on in Hebrew as he sat on the edge of the bed, the hands of soldiers, strong young men in khaki and black who blocked his view, resting on his shoulders while his own hands supported his head. He didn't understand a word of it. But something was terribly wrong.

Finally, a captain knelt by his side. Terry stared at the man uncomprehending, noting — absurdly, he thought for an instant — the crow's-feet around the officer's eyes and the deep scar along the man's neck and wondering where he'd gotten them. The Israeli put his arm around Terry's shoulder and squeezed.

"She is gone, Mr. Robinson. I'm sorry."

Sorry? Gone? Who's gone? Gone where? Gone how?

Then, he saw. Then he realized what he'd done.

The commando was laying Liz on a stretcher, oxygen mask obscuring most of her small face, still pushing down on her chest and counting the goddamn Hebrew syllables, "Echad, shtyim, shilosh, arba," and Liz, Liz, Liz's eyes were closed and — "Ooh, God — NOOOO!"

He screamed and lurched toward the stretcher where they were tying down the corpse of his daughter his love his child oh, God, no. "Please — God, take me now. Take me, take me, take me. Not her. Not Liz. Oh, please, God — Maggie — God, my baby, my baby. Dear God, no!"

Things went black and white. The soldiers held him down, he fighting against them, nauseated by the sweaty jumble of arms and bodies smelling of fear and death. From somewhere a hand with a syringe appeared and it went into his upper arm right through the shirt and then the room started to spin crazily, bright lights blinking neon like Piccadilly in the rain and he felt himself disappearing into a crystal vortex and the last words he heard himself scream were, "Don't you idiots understand? Take her teddy, take her teddy — there are monsterim."

MONICA WOOD

Unlawful Contact

FROM *Mānoa*

THE LAST TIME I saw my brother I came home burdened with
pretty things, ornamental nothings I'd come upon while browsing
through the string of perfumed boutiques in town. Except for the
earrings my brother bought for me on a whim, they were my pur-
chases: hair clasps, silk flowers, wind chimes, marbles. I had no use
for them and no one I cared to give them to, but that day in my
brother's presence their luster seemed necessary. While my brother
and I watched, salesgirls wrapped the trinkets in rustly, translucent,
pastel-colored tissue, then dropped them into shiny bags of the
same colors. The earrings I wore home.

I can imagine how we must have looked that day, my brother
lumbering behind me, his two years of prison a dull mask over his
face. He'd cut his hair and buttoned his shirt to the top, as if to
camouflage the length of days that trailed him; but they followed
him anyway, as visible as tin cans tied to the backs of his shoes.

Our meeting was a secret, though we met in a public place — the
park square downtown, in the heart of the waterfront shopping
district. He waited under the red sprawl of a sugar maple, head
down, hands thrust deep in his pockets. I could have ducked behind a building and gone home with a free mind, with nothing
further to hide from my husband and daughter, but I stood in the
open until he saw me.

We greeted each other like strangers, or worse than strangers: we
did not hug or shake hands; we simply faced each other and said
hello. We settled ourselves on a bench like people waiting for a bus,
looking straight into the emptiness before us. We said a few things,

about our mother's health, and our sister's upcoming wedding (to which my brother would not be invited), and the weather, and how hard it was to find work after prison.

"Do they know you're here?" he asked.

He was still a young man but looked so shockingly old.

"Meg?" he said.

"No." I was staring at the flower beds that ringed the park, the frilly summer flowers gone now, replaced by stiffer blooms in muted colors.

He pulled a pack of cigarettes out of his shirt pocket. I watched him light one and inhale. He shrugged, an apology. "You pick up some bad habits."

I nodded. The smell of cigarettes was a comfort because it was unfamiliar — he could have been anybody.

"It's not going to cost you, is it?" he said. "Coming out here, I mean."

I didn't answer until he'd smoked the cigarette down. He made a long sucking sound and then stamped the cigarette out with the sole of his shoe. He was thinly dressed for the weather but didn't appear to be cold.

"I did it for Mom," I said. "Fifteen minutes, I told her. Say what you have to say."

He lit another, and the smoke escaped with a small whistle between his teeth. "I wanted to see you, was all."

"That's it?"

"I miss you, Meg, I miss all of you," he said. "You, and Brent, and —"

"No," I told him, "don't use her name."

He whistled out more smoke. "It's you I missed the worst. I haven't talked to anybody in years. It takes a toll."

This much I understood. He had aged in prison, and I was reminded that I must have aged too, in the same way.

My brother and I had always talked. Even after we were both married he was a fixture at my house, stopping by on his way home from work, and we'd visit in the kitchen for a few minutes before getting on to the next part of the day. Sundays he dropped in to watch part of a ball game with Brent, or take the three of us out for ice cream. Brent had no brothers of his own and loved mine, and

Jenny adored her only uncle. He was always welcome in our home; after a while he didn't even bother to knock. He'd simply step through the door and join the family dance.

At that time, I believed he was still the brother of my childhood. I believed he could save me from some of the world's harms, given the right circumstances, as he had one summer saved me from the black and weedy water under our capsized canoe. We had dated each other's best friend; we had lied for each other to our stern, unyielding parents; we had accompanied each other in a silent vigil at our father's wake and funeral. Those days, white with distance, still bound us.

After his divorce Brent and I invited him over two or three times a week for supper. But he was a mess: he missed his wife, missed his house; he was drinking too much. He was a pleasant drunk, though, and we used to wait it out together, chatting in the living room until he was sober enough to drive home. Sometimes we reminisced about our childhood, our mother and father, our sister, Beth. Often we complained about our mother, who was getting cranky with age, or told each other little dramatic stories about people at work. He and Brent talked work, too, and sports. With Jenny, my brother played games: Go to the Head of the Class when she was ten, and Monopoly when she was eleven, and computer games when she was thirteen. When she was fourteen, they'd just talk. It was on one of these occasions, when Jenny was fifteen and a half, that my brother, long drunk and feeling generous, gave my daughter a taste of what a man's hand could find on a woman's body if it had a mind to.

She told her father first, moments after we got home. We'd been to a movie, one we'd chosen for a famous sex scene, which was shot low and which dissolved into black and white at the end. Our marriage had fallen dormant of late, a sleepy partnership that needed the shoring up we were happy to give it.

Every light in the house was on, and the radio, and the dishwasher, and the television, and the stereo — a clash of light and sound that was so wrong my heart was tearing up my chest before we got the door open.

"Who was here?" I asked her, looking around, thinking *burglar, rapist, one of those boys from her school.* She shrank against the wall, her pixie features lost and shriveled, and asked to speak to her father.

Wrestling, I heard her say as I eavesdropped, shaking, on the other side of the door. *He said he could teach me wrestling.*

Brent tore out of the house and went raging over to my brother's apartment, and by the time I got there it was done: the police had arrived and my brother — his face dirty with tears and blood — was wincing under the officers' questions. Brent was sulking by the door, his knuckles rubbed raw. It was my brother who had called the police, to save himself from harm.

She didn't tell me first because she thought I wouldn't believe her. It's true that I didn't speak right away, that I hesitated too long, that my first thought was not for her. My temples throbbed with the difficulty of believing them both, my head was crammed with two truths trying to fit into a space that would take only one. When finally I attempted to comfort my daughter, she found my arms unconvincing, my voice a small and suspect thing.

Brent believed her, believed such a thing of my brother, believed without a moment's thought, an instinct that — in the torment of therapists and victim advocates and assistant prosecutors that blotted our life for so many months afterward — made him the good parent, the one who could believe in evil on the turn of a dime.

We waited nearly a year for the trial, and in that time my family — I mean my first family, the one that included my brother — disintegrated as subtly as the afterimage of a fireworks. Everything we ever were as a family, everything we had ever shared — every morsel of food, every dog and hamster, every *yes* and *no* and *sorry* — was gone, replaced by the knowledge of what we might be capable of, what sin lay waiting in our souls.

My other family, Brent and Jenny, underwent an even subtler dissolution: we moved through the same house, ate at the same table, occasionally even laughed together or made each other proud. But I dragged around like a phantom limb the part of me that believed my brother, and in some unnameable way I knew my husband and daughter had stopped speaking to me.

The trial came, an unseemly ritual that held at its core my daughter's high, halting voice and my brother's tense denials. Strange men asked the questions I had not asked, for until the trial I'd had no wish for clarity. I listened to every word, and what I was listening for were the details — exactly where he had put his hands, the farthest reach of his fingers — so I would know how far I had to hate him, and how much room was left on the other side.

He had done *this,* but not *that.* They used real words, ugly words — *vagina* and *nipple* and *pubic hair* — words that dripped like a dirty rain from the domed roof. Brent sat next to me, his jaw set like a watchdog's, his fingers braided together, avoiding mine. My brother was found guilty of unlawful sexual contact and we all went home.

I got up, leaving my brother smoking on the park bench, suddenly bent on blending our secret into the cheerful clumps of midday shoppers picking their way over the cobblestones. He followed me and I let him. We eased into and out of the handsome little stores, and my brother watched as I picked up and handled every necklace and knickknack that pleased my eye. My brother's ugly shadow made me so greedy for pretty things; I wanted everything I saw, an embarrassment I carried around that day with the pastel bags I wouldn't let my brother hold for me.

It was a perfect New England fall day, sunny and cool, the city blazing all around us. If we had merely spoken on the phone, or perhaps met on the dark porch of our mother's house, or even if I had visited him once in prison — but our meeting was public in every way, and it was too late now not to claim him. That we were meeting, that I still hoped to find in his face the brother of my childhood were things I would have to account for.

The earrings cost forty dollars, money I know my brother couldn't spare, living with our mother and out of work. We spotted them at the same moment and reached for them, touching hands. He started to draw away, but I held his hand, and then picked up the other, as if they were two halves of a rock I'd found on the beach; I examined the tobacco stains, the starry cracks over the knuckles, the tattered fingernails, the healed-over cuts. Weighing what they might have done, I saw my brother's hands as a thing apart from him, and again I found myself believing they were what they seemed to be: the hands of my brother, not unlike mine in shape — narrow, innocent. I let him go.

Fashioned out of some sort of blue shell, the earrings had a graceful, bell-like shape and a thin lattice of gold around the bottom curve. Displayed alone on a tray of black velvet, they were heartbreakingly beautiful. And because they were beautiful I wanted them badly. I let my brother buy them for me; I understood that he was not buying them to make up for the cost of my meeting

him but because he too was taken with their beauty and he too —
on that crisp fall day amid scores of ordinary people and bright
storefronts and soulful dogs tied temporarily to lampposts — was
seized, unexpectedly, by hope.

"Remember that big shell we found one time at Silver's Beach?"
my brother said to me.

"No," I said. The earrings were on, I could feel their pearly shine.
I felt decorated, cleansed, acquainted once again with beauty.

"Don't you?" he insisted, a lilt creeping into his voice. We stepped
into the street, which was calm now, mostly empty. It was late. We'd
been together for hours. "I'm talking about the little cove at the
end, near the Crosbys' camp," he said.

"I'm sorry," I told him, though of course I did remember: the
most vivid pink shell, huge and heavy, planted there by my father,
who was given to grand gestures. But it belonged in the part of our
life that no longer existed.

"It was pink," he said, but he'd lost heart. He pulled out another
cigarette and held it between his ragged fingers.

We arrived at my car, and he opened the door to let me fill the
front seat with the delicate pastel bags. I wondered whether a pas-
serby would know that here was a man two weeks out of prison,
staring into the hole that was the rest of his life.

"Do you think we might, I don't know, get together again?" my
brother said. He stamped out another cigarette. "What do you say,
Meg?"

"We'll see," I told him. "I don't know."

"Meg," he said. His hands went to his pockets and he held his
elbows tight against his body. "Meg, it was only that one time —"

"Oh," I whispered. "Please, God." All this time he had left me
with the smallest hope, and in a word it was gone. I was weeping like
a child, for the part of me I'd held in reserve, for him, had cracked
open and joined the muddy slide of my heart.

He contorted his scarred, prisoner's face. "Meg, I'm so sorry."

"Don't." I put up my hands as if to defend myself.

"I'm not drinking anymore, if that means anything to you."

"It doesn't."

"Meg, if there was any way —"

"The only way is to undo it," I said. My voice was nearly gone.
"That's the only way," I said again. "Undo it."

I said it as if I believed he could. He hugged me hard then, knocking me off balance, and I might have let out a small cry of alarm — I think I remember seeing a man on the sidewalk stop and turn — but I recovered before falling and then he was off, lurching across the street like a fugitive. I watched him get smaller and smaller, until he finally turned a corner and disappeared.

When I pulled into my driveway, I sat in the dusk for a while, looking into the lighted windows of my house. Brent was already home, in his favorite chair in the den, and Jenny was moving back and forth in the kitchen, getting herself a snack. They were in different rooms, but something about their proximity was companionable, as if they'd been conversing through the doorway. Jenny was taller than she had been back then — a college girl now — and more graceful, though a certain furtiveness had crept into her carriage, a suspicion that I didn't remember from before. I got out of the car and circled the house, stopping to stuff my packages in the trash, then came in the side door, through the kitchen. Jenny's eyes — the wide-set, greenish eyes of my brother — moved from my face, to the earrings, and back again.

"You saw him, didn't you," she said. She stood at the counter, watching me over her shoulder, her palms flat down as if someone had hired her to guard the food.

Brent appeared then, folding his reading glasses, squinting in my direction. "Saw who?" he asked.

They had become strangers to whom I was irrevocably tied. We might have survived a train wreck or witnessed a murder, unable to meet each other again without evoking a physical memory. Our intimacy was an awkwardness we endured without naming, and it had erased the simple fact of mother-father-daughter that had once defined us.

My hand, of its own accord, went to my left ear.

"He gave you those, didn't he," Jenny said.

"Christ," Brent muttered. "I knew it."

It took me a long time to get them off. On one of the earrings especially, the post was a snug fit, and I had to work at it for a few moments before my family's unforgiving eye — the polished shell no doubt spewing little sparks of light all the while. I could have told them *I didn't say your name. I didn't say his.* For my family, however, betrayal was not a matter of degree.

I told them later that I threw the earrings out, flung them in a fit of remorse into the scrubby stand of trees at the far end of our yard. This was a lie, not my first. I kept them in my purse for days, and later moved them to the back of my top dresser drawer, rolled into a pair of cast-off gym socks, then I hid them again, and it has been long enough now that I can't say for sure where they are, only that they are somewhere in this house, two blue shells wrapped in a rustle of tissue. I hid them understanding that I would not show them or wear them or look at them ever again but would know, at times exactly like this, that they exist somewhere in all their original beauty, hidden but not altogether gone from this world.

Contributors' Notes

Born and raised in Northern Michigan, **Doug Allyn** majored in criminal psychology at the University of Michigan, served in military intelligence during the Vietnam War, and parlayed those credentials into a twenty-five-year career as a rock guitarist.

Since 1986 Mr. Allyn has published five mystery novels and fifty short stories. He has won, or been nominated for, every major literary award in his field, including the Edgar Award for 1995.

Mr. Allyn and his wife live in chaotic bliss in Montrose, Michigan.

▪ Some years ago I read an Aldous Huxley novel, *Point, Counterpoint,* in which Huxley structured his plot around the classical musical form of the fugue. I was attracted by the idea of transmuting elements of music into prose, but borrowing the structure of a work is a bit like breaking into a jewelry store to heist a display case. If you're going to steal something, why not filch the elements that actually empower music: passion and dynamics?

The story "Blind Lemon" is an attempt to do exactly that.

I can only hope it's half as effective as the performances of the original Blind Lemon Jefferson were.

James Crumley lives in Missoula, Montana. Since taking an M.F.A. at the University of Iowa, he has crisscrossed America as an academic tramp, published one collection of short pieces, *The Muddy Fork,* and six novels, most recently *Bordersnakes.* His work has been published in a number of foreign languages and awarded a Pushcart Prize and the 1993 Hammett Award.

▪ I hadn't written a short story since 1972 and had never written one about crime when Otto Penzler asked me to contribute one to his *Murder for Love* collection. Aside from the fact that my imagination doesn't seem to lend itself to the short story form, I discovered once again that the little devils are hard as hell to write. After a dozen false starts, I went over to Mike and Eve Art's Chico Hot Springs Lodge, planning a week floating the Yellowstone River trying to catch the brown trout fall run. It's Montana, right, and October is often the finest month. Of course it snowed like crazy. So I spent the week in a cabin on a bench watching the weather work the Paradise Valley — snow and freezing rain, occasional shafts of sunlight exposing the peaks through the low clouds, and steam curling off the hot spring pool. Somehow I was reminded of a story I had once tried to write while living in Mexico, started with that woman's dreams, layered with the scenery outside the window, memories of the Ozarks, football notions, and poker games. After more drafts than I care to remember, the result was "Hot Springs." Crime seldom pays, love seldom works. Thankfully stories, like fishing, occasionally work. In ways unexplainable.

Jeffery Deaver, former journalist, folksinger, and attorney, has written thirteen suspense novels. He has twice been nominated for Edgar Awards and is the recipient of *Ellery Queen's Mystery Magazine*'s Best Short Story of the Year for 1995. His recent *A Maiden's Grave* was an HBO film and his *The Bone Collector* is soon to be released by Universal Pictures. The London *Times* has called him "the best psychological thriller writer around."

  ▪ While my novels certainly have their dark side (a carping reviewer once wrote that the largest part of the film budget for a recent book of mine ought to go for fake blood), I nonetheless try to make sure that good prevails, that violence is unseen, and that readers arrive at the last page harrowed but happy, content in their knowledge that most of their favorite characters have survived the journey with them, principles and body parts intact.

  With short stories, however, all those rules go out the window. For a reason I have yet to figure out, when I write stories, I feel a refreshing license to be as dark as I can be and dance gleefully back and forth over that fishy boundary between good and evil.

  "The Weekender" is typical of my short fiction: A violent incident, a gothic setting, people pushed to extremes, psychological mind games, and a sense that nothing is quite what it seems to be. My influences are, not surprisingly, O. Henry, Poe, and *The Twilight Zone*.

Brendan DuBois grew up in New Hampshire and received a B.A. in English from the University of New Hampshire. A former newspaper reporter, he has been writing mystery fiction for more than a decade and still lives in his native state with his wife, Mona. He has published two novels — *Dead Sand* and *Black Tide* — and has recently completed a third. In 1995 he received the Shamus Award from the Private Eye Writers of America for best mystery short story of the year, and he has three times been nominated for an Edgar Award from the Mystery Writers of America for his short fiction.

▪ I've always been fascinated with the tale of the outsider intruding upon a closed community, and this is true in my story "The Dark Snow." The community in this case is a lakefront town in rural New Hampshire, with its own rules, mores, and ways of getting along. The people in this town are not necessarily bad or evil; they just have a certain way of doing things, and outsiders who come in and do things differently often come under uncomfortable scrutiny or, in the case of my story, outright hostility.

The main character in this story is an outsider in the truest sense — not only is he a stranger to the people of this small New Hampshire town but, after years of service in some of the dark corners of our government, he's also a stranger to the world of civilians. He does his best to adjust, he does his best to make friends with his community, and he does his best to try to ignore some old whispers that tell him what to do in the face of the hostility that's tossed his way. But doing your best doesn't always work.

With characters and a theme in place, the setting of the story was next. My parents once owned a cottage on a lake in New Hampshire, and my wife and I still vacation each year to a hideaway home on another lake, farther north. We have both come to love the times we spend at the lake, swimming, sailing, and stargazing at night. And a moonlight paddle in a canoe on water as still as glass, with the hooting sound of loons in the distance, is enough to raise the hair on the back of your neck. Lakewater can be comforting and soothing. It's often beautiful.

But as I proved in this story, it can also be deadly.

Elizabeth George published her first novel, *A Great Deliverance,* in 1988. It was recognized with an Edgar nomination, and it received an Anthony Award, an Agatha Award, and France's *Grand Prix de Littérature Policière.* She's been awarded the MIMI, Germany's award for international mystery fiction, and she's been nominated twice for *Svenska Deckarakademin,* by Sweden's Crime Writers Association. She's an instructor in creative writing, offering courses in universities, colleges, and with private students throughout the country. She divides her time between Huntington Beach, California, and London.

▪ I know exactly the moment when I conceived "The Surprise of His Life." It was the same moment in the summer of 1994 when I put together how O. J. Simpson had murdered his wife and Ronald Goldman. My story, however, isn't an attempt to explain the Simpson murder in any way. Far be it from me to question the conclusion of a jury sitting in a criminal trial.

On the contrary, the Simpson murders acted as a foundation for a set of ideas about the nature of obsession and where it can lead.

Since all of my novels are set in England, this short story was a departure for me. It's set in Newport Beach, California, and instead of my Scotland Yard detectives, it features a crusty private eye and a fifty-five-year-old man with prostate problems. Quite a departure, indeed.

It was a new experience, writing about my own back yard. I hope the effort proves enjoyable for the reader.

Jeremiah Healy, a graduate of Rutgers College and Harvard Law School, was a professor at the New England School of Law for eighteen years. He is the creator of John Francis Cuddy, a Boston-based private investigator who has appeared in eleven novels and thirty short stories. Healy's first novel, *Blunt Darts,* was selected by the *New York Times* as one of the seven best mysteries of 1984.

▪ The idea and title for "Eyes That Never Meet" came to me in an unusual way. I'd been asked by James Grady to contribute a piece to the anthology *Unusual Suspects,* benefiting Share Our Strength, a Washington, D.C., organization that fights hunger in America. On a trip to New York City, I happened to visit the Metropolitan Museum of Art during an exhibition of *stelae,* gravestones from ancient Greece in which the eyes of the departed and surviving spouses never meet, a symbol for the dead spouse no longer being able to see. It occurred to me, as it does to the fictional Marla Van Dorn in my story, that we who are fortunate seldom make eye contact with the homeless and hungry who beg on our sidewalks. Given the final twist in *Eyes That Never Meet,* I thought the title was particularly apt.

Melodie Johnson Howe lives near Santa Barbara. She is the author of two mystery novels, *The Mother Shadow* and *Beauty Dies.* Another Diana Poole short story, "Dirty Blonde," can be found in the anthology *Sisters in Crime,* fourth edition.

▪ Diana Poole was created out of my admiration for F. Scott Fitzgerald's *The Pat Hobby Stories.* His wry observations on Hollywood and his character's often funny and somehow sad attempts at regaining his past success are wonderful. I wanted to try to do something similar, but in the genre I write in and love — the mystery. So I created an out-of-work, middle-aged actress.

Being an ex-actress I have an intimate knowledge of the entertainment business. Hollywood reminds me of that old expression about New York: It's a great place to visit but I wouldn't want to live there. Hollywood is a great place to write about but I wouldn't want to work there.

The idea or need to write this particular short story came about when my husband and I were invited to attend a party for a rock-and-roll star. As it turned out, the star arrived after everyone had left. Some entrances, even in Hollywood, can be delayed too long. On our way home from the party I turned to my husband and in a theatrical, world-weary voice said, "Well, another tented evening." I knew in that moment I had a story to tell. I also knew it wouldn't be about a rock-and-roll star.

I put Diana Poole in the middle of a tented Hollywood party, created some guests, and the story almost wrote itself. When I realized that the story was really a long confession, I knew I would need a device to keep the tension and the suspense going. So I gave the party guests an almost phobic concern about the character Robin's singing. What didn't they want to hear? And what would happen if Robin did sing? While the questions regarding the murder are answered early in the story, I let these unanswered questions linger until the end.

I loved writing this story. And I'm glad the rock-and-roll star didn't arrive on time. Because if he had, well, who knows? I hope to group the Diana Poole stories together someday. When I do, I'll put them on the shelf next to Pat Hobby, who is still trying to sneak onto the studio lot.

Pat Jordan is a freelance writer living in Ft. Lauderdale. He is the author of hundreds of magazine articles (*New York Times Magazine, G.Q., Playboy, Men's Journal, L.A. Times Magazine, Life,* etc.) and nine books. This story, "The Mark," is only the second short story he's ever written. The first, "Bobby2" was published in November 1992.

▪ Sol, not his real name, was the best man at my wedding in January 1992. He was serving out the last six months of his six-year marijuana smuggling conviction at a halfway house for felons in Dania, Florida. I had to pick him up on the day of the wedding and return him to the halfway house a few hours later. He missed the reception. That part of "The Mark" is true. The rest is fiction. Sol is a little annoyed at the fiction part of the story. He thinks the story should have more accurately portrayed him as a heroic "Don Juan type of guy," rather than as "comic relief." Alas, you can't please everyone.

I am grateful, however, that I have been able to please Alice K. Turner, *Playboy*'s fiction editor, who ran the third story about Bobby, Sheila, and Sol this summer. She has encouraged me at every step to pursue these characters and is a willing and enthusiastic reader of each adventure I send her. All she demands of me is that I tell a good story.

Trained as a child clinical psychologist, clinical associate professor of pediatrics at USC School of Medicine, **Jonathan Kellerman** is the author of twelve best-selling novels translated into twenty-four languages, two volumes on psychology, and two books for children. His awards include the Edgar, the Anthony, the Samuel Goldwyn, and the Media Award of the American Psychological Association. He is married to the novelist Faye Kellerman.

▪ I don't write very many short stories. I could get all highfalutin and say it's because I enjoy developing characters gradually, subtly, adding layer upon layer of texture, mining deep lodes of exquisite psychological nuance. But a great short story writer can accomplish all that within the confines of the form. I know. I'm married to a great short story writer and I'm well aware that I'm not very good at this truncated, accelerated business. That's the real reason I shy away from anything briefer than a novel. If you're willing to suffer, it might as well add up to a book with your picture on the jacket.

But this story percolated in my mind for many years and I think I know why.

You don't have to be a shrink to realize that all fiction is, on some level, autobiography. I am a shrink, but sometimes it takes years for me to understand why I really wrote a specific book. So much for the value of a Ph.D. and all those insights acquired on both sides of the couch.

The big epiphany is: I'm a father. Boy, am I. Four kids with a fourteen-year age difference among them. Parenthood in my twenties, thirties, and forties. Sometimes it seems all Faye and I have done is play Maw and Paw. So far the young'uns have turned out great — despite the Ph.D. — and it's been tremendously fulfilling. Also a helluva lot of work.

We began our brood in 1978, when procreation was unfashionable and the only car seats around were designed by the Marquis de Sade. Yuppie scum looked down their rhinoplastied noses at us and preached about zero population growth. Waiters glared in horror when we schlepped our son into restaurants. (Twenty-four-hour places were best because he was up at 4:00 A.M., famished and ready to . . . play!) Undaunted, we continued through the eighties when the drive to self-perpetuate suddenly hit the yuppie scum like a sucker punch to the id, and we had to tolerate incessant nattering about how to develop perfect babies (usually something to do with flashcards and various canvas and titanium contraptions developed by light-starved, vengeful Scandinavians). Persisting into the nineties, too exhausted to notice fashion and foible, we mostly sleepwalked through the initial years of elderly parenthood, amazed that the newest edition seemed to develop quite nicely in the face of periodic senility.

So when I was asked to write a story about love, I thought about family love. Marital love. Parental love. All of the above. Since I'm trained as a social scientist, I also thought about Cosmic Issues: balancing family and career. Looking after one's own health, physical and mental, while not neglecting the Tiny Toon in the car seat. Trying to keep said Toon quiet in a restaurant. Changing diapers. Getting away with murder.

'Nuff said.

Andrew Klavan currently lives as an expatriate in London with his wife and two children. His last novel, *True Crime,* was an international bestseller. His new novel, entitled *The Uncanny,* is due out from Crown next year. Klavan is now at work on a mystery screenplay for Fox 2000.

▪ The first time I heard that TV cameras were to be allowed into U.S. courtrooms, I could not restrain a cynical laugh. For one thing, I have quite an attractive cynical laugh and like to show it off whenever possible. But for another thing, human folly always amuses me. Years ago, as a reporter covering courts in a small town in upstate New York, I had time to reflect at length on the similarities between the trial process and classical drama. Add cameras to the mix, I reasoned, and there would be nothing to distinguish the legal system from show business.

When the O. J. Simpson trial came along, I was proven right. American law and show business had become one. It's such a rare event for me to be proven right about anything that I thought I'd write a story about it. And that's how "Lou Monahan, County Prosecutor" came to be. I wanted to depict a regular guy, a stalwart guy — an honest public official like many I've known — who finds himself a part of the glamour and unreality of television simply by virtue of doing his job. It's a very intimate process, a seductive circle, or a vortex perhaps. Like everyone else, Lou expresses his most basic desires in terms of fantasy. Like all fantasies, Lou's have the elements of drama. That drama is reflected in the courtroom and that courtroom is going to be on TV, thus offering Lou the chance to fulfill his desires. There's a price, of course, and that's the heart of the story: how Lou reacts when the bill comes due.

My father was a performer and I've worked in journalism, so I've been around show business — and the news business, which is part of show business — all my life. It's very tricky stuff. No matter how you react to it, it can make you part of the act. You think people watch too much TV? Write a book about it and maybe I can get you on *Oprah.* You think undue publicity can cause a miscarriage of justice? Good story — you're on in five. Showbiz is like the make-believe tennis ball in the movie *Blow Up.* Pick it up — and you vanish. So that's the dramatic question of "Lou Monahan": Will our hero accede to the world of make-believe? Stay tuned.

Elmore Leonard has been writing fiction for the past forty-five years and claims he's still having a good time assembling characters to see where they decide to take him. When asked if he knows how a book is going to end before he gets there, Leonard replied, "If I know that, why write the book?" His thirty-fourth novel, scheduled for early 1998 release, is set in Cuba one hundred years ago, at the outbreak of the Spanish-American War. Quite a number of his books, including *Get Shorty*, have been adapted for the screen.

▪ I wrote "Karen Makes Out" to see if I'd like Karen Sisco enough to develop a novel around her as a federal marshal. I liked her a lot and *Out of Sight* was published in the fall of 1996. We will next see Karen on the screen in the film adaptation of the book. No one, though, has yet told me who will play her part.

Michael Malone was born in North Carolina and educated at Chapel Hill and Harvard. He's taught at various colleges on various subjects from fiction-making to the rise and the fall of the great American musical. Among his novels are *Dingley Falls, Handling Sin, Uncivil Seasons, Time's Witness,* and *Foolscap.* He's also written on the movies, as well as screenplays and television shows.

▪ I'm not an instinctive short story writer. My characters keep trying to be in novels and their stories get away from me. Back in the seventies I had considerable luck with women's magazines, writing a type of story about whimsical young men who'd had their consciousness raised, sometimes violently, by liberated young females, and I did a story for *Playboy* about Elvis right after he died but before anybody — except Southerners — expected he was immortal. But mostly I write long. So I was intrigued when Otto Penzler asked me to write a story about a murder for love. It was a mystery, which I love. It was an assignment, which is friendlier than an entirely blank page. Best, it was a theme of movie proportions — murder for love — and I immediately thought of a movie star to tell about.

As the vagaries of my career confess, I grew up infatuated with the movies. We had one small musty "art film" theater in my Piedmont town, and there as a teenager I fell in love every Saturday with a foreign woman — Jeanne Moreau, Simone Signoret, Melina Mercouri. Women worth dying for. Women who might kill you. The original image of "Red Clay" is a native goddess, Ava Gardner, one of the few American actresses with the epic beauty and grand gestures and sweeping self-destructiveness of a great star. Ava Gardner grew up in North Carolina and every Tarheel with any romance in his body sensed what an extraordinary gift we'd given the world in her. Stella Doyle in "Red Clay" is such a woman, on trial for murdering her husband. The story imagines an adolescent boy's coming to share the truth of his father's belief that any man who hadn't desired Stella Doyle had missed out on being alive.

Mabel Maney is a book artist and writer living in San Francisco. She is the author of the gay and lesbian Nancy Drew/Hardy Boys parodies: *The Case of the Not-So-Nice Nurse, The Case of the Good-for-Nothing Girlfriend,* and *A Ghost in the Closet.* Her short stories have appeared in many anthologies, including *Girlfriend Number 1, Beyond Definition,* and *Out for Blood.*

▪ I was in a cranky mood on the day Victoria Brownworth, a writer and editor, called me and asked if I could write a story for one of her mystery anthologies. Whenever I get tired of all the work it takes to get one girl and her small dog through the day, I think of my maternal grandmother, who sewed her own clothes, made bread from scratch, and made enough quilts to blanket the entire Great Lakes region. Then I feel crankier.

What better way to work oneself out of a bad mood than with a tidy little murder?

The setting is my grandmother's basement in Appleton, Wisconsin, where I spent many a stifling summer reading by flashlight in the cool darkness. Although my grandparents bear little resemblance to the nice couple in the story, I must confess I've never forgotten my grandfather's lesson on how to skin a catfish. "First, make sure your knife is sharp," and so on. Despite the fact that my grandparents were devout Catholics, and so considered even the thought of murder a sin, I think they'd be pleased that their home was the setting for this story.

Besides, few tears will be shed for the corpse. If anyone deserves his fate, it's our Mr. Feeley.

Joyce Carol Oates is the author, under the pseudonym Rosamond Smith, of several mystery/psychological suspense novels, including *Snake Eyes, Nemesis, Soul/Mate,* and, most recently, *Double Delight.* She has published mystery fiction in *Ellery Queen's Mystery Magazine.* Since 1978, she has lived and taught in Princeton, New Jersey.

▪ "Will You Always Love Me?" is one of a number of thematically related stories I've written in recent years that turn upon questions of love, fidelity, and the acknowledgment of or denial of "truth": Can our most intense love relationships withstand "truth"? Or is love, in a crucial sense, based upon the purposeful denial of certain elements of "truth"? The story leapt into my head after I'd heard just the skeleton of a tale of a woman haunted by her sister's brutal murder many years before. So far as the woman knew, her sister's murderer had been found and sentenced to life imprisonment. But, to me, that seemed only the start of another, more elusive and tantalizing story.

George Pelecanos was born and raised in and around Washington, D.C., where he has lived his entire life. He is the author of six novels, including the Nick Stefanos mysteries, *Shoedog, The Big Blowdown,* and *King Suckerman.*

 • "When You're Hungry" is the only short story I have written, and my sole work of fiction that is set outside of my native D.C. I wrote this story in the fall of 1993, during a three-month stay in Brazil, when my wife and I were in the process of adopting our second child.

At the time, with a one thousand percent rate of inflation, Brazil was on the verge of economic collapse, with no safety net provided for its people. Every day, standing on the balcony of my *apartamento* in Recife, I witnessed mothers and their children sifting through garbage bins in search of something edible, or simply lying down in the street from hunger and its attendant fatigue. In restaurants, tiny hands attached to painfully thin forearms reached beneath dividers, begging for table scraps. Meanwhile, receiving my daily English newspaper, I first began to read of the so-called "revolution" being touted in America, where our own welfare system would be radically restructured or completely eliminated.

This story is told from an American's point of view until it nears the end, where it switches, significantly, to the point of view of a Brazilian native.

As a toiler in the arena of crime/noir, I've often been tagged as a "dark" writer. "When You're Hungry" truly earns that description. There is nothing more horrifying than the sight of a starving child.

S. J. Rozan is the author of the Lydia Chin/Bill Smith series, which includes *China Trade, Concourse* (winner of the 1995 Shamus Award for Best Novel from the Private Eye Writers of America), *Mandarin Plaid,* and *No Colder Place.* Chin/Smith stories have appeared in *Ellery Queen's Mystery Magazine, Alfred Hitchcock Mystery Magazine, P.I. Magazine,* and numerous anthologies; "Hoops" was nominated for an Edgar Award by the Mystery Writers of America. S. J. Rozan is a practicing architect born, raised, and living in New York City.

 • "Hoops," like everything I write, is about motivation and moral ambiguity: what makes people do what they do and how they justify what they do when it results in evil. The characters in it are essentially characters I had used in my novel *Concourse;* I found I couldn't let them go so easily. The story, like so many stories, is about dreams unfulfilled and unfulfillable, and undreamt. It's also about people who have no power and very little experience with justice, using what power they can scrape together to demand justice — and, in the end, it's about the impossibility of justice: a word we use all the time, but one, I think, with no real meaning.

Allen Steele was born in Nashville, Tennessee. He received his B.A. in communications from New England College in Henniker, New Hampshire, and his M.A. in journalism from the University of Missouri in Columbia, Missouri. He became a full-time science fiction writer in 1988, following publication of his first short story, "Live from the Mars Hotel" (*Asimov's* mid-Dec. '88). Since then he has become a prolific author of novels, short stories, and essays.

His novels include *Orbital Decay; Clark County, Space; Lunar Descent; Labyrinth of Night; The Jericho Iteration;* and *The Tranquillity Alternative.* He has also published two collections of short fiction, *Rude Astronauts* and *All-American Alien Boy.*

His "The Death of Captain Future" received the 1996 Hugo Award for best novella, won a 1996 Science Fiction Weekly Reader Appreciation Award, and was nominated for a Nebula Award by the Science Fiction Writers of America. His novelette "The Good Rat" was also nominated for a Hugo in the same year. *Orbital Decay* received the 1990 Locus Award for best first novel and *Clark County, Space* was nominated for the 1991 Phillip K. Dick Award.

Allen Steele now lives in St. Louis, Missouri, with his wife and three dogs.

▪ Until the idea for "Doblin's Lecture" occurred to me, virtually all of my published novels and short stories were science fiction; although my last two novels are suspense thrillers, they're primarily SF in terms of genre classification. When I sat down to write this particular tale, though, I wasn't concerned about which genre it would fall into; I simply wanted to tell a good, scary story.

A couple of years ago, I read a brief item in the *New York Times* about how Jeffrey Dahmer, the convicted serial killer, had received about $30,000 since he had been sent to prison, principally in the form of small checks sent from people who apparently felt sorry for him; one of his benefactors had gone so far as to give him a Bible along with a check for several thousand dollars. I then recalled reading elsewhere that John Wayne Gacy made a tidy profit from sales of his paintings while he was on death row. Charles Manson occasionally receives royalties from the songs he wrote before he became notorious; a small indie label has released an album he recorded while in prison. And since the New York State Supreme Court recently struck down the "Son-of-Sam Law" as unconstitutional, there's nothing to prevent David Berkowitz from writing a best-selling memoir (a "kill-and-tell"). So why would anyone give money to these monsters, or pay for their mediocre art?

The answer is obvious: America is fascinated with serial killers. We regularly send books like *The Silence of the Lambs, Zodiac,* and *Mind Hunter* shooting up the bestseller lists, and we make movies like *Natural Born Killers* and *Seven* into box-office hits. Multiple murderers, both real and fictional, are staples of popular culture. Which person has better name-recognition: Stephen Hawking or Jeffrey Dahmer? Hawking is the most brilliant physicist since Albert Einstein while Dahmer slaughtered dozens of young men, but who is more famous?

Playing the "what if" game common to science fiction, I then asked myself: If Manson or Berkowitz (or, speaking in the past tense, Gacy or Dahmer) were put on a university lecture circuit, would I buy a ticket to see him speak? Yes, I probably would, if only out of curiosity. And if I knew that he would perform a demonstration of his . . . well, talent . . . during the course of his presentation? Probably not, but only because I'm squeamish about violence.

However, I'm sure I could easily scalp the ticket for a few hundred bucks an hour before showtime.

Brad Watson is from Meridian, Mississippi, and earned degrees from Mississippi State University and the University of Alabama. His first book, *Last Days of the Dog-Men*, was published by W. W. Norton in April 1996; Dell published a paperback edition in the spring of 1997. He has taught creative writing at the University of Alabama and currently teaches at Harvard University.

▪ "Kindred Spirits" grew out of a couple of anecdotes people told me while I was a reporter on the Alabama Gulf Coast. I heard the story of a man who repeatedly — with little effect — beat up his wife's lover. And I heard the story of a wild pig hunt that went wrong. When I first wrote my story, I dressed these anecdotes up considerably but had nowhere to take them. The stories of the murders — the narrator's story of a murder trial and the loss of his wife, and Bailey's story about his own ill-fated marriage — began to form around these early anecdotes as I worked on successive drafts. And I began to understand the kindred natures of these men and their stories, their patterns of violence, betrayal, and loss.

John Weisman is one of the select company of authors to have written both fiction and nonfiction *New York Times* bestsellers. He has written seven novels, including four in the current, best-selling *Rogue Warrior®* series. Two of his nonfiction projects, *Shadow Warrior,* the story of CIA agent Felix Rodriguez, and *Rogue Warrior,* the autobiography of Navy Commander Richard Marcinko and the top-secret unit Seal Team Six, were the subjects of *60 Minutes* segments.

Weisman and his wife, Susan, a State Department official, live in the Blue Ridge Mountains of Virginia with their three dogs.

▪ I hadn't attempted a short story since college. Then Jim Grady called and asked me to contribute one for a collection he was putting together as a way to raise money for a charitable organization called Share Our

Strength. With the perfect confidence of the naïf, I told him he'd have something from me in a couple of weeks. Then I sat down and tried to write. Nada. Bupkes. I must have false-started half a dozen times. Problem was, writing a short story was impossible. I write novels; that's marathoning — you grind out the words day after day. Grady needed a forty-meter dash. I had no idea how to start, how to dig down to get the right traction for this word-sprint.

Finally, I convinced myself that I wasn't writing a short story, but the prologue to a new novel. That worked. Indeed, once I'd shattered the initial psychological barrier, the characters broke away; started acting on their own, and the story told itself. One interesting sidebar to the little psy-op I ran on myself is that I definitely want to see a lot more of the protagonist of the story. And so, "There Are Monsterim" may turn out to be the prologue of a novel after all.

Monica Wood is the author of *Secret Language,* a novel; *Description,* a book on fiction writing; *Short Takes,* a teaching guide to contemporary fiction; and *12 Multicultural Novels: A Reading and Teaching Guide.* Her short stories have been widely published and anthologized.

▪ Forgiveness is a theme that runs through much of my fiction, and usually I don't recognize the theme until a story is well underway. "Unlawful Contact" is the first story I ever wrote that *began* with a theme. I asked myself, "Is it possible to forgive the unforgivable?" and set up a situation in which a character wishes to do just that.

My story's inclusion in a book of mysteries was, at first, bewildering to me. Otto Penzler, the series editor, assured me that the story fit the requirements because it involved a crime. As I reread the story myself I recognized not one but *two* crimes. The brother's act is a crime in a formal sense; the sister's desire to forgive him is, in the eyes of her family, a messier, even less comprehensible crime — as are all crimes of the heart.

Other Distinguished Mystery Stories of 1996

ADKINS, JAN
  Barratry. *Unusual Suspects,* James Grady, ed. (Vintage)
ANDREE, JAMIE
  Wishing Ball. *Fish Stories 2*
AUERBACH, JESSICA
  Police Report. *Unusual Suspects,* James Grady, ed. (Vintage)

BAKER, NIKKI
  Backlash. *Night Bites,* Victoria A. Brownworth, ed. (Seal Press)

CARLSON, RON
  On Killymoon. *Quarterly West,* Fall
CAUNITZ, WILLIAM J.
  Dying Time. *Murder for Love,* Otto Penzler, ed. (Delacorte)
CORN, DAVID
  My Murder. *Unusual Suspects,* James Grady, ed. (Vintage)

DAVIS, DOROTHY SALISBURY
  Miles to Go. *Women on the Case,* Sara Paretsky, ed. (Delacorte)

FREIMOR, JACQUELINE
  The B Rules. *Murderous Intent,* Summer

GORMAN, ED
  Famous Blue Raincoat. *Cemetery Dance,* Summer
GRADY, JAMES
  Kiss the Sky. *Unusual Suspects,* James Grady, ed. (Vintage)
GRINER, PAUL
  Boxes. *Playboy,* March

HAUTALA, RICK
Hitman. *Night Screams,* Ed Gorman and Martin H. Greenberg, eds. (Roc)
HOCH, EDWARD D.
The Problem of the Enormous Owl. *Ellery Queen's Mystery Magazine,* January
HOWARD, CLARK
The Banzai Pipeline. *Ellery Queen's Mystery Magazine,* November

KELLY, RONALD
Exit 85. *Cemetery Dance,* Summer

LAWRENCE, STARLING
Desire Lines. *Story,* Spring
LUTZ, JOHN
Shock. *Unusual Suspects,* James Grady, ed. (Vintage)

MCBAIN, ED
Running from Legs. *Murder for Love,* Otto Penzler, ed. (Delacorte)
MULLER, MARCIA
The Holes in the System. *Ellery Queen's Mystery Magazine,* June
MUNRO, ALICE
The Love of a Good Woman. *The New Yorker,* December 23 and December 30

OLMSTEAD, ROBERT
Rolling Stones. *The Midwesterner,* November/December
OLSON, DONALD
The Stone House. *Ellery Queen's Mystery Magazine,* June

SHEPARD, LUCIUS
Pizza Man. *Playboy,* September
SMITH, JULIE
Strangers on a Plane. *Unusual Suspects,* James Grady, ed. (Vintage)

WESTLAKE, DONALD E.
The Burglar and the Whatsit. *Playboy,* December
WHEAT, CAROLYN
Cruel and Unusual. *Guilty as Charged,* Scott Turow, ed. (Pocket Books)
WILLIAMSON, CHET
Dr. Joe. *Diagnosis Terminal,* F. Paul Wilson, ed. (Forge)